Half Faerie

Daughter of Light

Book One

A Young Adult Fantasy Trilogy by

Heidi Garrett

Half Faerie by Heidi Garrett

Half-Faerie Publishing

Find out more about Heidi Garrett at

www.heidigwrites.blogspot.com

This book is a work of fiction. Names, characters, places, brands, media, and incidents are either the product of the author's imagination or are used fictitiously. Any resemblance to actual persons, living or dead, actual events or locales is purely coincidental.

Cover Art by J.W.B.

Editing by H. Danielle Crabtree, Jennifer Ingman, and Vince Dickinson

ISBN: 978-0-9882068-4-7

Other Books by Heidi Garrett

Get All My New Releases! http://eepurl.com/wWKUj

Daughter of Light

(A Young Adult Fantasy Trilogy)

Isolt's Enchantment, A Prequel
Half Mortal, #2
War and Grace, #3

Once Upon a Time Today

(A Collection of Stand-Alone Modern Fairy Tale Retellings)

The Girl Who Believed in Fairy Tales: Three Short Stories
Beautiful Beautiful
Dreaming of the Sea
The Tree Hugger
I Am Lily Dane

In Collaboration with Billie Limpin

(A New Adult Paranormal Romance)

Cupcakes and Kisses

For my beloved

Elva

and

Jerry

Contents

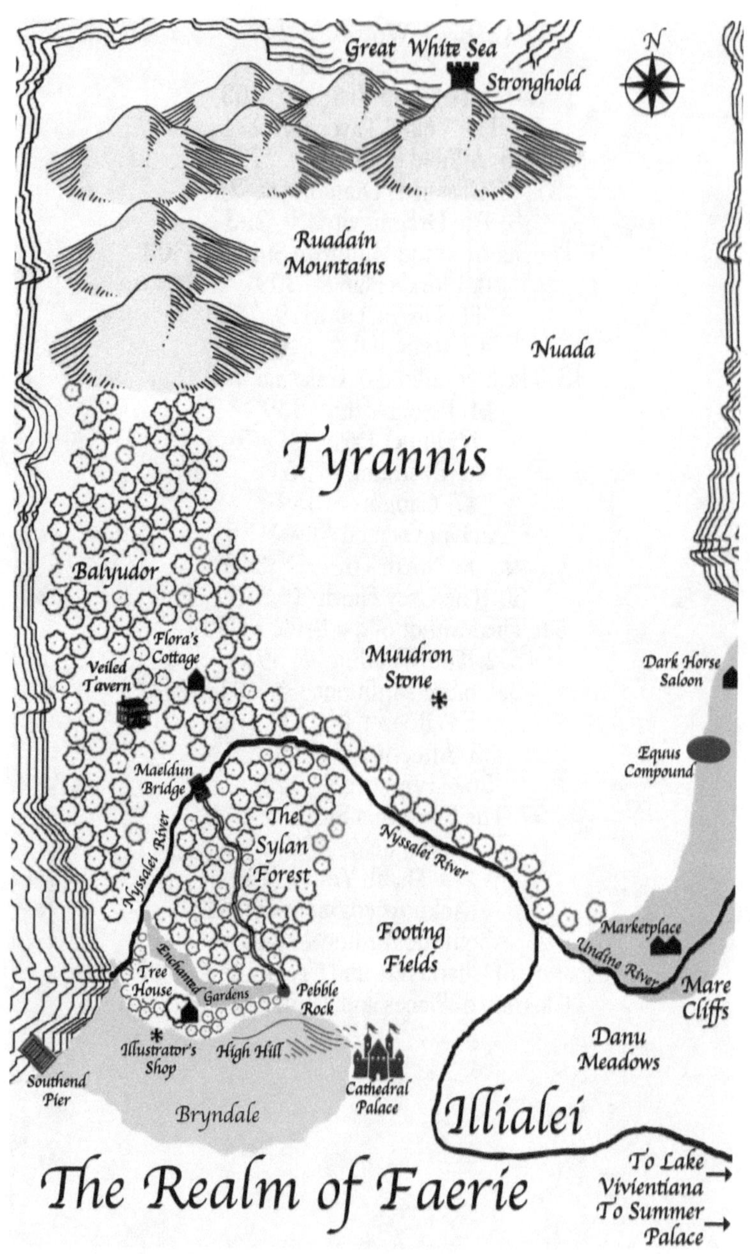
Great White Sea
Stronghold
N
Ruadain Mountains
Nuada
Tyrannis
Balyudor
Flora's Cottage
Veiled Tavern
Muudron Stone
Dark Horse Saloon
Equus Compound
Maeldun Bridge
The Sylan Forest
Nyssalei River
Nyssalei River
Footing Fields
Marketplace
Undine River
Mare Cliffs
Enchanted Gardens
Tree House
Pebble Rock
Illustrator's Shop
High Hill
Cathedral Palace
Danu Meadows
Southend Pier
Bryndale
Illialei
The Realm of Faerie
To Lake Vivientiana
To Summer Palace

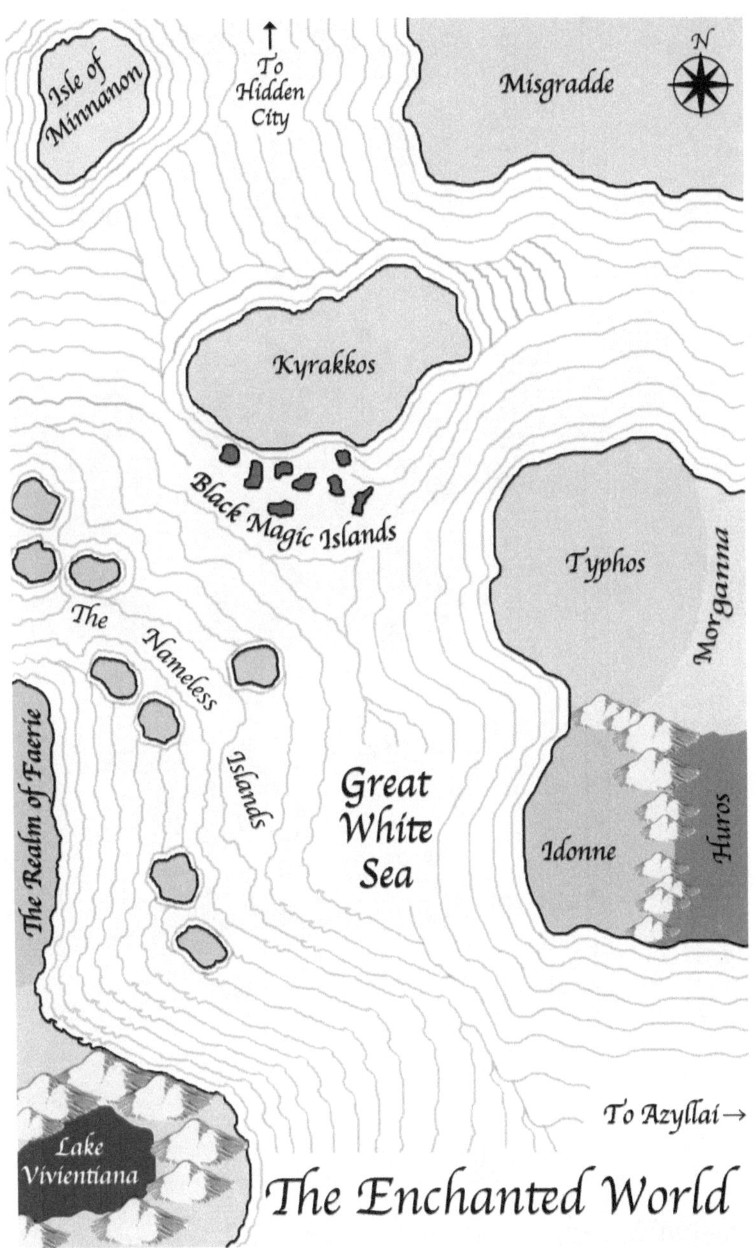
Isle of Minnanon
↑ To Hidden City
Misgradde
N
Kyrakkos
Black Magic Islands
Typhos
Morganna
The Nameless Islands
The Realm of Faerie
Great White Sea
Idonne
Huros
To Azyllai→
Lake Vivientiana
The Enchanted World

Idonnic Prophecy

When the Dark Master rises from the mist to breach the veil, and a Daughter of Light, denied the throne by virtue of birth, stands alone, beware. Cunning will test the Grey Sentinel's shield.

If the Iron Bridge falls, and the Ancient Doors close, the end is near.

The blood of innocents will soak Illialei's meadows, and dreamlessness will snuff all hope from the mortal world. Fear not. This apocalyptic union can be saved. Though grace is undeserved, the purpose is love.

These are the mysteries yet untasted, on the tip of your tongue, O Wayward Son of Idonne.

The Old Texts, Appendix VII

1. Ylandria

Defying the dark phase of the enchanted world's two moons, Melia imagined the light of a candle. A soft wind rustled the oak's leaves, and her timid inner flame snuffed out. She shifted on the tree's bough. "It's not going to work."

"Keep trying," Tatou encouraged her.

"It's hopeless."

Tatou's slight weight lifted from Melia's shoulder. A glowing orb in the pitch-black night, the pixie bobbed in front of her face. "Are you focusing on holding the flame steady?"

"Yes."

Tatou's natural radiance illuminated the half-faerie's slender hands and what was left of the ylandria clenched between her fingers. Melia held out her other hand. Tatou landed on the offered palm. "Are you relaxing?"

"How can I? Nothing is working." Melia's frustration bled into her voice. "Every thing I've tried to stop these stupid visions has failed." She smashed the ylandria butt against the tree limb before slipping the useless lump of faerie herb into her pocket. "One." She held up a finger. "Physical exhaustion. I ran across the fields until my legs gave out. Two." She raised a second finger. "A calming atmosphere. I buried myself in the meadows beneath morning glories and long grass–for an entire day! Three." She waved a third finger in the air. "Sleep deprivation. I forced myself to stay awake all three nights during the last dark moon phase."

Melia retrieved the burnt-out stub from her pocket and shook it in Tatou's face. "Now, this isn't working. What am I going to do?"

"Are there any seeds left?" Ylandria, a faerie herb whose vines wound through the tops of elm trees, was almost impossible to harvest. The pixie, eloquent in birdsong, had persuaded a swallow to gather the necessary volume for their experiment. She doubted she could do so again.

The half-faerie reached into her other pocket and fidgeted with the contents. "Yes, and another leaf."

"If you want to try again, I'll stay."

When Tatou had told Melia about the ylandria, and how it could help her control her inner eye, she couldn't wait to try it. Now, failure crushed her spirit. She couldn't even hold an imaginary flame steady.

Every second her desperation increased. What if she smoked more and it didn't make any difference? What if nothing ever made a difference? Why waste her friend's time?

"I don't want to make you later than you already are," Melia said.

Tatou was the only pixie who ever ventured beyond the enchanted gardens after midnight–and her late-night roaming made the other pixies wary of her. "A few more minutes won't matter."

"I'm sorry my mother stayed up so late." Pressina had returned to her study after dinner and lingered. "I wonder what she does down there," Melia mused, "in her room, carved out deep inside the oak's trunk."

"You know what she does ... black magic."

"But what kind of black magic?" Melia wondered out loud. "Other than Malachi, there's no evidence."

"Isn't he enough?"

"I suppose."

"Maybe you don't want to know what she's up to," Tatou said.

"You could be right about that," Melia huffed. But her mother's obsession with black magic aggravated her. "I'm just worried she's going to find out about these visions."

"How?"

"If Melusine or Plantine were to rummage through my mind while I'm having one, I'm sure they would tell her." The three sisters shared a telepathic connection.

Tatou puckered her lips with her fingers.

"Do you think they'd make me leave Illialei?" Melia asked.

"Who?"

"Whoever finds out"–Melia had given the subject a lot of thought–"my mother, or Queen Luisa, or a mob of flower faeries!"

"I've never heard of anyone being banished from Faerie before."

"Oh! And what about my father and every other mortal who broke a faerie troth?"

"That's different."

"I'm not so sure," Melia said. "What if they sent me back to the mortal world to live with him?" Her pulse quickened as her imagination leapt. She raised her palm higher to meet Tatou's gaze. "Or maybe they'd sentence me to death." Adopting a snooty tone, she mimicked, "Pressina bore it all in grim silence, a hard glint in her lilac eyes the only admission to the burden her middle child had always been."

Tatou giggled. "You sound like one of the flower faeries at the market."

Melia would have laughed at her own play-acting if she wasn't so afraid of what might happen if someone found out about the lifelike hallucinations of death and desolation that haunted her. She released a long, slow exhale.

"What?" Tatou asked.

"I was thinking about my thirteenth birthday."

"Why?"

Neither of them liked to talk about that day. Five years ago, after Queen Luisa's daughter, Lilliane, interrupted their celebration down by the river with a creepy joke about eating pixies, Tatou, Melia, and Plantine had trudged back to the tree house, their joy sapped. If that hadn't been enough to ruin the memory, Melia's father had telepathically interrogated her for the first time that night. He'd just discovered he shared the supersensory abilities his daughters possessed. None of them had been thrilled with the revelation. His attempts at telepathy were an invasion more than a conversation. Since then, during every dark-moon phase, gruesome images intruded into Melia's mind–gruesome images that she'd never seen or imagined before.

She knew it was all connected: her father's psychic trespass, the horrific visions, and the black nights when the enchanted world's two moons offered zero illumination.

"I had my first vision on the first night of the dark moon phase after that birthday," Melia said.

"What do you see, exactly?"

Melia's throat tightened. If her friend truly understood the images of slaughtered faeries and incinerated landscapes she saw–and the pleasure she took in witnessing them–she was sure Tatou would hate her or be frightened of her. She was frightened of herself, every time she experienced one. "It's better if I don't tell you." Tears welled in the half-faerie's eyes. She rubbed them away.

"What?" Tatou asked.

"When Melusine taught Plantine and me how to block Father's telepathic intrusions, I became the best at building interior walls." Sweat slicked Melia's palm. Tatou fluttered to the tree limb nearest the half-faerie's head. "I was certain that would stop everything."

"But it didn't," Tatou said.

"No."

"Do your sisters have them too?"

"No ... I don't know. I've never asked them." Melia's heart hammered in her chest. "I don't think so. I mean, I've never noticed them withdrawing the way I do." Or looking as guilty as she felt. No matter how many psychic walls she threw up, or how thick the walls were, when Faeries' moons went dark, the visions came. The most logical explanation made her uneasy. They weren't coming from outside her, they were bubbling up from within.

"Try the ylandria one more time," Tatou said.

Melia fished the last leaf from her pocket. It was as hard to roll the second time as the first, but this time its smoky haze seemed more potent. She coughed on the peppery fumes. The last thing she needed was to wake up her mother and sisters in the middle of the night. She muffled the hacking sound with her free hand as her eyes darted toward the tree house.

Everything remained quiet.

Relieved, Melia flicked ylandria ash into the engulfing darkness. When heat threatened her fingertips, she stubbed the glowing orange embers against the oak's branch and slipped the second butt into her pocket.

"What happened?" Tatou asked.

"The same thing. It flickered out."

"I'm sorry it didn't work. Are you going to be all right?"

"Sure. I'll see you tomorrow?"

"On the hill after school?"

Melia didn't remind her friend that she wouldn't be going to school tomorrow. She never went during the dark moon phase for fear of having a hallucination in class. The faeries and elves already kept their distance. How would they react if she fell into a trance right in front of them? "I'll be there."

The ball of Tatou's light shrank into a pinprick and then disappeared completely.

Melia slumped with her back bowing out, her elbows on her thighs, and her chin on the flats of her fists. They used to chase glow sprites on the shores of the Undine River, but now they experimented with faerie herbs. Maybe the ylandria wasn't working because she didn't want to know the truth. Her father's trespass had violated some inner boundary, one from which there was no retreat. It was a disturbing thought, to be forever transformed for the worse through no fault of her own, and at such an early age.

The ylandria's spicy fumes hung in the air. Melia sucked in a long breath. Her mind danced with energy. Focusing on a single flame seemed dull. She drew her knees up to rest her chin on them and turned her thoughts to her favorite fantasy. A pair of turquoise wings shimmered before her. Diamond chips laced the outer wings and lavender and emerald swirls patterned the inner wings. In her mind's eye, Melia reached out her hands and brushed an intricate mesh of downy feathers.

She dropped her legs, her feet swinging free, and gripped the branch she sat on with tight fingers. It helped her to connect the muscle and bone of her torso and shoulders with the wings in her mind's eye. With a gentle flutter, a slow flap, and a coordinated beating, she shot upwards. Delighted with her mental creation, she soared higher than any faerie of flower or field ever could.

The enormous oak cradling the tree house shrank below. She faced east, toward the meadows, but she wanted to fly toward the sea. She prepared to make the wide arc west–and froze. A familiar force wrested control of her mind. It erupted from deep within her and superimposed an alternate reality.

✧✧✧

I sniff the air. Something burns. I search the skyline for smoke. Heat and cinders explode beneath me.

I land on the ground. Sparks snap in the night. The tree house crackles. Flames run up its walls and prance across the roof. Bright tongues lick the towering oak. A wall of heat blisters my skin and scorches a trail to the Sylvan Forest. Heart-wrenching screeches explode in the night. I cover my ears. An enormous buck tramples the blaze, leading a stampede of deer. Following on their trail, an army of smaller woodland animals scurry from the inferno.

One of the oak's branches split, the tree house lurches.

Mother screams.

I can't see my father, yet from some hidden recess he encourages me, "Let it run wild."

I throw back my head and laugh.

✧✧✧

"Wake up." Her mother squeezed her shoulder, pinching her skin.

Melia twisted free of the grip. She was on the ground. Flat on her back. Everything throbbed. She must have fallen out of the tree.

"It's the middle of the night. What are you doing out here?" her mother asked.

Melia felt more than saw Pressina lean over her. She jabbed her heels in the dirt, pushing her body away. The ylandria had tasted sharp, not unpleasant. Could her mother smell its distinctive fragrance in her hair? Or on her nightgown? She couldn't tell. To Melia, the burning maelstrom of her vision still lingered. She wiped her nose with the back of her hand, hoping to clear the smell of charred wood.

"Do I smell ylandria?"

Melia rolled farther away and stood up. A twig poked through her nightgown. She brushed it, along with some leaves and grass, from her back. Her side felt tender, but nothing worse. She'd probably have some bruises in the morning.

"Answer me."

Honesty was useless. "I couldn't sleep."

Before she could dodge Pressina's hand, her mother's long fingers dug the two ylandria butts from the pocket in Melia's nightgown.

How had she managed that? Melia could barely distinguish her mother's shape–the slightest shade darker than the night around her.

Pressina grabbed her daughter's arm and pulled her toward the spiral steps circling the oak.

Resistance would only fuel her anger.

In the front room, Melusine and Plantine huddled together on their mother's favorite lime-striped chaise. They each held a candle. Otherwise the room was dark. Malachi, Mother's botched spell of a cat, hissed from the shadows as her mother dragged Melia into the kitchen.

"Melusine, Plantine, bring the candles," their mother commanded.

Her sisters pressed their melting sticks into the holders on the table. Melia formed a barrier over her chest with her arms. The flickering light drove home her failure; the ylandria had increased the power of her visions, not her control over them. While she'd dreamed of wings and flight, her timid inner flame–the one that had kept blowing out–ignited an inner inferno in some back corridor of her mind. She reached out to one of the kitchen chairs to steady herself.

Melusine's blue eyes burned with suspicion. Plantine's pained gaze was the one she always wore when Melia got in trouble.

"You were laughing hysterically," Pressina said. "It was so loud, you woke us up."

"Sorry I interrupted your beauty sleep."

"It was an evil laugh," Melusine said.

"All right, off to bed," their mother dismissed Melusine and Plantine. Neither dared challenge her, a testament to her angry state. Pressina pulled out a chair and eased into it.

Melia didn't move.

"What were you doing smoking ylandria?"

For a split second, Melia considered whether her mother might help. But Pressina resented the telepathic connection her daughters shared with their father. Bringing it up would infuriate her.

The color of her mother's lilac eyes deepened. "Where did you get it?"

Melia made a meal out of one of her fingernails. She'd be fending off her mother's glamour soon.

Pressina threw the butts on the table. Her ivory wings quivered.

Melia should have had an equally striking pair. But no, the Whole had played a cruel joke. As a half-faerie, she lived with a psychic bond to her mortal father–which she didn't want–and as a half-mortal, she lived without the one thing that she yearned for–which her faerie mother had–wings.

The shade of Pressina's eyes reached purple-black. A tendril of her will, an invisible leash, made her daughter's lip quiver with a desire to confess.

Furious, Melia dropped her gaze. It wasn't enough that her father's psychic probing had opened a doorway in her mind she needed to close, now her mother was trying to glamour her. She wasn't going to let her. Not tonight, not ever again.

Melia shifted her focus to the wax pearling down the sides of the candles. "I just wanted to try it."

"What am I going to do with you?"

"Send m-me to b-bed without sup-supper?"

The silly comment snapped her mother's concentration.

Melia tipped her head ever so slightly, to confirm the glamour had failed, but it was hardly a triumph.

Now, Pressina's eyes blazed with dissatisfaction. Faeries–always charming and graceful–didn't stutter. Her mother didn't need to say the words out loud. Pressina's harsh thoughts seeped beneath her daughter's skin: You're an abomination.

Melia gulped.

Pressina swept the ylandria butts into her palm, closed her hand into a fist, and jiggled them for emphasis. "The herbs in Illialei are potent, even to full-blooded faeries. Ylandria is toxic to mortals in large doses. When you decided to smoke this stuff, did you ever stop to think you're only half faerie?"

"How could I forget?" Melia pushed the words through clenched teeth.

"Stop feeling sorry for yourself. You don't know the half of it."

"Then tell me."

Her mother waved her hand, indicating there wouldn't be any telling tonight. Not surprising, Pressina forever hinted at a trunk-load of secrets she was either too afraid or too noble to reveal.

"If you're going to experiment with faerie herbs, get some reliable information."

Melia swallowed the challenge she wanted to make about reliable information. Her mother was winding down, no need to wind her back up again.

"Sh-sure."

"If you're not careful, you'll end up as wasted as one of those pathetic full-blooded mortals who comes to Faerie and loses their way forever."

"A pathetic, full-blooded mortal like my father?"

"We're done here," Pressina said.

Finally.

Melia stomped down the hall. She wished she could stomp right out of the tree house and into another life.

✧✧✧

The next morning, Melia feigned a headache. After she heard Plantine's steps on the oak's spiral staircase, she rolled over and waited for Melusine's slippered feet to patter by. The nest of blue jays who made their home in the oak chattered outside her window. Melia tiptoed over to say, "Good morning," to them. She caught sight of Melusine headed toward the river, probably off to the mortal world with her faerie friends.

Her mother's bedroom door creaked open. Melia dove back beneath the covers. If she was quiet, Pressina wouldn't notice her middle daughter was skipping school–again. Not that her mother cared. She was always distracted these days, disappearing into her subterranean room to study magic, or whatever else she did down there.

Melia didn't want to answer questions about ylandria–or anything else–this morning. She cracked her bedroom door open. When she heard the lock click on the door of her mother's study, Melia's body relaxed. Now, she just had to get out of the tree house and stay gone for the rest of the day. She ran her fingers through her long, dark hair as she tried to decide what to wear. A worn summer coat and several sleeveless dresses filled her closet. She reached for the orange one. As she pulled it over her head, she half-listened for her mother. The tree house remained quiet.

Barefoot, Melia padded down the hall.

The great oak's columnar trunk formed the central pillar of the tree house. From its axis, a single layer of branches spanned the front room, wheel-like, about two feet beneath the high ceiling. From his high perch on one of the limbs, Malachi fixed his strange golden eyes on Melia. When she passed underneath him, he hissed. Melia walked backward with curled fingers, taunting the odd creature as he continued to glower at her.

When he started to yowl, she spun and scooted out the door, running with light feet on the oak's steps. No doubt his annoying whines would draw Pressina from her study–they were about the only thing that did.

On the bottom stair, Melia's stomach growled. She headed in the direction opposite Melusine had gone, toward Bryndale.

A little while later, she wandered through the city's vegetable market.

The other shoppers stared more than usual as she sauntered by.

Yes, I should be in school. No, I'm not there. She stopped at the tomato stand to pick up a couple of Marguerite's famous beefsteaks.

"It was one of Pressina's daughters."

When she overheard her mother's name, Melia froze.

"She was *howling* outside the tree house."

A lump formed in the half-faerie's throat. Two old elves–she could tell by their thick, nasal voices–gossiped on the other side of the canvas wall in the stall that sold broccoli and cauliflower.

"If you ask me, it has everything to do with him. After all these years, he's still obsessed with Pressina."

The voices softened. Melia grabbed two ripe fruits and shoved past a group of field faeries. She pressed her ear against the divider to see if she could hear anything else.

"How long has it been? A decade? Almost two?"

"Longer than that in the mortal world."

"They say he's discovered a way to incarnate Umbra."

"Why does he want to stir up that kind of trouble?"

"He thinks it will change the laws between the worlds."

"So?"

"The old laws keep him out of Faerie, maybe the new laws will let him back in."

"Mortals!" The first elf's condescension rang out loud and clear. "What part of breaking a faerie troth does he not understand? You don't get a second chance. That's the point. He needs to move on. Forget about Pressina and incarnating Umbra."

"Are you going to tell him?"

"And miss my afternoon nap, when I've got dibs on the shadiest spot in the glen?"

Snort. "Have you seen the girls?"

"Pretty enough, but they don't have any wings."

"I heard the one involved in the incident last night is dangerous."

"They don't belong here. Pressina should have left them in the mortal world with him."

The elves wandered off.

Melia's impulse to rip aside the curtain and rain ripe tomatoes down upon the mouthy pair came too late. Red-orange juice oozed over her hands. Seeds and pulp splattered her dress. She'd squeezed the tomatoes so hard they burst.

A few feet away, a couple of flower faeries whispered.

"What are you looking at?" she demanded.

They tittered and preened, flaring their wings.

Melia stalked away.

He was the great mortal druid, Elynus–her father. Apparently, sowing her visions wasn't enough. Now, he was going to incarnate Umbra, whatever that meant.

Melia's jaw tightened as she hiked out of town.

Stupid elves. She was *laughing*, not howling.

2. The Prophecy

High Hill rose before Melia. As she ascended its grassy slope, the joyous sound of young brownies in the distance eased her frown. The hill's eastern side overlooked the Footing Fields where they played ball.

When she reached the hill's summit, Illialei spread out before her. To the west, the horizon of the Great White Sea sparkled in the late afternoon sun, and to the east, the rounded caps of the Rolling Mountains cradled Lake Vivientiana.

She headed toward the enclave of stone and towering pine where she and Tatou always met. After lowering herself to the ground, she leaned back on her elbows and swung out her legs. Falling out of the tree had left her with a stiff tailbone and a pale bruise on her hip. Not too bad, all things considered.

A flap of wings approached to her right–a flock of field faeries most likely.

Someone giggled.

Melia's body stiffened as she searched the hill's grassy incline for Tatou. If she were here, they'd leave her alone.

"What have we here?" Verbena, a loathsome flower faerie with the most gorgeous amber wings, entered Melia's field of vision. Her two best friends, Clementine and Brigitta, traipsed behind her. Specks of gold in Verbena's wings glinted in the afternoon sun. Melia had to shade her eyes with her hand to look at them. "Why, if it isn't Melia, daughter of the great mortal druid, Elynus," Verbena announced as if no one present knew who she was.

Clementine and Brigitta tittered. Their leader had said something clever.

Melia pressed her lips into a sullen line.

The haughty flower faerie stepped forward, pulled her skirt with a flamboyant swish, and folded herself into a graceful pose in the grass beside Melia. "Exactly who I was hoping to find."

Clementine's and Brigitta's mouths dropped open. Verbena patted the ground and her friends sat.

Still no sign of Tatou.

"You must be lost," Melia said. The hill wasn't where flower faeries usually gathered. They preferred the Danu Meadows, the banks of the Nyssalei River, and the shops in Bryndale.

Verbena winked at her friends. "We missed you in class today, didn't we?" Brigitta's and Clementine's heads bobbed. "Melusine thought I could find you up here."

Melia's heart thumped in her chest. She thought her older sister's best friend was Gisele, not this hag. Where was Tatou?

"I want to ask you a question," Verbena said.

The faerie's smug demeanor rattled Melia. She snuck a sideways glance at the flower faerie. Was she trying to glamour her?

Full-blooded faeries could affect a mortal's thoughts and emotions with a focused gaze, but faeries couldn't glamour one another, and most couldn't glamour Melia or her sisters. Pressina had always been the exception. Nevertheless, Melia made a point to look away. Her gazed settled on Brigitta's wings. They weren't as pretty as Verbena's, but their unusual color made them striking. Melia shifted her gaze to Clementine's sad, dandelion-colored wings–the plain appendages bolstered her.

"The rumors about your *father* ..." Verbena stretched the word to full effect.

Melia continued to avoid the flower faerie's gaze. "What a dull subject."

"Is he going to incarnate Umbra?"

"I don't know anything about it."

"I don't believe you," Verbena's tone turned nasty. She must have figured out her glamour wasn't working. "Everyone is talking about last night."

Melia imagined one of the tall pine trees cracking at its roots and smashing the flower faerie in the head.

"How you were laughing outside the tree house," Verbena's words dripped with malice.

At least she hadn't accused her of howling.

"I heard it was a horrible, evil laugh."

How did everyone know?

"Melusine said it made her skin crawl. She thinks you're going to help your father destroy Illialei."

Melia's head was spinning. Had her sister told every single creature she'd met on the way to the river this morning?

Melusine was a statuesque redhead who didn't stutter. Socially fierce, her lack of wings had never hindered her popularity among the flower faeries. Spiritually, she was one of them. Melia couldn't fathom how she managed it, and secretly envied her for it, but hated whenever her sister gossiped about her. Which was far too often.

"I think you're his spy."

The accusation stretched Melia's thin patience beyond its limit. "I don't even talk to him!"

"Did I touch a nerve?" Verbena's sickly-sweet voice rotted in the air between them.

Melia's heart raced so fast it threatened to escape her chest. "Leave me alone!"

"Or what, you'll turn me into a toad?" the flower faerie snickered.

If only she could–and splat her with one stomp of her heel. She needed to get away from Verbena, but it was too late. By the time she jumped up, her reality was already shifting.

✧✧✧

Acrid smoke burns the inside of my nose and lungs.

I turn in circles.

Tendrils of grey-white smoke rise as mist; charred tree stumps thrust jagged and menacing from the ground. Dark rivulets streak blackened rock.

Verbena's, Clementine's, and Brigitta's lifeless bodies lie a few feet from where I stand. More bodies–twisted and unidentifiable, form a grotesque heap farther down the hill. Mud, soot, and blood stain my fingers and palms–accusing me of slaughter.

Vindication possesses me; wave after wave of satisfaction washes over me.

My father's disembodied voice applauds.

✧ ✧ ✧

"Melia!" Tatou's bell-like voice called her back to the present.

Clementine's mouth gaped; Brigitta inched backward, eyes wide. Verbena smirked. Tatou shooed them away.

Melia collapsed on the grass, her body cool and clammy. When the flower faeries were out of sight, she propped herself up.

Tatou pirouetted to land on Melia's knee. The petite faerie reached for the pixie dust she always carried with her. Melia tamped down rage. Tatou blew the sparkling, powder-like crystals into the air. Melia inhaled the pixie magic. The sting of Verbena's accusations faded while the horror of her latest vision wavered. Although Tatou stood barely two hand-lengths tall, her heart was as big and as constant as the sun.

"I don't know what would have happened if you hadn't shown up when you did."

"I'm worried about you," Tatou said.

"You should be more worried about yourself. Haven't you heard? I'm dangerous."

Prisms of light shot through the pixie's gossamer wings. "Maybe the ylandria was a bad idea."

"I don't want to talk about it."

Tatou frowned.

Melia let her body drop flat against the ground. The thick throb at the base of her spine reminded her she needed to steer clear of Pressina and her questioning gaze for the next few days too.

"You're making things worse by keeping everything to yourself." Tatou fluttered near Melia's head. She reached out with tiny fingers to push a length of hair behind the half-faerie's ear. "You need to talk to someone."

Melia closed her eyes, reliving the flower faeries' deaths on High Hill. "I can't."

The pixie landed on Melia's stomach. She pivoted and settled cross-legged, facing the half-faerie's knees. "Pretend I'm not here, and tell me about the vision you just had."

Melia chewed her lower lip.

"Start any time," Tatou said.

"You can't tell anyone what I'm about to tell you, not even a whisper."

"I promise."

Melia squeezed her eyes shut and haltingly shared the vision in a cracked voice.

"Are you sure they were all dead?" her friend asked.

"Yes," Melia whispered.

"And there was blood everywhere?"

"Yes."

"This is what I think–"

Melia's heart pitched. She pushed herself up straighter. "Turn around," she said. "I need to see your face."

Her friend met her gaze. Melia's heart unclenched. She couldn't detect any judgment in the pixie's eyes.

"This is much bigger than you or your father," Tatou said.

"What do you mean?"

The pixie hopped down to the grass, gesticulating. "There's a poem that was written hundreds, maybe thousands of years ago. It's called the Idonnic Prophecy, What you saw describes an image written in one of the lines."

"What is the prophecy about?"

"The end of the Whole as we know it."

"That doesn't feel right to me."

"Why not?"

"What I see in these visions isn't about the Whole." The half-faerie rubbed her thumb against her lower lip. "It's about me–about something dark inside me."

Tatou pondered what her friend had said. Her eyes lit up. "According to the prophecy, there's hope."

"What kind of hope?"

"'The purpose is love.'"

Melia's heart sank.

"I know, I know." The pixie pressed her hands up and down mid-air. "You don't believe in love."

"You know I don't."

"Maybe some day you will."

Melia tossed her head.

"It could happen," her friend insisted.

"I don't think your prophecy is going to help me," Melia grumbled.

Tatou buzzed in front of her face. "It's not my prophecy."

Several weeks later, Melia and Tatou sat next to the stone wall that formed a perimeter around the enchanted gardens, where the meadow grass grew long enough to hide them. Tatou braided a crown of sky-blue asters.

"My life is over," Melia said.

"At least Melusine feels guilty."

Her older sister's genuine remorse was the only bright patch since Pressina had caught Melia smoking ylandria. "It's hardly enough," Melia said. "I can't go anywhere without some brownie staring or an elf pointing his finger. I was walking home last night and a flower faerie I didn't even know accused me of being a traitor. I'm surprised Queen Luisa hasn't thrown me in some dungeon."

"With all this talk about your father incarnating Umbra, everyone's getting worked up."

"Why won't they leave me out of it?"

Tatou puffed her cheeks. They both knew why not. Although Melusine had done all she could to stop the rumors from spreading, Verbena did everything but make daily announcements in Bryndale square; the flower faerie was determined to convince anyone who would listen that Melia and her father harbored a vendetta against Illialei. Her fixation bewildered the half-faerie.

"I've never done anything to Verbena. Why won't she leave me alone?"

"Envy?"

"Of what?"

Tatou hesitated. "You're prettier than she is."

Melia scoffed. "Everyone is. Her wings might be gorgeous, but her face looks like a smashed toadstool." Tatou giggled and Melia joined her. The tension in the half-faerie's jaw released, and her heart felt lighter. "Seriously, what am I going to do?"

Tatou placed the ring of asters on Melia's head. She lingered. "Have you thought about going to the Illustrator?"

Melia had seen the Illustrator's delicate, colorful artwork many times. Sometimes the faeries and elves at school wore spirals she'd painted, circling their arms and legs. Others favored budding flowers or crescent moons on their cheeks and foreheads. In the Bryndale market, she'd seen the skin of elders covered with more intricate patterns. "Why would I do that?"

The pixie settled on a nearby rock with her legs crossed, her elbows on her knees. "There are protective shields that can be painted on the body. They ward off bad things."

"You think she could paint something on me that could stop my visions?"

"Maybe. Maybe they'd protect you from Verbena's malice as well."

"That would be powerful magic," Melia mused.

"You can't hide out forever–skipping school, avoiding the market, never going to High Hill again."

"I'm not worried about missing school."

"But you're almost finished. Even Melusine finished school."

"Studying the *Old Texts* doesn't sound very appealing right now."

"You can't just give up," Tatou said. "Besides, you need to understand what you're up against. The *Old Texts* are full of information."

"I'll trust what's in my heart over anything written ages ago in some stupid book."

"It doesn't have to be one or the other."

The half-faerie rolled over. "Before Verbena made me her target, I overheard two elves gossiping at the market in Bryndale."

"What were they saying?"

"Besides talking about me? They were talking about my mother–"

"They shouldn't be talking about your mother at all."

Melia raised her eyebrows.

Tatou's wings twitched. "It's not polite."

"Manners." Melia studied the pixie. "That's old-fashioned."

Her friend disappeared into the gerber daisies that looked like orange lollipops with golden centers.

The half-faerie followed. "How old are you?"

"The longer you live, the less age matters," came Tatou's muffled response. It was the same answer the pixie always gave when asked about her age.

Melia let it go. "They were talking about my father incarnating Umbra, so he can come back to Faerie. Is that part of the prophecy too?"

Tatou's head poked from behind an enormous blossom. "There's something about the ancient doors closing."

Melia settled back down into the grass. "Nothing about the doors between the mortal and enchanted worlds opening?"

"No."

"Then I wonder what he's thinking?"

"Do you want to hear the prophecy?"

"You can recite the whole thing?"

"Yes."

Melia didn't believe a dusty old poem offered a solution to her problem. "Maybe another day."

"Fine."

"I'm so tired of all this." The half-faerie propped herself up on her elbows. "Maybe we could catch a ship at Southend and sail beyond Faerie, to a place where it doesn't matter that I'm the wingless daughter of Pressina and Elynus."

"Do you think that will stop your visions?"

"My mother wouldn't even notice I was gone."

Tatou frowned.

Melia rolled over and stared into the sky. "Maybe I'd be happier somewhere else. Maybe being happier would stop my visions."

The pixie zoomed from behind the daisies. She hung in front of Melia's face. "Go see the Illustrator. I'll go with you."

Melia hugged her knees to her chest. If she was going to go back to the

Illustrator, she'd do it alone. "Do you remember when I first came to Illialei?"

"Yes."

"I'd never seen a pixie before."

"I remember."

Melia held out her palm. "I thought you were more wonderful than anything I could have imagined–an enchanted bird who could talk. I followed you everywhere. You never tried to stop me. Why not?"

Her friend landed in her hand. "The other pixies never want to leave the enchanted gardens, but I want to explore."

"Then sail away with me. We can explore the enchanted world together."

Tatou crossed her arms.

Melia's chin quavered. "Fine. I'll go see the Illustrator." She didn't say when she would go.

✧ ✧ ✧

The first morning of the next dark moon phase, Melia curled beneath her covers, contemplating which illness to claim for the day. Another headache or strained ankle was sure to arouse suspicion.

"We're going to be late," Plantine yelled from the long hallway that ran between the sisters' rooms and dead-ended at their mother's.

"I'm not going to school today," Melia croaked.

Plantine peeked into her sister's bedroom. "I knew it."

Melia clutched her abdomen, conjuring up the appearance of as much distress as she could.

Her younger sister advanced with her arms behind her back. "Every dark moon phase an ailment strikes you. What is it this time? A sour stomach?"

Sometimes, Plantine knew her too well. "Too much raw dandelion weed, perhaps?" Melia forced her voice to quaver.

Her sister edged closer to the bed. When she was within arm's length, she produced the cup hidden behind her back. "I brewed this for you."

Melia jerked up. "When did you make it?"

Plantine handed her the cup. "It's been absorbing the waning moonlight on my windowsill for several nights."

The pale, milky liquid smelled delicious. "What is it?"

"The dust of flower petals, a bit of a crushed magnolia cone–one that fell inside the walls of the enchanted gardens, condensed water from that contraption in the kitchen, and an incantation I created on my own."

"Following in Mother's footsteps, are we?"

Plantine frowned. "It's no black magic."

"So you say."

"No one in Illialei could find fault with the ingredients or my spell. Drink it, and you'll be able to go to school today."

As they'd argued, the potion's pleasant grassy scent wafted around Melia's head in an invisible cloud. It begged to be tasted. After she took the first sip, she couldn't stop until every last drop was gone.

It felt like she'd swallowed a bottle of dappled sunlight. The gentle energy diffused her apprehension. It would be fine if she went to school today. Melia wondered at the spell's effect. "You designed this to soothe my stomach?"

"No," Plantine beamed. "Its intent was to counteract whatever ailed you. It worked didn't it?"

It was impossible to lie, and now it would be impossible to avoid school. At least the fear of having a vision in class wouldn't consume her.

"Hurry up!" her sister interrupted her thoughts. "We're already late."

Merry Nettle, a stalk-like flower faerie with crisp, sand-colored wings, wrote *Idonnic Prophecy* on the blackboard.

Melia sighed.

Tatou would be thrilled to know the poem was being taught in school.

After the teacher punctuated each word of the title with a thick line, she continued her scribbling. Melia watched until Merry wrote, *The blood of innocents will soak Illialei's meadows.* Beads of sweat collected on the half-faerie's forehead.

Why hadn't Tatou told her?

She gripped the sides of her wooden desk and snuck a glance at her nearest classmates.

In front of her, Plantine faced forward. To her right, Brigitta passed a note to Clementine. No one sat to her left. Verbena sat in the first row with her eyes riveted on their teacher.

Thankful no one paid her any attention, Melia slouched back in her seat. She tuned out her teacher's droning words–she'd already seen and heard too much.

The blood of innocents will soak Illialei's meadows.

No wonder Tatou was so concerned about her. Before Melia had been born, some anonymous priest in a faraway land had managed to describe the horror of her visions. Down to the last detail. How was that possible?

Melia's gaze returned to the chalkboard. *This apocalyptic union can be saved.*

Verbena's hand shot up.

"Yes?" Merry prompted her best pupil.

"Is it true *apocalyptic union* refers to Umbra's incarnation?"

Melia stared at her desk.

"The meaning is obscure," the teacher said, "but there are scholars throughout the enchanted world who have posited that theory."

"Then, I should think," Verbena's sharp voice persisted, "any loyal citizen of Illialei would be strongly opposed to the incarnation, and do all they could to stop it."

Melia crossed her forearms on her desktop and dropped her head into the cradle they made. Maybe it was time to go see the Illustrator.

A deep-voiced field-faerie joined in the discussion. "The passage is hopeful."

"If you call the death of innocents hopeful," Verbena sneered.

"Many believe it speaks of a new age."

"Not for those who will die."

"Some believe the death is metaphoric."

"And others believe it's literal!" Verbena screeched. "If Umbra incarnates, war will come to Illialei."

"Who needs Umbra when we've got Verbena?" another voice shouted.

Melia choked back a laugh and raised her head. As everyone chattered at once, she searched the classroom for the flower-faerie's detractor.

Merry rapped the board with the long, thin stick she used as a pointer. "Class, class, come to order!"

Melia couldn't determine who'd challenged her tormenter, but the class wasn't coming to order. One aisle over and two seats down, five pixies gathered on a single desktop. One hugged her knees as she twittered with her friend beside her. Two had plopped on their bellies–chins in hands, toes dangling over the desktop's edge–ready to nap in the drowsy heat of late summer. The fifth crawled toward the others, mischief in her eyes.

The uproar in the classroom fueled a sense of rebellion. Melia looked over her shoulder–the schoolroom door stood open. If she darted out the next time Merry turned to face the board, no one–not even Plantine–would notice.

As she watched for her teacher's back, the words on the chalkboard drew her once more. *Though grace is undeserved, the purpose is love.*

Melia rolled her eyes.

The fifth pixie pinched one of her sleeping friends. The friend's shocked squeak ignited a brawl among the tiny faeries. Pandemonium swept the classroom.

Melia dashed toward freedom.

3. The Illustrator

By the time Melia's pace slowed, she'd reached the outskirts of Bryndale, and the cobbled stones that formed neat geometric mazes around the town's central square were far behind her. As she searched the dusty alleys for the Illustrator's shop, a memory stirred within her–one she'd tried to forget: A much younger version of herself clutched her mother's hand and sobbed because she couldn't fly with the full-blooded faeries.

Just recalling the scene made Melia's cheeks flush.

It had been right after her father had broken his faerie troth. Plantine had just been born. The first scream from his youngest daughter had sounded, and their father had burst into their mother's bedroom. It was probably an innocent mistake, but it had violated the single promise her father had made when he'd married Melia's mother: to never view her in childbirth.

Faerie troths were that way, peculiar vows required by mortals, which prohibited specific acts toward the faeries they wed. Taking the vow allowed the faerie to live a normal life with their mortal spouse, undetectable as a creature from another realm. Breaking the vow undid all of that. It immediately ended the life the couple shared together without recourse.

Thus, Pressina was required to return to the enchanted world, and Melia was abruptly introduced to Illialei and full-blooded faeries with wings.

Pressina had kept her wings locked away in a metal box until they'd left Ireland. When that bitter day came, she'd slipped them on as if they were a splendid jacket. Her middle daughter had watched in awe as the ivory appendages fused seamlessly with her mother's back.

✧ ✧ ✧

"Where are mine?" Melia asked.

Pressina shushed Plantine, swathed in her crib.

"Where are my wings?" Melia persisted.

Her mother watched the window.

"Just tell her she doesn't have any," Melusine said.

Melia slugged her older sister.

"Don't do that," Pressina said. "It's almost twilight. We must go."

Melia refused to move.

Her mother leaned over to pick up Plantine. "Honey–"

Melia grabbed one of her mother's wings and tugged as hard as she could. Nothing happened.

Melusine ran for the door, laughing. "She thinks she's a bird."

"Can I help you?"

The question jerked Melia from her reverie.

The speaker, a slender, nut-skinned woman, sat on a wide porch. The Illustrator looked exactly as she had years ago when Melia had refused her services.

After crossing the borders separating the mortal and enchanted worlds, and discovering that all full-blooded faeries had wings–not only her mother–Melia had been inconsolable.

It had been a non-issue in the mortal world. There, Melia's faerie blood had rendered her uncommon in an appealing way, but here in Illialei, surrounded by the faeries of flower and field flitting about, she stood out in a graceless and lumbering way.

Asking the Illustrator to paint an intricate pair of wings upon her daughter's back had been Pressina's solution. But even at three, Melia had known that wouldn't make any real difference, she still wouldn't be able to fly.

She pressed her lips together. Soon after, she'd begun to stutter.

Recalling that painful visit from years ago strengthened Melia's resolve to move past her father's obsession with her mother, and her mother's obsession with black magic. It was time to forget prophecies as well, and to get on with *her* life. Stopping the visions would be a good start.

She opened the gate of the blistered, light blue fence that bordered the Illustrator's yard. Wild dogwood and sage crawled over the stones and dirt most faeries would have cultivated into a manicured garden. Luscious yellow and pink roses spilled into a lazy river, flowing down a weathered trellis.

"I was looking for your shop, for you," Melia said.

The Illustrator stood, a sun goddess rising. Pink and yellow scarves, matching the roses on her lawn, swirled around a carrot-colored shift which hugged her taut body. Stars and spirals twined her bare arms. She motioned Melia to follow her inside the unpretentious, but colorful, wooden building.

Melia had forgotten the Illustrator didn't have wings either. She traced the rocky steps to the front door.

"Come in," the invitation drifted from the interior.

As Melia crossed the threshold, cats–real ones, not botched spells like Malachi–froze, watching her. She felt as if she were a four-armed, blue-skinned sorceress from Kyrakkos who'd wandered into a crowded bar at Southend. She took another step. The creatures resumed their feline movement–re-curling in their high perches and stretching on the front room's magenta sofa.

A unique fragrance filled the cottage. Vanilla? Cinnamon? She couldn't quite place it, but it made her want to curl up on one of the sofas, alongside the cats, and take a nap. She forced herself to stand straight.

"Coffee?" The Illustrator's question came from the back of her studio.

Before Melia could answer, the woman returned with two plates. She set them on a table then brushed a fat black cat from its seat. The cat glared at Melia, straightened its tail, and padded from the room. The Illustrator swatted black hairs from the cushions and gestured for the half-faerie to sit. "Have you ever had coffee?"

Mesmerized by the woman's jet-black hair, neatly arched brows, and tiny nose ring, Melia fell silent. No one in Illialei looked anything like her.

"It's sinfully good." Her host winked. "Not that we worry much about sin here–one of the many reasons I don't go home." She pointed to the dark gems and slim biscuits on the plates. "With chocolate and biscotti, it's divine. Let me fix you a cup with a bit of cardamom and nutmeg. You'll love it."

She was so welcoming, maybe she hadn't heard the rumors about Melia or her father. "Thank you." Melia reached down to pet the grey cat rubbing against her leg, marveling at its soft coat.

"Call me Nandana. You're Pressina's middle girl, am I right?"

She had heard the gossip. Melia's face burned when she told the Illustrator her name.

"We'll chat about why you've come back to see me after all this time." The woman disappeared again. She returned with a cup filled with dark, steaming liquid, which she handed to Melia before sitting down across from her.

"Are you a muannaye?" Melia asked the question dancing on the tip of her tongue. She'd never seen a muannaye, but she'd heard they were beautiful and had no wings.

Nandana's laugh put her further at ease. "Oh no, I'm mortal." The woman seemed so comfortable in her home.

Melia wished she were as confident. "Do you enjoy your life here in Faerie?"

"You don't?" Nandana prodded.

"I love Illialei's beauty."

"It hurts when the faeries and elves spread lies about you, no?" Nandana′s kind response–so different from her mother's sharp, "you're my daughter, just ignore them" comments–sparked a craving in Melia to confide.

She blinked hard as tears formed in the corners of her eyes. She didn't want Nandana to find her pathetic or weepy. As Melia wiped her nose with the back of her hand, a single tear rolled hot down her cheek. She pressed her palm against her face to halt its wet trail. The grey cat curled up at her feet raised its head. Its luminous green eyes searched hers. When it seemed satisfied no greater outburst loomed, it went back to sleep.

Protestations tumbled from Melia's mouth. "I'd never destroy Illialei.

The rumors–the things they're saying about me–it's all lies."

"I believe you," Nandana said.

"You do?"

"Yes."

Melia bit her lip. Did Nandana know about the prophecy? If she was from the mortal world, maybe she didn't. But what if she did? Melia asked her about it.

"I've heard of it."

"Do you believe it's true?" Melia asked.

"Nothing is ever certain until it happens."

That was better than Tatou's conviction that the prophecy was some unavoidable edict.

The Illustrator smiled. "Why don't we talk about what else is troubling you."

Nandana's interest, so encouraging, drew Melia out. Before she knew it, she'd opened up to the Illustrator about her visions.

"You had the first hallucination after your father began probing your mind?" Nandana asked.

"He wanted to know things I didn't dare talk about." Things Melia was uncomfortable admitting: resentment of Melusine's circle of friends; envy of Plantine attracting the attention of every male who existed; shame over her inability to speak without tripping over her tongue–and her useless desire to fly.

Nandana never looked away. "The faeries and elves come to my shop for many reasons," she said. "Some want to mark their birthdays and weddings, others to celebrate the birth of a child. Some wish to adorn themselves for parties, and others come to honor death. All of them talk. These days, all the talk is of Umbra and Elynus. How much do you know about Umbra?"

"M-my father wants to incarnate him. N-nobody else wants him to do it." Melia's stammering embarrassed her. She stopped talking.

Nandana held her cup with both hands, but didn't drink any of the coffee. "Umbra exists in the Void, beyond the Parallel of Shadows. Although he's incorporeal, he's considered to be quite dangerous." Her eyes darted to the front window as if she might find his disembodied form hovering there like a storm threatening Illialei's perennial blue skies. "He's the dross of human consciousness."

"I don't understand."

Nandana set down her cup. She used her hands to show how mortal essence divided. Unfinished souls were reabsorbed into the Primal Essence, while evolved ones traveled on to the Unknown Beyond. The problem was the in-between souls. They were neither unfinished, nor fully evolved, and upon death they split, creating ember and ash. The ash was a toxic residue. Nandana called it psychic ash, and explained how it fueled Umbra's growth. Melia's heart pumped. The room felt hot, her palms damp.

"The Whole is out of balance," Nandana said. "There are some who believe Umbra's incarnation is an opportunity to correct that imbalance, but not without a war–the outcome of which is uncertain. That uncertainty causes great fear." The woman shifted back in her seat. "I fear this war too. It will be like nothing anyone has ever seen."

Melia's mind leapt. Had she seen? What if every vision she'd had for the past five years had been a premonition of war–not proof that some virulent evil existed within her?

The startling connection dismayed her as much as it relieved her.

Everything always came back to Elynus. His determination to incarnate Umbra either aggravated her visions or caused them.

If only he would stop!

A familiar pressure steeled the half-faerie's jaw.

The walls of Nandana's cottage implode.

Wood splinters into violent shards. The cottage roof collapses in a single thunderous roar.

Cats hiss and yowl.

The floor ruptures, and a rotten smell saturates the air. I turn.

Nandana sprawls on the floor. Her scarves twist around her. Dried blood cakes a gash on her forehead. The grey cat with the soft fur lies beside her–its belly split wide.

"There are no innocents in Illialei," my father whispers.

"Melia!" Nandana stepped on the grey tabby's tail. It hissed and ran from the room. She brushed the half-faerie's forehead with the back of her hand. Her fingers were cool. The woman pointed to the cup of coffee on the table. "Drink, then tell me what just happened."

Melia mumbled as much as she dared between sips of coffee and bites of chocolate. Plantine's potion had made her careless. She should have come to talk to Nandana another day. But after the lesson in school had shaken her, she'd finally decided to follow through on Tatou's advice.

Nandana pressed for details. When Melia evaded, the Illustrator insisted she drink a second cup of coffee. Although it burnt her tongue, her weepiness subsided, her exhaustion faded, and her insides hummed. The steaming liquid girded something within her. She felt able to face the horror of what she'd seen. She shared more with Nandana, and the woman absorbed every word with grave respect.

When Melia finished, she sat back in her chair. While her impromptu confession had been cathartic, the purpose of her visit hadn't changed: No matter what their source or what their meaning, she wished to be done with her visions. "I've heard there are symbols that can be painted on the body for protection."

Nandana's eyebrows rose the slightest bit. "That's true."

"Do you know how to make them?" Melia pressed.

"Most of the work I do is decorative–and impermanent."

Melia remembered sneaking into Princess Lilliane Albiana's declaration ceremony years ago. The Illustrator's designs–ornamenting cheeks, foreheads, arms, necklines, throats, and hands–had rivaled the artistry of the gowns and the sparkle of the gemstones.

"Can you draw the shields?" Melia asked.

Nandana's eyes widened, but she recovered her composure quickly. "It's an unusual request. The symbols are treacherous. There are multiple interpretations. If drawn improperly, or in the wrong combination, they invite evil rather than protect against it. I've never done this work. There's a dragonwitch in the muannai valley, and she's a master at this. Her name is Sevondi."

Melia twisted her fingers. The muannai valley was across the Maeldun Bridge in Tyrannis–the Realm of Faerie's other country. No one crossed the bridge these days. The two countries and their populations had become divided as if the Undine River was a line drawn between two different worlds.

The split had happened before Melia came to Faerie, and crossing the bridge sounded intimidating.

Nandana leaned forward. "I know they're difficult to receive, but don't assume stopping your visions is the task before you. You must gain more knowledge before you commit to any path."

The question Melia had dreaded to ask, even of herself, spilled out. "But why do I take pleasure in the destruction I see? Why do I laugh when the Sylvan Forest burns, and the blood of flower faeries stains my fingers?"

Nandana pulled Melia's hands into hers. She rubbed her thumbs across the half-faerie's open palms. "The veil between your mind and your father's has grown thin. His dark passion infects you. Elynus doesn't grasp the full consequences of his ambitions. He imagines an opportunity to reunite with his beloved wife–nothing more. Perhaps your ability to see is greater than his."

"Do you mean I must stop him?"

"He has his path to follow, and you have yours. But I fear they're connected. Come."

The Illustrator pulled Melia into the next room where high oval tables, cluttered with ink jars and brushes, stood between several long, padded benches. Overfilled bookshelves lined two of the walls, and etchings covered a desk pushed into an alcove. More cats, perched about the room, turned their furred heads. An energetic ginger cat slid across the floor. Nandana guided Melia to an altar in the room's far corner.

Before the half-faerie could stop her, the woman pressed her thumb into a saucer of ink, uttered something unintelligible, and pushed her thumb pad against Melia's forehead.

The half-faerie tried to pull away. "What–?"

"He will help you." Nandana maintained a firm grip on Melia's hand as her glossy eyes stared into space. "Yes. I feel his presence in the Parallel of Shadows." Her gaze gradually refocused on Melia. "Like you, he lives in a world where he doesn't belong. And like you, he comprehends the horror that threatens and searches for answers." She placed her hand over Melia's heart. "This mark will call him to you."

"I don't understand."

Nandana pulled Melia closer. "There are reasons you can see what your father calls forth but cannot bear to witness. Trust that."

The prediction did nothing to calm Melia, but it resonated with an inner knowing she could no longer deny. Her father's obsession with Umbra had breached her inner world.

She had to stop him.

4. Sisters

Melia took the long way home to avoid any traffic from Bryndale. When she reached the Nyssalei, she stopped at one of the spots where the river eddied, creating a good-sized pool. Staring at her reflection in the water, she gasped. A dark stain marked the place between her brows. Splashing it with water did nothing to dilute it, neither did scrubbing it with the hem of her dress.

She frowned at the grape-shaped blotch.

The pool's surface rippled. A single circle expanded outward. A second tight spiral formed, then two more. The crests of the tiny waves frothed.

A hand broke the water, followed by a head of wet, copper hair. The water-soaked creature laughed. It was Melusine. Her faerie friends bobbed around her as if they were apples on Samhain's Eve. Melia ducked into the shadows, but the birch trees proved poor camouflage.

Her sister called her name.

Melia groaned.

"The water is delicious. Come, join us," Melusine invited.

As if she ever had, or would. Melia walked away quickly, so no one could see Nandana's mark. Behind her, bare feet pattered in the grass. Slick fingers grabbed her elbow, spinning her against her will.

Melusine pointed at her sister's forehead. "What's that?"

The flower faeries exited the water to gather around Melia, staring. At least Verbena wasn't among them.

"N-nothing," Melia said.

Melusine's slim fingers gripped her sister's chin, turning her face from side to side. She was stronger than she looked. "Did Nandana do that to you?"

Melia wished the ground would open and swallow her. "Y-yes."

"Well, it's not her usual work." Melusine huffed. "I'll say that. Has Mother seen it?"

"Nnn-o," Melia struggled to keep the word whole.

"I want to be there when she does." Melusine waved to her friends. "See you tomorrow. I'm going to make sure my little sister doesn't get lost on her way home."

The faeries tittered, flapping their wings. Gisele hugged her. Melia thought she heard her whisper a wistful, "Lucky you," but couldn't be sure over the chatter of their departure.

"D-did you have to d-do that?" Melia snapped, as her sister squeezed a puddle of river water from her hair.

"Do what?" Melusine asked.

Melia tipped her head in the direction the faeries had flown. "Embarrass m-me in f-front of them?"

"They don't care."

Melia hurried toward the tree house. "M-maybe I d-do."

"Slow down. I've told everyone I know that you're not conspiring with Father."

"*After* telling them I was!"

"Melia, wait!" Melusine skipped beside her. "I want to show you something."

Melia couldn't remember the last time her sister had wanted to show her anything. Curious, she stopped.

"I've grown close to someone, a nobleman in the French Court of Charles VII." Melusine held her hands behind her back. "He's mortal, like Father, and I want you to meet him."

Melia wondered what had come over her sister who usually found her as distasteful as sour milk. "I thought you found the mortal world dull."

"That's only Achill, in Ireland. There are so many other places–and centuries–where mortals are elegant and don't stink of the sea. Raymond wears silk shirts. And when he hunts, he wears leather riding boots that accent his muscled thighs." She brushed her fingers across her leg. "He composes poetry, and his black hair curls just so on the nape of his neck." When Melusine twirled her orange-blonde curls, a large stone glinted in the last rays of daylight.

"What's that?" Melia asked.

Her sister held up her hand and spread her fingers wide. A white diamond sat in a white gold band on her fourth finger. "I'm betrothed."

Melia felt a momentary spate of relief. Certainly, that news–and that gemstone–trumped Nandana's blotch.

Melusine tugged on her elbow. "Will you be my maid of honor? You must! Don't tell me you won't."

Melia yanked her arm free. "After what happened between Mother and Father, how can you even consider marrying a mortal?"

They rounded a corner, leaving the banks of the Nyssalei behind. The enormous oak that cradled the tree house loomed against the sunset.

"Are you jealous?" Melusine asked.

"Worried about what's gotten into you is more like it. Every mortal in history has broken his faerie troth. What makes you think Raymond will be any different?"

Melusine took a step backward. "Why are you ruining my moment?"

"Faithfulness to any vow is the standard of the enchanted world. There are no exceptions, and mortals don't grasp fidelity. That's why Mother warns us against romanticizing full bloods. In spite of Father–because of Father."

"You're still angry about–"

"The lies you spread about me."

Melusine pressed the gauzy layers of her short, berry-colored skirt against her upper thighs. The thin fabric had already dried. "I told you that was Verbena, and we're not friends anymore."

Melia pointed to her engagement ring. "Does Mother know?"

"No."

Plantine appeared out of nowhere. "Does Mother know what?" She lugged a large package wrapped with parchment and twine. She must have gone by Bryndale on her way home from the library.

"Nothing," Melusine snapped.

"What's that on your forehead?" Plantine asked Melia.

Melusine moved to the middle of the narrow dirt path and crossed her arms. "Yes, tell us what inspired the Illustrator to mark your forehead with such a plain spot. It would be so much more attractive if it were a flower, or maybe–"

"You went to see Nandana?" Plantine echoed.

Melia wasn't about to tell them about the lone seeker in the Parallel of Shadows, or how Nandana believed the spot on her head would call him. Melusine would tell everyone, and Plantine would fall silent, convinced any seeker from anywhere would prefer her to her crazy sister.

Crickets filled the strained quiet. They waited. Melia racked her brain for something to tell them.

Melusine pointed at her. "She's working on a story."

The three sisters had taken their telepathic abilities for granted until their father had found them in Faerie. He'd discovered that he shared their gift, only after they'd left Ireland. After his visits had become too intruding and too frequent, Melusine had taught her younger sisters how to keep their thoughts from him. Melia's mental shields were the strongest. Melusine could no longer penetrate her mind. However, that didn't stop her from ganging up with Plantine in moments like these.

Drained from her encounter with Nandana, Melia's mental defenses slipped. Her sisters ferreted through her thoughts.

"It's about Father," Plantine shouted with annoying glee.

Melia redoubled her efforts to close her mind. Plantine continued her gentle probing. Once she'd gained a foothold, it was hard to push her out.

"It's something to do with the rumors about Umbra," Plantine said. "Are you still worried about that?"

"Did you hear what Verbena said in class today?" Melia asked.

"Verbena is a fool," Plantine said. "Whatever Father's doing, it's the right thing. No matter what anyone in Illialei says."

Melia pressed her lips into a tight line. Her sisters wouldn't listen to her. They never did. As soon as they let her go, she was going to find Tatou and tell her everything that had happened today.

Melusine circled behind her, clamping her strong hands onto Melia's shoulders. "Anything else going on in that silly head of hers?" she asked Plantine.

Melia tried to shrug Melusine off, as Plantine struggled to tease more information from thoughts Melia jumbled on purpose. When her younger sister leaned in to press her hand against Nandana's mark, Melia was caught off guard. Energy surged between the two girls. An image of the Illustrator, lying dead with her grey cat, flashed through Melia's mind. Plantine jolted backward, and the bulky package she'd struggled to hold crashed to the ground.

"Why is there a picture of Nandana's death in your mind?" her younger sister's voice quavered.

"What's wrong with you?" Melusine flared.

Melia tried again to shrug off her firm grasp, but her sister's nails pressed deeper into her shoulder blades.

Plantine's huge, sky blue eyes darkened. "Have you been smoking more ylandria?"

"No, it's nothing like that," Melia said.

Melusine let go of her shoulders. "Then, what is it?"

Plantine threw her arms around Melia. "Push those awful pictures out of your mind. They're frightening."

Something citrusy–fresh oranges?–clung to her younger sister's hair. "I'm trying," Melia said.

"Will that mark help? Is that why Nandana put it there?" Plantine asked.

"Sort of."

Plantine leaned over to pick up the dropped parcel. She brushed several straw-like blades of grass from the twine. "I hope it works."

Melia pointed her chin at the unwieldy object Plantine held. "Is that for Mother?"

"Yes."

"Another package from Kyrakkos?" Melia asked.

"Probably."

"What did old Eli say?" The elf was the Bryndale postmaster.

Plantine plucked at the package's twine.

"Let me guess, he mumbled something everyone standing in line could hear? Something about how black magic shouldn't be practiced in Illialei," Melia said.

Plantine glared at her. "You worry too much about what others think."

"If everyone in Illialei thought you wanted to kill them, you'd worry about what they thought too."

Her younger sister sighed. "Always so dramatic."

Melia wanted to shout, "Father's not doing the right thing, and Mother's obsession with the dark arts is out of control," but Plantine preferred to see their parents as perfect. Melia said, "Melusine's engaged," instead. "To a mortal. And she wants us to attend the wedding."

"Of course we will!" Plantine squealed.

Melusine loosened her grip on Melia's shoulders. "We can't tell Mother yet."

Their younger sister promised not to, as she oohed and aahed over the diamond.

Melusine slid the ring from her finger, concealing it in her pocket. She shot Melia an I'll-deal-with-you-later look and placed her arm around Plantine's shoulder. The pair turned toward the tree house.

Melia ran to the enchanted gardens and Tatou.

The blood-red sunset–swiped with lavender, fuchsia, and orange–signaled the approach of a pitch-black night. Melia waded across one of the Nyssalei's sandbanks. The river was an in-between place, the waters unpredictable during the moons' dark phase. But it was the quickest route to the enchanted gardens. She'd had to choose–risk the waters and reach the enchanted gardens under the safety of twilight, or end up running through the Footing Fields in total darkness.

When the vision overtook her, she stood with one foot on the Nyssalei's bank and one foot in the water.

Warships approach. Their dark cannons smite the land with ear-shattering blows, leaving only death and roiling smoke in their wake.

The banks of the Nyssalei wither, all life extinguished.

Illialei is black and brown and grey.

I stand with one foot in the river. A luminous thing drifts to the water's surface. Gold swirls frame it. I take a closer look. A mermaid. Drowned in the sewage of destruction.

Not a hint of compassion touches my heart.

"And why should it?" My father's disembodied voice slithers through my mind.

"Melia," someone other than my father calls me.

I search for the speaker. He stands in the east—a male with dark hair, sunburnt skin, and emerald eyes. I want to swim in those eyes.

He holds out his hand. It doesn't reach me. A brown cloak billows behind him.

I want to move toward him, but my feet are rooted.

"I'll stay with you," he says. "No matter what."

"Who are you?" I ask.

The icy water pooling around her ankles brought Melia back to reality. She touched her forehead. Was the man with the emerald eyes the one Nandana had spoken of? How had he come to her so soon? It was positively eerie.

But he wasn't.

He was a dream.

5. The Renegade Priest

Ryder stared at the sword enshrined in the glass case. The blue shimmer of its blade lit the room. Named Koldis, a single ruby crowned its hilt.

It was well past midnight. The halls of the library–famous throughout the enchanted world and the purpose of the Order of the Idonnai's existence–stood silent.

The young priest's ragged breathing filled the room.

The first time Anton had brought him here as a seven-year-old boy, Ryder had wanted the sword. When he'd asked if he could have it, his mentor had boxed his ears and said, "Idonnic priests do not fight."

It had been the first and last time he'd kicked Anton in the shin. His pious mentor hadn't administered the whipping that had left three thin white lines across his back, but he'd watched until the young boy had stopped calling out for Garrick.

Ryder had been abandoned at the citadel gates as an infant. Garrick, a baker, had been the one to find him. In the emotionally remote world of the priesthood, Garrick and his wife, Shilda, were Ryder's only source of affection.

Now, Anton was the head of the order. He'd never forbidden his protege's visits with Garrick and Shilda, but after Ryder had risked his life to save the couple during a ferocious sandstorm, he'd made it clear he didn't approve of Ryder's fondness for them.

Ryder tightened his grip around the large rock in his hand. He'd scoured Idonne's rocky seashore for months, searching for the perfect stone. The first stone he'd brought back to his austere quarters had had a single sharp plane. He'd traded it out with four more before he'd settled on the one he held tonight. One of the stone's edges sharpened into a jagged point. For weeks, night after night, lying awake on his pallet, he'd practiced shifting it into the right position. He didn't need to look down now to know the stone's point was centered.

Garrick and Shilda would be disappointed with his decision to become a common thief. As far as he could tell, that was the only flaw in his plan. But there was no way around it.

For over a decade, Ryder, now nineteen, had been trained in the rigors of Idonnic research and documentation. Despite his lack of passion for the work, he had a talent. As Anton's favorite, he'd been assigned to a closely guarded branch of Idonnic knowledge: the study of Umbra.

He'd read and reread every scrap of information the priests had collected about the mass of psychic ash accumulating in the Void. A product of mortal impotence, frustration, and failure, Umbra had formed a discrete identity, and become self-aware over the eons. He intended to enter the realm of the material plane. He'd discovered a means to do so. He meant to destroy the Whole.

The priesthood would do nothing to stop the incarnation, and the Oath of Non-Interference Anton had contrived Ryder into taking a year ago–to the day–choked him. Vowing to chronicle and observe, but never to act, violated every fiber of his being.

There was also the ill-defined thing the young priest couldn't name which called him. It radiated from deep within his heart, and of late, it left him sleepless most nights. As the summons grew more insistent, the need to leave Idonne dominated his thoughts. But he couldn't leave without the sword.

He understood the consequences. If he took one step closer to the case, if he raised his arm to shatter the glass with the stone, if he took the sword and fled Idonne, he'd be a fugitive throughout the enchanted world for the rest of his life.

He examined the room. There were no guards, no spells of enchanted protection. Only the library's labyrinth of marble halls hid Koldis from the rest of the enchanted world. The sword wasn't safe. Rumors had already reached his ears. Sorcerers and witches from Kyrakkos sought the blade and its counterpart, the bejeweled basin Ormrun.

The magical sword and basin opened a portal in the veil between the worlds. Plunged into Ormrun, Koldis became the key to unlock the ancient door. Umbra could leave the Void and travel through the Parallel of Shadows. He could incarnate his consciousness into a vessel of his choosing.

Last week a war captain from Huros had dined with Anton. He'd asked about Koldis. His tone had been casual, but Ryder was convinced the pretense for the visit had been a charade. The captain sought the sword.

Ryder raised his arm. No one who wanted Umbra's power for themselves was going to get it.

He would sail to Faerie with Koldis.

Although there had been no sightings of Ormrun for over a hundred years, there was no evidence the bowl had ever left the Realm of Faerie's shores. The dwarves, Haff and Gweff, had forged the sword and the basin in the bowels of the Ruadain Mountains for the ancient water elemental, Isolt. But Umbra had appropriated the basin's power.

Ryder had no faith in the prophecy or the slight hope that it offered. However, he did have faith in himself. He believed he could find Ormrun and take it, with Koldis, to the Grey Council on the Isle of Minnanon. The grey faeries who sat on the council were the only creatures in the Whole immune to the siren call of Umbra's power. They were the ones to safeguard the sword and the basin for eternity. Umbra could never incarnate.

The young priest tightened his grip on the stone. *Yes*, his heart said, *sailing to Faerie is the right thing to do*.

He brought his arm down with all the force he could summon. A line appeared in the glass casing. The shield was stronger than it looked. He raised his arm and smashed the case a second time. Cracks spider-webbed across the surface, but the glass remained intact. The third time, he aimed the rock's sharpest point at the web of cracks. When his hand crashed through the glass, he dropped the rock and grabbed the sword's hilt.

He wrestled the blade through the jagged hole. A sharp edge sliced the back of his hand. He didn't feel any pain, but he saw the dark line of blood. The blade was lighter than he'd imagined. He ripped a strip from the length of cloth he'd thought to bring, made a rough bandage for his hand, and then wrapped the remainder around the blade. He shoved the whole thing into his belt.

He eased through the door and slipped into the hall where a few oil lamps cast a dim light. Although his impulse was to run, he forced himself to walk and catch his breath. On occasion a zealous novice studied through the night. If there was one nearby, running would bring unwanted attention.

By the time Ryder reached the library's exterior stairs, sweat gathered on his brow. He'd made no specific arrangements to cross Idonne, but if he walked toward the mountains–and Garrick and Shilda's home–there would be traffic on the road when the sun rose. He looked down at the patched brown pants Shilda had brought the last time she'd visited. His work shirt and bare feet would help. Although with his dark hair and muscular build, he stood out among the tall, slim, fair-haired Idonnai, without his robes, he could pass as a foreigner traveling to Typhos.

✧✧✧

"This is good," Ryder said.

The cart pulled to a stop.

It was still a long walk to Garrick and Shilda's home, but the less the craftsman knew about where he was headed, the better. Ryder slipped a silver coin into the man's rough hand. It was probably too much, but he'd ferried him the entire length of Idonne's dry, dusty roads, and hadn't asked any awkward questions about the bloody bandage on his hand, or the sword.

The man slipped the silver into his pocket and cracked the reins. The cart pulled away with a jolt.

It was late afternoon. Ryder headed toward the mountains that divided Idonne from Typhos. He longed to pull the blade from his belt and test it, but any bird hidden among the trees along the foot of the mountain could be a spy.

Every spring, a variety of birds were hatched in the citadel aviary. Half were trained to carry messages, the rest to gather information. Speaking in birdsong was common in the enchanted world, and the priesthood boasted its fair share of monks who had mastered the skill although Ryder wasn't among them. He'd traded his lessons in the aviary for training with the guard.

He left Koldis in his belt.

As if to confirm his wariness, when he rounded the next bend, he saw Garrick conversing with a falcon perched in the sycamore tree next to his home. Dressed in traditional Idonnic garb, sand-colored tunics and pants, Garrick's eyes widened as Ryder approached.

"We didn't expect to see you until our next visit to the citadel," Garrick said.

Ryder pulled up short. "I–" Standing in front of the man who was like a father to him, he didn't know how to explain his unexpected arrival.

The tall man hugged him.

Ryder leaned heavily against him.

"Whoa," Garrick said.

The dizzy spells that had begun last night were becoming more frequent. "It must be the heat." Ryder forced himself to support his own weight. As he pulled back, Koldis hit Garrick's thigh.

"What's that you've got there?"

Sitting in his tiny room in the priesthood dormitory, Ryder couldn't imagine leaving Idonne, for good anyway, without saying goodbye to Garrick and Shilda. But now, Ryder wished he hadn't come. By bringing Koldis here, he'd placed them in danger. He needed to make his goodbyes as hasty as possible.

"Since when do priests carry swords?" Garrick asked. "And what happened to your hand?"

Ryder tried to hide the bandaged mess behind his back, but Garrick caught his forearm and pulled it toward him. "The wound is festering."

"What a nice surprise." Shilda's greeting rang out behind them.

"Let her treat the infection," Garrick said.

The throbbing in Ryder's hand extended to his shoulder. His skin had grown clammy. It was at least a three-day trip over the mountains to Typhos, and another day to reach the seaport. The bloody bandage would make him easier to identify if anyone asked questions. Shilda was a skilled herbalist. It would be foolish not to let her take a look at it.

"You would have died by this time tomorrow," Shilda said. "The glass that made the cut was treated with a lethal poison."

Ryder squirmed. He refused to let himself believe he'd made a mistake. "I didn't know."

"Anton won't stop until he's found you and the sword," Garrick said.

"I'm taking it to the Isle of Minnanon. Once I've delivered it to the Grey Council, Anton can do with me as he pleases."

"It's a long way to Minnanon," Garrick said.

Ryder didn't mention Faerie. The less they knew about his plans, the better. He didn't try to explain the hope swelling in his heart, either. To tell Garrick and Shilda that Idonne had never felt like his home, in spite of their genuine care, would hurt them for no reason. He loved them, and they'd made the years he'd lived with the order bearable. They deserved his gratitude and nothing else.

"I can catch a ship in Typhos." Ryder counted on eluding Anton's grasp in the busiest seaport in the enchanted world.

"Do you have coin for passage?" Garrick asked.

The heavy weight of a coin bag rested against the young man's thigh. "I've earned enough tutoring."

"I don't need to warn you of the risks," Garrick said.

"I've thought about this a long time," he said. "It's the right thing to do."

"If it's any consolation, we never thought you were suited to the priesthood," Shilda said.

Ryder laughed as his dread of their judgment slipped away. How could he have doubted the two people who'd been like a mother and father to him all these years?

The unmistakable thunder of galloping horses approached. Worry pinched Shilda's face.

Garrick walked to the small window cut into the thick dirt wall of their home. "It's the Idonnai Guard. You need to leave."

Shilda squeezed Ryder's hands harder than she ever had before. She wanted to prepare a bundle of food, but there wasn't time. They pushed him out their back door with a packet of ointment for his wound.

He didn't look back as he took cover in the thick brush that crawled up the mountain. He had friends in the guard, but he refused to involve them with his crime.

Ryder took advantage of a shadowed grove of trees as dusk fell. He kept an eye on the large, dull structure across the way. Used to Idonne's pristine architecture, the sight of the sagging wood building shocked him. It looked as though a strong wind could topple the whole thing with a single gust, yet a steady stream of patrons came and went.

He removed the cloth binding his hand. He'd applied the ointment Shilda had given him, twice a day, for the past four days. A fresh layer of skin had already sealed the cut. He flexed his palm. Other than a slight numbness in his fingers, it was as good as new.

He stuffed the cloth in his pocket, made sure the blue shimmer of Koldis' blade remained hidden in its makeshift cloth scabbard, and headed across the road. All he needed was the name of a ship–one that sailed to Faerie.

The name of the tavern was scratched in the building's weathered exterior–The Crossroads. Ryder followed a group of grizzled sailors through the barn-like doors. Inside, it was loud and crowded. The floor was sticky to his bare feet. Trained to observe, he walked behind the sailors until he saw an empty, out-of-the-way table. He settled there to watch.

A long bar lined the hall's back wall. Nine barkeeps, of varying age and race, poured drinks, wiped down the counter, and laughed with, snarled at, or ignored their customers. Most of The Crossroad's clientele clumped in large groups, although there were a few tables with only one or two drinkers. Ryder guessed the majority of patrons were Typhons from their wiry builds. There were a few light-haired Hurons, Idonne's eastern neighbors, but he didn't see any Idonnai. That was a relief. He recognized many of the enchanted world's other races from pictures he'd seen in books. It was exhilarating, seeing them breathing and alive.

A few tables away a crowd of stocky, ebony-haired Morgannai shouted at a slight male with cinnamon skin. The male wore a bright yellow turban and crimson pants, but his chest was bare. The fierce Morgannai–the enchanted world's warrior race–pressed in on the thin man.

Ryder stood. The confrontation had gotten the attention of some of the surrounding tables. One of the Morgannai punched the bare-chested man in the face. The man reeled but didn't defend himself. A crowd gathered. They laughed and elbowed one another. A second Morgannai hit the man, and he fell against the table. Drinks and piles of coin toppled. When the third man pulled the small man up, Ryder reached for Koldis' hilt. He'd trained enough to know how to handle the sword, but he'd never experienced anything resembling real combat.

His eyes swept the audience. If he brandished Koldis, who would attack him?

The small man had slipped to the ground. The Morgannai who'd landed the first punch straddled him. He pulled on the yellow turban. Everyone laughed.

It wasn't a fair fight, and Ryder couldn't stand by and watch the man get beaten to death. He moved.

A hush fell over The Crossroads. Ryder stood over the unconscious man. The Morgannai surrounded him.

"It's not a good time to play the hero," the closest one said.

"He owes us money, and he can't pay," another one added.

"You won't beat him to death in my presence." Ryder's words were calm, but adrenaline pumped through his body. He'd fought a Morgannai before–and been carried away on a stretcher. He raised the sword. The Morgannai race possessed a type of pre-cognition in raw physical combat, and the metal in his hand was Ryder's only defense against it. It disrupted their sight. He didn't want to use the blade, but if any of the them inched closer, he would.

One of the barkeeps approached. "What's your problem, Jack?"

"He"–Jack pointed to the man Ryder protected–"wanted to join our game of Spit Five, and we were friendly enough to cut him in."

"Yeah," one of the other Morgannai jumped in. "Then when he lost, he said he didn't have any money."

"He meant to take ours," Jack said. "But we beat him, fair and square. We're gonna take what he owes us out of his hide. Them's the rules at The

Crossroads, right?"

"What's your story?" the barkeep asked Ryder, but he stared at Koldis. The blade's blue shimmer had attracted the attention of the entire bar.

Ryder had plenty of money in his bag. Maybe he could cover the man's debt. "He's my friend. I was supposed to meet him, but I was late. I have his money. How much does he owe?"

"Why didn't you speak up sooner?" Jack asked.

"How much does he owe you?" Ryder needed to get out of The Crossroads before anyone got his name or a better look at him.

Jack looked at his friends. One of them flashed his fingers and a thumb. "Five silver and one gold."

That was a lot of coin. Ryder looked down at the man on the floor. What had he been thinking?

"I don't have any gold. What about twenty-five silver and call it even?" It was a fair offer, but gold was gold. Ryder knew the Morgannai didn't have to accept it.

The group huddled. The crowd was talking, but they weren't nearly as loud as they'd been before Ryder had pulled out Koldis. Jack broke away from the group.

"Yeah, we'll take your stinking silver. But you tell your friend, if he's gonna play at The Crossroads, he better have his money on him."

The barkeep nodded. "Them's the rules. Everyone abides by them."

Ryder returned the sword to his belt, but he'd lost the cloth he'd used to cover the blade. What a mess. He crouched next to the man he'd saved. The barkeep returned with a glass and towel. He poured what looked to be water in the man's face. The man sputtered. The barkeep tossed the towel at him and left.

Ryder lugged the man out of the tavern to the grove of trees across the road. He propped him against one of the trunks and waited for him to say something. He checked to make sure no one had followed them.

The man snored.

Ryder didn't want to sleep under the trees. Besides, it wasn't safe. The enchanted world's two moons were full and high in the sky–anyone walking by could see them. Everyone in the tavern had seen Koldis. Who knew what a group of hooligans might try if he let down his guard?

He crouched beside the man. "Hey," he said. The man shifted, but continued to snore. "Hey," Ryder repeated.

The man jerked.

"Twenty-five pieces of silver is more than I'd planned to waste on someone else's gambling debts," Ryder said. "The least you could do is let me know whether you're okay."

The man opened his eyes. "You paid them?"

"It's the only reason you're still alive."

"I can replace your money. But saving my life"–the man shifted, turning his back to Ryder–"why did you have to do that?"

"I don't need empty promises. Just tell me you're going to survive the night."

"You're not going to let me sleep, are you?" the man asked.

"You can sleep, but I can't stay here and protect you."

"Why not? The sea air smells good after the stink of that bar." He patted the ground. "You're looking at one of the best rooms in Typhos. The beds in the inns are hard as rocks–I know–I've slept in most of them. The price they charge for a single room, let alone two of them, is robbery."

Five men walked down the road. Two of them looked back at Ryder and the man he'd saved.

"I get it. You're on the run." The man pushed himself to his knees. When he stood up, he brushed the dirt from his billowy crimson pants and righted the bright yellow turban which had twisted on his head. "I was feeling lucky tonight. I didn't think I'd lose."

He surveyed their surroundings–the five men were gone–before he pulled a multicolor scarf from his pocket. "It's dangerous for me to do this, but I do owe you." He unfurled the flimsy cloth, tossed it into the air, caught it, tied it into several knots with lightning quick movements, and then shoved it back in his pocket. When he pulled his hand out, he pushed two gold coins into Ryder's palm. "My name's Sinjiin. That makes us even as far as the coin."

Ryder had read about magic many times but never seen such a display. He was speechless.

"It's real," Sinjiin said.

The young priest slipped the coins in his pocket.

"Watch out!" Sinjiin yelled.

The five hooligans had returned. They came at them with rocks and sticks.

Ryder pulled Koldis from his belt. Again, he registered how light the sword was. The blue blade shimmered. It felt comfortable in his hand. The many nights Ryder had trained with the Idonnai Guard had been worth it. He slashed the sword through the air.

A deafening roar erupted behind him.

The men screamed, dropped their sticks and stones, and fled.

A second, closer growl made Ryder's blood run cold. He slowly pivoted.

An enormous tiger crouched before him. Where had it come from?

Ryder searched the night's shadows for the mage's slight form. Had he run away?

The tiger flattened its belly against the ground, resting its shaggy head on its forepaws.

Ryder took a step back.

The tiger rolled over and kicked its giant paws in the air.

Ryder could have sworn the big cat was laughing. "Sinjiin?"

6. Elynus

Icy water bit Melia's toes. The many times she'd watched Melusine and her friends dive into this frigid stream was the only thing that convinced her it could be done. She rubbed her arms to generate some warmth, but it didn't work.

"Can you picture Achill in your mind's eye?" Tatou lounged a few feet away on a large rock, coaching her. Although the pixie had never been to the mortal world, she assured Melia she understood the principles. "Or maybe it would be easier to concentrate on your father."

She had a point.

Melia closed her eyes and struggled to form a concrete image of Elynus in her mind. Calling her father by his given name offered an emotional distance she found comforting. However, it did nothing to help her accomplish the task at hand. Rather than seeing her father's tawny hair and blue eyes, she kept seeing the mysterious stranger with green eyes.

"Well?" Tatou asked.

"I keep seeing *him!*" Tendrils of energy as fine as a spider's thread spilled from the center of Nandana's mark. The sensation continued until Melia's entire forehead thrummed.

Tatou was in front of her face. "Stop it."

"Stop what?"

"Stop obsessing about him. You're worse than Melusine going on about

'Raymond, Raymond, Raymond.'"

Since the night Nandana had painted the mark on Melia's forehead, she'd had three more visions. *He'd* appeared in each one. *He* was always reaching through the carnage–to protect her? Save her? Warn her? Was he the lone seeker Nandana had spoken of?

She couldn't be sure, but whenever she thought of those unwavering eyes set in that broad face ruddied by days in the sun, Nandana's mark stirred, prompting Melia to wonder what kind of power the Illustrator possessed.

"Do you think appearing in my visions counts as entering my life?"

"I don't know," Tatou answered.

"Nandana told me he walked the veil between the worlds, in the Parallel of Shadows."

"That's why you need to stop thinking about him. What if he does exist there–in the veil separating the enchanted and mortal worlds from the Void? You could end up there instead of the mortal world and never come back." Tatou jabbed her tiny finger in the air to emphasize each word.

"I should have asked Nandana more questions."

"I thought you wanted to see your father."

"I don't want to see him," Melia said. "But I need to."

"Do you think you can stop him from incarnating Umbra?" Tatou asked.

"I need to try."

The pixie zoomed back toward her rock. "Then concentrate on Elynus, because if you end up in the wrong time and the wrong place and can't get back, I'll never see you again."

Melia reluctantly pushed aside thoughts of *him*. "You're right."

"Describe him to me," Tatou commanded.

"Who?"

The pixie tapped her foot. "Your father."

Melia shifted her focus from the mysterious stranger in her visions to her father. "He has the same gold hair Plantine has with blue eyes similar to mine."

A portrait of Elynus's weathered face exploded in her mind. *"Melia?"* He'd aged.

The lifelike apparition crushed every other thought in her mind.

"How unexpected."

And unwanted. Apprehensive of their psychic connection and its poisonous residue, Melia searched for an image–anything to push his looming visage away.

He blocked every exit.

She couldn't see anything but him. *"I–we–could–"*

"You're troubled."

She needed to regain her equilibrium. "*No. Yes.*"

"Talk to me, Little Bird."

Melia's stomach knotted at the familiar nickname. Even as a child in the mortal world, she'd longed to fly. *"The elves and faeries–everyone in Illialei is talking about you."*

"Things must be boring in Faerie." He laughed.

"No, Father. They're afraid of you."

"Afraid of a mere mortal, one exiled from the enchanted world to boot? The creatures of Illialei have grown cowardly under Queen Luisa's rule. Fearful," he mused. *"That's not how I remember them."*

Her father's observations touched a nerve. Her mother had never disguised her contempt for Luisa, either.

Melia forced herself to focus. This conversation wasn't supposed to be about the queen, it was supposed to be about stopping Umbra's incarnation. *"The rumors claim you intend to incarnate Umbra. Is that true?"*

"Little Bird–such a kind-hearted girl. A bit headstrong at times, but always–" Her father paused. She could feel him search his mind. An image of Melusine drifted by, the thought *"beautiful"* arose. A picture of Plantine followed with the thought *"ambitious"* then Melia ... and the word *"sweet."*

Her teeth clenched. She didn't even like honey. A familiar rage stirred within. In her visions its bottomless pit frightened her, but now she drew from the dark well instinctively. *"You can't incarnate Umbra."*

"Don't challenge me, Little Bird."

Nandana was right–he meant to go through with it. *"I've seen what will happen. Illialei destroyed. Innocent faeries slaughtered. You can't possibly want that."*

"Your imagination has always been spectacular," he responded sourly.

"I'm not imagining–"

"Illialei's wrongs must be rectified."

"What about your wrongs?" Melia exploded. *"After all these years, Mother still cries herself to sleep every night."* She stopped.

Pressina hid her tears. If she knew Melia and her sisters heard, or that Melia had told their father, she'd be furious.

"Incarnating Umbra will remedy that."

"How?"

"You must trust me."

Melia recoiled. How could she trust him when he wouldn't listen to anything she had to say?

A black cloud descended and he was gone.

Had she pushed him away?

"Melia." Tatou's voice broke through the dark spell.

The half-faerie's neck and shoulders burned, her teeth chattered. She brushed at something on her cheek–tears. Her calves and feet were freezing in the Nyssalei's waters.

"What happened?" Tatou asked. "I kept calling your name, but you didn't hear me."

Melia waded to the river's grassy bank and crumpled on the soft green pallet. She stared up at Illialei's periwinkle skies. She'd snuck from the tree house at dawn, and now the sun was at its height. Tatou hovered, her eyebrows and lips puckered with worry.

Melia's throat tightened. "He's not going to stop."

Tatou's eyes widened. "Oh dear."

A few days later, Melia found herself seated in the darkest corner of the Hive with Tatou and a tree elf named Tuck.

The Hive was a dilapidated but reputable café in Bryndale. It catered to wood elves and its specialties included: biscuits and honey, honey vanilla cake, honey fruit pies, honey mead, innumerable teas served with honey, and pretty much anything baked, brewed, stewed, or fermented with honey.

It was mid-afternoon and boisterous, chatty elves packed the place. No one seemed interested in their hushed talk.

"You'll do fine," Tuck assured her. His striking appearance contrasted with the short, stout wood elves seated at the tables around them. "Focus on this image, not your father." He tapped the picture of a sea cliff in a large picture book. Tall and angular, his straight, dark hair fell over piercing brown eyes.

Tuck was an apprentice at the Cathedral Palace Grand Library. Tatou had asked for his help because she trusted the elf's knowledge and discretion. Meeting at the Hive had been his idea when Melia had refused to go to the palace library.

She didn't want to run into Plantine. Her younger sister went to the library almost every day after school. She also knew what little value Melia placed on books. If Melia showed up at the library out of the blue, Plantine would probably ask if she'd been smoking more ylandria. Besides, her sister always defended their father.

"You sure you're not hungry?" Tuck asked again. An empty bowl, plate, cup, and saucer sat before him. Tatou nibbled on a honey-walnut cookie. Melia hadn't ordered anything.

"Yes." She would have killed for a savory soup or sautéed greens, but the Hive's reputation was built on "Honey in Every Dish." Disliking honey was viewed with raised eyebrows in Illialei. It was better to just lie.

Melia appraised Tuck. "Have you ever been?"

"To Achill?" he asked.

"To the mortal world."

"No," he said.

Her lips twisted. She couldn't help but wonder if his advice would be any improvement upon Tatou's. It was possible that the principles of travel to the mortal world–concentrating on a time and a place or person–might involve subtle intricacies difficult to grasp if one had never actually done it.

"Perhaps the strain in your relationship with your father, and your fear concerning his determination to incarnate Umbra, is hindering you," Tuck said. "Try drawing on a childhood memory of Achill instead, some moment when you experienced intense joy. Happier emotions will improve your chance for success."

That was something Melia could do. She'd shared many wonderful days with her mortal friends as a child.

"It's not necessary to focus on your father, per se. As long as you can reach the beach, you'll be fine. Our sources assure us, he remains in Achill."

"Your sources?" Melia asked.

"Contrary to popular opinion," the tree elf said, "even though they are much less traveled these days, the borders between time and space are still porous. Although the thresholds do seem to stick from both sides from time to time. Just remember, the greater the internal energy, the greater the momentum to push through. Sometimes our thoughts need a little help from our emotions. Love and joy generate the most energy, thus the most helpful.

"On your first attempt, did you completely submerge yourself in the river?" he asked.

"Hardly," Melia said. "The water is freezing."

"You're not going anywhere standing at the river's edge. You must immerse your body."

"No wonder so few creatures travel between the worlds these days." She already dreaded her next attempt. "Has the Nyssalei always been so cold?"

"Melia." Tatou pointed.

Plantine stood at the entrance of the Hive, squinting as she searched the crowd.

The last thing Melia wanted was to get into an awkward conversation about their father with all the elves watching. She slid from her seat and crouched beneath the table. Her reaction drew a few quizzical looks. She sighed. How much time would the Bryndale gossips allot to her crawling under a table at the local café? She hoped it would be much less than to a juicy argument between her and her sister about whether Elynus should incarnate Umbra.

"Did she see me?" Melia asked Tatou.

"She sees Tuck, and she's making her way to our table."

An uncomfortable quiet descended upon the café. Did every elf in the Hive watch Plantine approach? "What is she doing?" Melia asked.

Tatou waved her silent.

"Tuck, Aldous told me I could find you here." Plantine's voice oozed something syrupy that Melia had never heard in it before. "Tatou." That short greeting sounded more like the sister Melia knew.

"Good afternoon, Plantine. Tuck and I were just–"

"Getting a bite to eat," he finished the pixie's sentence.

"I thought–" Plantine paused. "We were going to–"

"We are." He pushed back his chair. "I lost track of the time."

"Tatou hasn't finished her cookie," Plantine said.

"Yes, I have. You two go on."

"You're sure?"

"Oh yes," Tatou said.

From beneath the table, Melia could see Tuck stand next to Plantine. They turned. She heaved a sigh of relief.

Plantine spun back around. "Have you seen Melia?"

"No," Tatou squeaked.

Plantine laughed. "You might want to look under the table."

Tuck and her sister had reached the door by the time Melia stood straight. She couldn't believe Plantine hadn't waited to needle her. "She just left? Was she all right?"

Tatou landed on the table. Conversation resumed around them. "He has that effect on her."

Melia settled back into her seat. "Elves don't possess the ability to glamour."

The pixie batted her eyelashes. "It's not that kind of effect."

"What are you saying?"

"They've become close."

"And you're telling me this now, after I've confided in him about my father? He'll tell Plantine everything."

"No, he won't," Tatou said. "I told him not to and he said he wouldn't."

"And you believe him?"

Tatou crossed her fingers over her heart. "Honestly, as long as he keeps your secret, why do you care what's going on between them? You don't believe–"

"In love," the half-faerie finished her sentence.

Her friend nodded. They'd had that argument too many times to count. Melia let it drop while she ran through the list of suitors Plantine had already rejected. "Tuck is a tree elf."

Native to eastern Illialei, tree elves had a reputation for being clannish. Few ventured beyond their enclaves to the east of Lake Vivientiana.

"He is," Tatou replied.

"It's hard to believe Plantine would fall in love with a tree elf, that's all."

"You saw him."

"He is handsome."

"Plantine baked him a cherry tart the other day."

Melia's mouth gaped as she imagined her sister sweeping through the halls of the palace with a burnt but well-intentioned offering.

Tatou somersaulted midair and spun around to face her. She clasped her hands over her heart. "Tuck's of the Wild Cherry Lineage. They love anything and everything cherry. He was most touched."

Melia shook her head. "If Melusine's engagement to a mortal doesn't kill my mother, Plantine's falling for a tree elf will."

Tatou popped the last bite of cookie in her mouth. "She might understand more than anyone that the head can't rule the heart."

"You can't possibly be talking about my mother now," Melia said.

The pixie raised her eyebrows.

"Only a prince or king will satisfy Pressina's ambition for her most eligible daughter. She wants to see Plantine on a throne."

Tatou choked.

"Are you all right?" Melia asked.

The pixie banged on her chest and signaled for water.

7. Heartache

Plantine pushed the shop door open. She frowned at the numerous cats gathered in the front room.

The Illustrator was in her studio, perched on a high stool with pen in hand. "May I help you?"

Plantine closed the door behind her.

Nandana crossed beneath the arch separating the two rooms. "What can I do for you today?" She reached for the half-faerie's hand, trailing her fingers along her forearm. "Perhaps some delicate spirals?"

"No, thank you."

The mortal woman released her hand.

Plantine wondered if Melia had declined the popular spirals as well. She was dying to know if her sister had requested the mark on her forehead, but how would Melia have known to ask for such a thing? Plantine had never seen anyone else in Illialei with such a design. She pushed away a twinge of envy. Everything about Melia was different. She wasn't sure why that irked her, but it did.

Nandana waited.

Plantine sensed the customary pleasantries wouldn't help her cause. Perhaps the woman would appreciate her being direct. "My sister has been acting strange since she came here." She recalled the embarrassment she'd felt at the Hive. What had Melia been thinking, hiding under the table–that she was blind?

Nandana waited for her to say more.

"Since she came home with that"–Plantine searched for a word that wasn't insulting–"emblem on her forehead."

"She sent you here?"

Plantine didn't know whether Melia had returned to the Illustrator's. She couldn't be sure about anything regarding her middle sister these days. But if she lied, and Nandana found out, it wouldn't look right. She decided to stick with the truth for now.

"No, she'd never ask for my help. But she's my sister and I'm concerned. We all are."

"We?"

"My mother and older sister." Certainly, Melia's peculiar behavior and change in attitude hadn't gone unnoticed by Melusine, or their mother. "She's rarely at the tree house these days and she–well, she's been absent from school."

Nandana settled into a chair. "You miss her?" A grey cat–Plantine recognized it at as the one in Melia's vision–jumped into the Illustrator's lap. The half-faerie felt herself pale. The woman motioned to a well-worn sofa. "Sit."

It was covered in cat hair, but it wouldn't do to appear rude. Plantine balanced on the sofa's edge.

"You miss her?" Nandana asked again.

It was a strange question. Why would she miss her sister? Other than walking to school in the mornings, their lives were not entwined. Plantine lived in the palace library, studying everything about Faerie's history with the elves, while her sister roamed the fields and meadows with Tatou.

"It's more that she's not been herself," Plantine said.

"And you know your sister well?"

Heat rose in the half-faerie's cheeks. She'd come here for answers, not to be questioned. "I know her well enough."

"Perhaps you should be asking her these questions."

Plantine tried to find fault with the Illustrator's response, but her simple answer had been spoken without emotion. She shifted on the sofa. "Do you think I need one of those marks?" She pushed away a fat black cat who tried to settle at her feet. "Like the one you gave Melia."

Nandana reached for the heavy cat, perched it in her lap, and then proceeded to rub the creature behind its ears. The cat purred loud enough for Plantine to hear. "Sometimes it's hard to let those we live with be themselves. We think we know them. Sometimes we think we're the same, or that we should have the same things they have, but each of us is unique. I think it would be a mistake for you to compare yourself to your sister."

Plantine took a deep breath to quell her temper. She wasn't used to being censured. "You don't know Melia. She appears sincere, but she's often confused."

"How is Pressina?" Nandana asked.

The half-faerie forced a smile. "Mother is fine."

"And your father, do you hear from him often?"

Plantine's fingers flew to cover her mouth before she could control the gesture. She'd never admit her father never contacted her. Not to anyone. She repositioned her hand beneath her chin then let it fall to her breast. "He's fine as well."

"That's good to hear," Nandana said. "All the rumors–"

"My father would never hurt anyone."

"That's good to know."

The half-faerie stood up. Nandana remained seated as Plantine excused herself.

✧ ✧ ✧

Plantine assessed the sky. Twilight approached. Going to the Illustrator's had been a mistake. She brushed at her sleeves as if that could remove the discomfort of the visit.

The last person she wanted to see right now was Melia. These days she was so unpredictable. Who knew when she might pop up at the tree house? Instead of heading home, Plantine wandered toward the Nyssalei.

When she reached the river's banks, she offered a perfunctory wave to a small group of flower faeries. Rather than go east, toward the stretch of popular beaches she often frequented with Tuck, she chose to follow the setting sun. She needed an isolated spot to contact her father.

She walked faster as the sun dropped in the sky. By the time she stumbled upon the inland cove, she could hear the roar of the Great White

Sea. She wondered how close she was to the shoreline, but there wasn't time to investigate. She settled upon the trunk of a fallen tree. Washed over time by water that ebbed and flowed, it was as hollow as driftwood.

When she was certain she was alone, she closed her eyes and imagined her father. She sent his name, pushing it beyond the enchanted world with her mind.

It was difficult. She had no memory of the mortal world. As far as she was concerned, Illialei was her home, the Realm of Faerie her country. She was different from Melia, who questioned everything, including why she was a half-faerie without wings. She was also different from Melusine, who went to the mortal world behind their Mother's back.

Unlike her sisters, Plantine trusted her mother and father. Why didn't her father know that?

She opened her eyes. Getting agitated wasn't going to help her reach him. She stood up and walked a circle in the sand between the dead tree and the river. She needed to focus on her father, not Melia or Melusine. She sat back down on the tree trunk.

"Father?" she called again and again. Each unanswered attempt made her more determined to succeed. It was dark before she could admit her failure.

When the tears came, she made no attempt to stop them. When her hiccups became loud sobs, she gave them full rein. Her sorrow crested, fueled by the rejection of the one man whose attention she sought.

"Why won't you answer me?" she screamed into the night.

The lack of response was deafening.

On the long walk home, Plantine fortified herself with stoic thoughts. Soon her mother and father would comprehend their youngest daughter was their most worthy daughter.

8. Achill Island

Melia stuck her toe in the Nyssalei. "It's still freezing."

Tatou lounged on the same rock she had days before. "You'll acclimate."

Her cheerful encouragement made Melia want to growl.

"Remember what Tuck said, happy thoughts."

Melia forced herself to wade deeper. The river's sandy bed molded itself to the soles of her feet, but the water was frigid. She rubbed her upper arms as she looked up at the summer sky. *This is the right thing to do*, she told herself, before plunging in up to her knees.

"Take a deep breath and dive. Concentrate," Tatou said.

Melia stood up, reached her hands over her head, pressed her palms together, bent her knees, and launched her body forward into the water. The current dragged her sideways. She came up shivering and spluttering for air. An odd sensation had startled her, breaking her concentration.

Tatou buzzed up and down the river's edge, clapping as if Melia had actually done something. "That was great!"

Melia let her body slip back into the water. It didn't feel so cold. "Something happened."

"What?"

"A pulling."

"Tuck said that would happen. Try again."

Melia returned to one of her happiest memories of Achill. It had been late in the day. She and several of her mortal friends had chased one another around a bonfire on the beach. Screaming and racing the tide, they'd danced as the sky turned crimson. Melia had been the beloved faerie princess, delighting her tiny companions with her vivacity.

Her heart swelled. She breathed as Tuck had instructed her. A warm glow suffused her chest; it extended outwards through her arms and legs. She stood up, centered her feet in the river's sandy bed, prepared her body, and dove headfirst.

The pulling sensation sucked her in, but this time she was prepared. She continued her rhythmic breathing. The water turned to air, the pulling intensified, and she felt wind against her face as she fell into a weightless, timeless space. Her body spun, not out of control but as if it searched for the right direction. Shutting out all other thoughts and images, she brought the picture Tuck had shown her of the sea cliff to mind. She recalled every detail: the white froth capping the blue-green sea, the brownish-red shade of the cliff's sandy rock. Then she heard the exuberant rush of the tide and inhaled the tang of salt in the air. An invisible force evicted her onto a wave-kissed beach.

She'd reached the mortal world.

Three days later, Melia stood before a small stone building. She raised her fist to knock on its door; her hand stilled midair. More than one shopkeeper in the village had told her she would find the great mortal druid, Elynus, here. She dropped her fist and stepped back down the steps. Her body trembled.

Elynus' simple stone abode stood as though it were the solitary sentinel on the sweep of an elevated promontory–Achill Head, the shopkeeper had called it. A thin trail of smoke blew from the chimney, dissolving into grey clouds overhead. Seagulls clacked in the bay to the south.

She paced in the short grass, staring at the three steps that led up to the cottage. The locals held her father in high esteem. Did she dare confront him? After all, he was a great druid. Who was she to question his work?

Melia felt weak and confused. She hadn't realized when she'd arrived on the beach that she would have to roam the countryside to find her father.

For some reason, she'd expected to arrive closer to where he lived. Maybe she should have swallowed her pride and asked Melusine for help. But that was her hunger talking. Although it had taken a generous fisherman and a benevolent grocer to keep her from starving, and every single muscle in her legs and feet ached, she told herself she was fine.

She touched her hand to her forehead. She couldn't feel Nandana's mark, but knowing it was there gave her a sense of purpose. She saw things her father couldn't bear to witness. Didn't that mean some part of her was stronger than some part of him?

The wood door swung open. Melia faced a young lady in clean but well-worn clothes. She carried a wicker basket on her hip. Their eyes met.

"He's busy, he is," the young lady said, closing the door behind her. "Best to come back later."

"I can't."

"Suit yourself." The young lady pushed by. "His mood's dark; it's all I'm sayin'."

Melia watched the young lady retreat into the distance. When she was a black stick on the horizon, Melia raised her fist to the door. This time she knocked.

"Go away!"

Her body trembled again. She recognized her father's voice. "It's M-Melia."

The door swung open. Her father stood before her, a sour look on his face. He backed away from the door. "You shouldn't have come."

Melia followed him inside. "I need to talk to you."

They stood in a bright room overwhelmed by the massive desk in its center; a leather-bound book, an ink pot, several quill pens, and a stack of parchment covered the desk's surface. Bookshelves lined three of the walls. A fire popped and crackled in the hearth. To the right, two large oil lamps provided additional light. A single shadowy doorway stood to the far left of the fireplace.

A stew of emotions simmered in Melia's stomach. They bubbled up into her ribcage and made her throat feel hot. Over the past three days, wandering around Achill Island, she'd wondered how it would be to see her father for the first time in more than fifteen years. Although she'd never welcomed his intrusions in her mind, there'd been a time she'd loved him deeply.

Any lingering affection scattered in his presence. He was as stiff as a fence post and made her feel about as welcome as a horsefly.

He pointed to a chair in front of his desk as he settled himself into a larger one behind it. He steepled his fingers, steadied his gaze, and penetrated her mind.

Traveling to the mortal world had strengthened Melia's confidence. She pushed him away, but not before she felt his resentment; that she was freer than he was, banned as he was from the enchanted world and Faerie. The look in his eyes told her he was surprised by the force with which she'd closed her mind.

"Little Bird is not as small as she once was," he mused. "Yes, you've grown up into quite a lovely young lady, I daresay."

His compliment caught Melia off guard. He opened one of the desk drawers and pulled out a bit of cloth. He handed it to her. "You've got some dirt"–Elynus brushed his fingers between his eyebrows–"there."

Melia twisted the rag in her hand. "It's not dirt. Nandana–"

"Say no more. I usually recognize the Illustrator's work. It's usually more–"

"Delicate," she said.

He smiled. "Yes, that's the word I was looking for. But young people have their own styles, don't they? It's quite unusual–gives you an exotic look. Does it serve some purpose? Awaken your third eye, perhaps?"

She didn't know what he was talking about. Nandana hadn't mentioned anything about her eyes, let alone a third one.

"Did you know Nandana's Hindi?" her father asked.

"No."

"Her husband died. He was young, and so was she. Her culture dictated a faithful wife go with him. They were going to burn her alive on his funeral pyre. She was frantic, then she found her way to the Realm of Faerie. I don't think she's ever come back to join us mortals. No reason she should. Illialei is much safer for her these days."

"She didn't tell me." Would Nandana have told her, if Melia had ever gone back to visit her? How many times had she wanted to return to the

Illustrator's shop and talked herself out of it? A pang of sadness settled in her chest. She'd have to fix that when she returned to Illialei.

Once again, her father had turned the conversation away from himself. On the shores of the Nyssalei, he'd talked about Queen Luisa; now he talked about Nandana. Melia shifted her gaze to the fire–its heat stifled. She recalled the horrible vision of the Illustrator dying with her grey cat beside her. "You can't incarnate Umbra. You must think of others besides yourself." The clarity of her speech was a small, yet important, victory.

Her father's eyes hardened, but he said nothing.

His silence unnerved Melia more than any outrage she'd anticipated. Although her heart raced, she was determined to match his quiet.

In those still moments, Melia recognized her father's strength within her. She'd always dwelled on her faerie blood, and the gifts it had bestowed and denied. Not once had she considered what traits might have come to her by way of her father's blood. By matching his resolve that afternoon, it became clear strength of will was one of them.

Finally, he spoke. "I can incarnate Umbra. I will incarnate Umbra. And who I do or do not think about is none of your concern."

"But why must you attack Illialei?"

He reached for a quill and began smoothing its feathers. "Perhaps its population is not so innocent as you imagine them to be."

"Faeries are innocence." Melia tried not to think about Verbena. "M-mother told us: All good things in the mortal world come from Faerie." The appearance of her stumbled words wasn't a good sign.

"Ah." Father set down the quill, rested his elbows on the desk, clasped his hands, and leaned forward. "It's the energy of the enchanted world itself which feeds the dreams and imagination of mortals, not its creatures. What are they teaching you children in that school in Bryndale?"

How did he know about the school?

"Melusine used to visit," he answered.

Melia startled; he'd read her mind. Her sister had never told her about those visits.

Her father slammed the desk with his hand. "Enough. Crimes have been committed in Faerie, horrible crimes. They must be righted. I'm not at liberty to speak to you on these matters–your mother has forbid it. But rest assured, the power of Umbra is the only power in existence strong enough to confront the forces we must subdue."

"Crimes? There is no c-crime in Faerie." Melia bit the tip of her tongue. Was gossip a crime?

"It's what Queen Luisa would have you believe."

Melia's mind tripped and spun. She knew so little about the queen. "But a terrible war will come to Illialei," she pleaded. She shut away the pleasure that came with her visions. The thought that her father might be right, even if only a little, didn't make sense.

"I can't teach you," her father said, "in one afternoon, everything you must comprehend to trust my judgment. I've not made the decision to incarnate Umbra lightly. It's only after a thorough study of the facts"–he swept his arm wide, indicating the numerous books in his home–"that I've come to understand what needs to be done and why."

"But you don't understand!"

Elynus glared. "Does your mother know you've come here?" Before she could speak, he answered himself, "No, of course not." He waved his hand. "Return to Faerie, play with your friends, and fall in love. Leave matters you can't begin to comprehend in the hands of your elders who do."

She stood up and leaned over his desk. "You haven't seen what I've seen."

Elynus sat upright in his chair, his rigid body betrayed the impatience he barely contained. "Your visions–they're an interesting phenomenon, but you let them trouble you too much."

Melia pointed to her head. "Th-they started with y-you invading my m-mind. You're always in them. Urging m-me on."

He rubbed his chin. "I admit it's an unfortunate–and unforeseen–consequence of my work."

Her eyes stung.

He tapped his fingers on his desk. "I can tell you this: The Whole is bound by natural cycles which conserve and balance its energy. Do you understand what that means?"

Melia sank back in her chair. The Whole referred to the single universe that contained the enchanted and mortal worlds.

He continued his lecture. "Death and birth, grief and joy, nightfall and dawn, light and dark are eternally bound. The creatures of Illialei have chosen to shun the dark these long years. It's a farce that cannot continue. I will not allow it."

"You won't allow it?"

"Don't think you're going to stop me."

"I'll find a way," she said.

Her father's jaw tightened.

Panicked, Melia searched for some point to convince him. "What good can come from freeing the dross of human consciousness from the Void? It's where the Whole put it. Doesn't it need to stay there?"

When he spoke again, Elynus' voice was so soft and low she had to strain to hear it. "When the creatures of Illialei no longer deny the truth of what they have blessed with their ignorance; when the tears of earnest grief have cleansed their hearts and souls–the tyranny of the first-born Albiana will end, their poison rendered impotent."

"Their poison? You talk as if the faeries are black witches, and the brownies and elves are sorcerers from Kyrakkos! They're like children–prone to play. Maybe they tell tall tales ..."

Her father paced behind his desk, a rhythmic march that distracted her. "I'm talking about the Albiana. You're bewitched by them, as is everyone else in Illialei."

"B-bewitched?"

He stopped his back and forth movement. "By an appearance which bedazzles the eyes as it suffocates the very beauty of the soul."

"You speak of appearances?"

"Illialei's queens are not so pretty as they wish you to believe."

"Yet–"

"Melia, you must accept that you're mistaken in this matter. Your vision is narrow."

"Do you know of the prophecy?"

She'd caught his attention. He glanced down at his desk as he rolled up one sleeve, then the other. Melia's breathing shallowed as she waited for his response. Maybe he would finally take her concerns seriously.

"The Idonnic Prophecy?"

She nodded, afraid to say anything.

"I'm surprised you've heard of it," he said.

"It's included as an appendix in the *Old Texts*."

Her father's blue eyes pierced her.

"Those are the books they use in the Bryndale school," she offered.

"The Queen's propaganda."

Melia blinked. "But–"

Her father leaned forward as if he were about to confide a carefully kept secret, then pulled back as if he'd thought better of confessing. He shifted the piles of parchment on his desk.

"What?" Melia pleaded.

"I'm surprised that dusty poem is taught in your school."

"Do you think it's true?"

Elynus crossed his arms. "In my experience, foretelling is an unpredictable science." Melia wanted to hear more of his opinion. She bit her lower lip and waited. Her silence was rewarded when he continued, "The prediction itself affects all outcomes."

"Then, you don't think it's true."

"I choose not to dwell on it."

"But you must have some opinion about it."

"I know the *Old Texts* are not that old. Their purpose is to brainwash Illialei's youth and secure the Albiana reign. As I interpret it, the prophecy is about a revolution, albeit a risky one. Regardless, I'm puzzled that it's included in the texts you study."

"Why?"

"Because many believe it foretells the end of the Albiana queens. It became popular after ..." He collapsed in his seat and massaged his forehead. "Perhaps that's why it was appended to the *Old Texts*. It's more effective for the Albiana to refute the verse in public than let its scant hope feed some underground rebellion."

Melia blinked. She could hardly imagine Illialei's sunny inhabitants mounting an insurrection against their queen.

Before she could formulate an adequate response to her father's strange musings, Elynus straightened in his chair and re-focused his full attention on her. "I've said too much, and that after promising your mother I wouldn't speak of these things with you or your sisters. I've already broken one promise to her." He shuffled his parchments, evading Melia's gaze. "I'll not break another."

"You've spoken to Mother about these things?"

He stopped sorting through his papers and cradled his jaw in his hand. He closed his eyes. The flame from the fire had died to embers, and the room had turned dark. A strained silence waxed between them. Melia shifted and the floor boards creaked.

"Not in so many words," he said.

"But she knows about all these things?"

"If it's as you told me, and the entire population of Illialei is gossiping about them–"

"She never leaves the tree house."

"Melia." He pressed his palm on the cover of the large leather-bound book before him and stared at it. "I have work here I must finish. These things don't concern you. It's time for you to return to Illialei."

"But Father–"

When he raised his face, his eyes were hooded, his lips flattened. "Please, you must go."

"Then, you will proceed with the incarnation?" Melia asked.

"I've already said I will."

Melia returned to the beach, heartsick. Although no one else stood on the shore, she searched for a private spot to mourn her failure.

A short distance away, waves rolled into three sea caves that appeared to yawn as though they were giant mouths. Next to them, the foamy tide lapped at several large boulders piled on their sides. She clambered up onto one of the orange-brown mounds and stared into the horizon.

She sifted through her conversation with her father–because she wasn't giving up–and settled upon his explanation of the prophecy. Everyone ascribed it a different meaning. Tatou believed its poetry encoded actual events, destined to unfold, and took Melia's visions as confirmation of that. Verbena believed it was a warning against Umbra's incarnation. Nandana didn't believe anything could be counted on until it happened, and yet, she feared the war it predicted, and her father thought the writing of the prophecy had already altered the course of events.

Melia hated to agree with Verbena, but after seeing her father in the flesh, the conviction that it was wrong for him to incarnate Umbra had only grown stronger in her. How was she going to stop him when he'd been so adamant and dismissive?

A faint melody put an end to Melia's ruminations. Words Melia didn't understand formed a sweet song. She looked around for the singer. Low tide had revealed a series of pools. A mermaid surfaced in the nearest one. Melia clambered down from her rock. The golden-haired water creature fell silent.

"Please, don't stop," Melia said. "Your voice is lovely."

The mermaid swished her tail and resumed her singing.

Melia dangled her feet in the pool. The perfect moment transformed the ache in her heart from the smart of defeat to a twinge of longing. She wished Tatou were here with her.

The mermaid finished her song. "You look so wistful."

"I suppose I am," Melia said. "I came here to do something, and I've failed. I wanted to feel sorry for myself, but your song was so enchanting, it's given me some hope."

"You're not mortal," the mermaid said.

"Half."

"Are you one of Pressina's daughters?"

Melia laughed. "Is there a sign on my forehead?"

"There's a mark." The water creature gave a playful laugh. "My name's Evangeline. I know your sister, Melusine. She used to visit this place quite often. Your eyes are the same color as hers."

"That's about all we share."

"Did you come to see your father?" Evangeline asked. "That's why Melusine used to come."

"Yes, and it was a disappointing visit."

"I'm sorry," she said. "Elynus is stubborn."

"You know him?"

The mermaid shrugged. "He's a druid. Everyone who comes here from the enchanted world knows him. There aren't that many of us."

"But you're fond of him?"

"You're not?"

"He's committed to doing something he shouldn't do. I'm scared for him," Melia said.

"He's lonely. He misses your mother."

"That's the problem."

"Tell me," Evangeline said. "I can weave your burdens into a song and send them across the ocean."

"I wish someone could help me stop him from incarnating Umbra."

"Oh, that. He's been talking about that for ages."

"You don't care?"

"Well, he hasn't done it yet," the mermaid said.

"If nobody stops him, he will."

Evangeline swam closer. She put her hand on Melia's knee. Her touch cooled the half-faerie's returning frustration. "You made a wish in my presence, now I'm bound to help you."

Hit with a sense of wonder, Melia was torn between the desire to hug Evangeline and take back her words. If she'd known speaking her wish aloud would bind the mermaid to her, would she have done so? What could the mermaid do to stop Elynus, after all? "I had no idea."

"It's true." The mermaid's eyes hooded as though she was thinking hard. "Do you know any spells?"

"No, but my younger sister is good at them."

"Then, you'll need to bring her here."

Persuading Plantine to help them wasn't going to be easy.

"She'll need a spell that's strong enough to move one of these boulders. I'll recruit some of my friends. It will take our united voices to lure Elynus from his home."

Melia was still trying to figure out how she could persuade Plantine to help them.

The mermaid trailed her hand in the water. "Maybe a good scare will bring Elynus to his senses."

Melia wasn't convinced, but Evangeline was hopeful. They agreed to meet on the beach in a fortnight.

9. The Rose Garden

Plantine walked with Tuck through the Cathedral Palace rose garden. She'd chosen the garden for its privacy and the sweet scent of its velvet blossoms; they calmed her. The topic she wished to discuss with the tree elf made her anxious. She feared his position on her dilemma differed from hers and meant to choose her words with care. "Melia has asked me to travel to the mortal world with her and Melusine, to speak to our father."

"About Umbra's incarnation?" he asked.

"Yes." Usually, she preferred to walk with Tuck along the banks of the Nyssalei in the late afternoon. The covert glances from the flower faeries, who invaded those shores at that time of day, affirmed her peculiar beauty and fortified her confidence. But today she didn't want to be overheard.

"Will you go?" he asked.

If she could see his face, she could better gauge his reactions to her words. Walking, he stood as tall as the Albiana, towering over her. She tugged his arm, pulling him toward one of the ornate seats hidden in a recess of blooms. He didn't resist. When they sat, she settled her skirts.

She'd made sure to select her most attractive day dress this morning, its blue color matched her eyes, and its full skirts–falling just below her knees –accented her tiny waist and slim calves. Like most of the faeries in Illialei, she preferred bare feet to slippers.

She opened her eyes wide for the effect of innocence. "Do you think my father is wrong?"

"Love is never wrong," Tuck answered.

"Then you think he's right to incarnate Umbra, so he can reunite with our mother?"

"It's a dangerous quest."

"But you're not opposed to it."

He reached for one of her hands. She treasured the feel of his fingers against her palm. Although the mores of Faerie didn't preclude young romance, Plantine limited her physical contact with Tuck to affectionate gestures. The tension of restraint fueled her sense of control as much as it gave her time to consider her options. As her mother never failed to remind her, she had many.

Tuck opened his mouth, then closed it.

A sharp pinch tweaked Plantine's heart. "Then, you're opposed?"

"Umbra's consciousness can't be contained by a mortal," he said.

"What do you mean?"

He dropped her hand and rubbed his palms against his thin wool breeches. His chestnut hair covered his eyes. She longed to brush it aside, but sat on her hands instead.

"We've been in communication with the Order of the Idonnai," he said. "They're much more knowledgeable about Umbra than we are."

"You mean yourself and Aldous?"

"Yes."

"And they've told you this?" she asked.

"It's believed that, were a mortal to attempt to serve as Umbra's vessel, the incarnation would cause the mortal's death."

She got up from the seat. "And when did you plan to tell me this?"

"At this point, it's all speculation. We don't know the details of Elynus' plans. We don't know who he intends as the vessel. Whether it's him or some other."

"Some other?"

"We don't know."

"But you would let him attempt it and die, without a word of caution?"

"Plantine, your father is not known as the great mortal druid without reason. His research has been thorough. Despite his exile, he has amassed an intricate network of spies, investigators, scholars, and witches throughout the enchanted world."

"Have any told him he risks his life if he acts as Umbra's vessel?"

"We don't know. But he can't proceed with the incarnation without certain artifacts. And we're certain he doesn't possess them." He grinned. "It makes the question rather moot."

She didn't find the humor in his assessment. "I should warn him."

Tuck raised his eyebrows. "He might not listen."

"I'm his daughter."

"I'd hate for you to be disappointed."

Plantine could feel the blood rush to her face. "You don't think he'll listen to me?"

He held out his hand; she ignored it. He rested his elbows on his knees and stared at the ground. "Your father broke his faerie troth the day you were born."

Her arms and legs quivered with rage. "Must you remind me?"

"I don't mean to hurt you, but think it through. If he blames you in the least for the loss of his wife, will he heed your warnings?"

He brought up the critical doubt she chose to overlook, her father's uncertain feelings for her.

"It's been hard for you, living your life without knowing him," he offered.

Plantine relented. Her connection with her father was abstract, her only memories being their sparse, telepathic encounters years ago. He'd always been more attached to Melusine–even Melia. Plantine told herself it was because he'd never gotten the chance to know her.

She was sure that he longed to. "Do you think I should help Melia?"

"It's doubtful Umbra's incarnation can be stopped forever, but there's a question of timing. The vessel of incarnation will determine the outcome of the war. That much is known. Umbra, as an incarnated entity, will be a fierce energy which must be harnessed. It would be wise for all who have a stake in the Whole to steer the choice of vessel with great thought."

"And you don't think my father is the best vessel?"

"Plantine, it will kill him."

The thought of saving her father's life infused Plantine with noble purpose, a spiritual rectification for her role in the loss of his beloved faerie wife. She clasped her hands together. "This information you and Aldous have received from the priesthood, it's confidential?"

"Yes."

Her sisters didn't have to know the reason she agreed to help them. They had their own selfish reasons for stopping the incarnation. Melia believed her father would destroy Illialei, and Melusine wanted to challenge him as a warning to Raymond: Witness the dire consequences of breaking a faerie troth.

Plantine was also concerned for her mother. Years had passed since they'd returned to Illialei–Plantine was fifteen–yet Pressina still wept in her room every night, assuming her daughters didn't hear. Her mother's tears troubled Plantine. They professed a love Pressina wouldn't admit, a love which contradicted the ambitions she encouraged in her youngest daughter. Some nights, Plantine thought she'd do anything to bring her mother peace. "There's nothing I can do to reunite my mother and father?"

"I wish that you could," Tuck said.

His response increased her frustration, but if she couldn't help her mother, at least she could save her father from his own ignorance.

She returned to Tuck's side. Her knee touched his. "I'll go with them. Melusine will try to persuade him first. If he won't listen to her, Melia wants to scare him to his senses. She doesn't know any spells. That's why she needs me."

"With your perfect memory for incantations, you'll be a great help."

She glowed. His attention touched a deep crack in her being. She couldn't put it into words, but Plantine sought him out whenever she could. "I must bake you another tart, as a way of saying thank you."

He took her hand again. This time she let him. "Sitting here with you is treat enough."

She relaxed. It would be hard to explain another baking project without raising her mother's suspicions, and her mother's reservations about her youngest daughter falling in love with a tree elf was a conversation she intended to avoid–especially when her own emotions confused her so.

Plantine couldn't understand why she wanted to spend every moment with the humble Tuck. He was breathtaking to look at, and being the apprentice to the head librarian of the Cathedral Palace Grand Library was an honorable vocation. Yet, she had always dreamed of more.

"The sun will set in not too long. Would you care to join Aldous and me for tea?" Tuck asked.

Plantine hesitated before she declined.

10. The Siren Call

Several days later, a compelling melody drew Elynus' attention from his writing. It had been a half-moon cycle since his middle daughter, Melia, had traveled to the mortal world, challenging his judgment and demanding he stop his work. He forced himself to laugh out loud at her foolishness.

One day she would thank him.

From beyond his cottage walls, the music insisted. Elynus sprinkled a fine sand across the wet ink.

He poured the crystals back into his sander bowl. When he brushed his fingers across the page, they came away clean. He shut *The Book of Umbra's* heavy cover and reached for the leather satchel he kept in his desk's bottom right drawer. He untied the satchel's flap, felt for the letter he'd written many years ago to Lord Goring, then slid his greatest work inside.

Elynus performed this ritual every time he left the cottage. If anything ever happened to him, his courier (the troll named Moog, who ferried all communication between himself and the enchanted world) would take the satchel straight to Lord Goring.

Years ago, when he'd made these arrangements, he'd trusted the muannaye implicitly. Their commitment to incarnating Umbra had united them, but over time, the muannaye's fondness for Elendah pricked at Elynus. Of late, the thought of altering his instructions to Moog grew on him. If anything happened to him the satchel should go to Pressina.

He retied the satchel's flap, balancing it upright in his chair. He'd change Moog's instructions when he returned. He'd do it tonight.

The song that compelled Elynus to leave his work filled his mind.

He went to the bedroom for his coat. He couldn't remember the last time he'd taken a midday break. The alluring tune filled his mind with images of the beach at Ashleam Bay.

✧✧✧

Mermaids.

Elynus should've guessed.

A ring of the enchanting creatures sang in the sea cave's semi-darkness. Where their luxurious hair left them naked, the porcelain skin of their arms and torsos gleamed. Their sinuous tails splashed and dipped, shimmering in the cove's shallow waters.

Entranced by their presence, Elynus settled on a rocky shelf, a short distance beyond their circle.

A loud boom jerked him from his reverie. The cave was dark, the air cold, the mermaids silent. He must have dozed off.

"Father!"

Was that Melia?

He struggled to gain his equilibrium in the pitch black.

"Father, can you hear me?"

He stumbled toward the sound of his daughter's voice, his arms stretched out in front of him. Water splashed his boots, the tide rose. High tide would flood the cave. How much time did he have?

"Melia?"

"We're all here."

"Melusine?" he called.

"I'm here too, Father."

Elynus stopped his forward movement. "Plantine?"

"We've agreed you mustn't incarnate Umbra," Melusine shouted above the crash of waves her father could no longer view.

"When you promise you'll stop, we'll release you from the cave."

Melia.

He could find no words. His heart beat in his chest–clammy sweat gathered on his brow. He sloshed toward the sound of their voices. Seawater reached his knees as he concentrated his furious energy on the boulder blocking his exit. Whatever magic his daughters had cast, it rendered his own efforts impotent.

"Are you going to incarnate Umbra?" Melusine shouted.

He heard their muffled voices. "HOW DARE YOU IMPRISON ME."

"Father, if you promise you won't incarnate Umbra, we'll lift the binding spell from the stone."

"I'll make no such promise! I'm your father! Release me now!" His shouts returned to his ears in furious echoes.

"Why won't you reconsider?" Melia's voice quaked.

The water had reached his waist. It was freezing cold. Already, he'd lost all feeling in his toes. He paddled clumsily, searching for higher ground with his hands. "DO YOU WISH TO DROWN ME?"

Again, he heard their muffled voices. Plantine's voice separated; she chanted. He strained to hear her words. When her sister's voices joined in, he caught the final verse:

"Wind that carries air with mighty force,
Roll this heavy stone with one slight breeze."

Thank goodness, they'd come to their senses. He waited.

The chanting rose to a frantic pitch.

The sea cave remained sealed.

"Plantine!" Elynus called.

Water reached his neck; he bobbed, feeling for a handhold, something to cling to.

The icy sea numbed his limbs.

"I can't move the stone. Father, are you all right?" Plantine's tearful voice pleaded.

Elynus gulped great mouthfuls of water. The rising tide showed no mercy. In his wildest imaginings, he'd never conceived his life would end by patricide. He tried to remember Pressina, the last time he'd held her in his arms.

"FATHER!" Melia's panicked cry came from far away.

11. An Investigation

"Plantine, DO SOMETHING!" Melusine cried. She was the only one still dry. "Evangeline, our father is drowning! Can't you help us?"

One of Evangeline's hands covered her mouth, the other treaded the rising water. The horror in the mermaid's eyes confirmed what Melusine feared. They were killing their father. Evangeline's friends, silent behind her, formed a solemn group of witnesses.

Trapped on the highest patch of ground, the bluff that overhung the sea cave, Melusine felt helpless. She knew no spells, no incantations. The study and memorization of the intricate relationship between words and the natural world had always seemed tedious, when her natural beauty and faerie glamour had always been enough to get her whatever she wanted. Until now. She wanted the sea cave unblocked and her father safe and alive.

Below, Melia sloshed through seawater. She headed toward Plantine who clung to a spindling tower of rock, choking and sobbing. Melusine screamed at Plantine again. The tide had come so fast, the strip of beach in front of the cave, and most of the boulders around it, were submerged. Melia tripped and slipped in the seething swells. Her head appeared and disappeared in the waves. The water continued to rise.

Melusine watched the scene below, unbelieving.

Melusine pushed through time and space. Her head broke the water's surface. The familiar banks of the Nyssalei did nothing to staunch the sickening weight in her gut. Beside her, two small circles of waves announced her sisters' return from the mortal world. Plantine first, then Melia. In a truly enchanted world, their father wouldn't be dead, and her sisters wouldn't exist.

She pushed through the river water. Silent. Angry.

The three sisters huddled on the riverbank. The sun was gone from the sky, but in the dim light before night fell complete, Melusine saw they were alone. She decided to be thankful for that minor reprieve. "We have to act as though nothing's happened," she said.

Plantine's lips quivered. "Why?"

"Well," Melusine said. "Let's think it through. We could go to the tree house and march in hand-in-hand. When we sit Mother down to tell her what happened, it will sound something like this: 'We decided to picnic in the mortal world today, and by the way, when we were there, we accidentally killed Father. Funny, how some days things don't go as planned.'" She pierced Melia with a searing gaze.

"Don't blame this on me," her middle sister said.

So predictable. "Whose idea was it to go to the mortal world and give Father a little scare?" Melusine asked.

"Ac-actually, it-it was Evangeline's."

"Blame it on the mermaid."

"I didn't make you go. You wanted to go. You wanted to teach Raymond a lesson. You wanted to make sure he understands what breaking a faerie troth is all about. That's what *you* said."

"Yes, I said, 'teach Raymond a lesson,' not *kill* our father!"

"I didn't do it," Melia said. "P-Plantine's spell–the rock–"

"Don't blame her." Melusine looked at her youngest sister. She wanted to strangle her, but she was sure Plantine hadn't sealed the cave on purpose. The girl worshipped Elynus.

"You s-saw what happened," Melia said. "How c-can you blame me?"

Melusine pressed her finger against Nandana's mark. "Ever since you got that thing on your forehead, you've been acting strange. Nandana's the one who put you up to this, isn't she?"

"Leave her out of this," Melia said.

Melusine chopped the air with her hand. "Then don't blame Plantine. Look, no one has to know we were there when he died." She rubbed her temples. In many parts of Illialei, news of Elynus' death would be greeted with enthusiasm–no one had wanted him to incarnate Umbra–but their mother was unpredictable. Pressina would be angry enough when she found out her oldest daughter was betrothed to a mortal. There was no way to predict how she might react to her daughters' involvement in their father's death.

Melusine could bear only so much of Pressina's rage as she prepared for her wedding. Her sisters needed to keep quiet. "We all know Mother." It was hard to put her feelings for Pressina into words. "We don't know how she's going to take this. What good will come of a confession?"

Plantine stared at the ground.

Melusine put her fingers under her younger sister's chin and lifted it. "You're so good with spells. I couldn't believe when you moved that enormous boulder in front of the cave."

Plantine began crying, hard. It sounded like the high squeal of a horse in unbearable pain.

Melusine pulled her youngest sister close and stroked her hair. She'd intended to soothe her younger sister, not set off her dreadful sobbing again. "Shh. Shh. It's not your fault the rock got stuck."

Silent shudders racked Plantine's body. Melusine held her until she was still. When she pushed her away, Melusine watched Plantine to see if she could remain calm. "Better?"

Her youngest sister shrugged.

Melia stood a few feet away, defiant. "Fine, we won't say anything. But what about Evangeline and her friends? What if they tell someone?"

She still didn't understand. "They won't," Melusine said.

"How do you know?" Melia asked.

"They're in the same situation we're in. They lured Father there, but they didn't expect him to die. What are they going to do? Volunteer it was their idea? It was their idea, right? That's what you said."

"I already told you. I didn't know when I made the wish in front of Evangeline she had to help me make it come true."

"Well, she did do that. Make your wish come true."

"I didn't wish for Father to be dead."

"He won't be incarnating Umbra."

"Can you believe this?" Melusine asked.

Raymond held out his hand for the letter addressed to Queen Luisa Albiana.

"She's the bloody queen of the enchanted world. How did you get a hold of this?" he asked.

"Luisa is not the queen of the enchanted world." Melusine sighed. "How many times have I told you? The Realm of Faerie is a single land mass in the enchanted world. It has two countries: Illialei and Tyrannis. But there's also Azyllai, home of the gods, including the lesser ones; Kyrakkos, home of witches, sorcerers, and other practitioners of the black arts–"

"Shouldn't your mother move there?" he asked.

Melusine worked to keep her expression serious. She'd imagined her mother immigrating to Kyrakkos many times herself, but it didn't feel right to admit it to Raymond. She ignored his joke and continued her lesson. "And Misgradde where most of the dwarves live–"

"Most, but not all," he said. "There's a stubborn population residing in Tyrannis. They're reputed to be the best chefs in the Whole, even better than the ones in France."

She laughed. It felt strange–smiling. Any sense of gladness felt as if it were a betrayal of that dark afternoon when she and Melia had helped Plantine chant the spell that sealed their father's death. She wondered if the secrecy binding them and the mermaids had made things worse. Well, it was all going to come out now.

"Where have you gone, sweetheart?" Raymond stroked her hair, calling her back to the present. She touched the back of his hand, grateful.

As soon as she'd settled Melia and Plantine the night they'd returned from Ashleam Bay, she'd returned to France to find her fiancé. He'd been wonderful, assuring her that terrible accidents did happen, that she and her sisters weren't at fault.

Why couldn't she believe him?

But Melusine didn't want to dwell on her guilt. "I see you've been paying attention to my geography lessons."

"Yes, I have, love."

"Then you should know, Luisa is not the queen of the enchanted world. She's not even the queen of the Realm of Faerie. She's only the queen of Illialei."

Raymond's eyes twinkled with mischief. "Does that make your possession of this letter any less of an achievement?"

"I do have friends."

"And beauty, and that faerie glamour." He hugged her, crushing the letter between them. After he kissed the tip of her nose, he read more. "*Lord Zachariah Goring*—who's that?" he asked.

"A damn muannaye who used to work with Father."

"*Petitions for an official investigation into the suspicious death of the great mortal druid, Elynus.*" Raymond looked over the top of the letter.

She rolled over onto her stomach and plucked the blades of grass. She wouldn't cry, not out of frustration, not out of sadness, and not out of guilt. "They're going to find out we were there."

He placed his hand on her shoulder. "It was an accident. They'll find out about that well in the cave too."

"As if the gossips in Illialei don't have enough to tattle about. Melia mopes around with that odd mark on her forehead. Now there's a rumor Plantine's fallen in love with a tree elf. Mother is going to be livid."

"At least no one's talking about your father incarnating Umbra," he said. "What was that all about, anyway?"

Irritated by his curiosity, Melusine snatched the petition from his hands. "Now they're chattering about the strange circumstances of his death." Her fiancé had missed the point of her participation in Melia's scheme. "You know, none of this would have happened if my father hadn't broken his faerie troth."

Raymond laughed out loud. "Love, are you still worried about that?"

"Mother's always warned us against you full-bloods." She was half-joking, half-serious.

"I'm not your father," he said. "I can keep a promise."

When he kissed her, she stopped thinking about everything.

12. Black Smoke

They formed a half-circle in the front room of the tree house. Melia held her breath, Melusine shifted from foot to foot, and Plantine fidgeted.

They were focused on their mother.

Pressina had been staring at the ring on the fourth finger of her left hand far too long.

The carved band had been a gift from Elynus on their wedding day. That the gold winked in the morning light as her hand jerked seemed a final, cruel joke.

No one laughed.

Pressina's hand wouldn't stop shaking. Each bob of her wrist made the thin parchment between her fingers rasp, reminding Melia of the news written there, scrawled in long black letters. She wanted to grab her mother's arm and stop the rattle. Instead, she flattened her sweaty palms against the sides of her dress and stole a guilty look at her sisters–all of this was her fault.

When their mother's voice broke the taut silence, the torrent of her grief bewildered Melia. She'd never heard her mother speak fondly of their father. In fact, she'd never heard her speak of him at all since they'd returned to the enchanted world.

"How is it possible that Elynus is dead?" her mother asked, lilac eyes wide. She collapsed to her knees as her peacock-blue skirt billowed around her.

Melia had never seen her like this, limp and helpless. What was worse was that her response seemed genuine, not her usual histrionics.

Plantine stumbled to grasp her shoulder. "I'm so sorry."

Pressina twisted to push her youngest daughter away. "Don't touch me."

Melia's younger sister wavered, wild-eyed and off balance.

Melusine patted the lime-striped chaise. "Come sit."

Their mother bristled. "I'm not some pet."

"Please," Plantine said.

Melia tugged on a strand of hair.

Pressina pulled herself up to standing. A mask of fury erased the visible sorrow clouding her face. She crushed the parchment in a single fluid motion.

If nothing else, she was graceful, even in a rage.

"How could you?" Their mother shook the crumpled wad in her fist. It was the official pronouncement–the result of the investigation prompted by the muannaye, Lord Zachariah Goring–certifying their father's death had been an accident.

Desperate to explain, Melia tried. "We didn't mean–"

"To kill him." Melusine stepped next to her, shoulder to shoulder.

A single vein on Pressina's forehead throbbed.

She was making things worse. Melia sent a telepathic message to her older sister. *"Don't say anything else!"*

Melusine, her eyes gleaming with conviction, ignored the warning. Her chin jutted forward. "He should have honored his faerie troth. Not betrayed you."

Pressina's fury boiled over. "You dare credit your actions to me?"

Plantine broke rank. Kneeling, she reached for their mother's hand. "So many nights we heard your tears ..."

Pressina freed her hand with a violent shake. "I never made my sorrows your burdens. What made you think–what made you dream–that harming your father would please me?"

Waves of doubt spread from Melia's chest, down to her stomach, and back up into her throat. She thought her mother cried every night because she hated Elynus. By breaking his faerie troth, he'd forced their return to Illialei and planted the seed which had blossomed into Pressina's bitter existence. She'd never imagined her mother's grief was for the loss of a shared life with her husband.

How could she have been so wrong?

Father's death hadn't stopped her visions, either.

She risked two sideways glances. To her left, Melusine's toes traced the sunbeams spilling through the open windows. The side of her older sister's lip curved upwards in the faintest hint of a smile. Melia didn't want to know what she was thinking. To her right, Plantine's slender shoulders slumped with guilt. Her younger sister's flaxen hair hid her face, but she twisted her fingers into knots.

As Melia chewed on her thumbnail, she considered sending a telepathic message to her younger sister. She'd need to be careful, because if their mother caught them–

"Stop that!" Pressina's face was inches from Melia's. She pulled her middle daughter's hand away from her mouth.

Melia's jaw set as her mother's hardened eyes bored into hers. Was she trying to glamour her?

"Wasn't Father evil?" Melusine's question ended their silent battle of wills. "Didn't his wickedness bar him from the enchanted world forever?"

Their mother advanced on Melusine, the sisters' usual ringleader, with curled fingers.

"Evil? You have the nerve to ask if he was evil, after you entombed him in Ashleam Bay? Might it have been more just to have this conversation before"–seemingly aware that her pitch rose to a frenzied shriek, Pressina paused to collect herself–"before you murdered him?"

Melusine's eyes narrowed. Plantine gasped.

"It was an accident! The official letter explains about the well and the rising tides. Did you read it?" Melia asked.

Pressina shook the parchment in her face. "These are only words on a page. They're meaningless. No one in Faerie cares about Elynus, or me–not even our daughters."

Melia lifted her hands, then let them fall to her sides. Her mother was being impossible, but she couldn't let her believe they'd killed their father on purpose. "When w-we sealed the sea cave, we only meant for Father to reconsider his commitment to incarnate Umbra. We never m-meant–"

Her mother's nostrils flared.

"We never m-meant ... we had no idea the tides would rise so fast. There was no m-murder." Melia hadn't fully grasped the reality of her father's death until this moment. Now, his absence seemed to swallow the entire tree house, even though he'd never stepped foot inside it.

Pressina sank down onto the chaise.

Had she even heard of Umbra? Or the war that would come if Umbra was incarnated?

Other than the infrequent visits from foreigners at odd hours, their mother led an isolated existence. Through the years she ventured less and less to the Bryndale market, preferring to send Melia or Plantine.

Was it possible she'd never heard the rumors regarding their father?

Melia tried to remember the last time Pressina had spoken of Nandana, other than to curse her for blemishing her daughter's forehead. She couldn't. When she tried to remember what her father had told her about what her mother knew, she could hardly think beyond the dreadful cries he'd uttered the moments before he'd died.

She had to make her mother understand why they'd done what they'd done, why she'd done what she'd done. "Father was going to incarnate Umbra." Melia waited for her mother's protests.

Pressina looked from Melusine to Melia. She waved the balled parchment between them. "Which is it? Did you kill him to avenge my honor or because he intended to incarnate Umbra?"

Melia took a step back. "You don't care that he wanted to bring Umbra from the Void?"

"Do you honestly think"–a light rap on the front door persisted –"nych!" Pressina forbade her daughters to move.

Melia fell back in line with her sisters.

Tatou's sing-song voice drifted through the front room's open window. Melia opened her mouth, but her mother raised a warning hand. Pressina's high-heeled boots clicked against the polished wood as she marched to the window closest to the front door. Melusine rolled her eyes; everyone else in Illialei wore slippers or went barefoot.

"Good morning, Pressina. Is everything all right?" the pixie asked.

A number of swallows chirped in the background, as if she voiced their concerns.

"We're fine, Tatou."

Melia searched the leaves outside the window but couldn't pick out the shape of her friend fluttering among the greenery.

"Lots of smoke coming from the chimney," Tatou said.

Finally, Melia saw her friend's golden curls as she settled upon a wide limb.

Pressina's wings quivered, whether from rage or the light breeze blowing the window's sheer curtains, Melia couldn't be sure; she suspected the former. Pressina hated when the pixies complained about the smoke. "I've been cold," she snipped.

"Sky over the oak is black. You can see it from the enchanted gardens. We were worried."

"Very thoughtful of you to check up on us." Pressina nettled as Melusine snorted. "I told you, we're fine. Run along, dear."

Melia's heart sank. Their mother wasn't finished with them yet.

"A chimney shouldn't put out that much smoke. Maybe you could get someone to clean it." Tatou was doing her best.

She'd encouraged Melia to tell her mother about what had happened with their father before the official pronouncement was released. But every time Melia had tried to speak up, the courage had escaped her. Now it was too late. Her mother had been blindsided by the news, and she was furious. Tatou's efforts to distract her were hopeless.

"Will do." Pressina slammed the shutters before Tatou could get in another word. She already knew why the chimney winding around the oak's trunk dirtied the sky.

"A consequence of practicing the black arts in Illialei, my dear," the sorcerer from Kyrakkos had told Pressina. "Residue from spells and potions you've brewed over the years interacts with the mud of the chimney's bricks."

A chill traveled Melia's spine. They'd tried to excuse their mother's strange obsession with black magic as an eccentric hobby. Now, she seemed untroubled by their father's desire to incarnate Umbra.

What was going on?

It wasn't that magic wasn't practiced in Illialei. It was. But the dark arts crossed the line from reining or amplifying the energies of the enchanted world to perverting, corrupting, or subverting them. It was the difference between an herbalist with a talent for healing and an alchemist who had mastered the art of poison.

Across the Maeldun Bridge, in Tyrannis, the muannai were obsessed with black magic, and Kyrakkos was its font. But the elements–air, fire, matter, and water–were more potent in Illialei, so black magic had always been shunned in its borders.

Melia's gaze swept the spare yet elegant room they stood in. No telltale sign evidenced the craft Pressina studied, but her daughters–and everyone else in Illialei–knew. Black smoke hovering above the oak wasn't the only clue. Although she'd done her best to segregate her occult studies to the single locked room, carved deep beneath the oak tree's massive trunk, faeries and elves were gossipy folk. Melia and her sisters had grown practiced at shrugging off the whispers in Bryndale when they ventured out.

"Pressina entertains strange guests late at night."

"Packages arrive from Kyrakkos."

"She receives weekly bundles from Tyrannis–the Inker's drivel–why would any decent faerie keep up with the copper sheets?"

Malachi had joined their family courtesy of a spell gone awry. Pressina, advancing in her studies, had meant to change a chipmunk into a blood hound. When the rodent had transformed into a yellow-eyed, plump-cheeked, cat-like creature with stripes running lengthwise down its back, she'd insisted on keeping it as a pet.

The ill-tempered beast padded through the tree house, claiming every last inch as its territory. Ridiculously attached to Pressina, it never failed to hiss if Melia or her sisters challenged its dominion. On the rare occasion their mother did leave home, it shadowed her, skulking through fern and brush.

Melia searched for the misshapen feline now. Predictably, Malachi perched on one of the wheel-like branches spanning the room, keeping an eye on his mistress. A nauseating feeling gathered in the pit of Melia's stomach.

Her mother stormed to the remaining windows and locked the shutters. With each slam and bang, Melia felt more like her prisoner and less like her daughter. Pressina swept toward the enormous fire roaring in the grate against the far wall, the cause of the smoke. Her clenched fist still gripped the crumpled parchment. She bent over and pushed it through the grill.

The firelight cast menacing shadows as the husk burned. When their mother turned, Melia recoiled. Her sisters must have recognized the same fierce determination on Pressina's face that Melia did–the three of them backed away together.

Their mother raised her arms. A gust of wind burst through the darkened room.

"Stop it!" Melia yelled.

Plantine whimpered as Melusine stomped toward the door.

Pressina clapped her hands. The sound of thunder reverberated through the room. Melusine stopped involuntarily. The abrupt halt in her forward movement sent her crashing to the floor with a graceless thud. Fear erased defiance from her eyes.

"Why do you care if Father is dead?" Melusine panted.

"He was my husband," their mother's voice quaked.

Melusine struggled to her feet. "You never spoke of reconciliation. Not once."

"You never spoke of loving him," Plantine chimed in.

"What do you know of love?" their mother hissed. "What you read in your silly books at the palace library?"

"You're in shock," Melia said. "Let me make you some tea." She bit her tongue as soon as the useless words had passed her lips.

Her mother whirled to face her. "You've killed your father and you offer me tea?"

"Why aren't you proud of us? What we did was heroic," Melusine boasted. "Don't you see? We've stopped Umbra's incarnation. Without war. Everyone else is relieved."

If anyone in Illialei was relieved, it was news to Melia. Everyone still gave her wide berth as if she was the murderess Pressina accused her of being.

Their mother glared at them, one by one. "Yes, I imagine Luisa's puppets are thrilled."

Plantine broke down. "I meant to save him."

Melia whipped her head. She got a mouth full of hair. "It was your spell that–"

Plantine's eyes looked as if they were going to explode. "You!"

Before she could say another word, Melia stepped in front of her to address their mother. "We stopped the war that Umbra's incarnation would have brought to Faerie. Doesn't that mean anything to you?"

"It means you've killed your father for nothing."

"But–"

"I've raised three fools if you believe you've stopped anything."

"You defend Umbra's incarnation?" Melia's head felt so light, she thought it might float away. Everything around her seemed unreal.

"Your father's devotion to Umbra served *me–*" Pressina caught herself.

The room fell silent. Melia held out her hands to her sisters. *"We need to form a mental shield."*

Pressina continued to yell.

Melia squeezed her sister's hands. *"She can't last much longer."*

Pressina ripped Plantine's hand out of Melia's.

Melia tried to call her younger sister back, but she was gone. The shock broke Melia's concentration.

Pressina jerked her older sister's arm.

"Melusine–" She slipped away too. It was over.

"You'll atone for your trespass," Pressina said. She began to chant, using a tongue Melia didn't understand. The chant heightened into a single high-pitched hum. Melia covered her ears.

Silver strands exploded like new growth from every branch of the oak. Malachi screeched and landed on the floor in a single leap. Pressina's strange hum lowered in pitch.

A soft wind gathered the disparate glimmering threads reaching from the oak into a single swirling tower. Pressina chopped her palm three times with the side of her hand. The tower divided, isolating each sister in one of three vertical silos.

Melia tried to run. Too late. A fog rolled into her mind. A cyclone of energy, within the shining column, paralyzed her body. She could see and hear, but not speak. She tried to formulate one last silent communication to her sisters. It got trapped in the vibrating strands of light that restrained her. All she could do was stare straight ahead.

When had her mother become so good at magic?

13. Spellbound

Pressina could count on one hand the times she'd responded to Elynus' hundreds of letters. She'd always doubted him. Now, the burden of that doubt crushed her.

Elynus had promised: *Incarnating Umbra will change the laws governing the mortal and enchanted worlds. I'll return to the Realm of Faerie and crown you my queen.*

All these years holding her breath, never letting herself hope. What if she'd believed in him? Could things have turned out differently?

Pressina wanted to scream her throat raw.

The truth was she'd never forgiven him for breaking his faerie troth. Now, it was too late. Her beloved Elynus was dead.

He'd never know how much his letters had comforted her, or how much she'd learned from them.

She paced the floor, deliberating her course of action. He'd taught her Umbra's consciousness could be melded with her own.

Like riding a wild horse, he'd written. *But you must give it rein.*

She interlaced the finger of her hands and pressed her palms against the back of her neck. Did she dare call the dark master her husband had worshipped? Umbra had been his obsession, not hers. Through the years he'd written her so many letters. How many times had she read each one? Their instruction came easily now.

The dark master feeds on the shadow within our hearts. Whatever is hidden there–resentment, envy, loathing–when offered to Umbra, its power will increase tenfold. Neither talismans nor black charms are a necessity, he'd detailed. *But either may be useful as a tool to steady your concentration.*

She let her arms drop. Although Elynus had warned her against calling Umbra from Illialei, an irresistible impulse seized her. She had nothing to lose.

Focusing the anger coiled snake-like in her belly, Pressina stepped in front of Plantine's shimmering cell. She recalled the day of her youngest daughter's birth, the day Elynus had broken his faerie vow.

She reached through the silvery bars to twirl a strand of her daughter's straw-colored hair. "It was your fault," she whispered. "If you'd never been born ..." Her anger smoothed into a heated pulse.

All marriages between mortal and faerie required a troth. The promises were seldom onerous, considering the price of their violation. Yet Pressina couldn't remember a single one throughout the history of mortal and faerie unions that had not been broken. The realization didn't make her more forgiving.

She looped Plantine's hair around her fingers. What foolish impulse had sent Elynus rushing to her side the minute her third daughter had kicked hard in her belly?

"It's your fault your father broke his faerie vow," she whispered. The words fueled the pulsing heat building within her. "It's your fault I've had to live alone all these years, disgraced. It's your fault."

As Pressina voiced her seething resentment, welcome heat radiated through her body. It warmed her fingers and toes, her cold, aching bones. As she surrendered to the penetrating fever, it was almost as if Elynus stood beside her. A chant boomed from her lips:

"From the moment of your birth,
Precious time with my beloved–Gone!
What has left cannot return
Let it leave you too.
Day by day, you will fade

To nothing but dust."

A brief respite of thrumming energy snapped Pressina from her trance. She wiped the perspiration from her forehead. Her cheeks flushed with an uncomfortable warmth. Blinking, she gazed into her youngest daughter's terrified eyes.

Had Umbra reached through her? Describing his experience channeling the dark master, Elynus had written: *The effects are subtle, often unrecognizable to the practitioner, but the results are beyond question.*

She backed into a small table. A vase of freshly cut flowers cracked hard against the floor. Streams of water spiraled across the polished wood. A band of pressure encircled her head; her cheeks were wet.

No! She'd wanted to teach Plantine a lesson. Not end her life.

Glass splinters lanced her skin; the sight of blood sharpened the moment. Pressina rose, searching for visible evidence of Umbra's presence.

The front room looked strange–shuttered and swathed in firelight and shadows–but there was no plume of smoke or shimmering cloud to prove the presence of another consciousness.

Silly me, she thought. Certainly she didn't believe she'd called the dark master on her first attempt. Her lips curved and she laughed at herself. *I'm simply too angry, and Plantine deserves a remedy.*

She straightened her back. This time her spoken words trembled, "True love's first kiss will make you whole." She repeated the petition several times. With each recital her voice evened out.

Although Melusine was arguably her most beautiful daughter, Plantine had been born with a numinous quality no full-blooded faerie possessed. Suitors from all corners of the enchanted world already vied for her youngest daughter's hand. Consumed with her studies, Plantine had refused them all. Nevertheless, Pressina convinced herself true love's first kiss would find her youngest daughter in time.

Satisfied, she paused to consider her course.

Melusine and Melia were hardly innocent. She'd proceed with their punishment, but without further appeals to Umbra.

Slipping her fingers through silvery strands, she brushed Melia's cheek with the back of her hand. The ice in her daughter's blue eyes admonished her for practicing the black arts in Illialei. Pressina pulled back.

Melia's ideas about right and wrong had always been strong, but that she would judge her own mother and father broke Pressina's heart. She'd never expected her middle child to turn against her.

"How dare you question my love for your father? How dare you question any of my choices?" she growled. "The last one I expected to betray me was you." She shook her head. Why Melia had followed her sisters to the mortal world to challenge Elynus, she would never know.

Pressina frowned. It would be hard to punish her most vulnerable daughter–the one who stammered and hid–the one who despaired of having no wings. But Melia needed to face the consequences of her role in Elynus' death. Pressina closed her eyes and let the heat in her belly surge.

Again, Elynus felt close, as if he stood beside her. Little Bird. Yes, Melia had always wanted to fly.

"From this day forward, dusk to dawn,
Find a black-winged eagle, not a faerie,
Bound by a predator's instincts.
When true love's first kiss,
Breaks the spell,
You will never fly again."

Pressina pressed the sides of her temples. An image of a black eagle soaring high above the clouds filled her inner vision. No feelings of sorrow or regret attached to the bird. Would her middle daughter deny true love to preserve her freedom?

She shuddered. More words twisted on the tip of her tongue, but she bit them back. It was too late to alter the spell or its remedy. Twice she'd missed the mark. Frustrated, she turned to face her eldest daughter.

Melusine stared a challenge through the silvery tower binding her. Her impudence ignited embers still hot in Pressina's belly. *She knows no shame,* Pressina told herself as she envisioned her eldest daughter's beauty spoilt.

"If I wasn't your mother, you wouldn't be so pretty."

Melusine's gaze hardened.

Pressina slowed her thoughts as the now familiar heat flooded her limbs. Her words fell like fire:

"Each week, on the seventh day, from sunup to sundown,
Crawl upon your belly like a writhing serpent,
Leathery wings marred by scaly ridges on your back.
All who see you will name you an abomination.
Should you marry mortal, your husband's troth:
Never witness your vile change.
If the vow breaks: Crawl upon your belly beyond the seventh day;
Crawl upon your belly through eternity.
Thus spoken, marry wise."

Pressina staggered as sobs rose in her throat. Wilting upon the nearby chaise she grabbed an embroidered cushion and covered her mouth. Across the room three pair of eyes glared daggers through their silver bindings.

She turned away. Elynus was gone; their daughters had killed him.

A gust she hadn't summoned blasted through the tree house. It extinguished the fire and sucked all warmth from the room.

14. First Flight

Melia didn't know what she expected to see when the shimmering tower that imprisoned her dissolved. Her mother had left the room. Melia wasn't sure whether or not she'd left the tree house, and she didn't care. If their mother believed they'd murdered their father, she didn't ever want to see her again.

Her sisters looked as bewildered as Melia felt, but Plantine wasn't fading, and Melusine wasn't on her belly writhing like a serpent.

Melusine spoke first. "Little Bird gets to fly. What punishment for you."

Plantine swooned. Her sisters raced to catch her. Melia refused to make eye contact with Melusine as they helped their little sister lie down on a coral-colored sofa.

Melia went to get Plantine a glass of water. She handed her the glass. "Here."

Melusine glared at her middle sister. "This is your fault."

Melia wasn't going to argue. "You don't look any different," she said to Melusine. She pushed a sticky strand of hair from Plantine's damp cheek. "Neither do you."

Although Melia had heard every word their mother had said, she didn't believe the spells would work. How could they? She looked for Malachi. The misshapen creature was proof her mother lacked mastery over the black arts.

The cat was nowhere to be found.

"It's not Sunday," Melusine said. "And Plantine's fading will be gradual."

Melia preferred to believe their mother's curses were ineffective. "I don't feel any different," she said. "Do you actually think she spelled us?"

"Let us know what happens at sunset," Melusine said.

The first thing Melia noticed when she stepped out of the tree house was the fresh scent in the air. Halfway down the oak's spiral staircase, she noticed the steps were damp.

"Pssst." Tatou landed on her shoulder.

"Were you here the whole time?" Melia asked.

The pixie nodded. "What happened?"

Melia continued down the stairs. "Did you hear anything?"

"Not after she closed the windows. But a bright light spilled from the sides of the shutters."

Melia still couldn't believe what she'd seen her mother do. "She locked us in these towers. They were made from strands of light she pulled from the oak tree. We were separated and couldn't move or talk. It was terrifying. Then she accused us one by one and spelled us."

"Wait. Your mother did not spell you," Tatou said.

"She did. And she knows all about Umbra. Father was doing it for her." Melia sucked in another deep breath. "Did it rain?"

"There was a big storm. Thunder and lightning," Tatou said, "but it was only over the tree house."

The sky was clear now. Crystal.

Melia ran.

Tatou's fingers gripped her hair. Melia kept running. If she stopped, she might believe she was going to turn into an eagle at sunset.

✧ ✧ ✧

Melia followed the enchanted gardens' stone wall. Winded by the time she reached the magnolia grove on the gardens' far side, she stopped and gasped. A light, musky scent filled the air. The trees were in full bloom. Beneath their towering shade, it looked as though the sun had already set.

Tatou left Melia's shoulder and perched on a lower branch next to one of the creamy blossoms. The flower was as big as she was. "Can you make it to Pebble Rock?" Tatou asked.

"What difference will that make?" Melia's world spun around her. She tried to untwist the tangle of events that had brought her to this moment. "Do you think I'm going to turn into an eagle? Is that even possible?"

"Oh, it's possible," Tatou said. "But it's a kind of magic that's not often practiced in Illialei."

The half-faerie raised her eyebrows. "Great–another thing for everyone to gossip about." But ... an eagle. What would that be like? "Do you think I'll be able to fly?"

"Of course you will."

In spite of everything, the corners of Melia's mouth turned up. Then she thought of her mother's bizarre pet. "What if I turn out misshapen like Malachi? I should have run away when I had the chance. But my sisters–"

"What did she do to them?"

"Melusine will have leathery wings and slither on her belly every Sunday, like a snake, I guess."

"Eww."

Melia paced. "Mother couldn't have come up with a worse punishment for Melusine. Being ugly–even if it's only for one day of the week–is going to kill her." She couldn't look at Tatou. "But Plantine ... she is is going to fade to dust." Melia picked up a stick and threw it as far as she could.

Tatou stood up on the branch. "Your mother has gone too far."

"She gave each of us remedies." Melia chewed on a fingernail. Her mother's rage had come out of nowhere. Or had it?

Melia had been afraid to tell Pressina about their father's death because the smallest things set her off. And that afternoon at Ashleam Bay was hard to explain. Whenever Melia tried to sort through what had happened, she never got past the point when the tide had poured in, and Plantine's second spell–the one to lift the boulder–had failed. "Do you think my mother loved my father?"

"Everyone thought she did."

Melia covered her face with her hands.

"Your father's death was an accident," Tatou said.

"Mother doesn't believe it."

"Your mother–" Tatou looked around.

"What?" Melia asked.

"Your mother–" The pixie flew in a wide circle around the clearing's perimeter.

"What are you doing?"

"I need to make sure no one is listening." Tatou flew back to Melia and hovered in front of her face. "There's a lot more to your mother than you know."

"Like she wanted my father to incarnate Umbra?"

"I don't know about that. I'm only saying, it's a lot easier for your mother to take her anger out on her daughters than on"–the pixie looked around the grove of magnolia trees one more time–"who she's really mad at."

"I thought she was angry with my father for breaking his troth."

"I'm sure that didn't make her happy."

"But she still loved him, I guess."

"Tell me about the remedies," Tatou said.

"Melusine's isn't a remedy as much as it's a condition. If–when–she gets married, her husband isn't ever to see her on Sunday when she changes. If he does, she'll keep her serpent tail and dragon wings forever. Oh no! She's going to marry Raymond. He's never going to be able to keep that promise."

"Then maybe she shouldn't marry him," Tatou said.

"Who's going to stop her?"

The pixie shrugged. "She's not going to listen to either of us."

"I know," Melia said.

"What about Plantine's remedy?"

"True love's first kiss will reverse the spell, and the curse will end. Her fading will stop forever."

"Sounds like a job for Tuck."

Melia rolled her eyes. "And what if there's no such thing as true love?"

Tatou pointed at her.

Melia's legs twitched. Her toes spread wide and dug into the ground. Air vibrated around her. She looked at her hands. Her fingers thinned and curved into sharp talons. Her body temperature cooled as her torso pitched forward. She felt her mouth and tongue contract. Her nose elongated into a hardened beak. Her arms extended to their limit as her sleeveless dress and skin transformed into thousands of black feathers.

She had wings.

It had only taken seconds, but Tatou's mouth hung open.

Melia hopped. She flapped her arms, which had become light and strong. She felt a slight lift, but that was all.

The world grew loud around her. Pixie chatter came from the other side of the garden wall, and birds argued in the Sylvan Forest. In the distance, the Nyssalei rushed to the Great White Sea.

She craned her head. Every movement and sensation felt both odd and natural.

"You're an eagle," Tatou said.

Melia looked at the ground, inches from her beak. She spread her wings, but she wasn't quite sure what to do with them. She flapped them up and down. Again, nothing happened.

Tatou landed next to her. She ran her fingers over Melia's feathers. "You look amazing."

The half-faerie's lips were gone; her beak was hard and immobile. She tried to say, "Yes." It came out as a chirp.

"How does it feel?"

In spite of everything, a sense of joy bubbled inside her. "Wonderful." She was speaking in the tongue of eagles.

Tatou, eloquent in birdsong, understood. "Follow me to Pebble Rock," the pixie said. "I'll call some birds. They can teach you to fly."

Melia craned her head. Was that a mouse? "Wait a minute." She jumped through the long blades of glass. Devouring the small furry animal was all she could think about.

"Tell Tatou I'll find her in the morning," Melia cawed.

The falcon and two orioles peeled away.

Melia soared higher than any faerie.

All night she spiraled, glided, coasted, and dove.

She could fly fast.

After losing a flock of gulls on the shores of the Great White Sea, she followed the Nyssalei to where it split and wound through Tyrannis as the Undine River.

She swooped from the Mare Cliffs.

Glow sprites! She squawked her excitement.

When a slit of light appeared to the east, she circled back to the enchanted gardens.

Melia stared into the bruised sky. The harsh sunset promised dark moons that night. It would be the third dark moon phase since her father had died, half a moon cycle since her first flight.

Tatou stood next to her on the enchanted gardens' stone wall, their new hangout since Melia never went home anymore.

"The visions are getting worse," Melia said. "It's as if my guilt over my father's death and my sisters' curses feeds them."

"Does the stranger with the green eyes still try to help you?" the pixie asked.

Melia touched her forehead. "Sometimes. Do you think this will go away if he never shows up?"

"Do you want him to?"

"Nandana didn't say anything about love, but I–"

"Don't want to kiss anyone and stop turning into an eagle?"

"It doesn't seem right, does it?" Melia asked.

"That you love to fly?"

"I saw Melusine in Bryndale yesterday. When I walked toward her and waved, she turned and went in the other direction. I tried to shout to her–in my mind–but she didn't respond."

"Ouch."

"Do you know if Plantine still goes to the library to see Tuck?"

"Not since–"

"My mother cursed us."

"She's holed up in the tree house," Tatou said. "No one has seen her."

"I've tried to contact her a few times too, but I get nothing. I'm worried. Do you think our curses have affected our abilities to communicate telepathically?"

Tatou shrugged.

Laughter drifted from the gardens. A group of pixies danced around a bed of peonies. Some turned cartwheels and somersaults. Melia watched, envious of their innocent exhilaration.

A black vision erupted from within. Ruin superimposed the picture of carefree joy.

✧ ✧ ✧

Every flower in the enchanted gardens is dead. It looks as if an enormous animal has taken a bite out of the ground. There is no grass or leaves. There is no green.

I step forward to get a better look. Tiny bodies contort into impossible positions. Silvery wings–ripped and torn–belong to no one. An enormous ash tree smolders on its side. Slimy roots coil like snakes.

All life has been excavated.

My green-eyed stranger stands on the other side of the crater. "You don't have to do this."

"It's not up to me."

"It can be," he says.

I press my hands against my dress. They leave dark stains. "You're too late," I say.

"Then wait," he says.

"I can fly now."

"Don't fly away," he says.

I flap my wings. "Umbra is coming–"

✧ ✧ ✧

"Melia!" Tatou shouted.

The half-faerie lifted heavy eyelids. The vision receded but left its taint. Melia couldn't tell her friend what she'd seen. She wouldn't.

15. The Lucky Seahorse

Ryder snapped awake. Something was wrong. His heart thundered in his chest. He reached for Koldis. When he found the blade, unyielding and wrapped in rough cloth, he swallowed hard.

What had pulled him from sleep with such urgency?

The night was black, but the gentle lap of seawater against the ship's hull oriented him. He sailed on a ship to the Realm of Faerie. He shifted his gaze in the direction of the porthole, but saw nothing. The enchanted world's moons were dark.

His heart continued its race. A vague threat thickened the air. The name Umbra entered his mind. He settled his hand upon the sword's hilt. Did Koldis call the one who gathered energy, yet remained formless in the Void?

The moment passed.

Ryder reached toward the floor. Nothing. He'd expected to touch Sinjiin's shaggy head, at least a paw. He reached farther. His fingers scratched the pallet upon which the big cat slept. "Sinjiin?"

Ryder stood up and slid the wrapped sword into his belt. He slept fully dressed; the crew's suspicious eyes, following him everywhere, kept him on edge. He couldn't blame them. How many passengers, even in the enchanted world, traveled with a six-hundred-pound clove-colored tiger? "Sinjiin?"

With no light, Ryder moved by touch. The wood bolt that locked their cabin door from the inside was out of place. Ryder pushed the door open. The passageway was dark, and the Lucky Seahorse was quiet. He moved toward the main hatch, letting the wall guide him. A dull noise caught his ear. He stopped to listen. It was only the sound of the sea.

A corner of hard wood collided with his knee. The stairs. Blessed Idonne, it smarted.

When he reached the top step, he hesitated. A few oil lamps swung from the masts, but a heavy fog swirled over the ship. As far as Ryder could see, the deck was clear, but the Lucky Seahorse was a long ship–a carrack–built to carry heavy loads of cargo. He looked behind him. Two men faced each other on the bridge. The distance was too great to distinguish their features, but one wore the captain's long coat. If Ryder was quiet, and kept to the shadows, he could remain hidden from view. A faint sound of singing drew his gaze to the bow. He crept toward the sound. Three sailors stood beneath the mizzenmast, their backs to Ryder.

"Can you believe it? A mage from the Hidden City."

"We'll have all the gold in the world from him."

"But how are we going to make him give it to us?"

"We'll figure something out."

"What about his friend? He'll be looking for the tiger in the morning."

"Maybe we'll tell him he jumped ship."

"Yer, the big cat wanted a swim."

"He was hungry for fresh fish."

The trio guffawed.

The first sailor pulled something from his vest. He showed it to the others. "Or maybe, we'll turn him in. The Order of the Idonnai is willing to dish out a nice bounty to whoever can deliver him and that sword he thinks he's hiding in that heap of rags."

The second sailor grabbed the parchment. "Looks just like him."

"Maybe we should grab him now."

"While he's asleep."

The third sailor kicked something. It groaned.

"You got more of that rope? We'll need it for the priest–he's no lightweight."

"There are three of us. Plus, it's late. He'll be asleep by now. We can catch him off guard."

"Where're we gonna keep 'em? It's a whole moon cycle 'til we reach Faerie."

"Captain only cares about the cargo. He gets paid for what he delivers, but the passengers"–the second sailor spit–"they've already paid. He could care less what happens to them."

"We could lock 'em in their cabin, or maybe throw 'em in the orlop, and take turns keeping guard."

"Good idea."

"Wanna take this one down now?"

"One of you is going to have to cut him–deep."

"Cut him?"

"If they're hurt bad enough, they can't shift."

"Why don't you cut him?"

"I found him out. You want your share of the gold, you're gonna cut him."

"Wait, how're we going to get him to make us gold?"

"I said we'll figure something out."

"Fine." One of the sailors pulled out a dagger. Ryder prepared to tackle him. The sailor who said they needed to cut the mage stayed the other sailor's hand. "Bloodying the decks will raise too many questions. Let's get the priest and the sword tied up nice and tight, first."

"What if he shifts while we're gone?"

The de facto leader kicked the bulk at their feet again. This time it remained silent. "Nah, he'll be out for a while. Good and drunk he is, appreciates his rum. After we've got the other one tied up, we'll come back for this one. Cut him after we take him down below."

Ryder crouched in the shadows. When the sailors walked by, stinking of rum, they didn't see him. He hurried to where they'd stood moments before. A pair of black slippers protruded from a pile of netting. Ryder threw the corded mesh aside. Bulky rope coiled Sinjiin's body. After he cut the mage free, he shook him.

The sailor was right. Sinjiin was out. Ryder rolled him up and over his shoulder. He carried him toward the bow, searching for a place to hide. He spotted a small hatch that led below deck. By the time he reached the bottom of the companionway, Sinjiin had grown heavy. Ryder set him down. Someone shouted from the deck. Probably the sailors. Sinjiin groaned.

Ryder leaned over the mage. "Wake up!"

Footsteps pounded overhead.

Ryder grabbed Sinjiin's wrists and dragged him down the dark passageway. Once again, he followed the wall. He pushed his weight against every door, hoping one would open. Light bobbed behind him in the companionway. He kept going. His back hit a wall–a dead end. The light approached. Ryder dropped Sinjiin's arms. He pulled Koldis from his belt, stuffed the cloth scabbard into the back of his pants, and moved into a protective stance in front of the mage. The blue light from the sword's blade shimmered.

"That's a fancy weapon you've got there."

Ryder raised the sword. "Stay back."

The captain of the Lucky Seahorse stepped into the circle of light. "No need to make threats."

Ryder looked past him for the sailors who had tied up Sinjiin.

"I'm alone," the man said. "Your friend there looks as though he's in bad condition."

"He drank too much rum."

The captain pointed down the hall. "That's my cabin. Let's have a look."

Ryder weighed his options. Attacking the Lucky Seahorse's captain didn't seem like the best one. Neither did refusing his request. He lowered Koldis.

The man whistled a cheery tune while Ryder wrapped the sword back in its cloth and returned it to his belt. He heaved the mage over his shoulder a second time and followed the captain into his cabin.

It was four times the size of the one he shared with Sinjiin in the lower hold. A fire burned in a fireplace. Dark polished furniture filled the room: a large table, chairs, a desk, and several cabinets.

The captain pointed to a massive bed. Ryder settled the mage on the covers. The captain held his lamp over Sinjiin's face. "I know everyone on board this ship, but I've never seen him," the captain said. "Where's your tiger?"

Ryder shrugged.

"A pet that size is hard to lose." The captain took a closer look at Sinjiin. "I met a fella dressed the same as him once before. Well, he didn't go around bare-chested like that." The captain pointed to the skin that Sinjiin's black vest left exposed. "But he had the same kind of head get-up." He pointed to the turban. "And he wore the same kind of funny-looking bloomers and shoes. He was a mage from the Hidden City. What do you think about that?"

Ryder didn't answer.

The man walked around the bed, holding his lamp high. He didn't take his eyes off Sinjiin. "I think he's one of them. And I think I've found your tiger." The captain walked over to his desk. He picked up a piece of parchment. "I believe in luck," he said. "That's how the Seahorse got her name." He handed the piece of parchment to Ryder. It was the wanted poster from Idonne. "So when I realized a powerful mage and a thief with the magic sword he stole from the priests of Idonne sailed on my ship, I thought to myself, Tom, that's pretty lucky; you should have a drink." He nodded toward the bed. "Looks like your friend had the same idea." Tom laughed. "Now, while he's sleeping his off, why don't you and I talk about what this bit of luck is going to do for me."

Ryder wanted to throttle Sinjiin.

The captain walked to one of the cabinets. He took out two glasses and a clear bottle filled with amber liquid, which he set on the table. "Sit," he indicated the empty chair across from him.

Ryder wasn't in a position to refuse.

Captain Tom filled the glasses. He raised his and waited for Ryder to do the same. "We're going to have to keep this to ourselves. The crew might get greedy if they knew." He wiped his mouth with the back of his hand. "I can keep them on a tight leash most of the time, but greed won't bring out the best in them."

✧ ✧ ✧

Ryder paced the small strip of bare floor in their cabin. "Why?"

Sinjiin lay curled on his pallet. After the effects of the rum had worn off, he'd paid the captain's asking price for keeping quiet, then resumed his tiger form.

Ryder glared through the tiny porthole. "You said if anyone knew you were a mage, your life would be in danger. Do you think Captain Tom is going to keep our secrets when he returns to Typhos–if he keeps them that long?"

Sinjiin lifted his head and showed Ryder a row of sharp teeth.

"Don't threaten me."

The tiger rested his head on his paws and closed his eyes.

"I can't believe you risked everything for a bottle of rum. No wonder you were evicted from the Hidden City. You have no discipline."

Sinjiin growled.

"How does that work?" he asked. "If you kill me, while you're indebted to me for saving your life? Twice."

The tiger rolled over. The bulk of his weight landed on Ryder's foot.

The priest shoved the big cat.

Sinjiin twisted and landed on his paws before Ryder could react. The tiger's muzzle was inches from his face. The big cat roared. The cabin shook.

"Fine," Ryder said. "Get some sleep."

Sinjiin leaned back on his haunches and licked his fur.

"I need some fresh air." Ryder stalked out the door.

Sinjiin followed after him.

Ryder ignored the big cat padding behind him. In Typhos, the mage had informed him that, as a citizen of the Hidden City, he was indebted to Ryder for saving his life. Sinjiin was bound to serve the priest until Ryder saw fit to release the mage from said debt.

Ryder had told him about his plans to sail to Faerie, then to the Isle of Minnanon. If the mage would help him find Ormrun, he'd release him from his service when the Grey Council took possession of the basin and the sword.

Sinjiin vowed to pay his debt in full. By the laws of the enchanted world, they were stuck with each other until then.

It had seemed like a good idea at the time.

16. A Serpent's Tail

Melusine raced across Footing Fields. It was the third Sunday since her mother had cursed her. How could she have grown so careless?

The first Saturday night, she'd camped along a secluded stretch of the Nyssalei. At the first twitch in her abdomen the following morning, she'd submerged her lower body in the river. Strange sensations had traveled down her legs and up her spine. As she'd felt beneath the water for a ledge –some place to sit–the dull gouging had intensified. When her fingers found a shelf of rock, she'd settled there, holding tight, while her body metamorphosed into an unrecognizable thing.

She'd caught a glimpse of her dragon wings reflected in the river water. The lumpy, leather masses repelled the eyes. What would the flower faeries say, if they ever saw them?

Melusine sank deeper until the water reached her chin. She could never let that happen.

A burning anger turned her silent tears into noisy sobs. Why couldn't her mother have condemned her to suffer as a mermaid or a sylph? Even a melancholy and treacherous siren would have been better than a snake. It was all Melia's fault. And what had been her punishment? To shift into a stunning black eagle at sunset.

Melusine ran harder. No one had seen her disgusting transformation, and she meant to keep it that way. After her success at concealing herself the first Sunday, she'd allowed herself a bit more leeway on the second one. Rather than spend the entire night by the river, she'd made sure she was up early enough to reach the Nyssalei before dawn.

But last night, the eve of the Annual Rolling Ball Tournament, Gisele had thrown a party on the shores of Lake Vivientiana. Melusine had been determined to attend, even though the lake was a good day's hike from the tree house. A long, exhausting hike that Melusine always made alone. The less opportunity she gave the flower faeries to notice her lack of wings, the better. She'd learned that lesson when she'd first come to Illialei.

Her side cramped. She stopped to take a deep breath.

The party had been dull–the faerie cake its most dazzling feature. Unusual for her, Melusine had heaped her plate with the airy confection.

Now, halfway between the lake and the isolated shores of the western Nyssalei, she wanted to lie down and sleep, let her dreams take her. She dropped to her knees. If she could close her eyes, only for a moment ...

Melusine startled in the grass.

The purple-grey dome of pre-dawn arched across the sky.

What had she *done*?

She jumped to her feet and ran faster than she'd ever run before. She pumped her arms and ignored the deep ache in her calves. Her hair flung and tangled in the wake of her desperate speed. Salty beads of perspiration lined her forehead. They trickled down and into her eyes. She swiped them away with the back of her hand. When she reached the far side of the fields, her heart exploded with ecstasy. She was going to make it.

Her lower body jerked.

No!

Why hadn't she worn a longer skirt?

Her pelvis throbbed.

It felt as though someone dug a dull knife down both sides of her spine.

In a few hours, the Rolling Ball tournament would begin. The Footing Fields would be jammed with the brownies who competed and the faeries and elves who came to cheer their favorite teams. Queen Luisa might even return from the Summer Palace.

Melusine took one last look over her shoulder. The sun's crown peeked over the Rolling Mountains. Her left cheek slammed into the long grass.

She screamed her frustration into the dirt as her legs twisted into a single tail.

The agonizing pressure peaked.

She had to get out of the fields before the players and spectators arrived.

Melusine pulled herself forward on her elbows.

When the ball bounced off her butt, Melusine pressed her torso flat. Maybe whoever had thrown it wouldn't see her in the waist-high grass.

Someone tripped over her tail.

She held her breath as they crashed beside her.

"Wait up, Toby."

It was a brownie, for sure.

He wiggled next to her. Melusine prayed to the gods of Azyllai. *Please, don't let him see me.*

Someone else circled back. "What'd you do? Fall over a log?"

Melusine cringed.

"Take a look at that snake."

She rolled her eyes.

"Is it dead?"

Someone kicked her tail.

"Maybe, it's huge."

"And ugly."

No one had ever used the word ugly to describe her before. Why didn't they just go play ball?

Something poked the end of her tail. The poking traveled up the length of her lower body.

She couldn't believe her bad luck.

The poking stopped. The grass rustled around her. "What is it?"

"Look at those wings."

Something poked the side of her body. "Stop it," she said.

They jumped back. "Did you hear that?"

"Yeah, it said something."

"Go play ball!" Melusine said.

Two pairs of brown feet smashed down the grass in front of her face. The feet were attached to two pairs of tanned legs in orange breaches. Two round, brown-eyed faces peered down at her.

"What are you?" one of them asked.

She heaved a sigh. "I need to get to the river. Will you please just let me pass?"

The brownies looked at one another. Their eyes widened. They looked down at her. "Are you Umbra?"

Melusine snorted. "Are you kidding? Didn't you hear? That crazy druid is dead. Umbra's not coming."

"Yeah, Ben." One of the brownies–Toby, she presumed–elbowed the other one. "That's true."

Toby took a step back. "Wait a sec. You're his daughter."

Ben edged closer, his brown eyes taking in every inch of her. "Your mother cursed you and your sisters. You're the one"–his gaze followed the length of her body–"who turns into a ... a–"

"Thing with a serpent's tail and dragon wings on Sundays." Melusine helped him along.

Ben stared at her. "Yeah, that."

"Has anyone else seen you?" Toby asked.

"No."

The brownies bumped their fists. "All right!"

"Could you please let me pass? I need to get to the Nyssalei."

They stood aside. "Sure," Ben said.

Melusine pulled herself forward.

The two brownies ran toward the playing fields.

It could have been worse.

She'd reached the banks of the Nyssalei, the water at her fingertips, when she heard the jeers from behind. Ben and Toby led a small army of players in her direction. A couple of flower faeries were with them. Oh my god–one of them was Verbena.

Melusine dragged herself forward. Her fingers were covered with small cuts and bruises. Her elbows were raw, and her arms felt like they were going to fall off.

"Coming to the games?" Verbena's sick-sweet voice asked.

Melusine gritted her teeth.

A high-pitched squeal followed. "She's hideous. Absolutely hideous."

Clementine. Melusine closed her eyes as she slipped into the river. She'd never live this down.

Someone watched her.

Melusine opened her eyes. Melia stood on the other side of the river.

"Don't say anything."

"Are you all right?" Melia asked.

"No, I'm not all right."

"I heard about this morning–all the brownies and Verbena seeing you."

"You know better than anyone, gossip travels fast in Illialei."

Melia waded into the water.

"Please, don't keep me company."

Melia stopped. "Okay."

Melusine looked at her sister. When had Melia stopped arguing with her? Was it after she'd apologized for telling Verbena about the ylandria or after their father had died?

"Have you seen Plantine?" Melia asked.

"No."

"Tatou said she's hiding out in the tree house, with Mother. Why would she do that?"

Melusine thought it was weird too.

"Have you tried to contact her?" Melia persisted.

"No." That was a lie.

"I've been trying to contact both of you, telepathically. Why haven't you answered me?"

Melusine shrugged. "Maybe we don't want to talk to you."

"Then it's not Mother's spell."

That's exactly why they didn't want to talk to her; Melia's curse wasn't a curse at all. When would she get the message and leave them alone?

"I was afraid our curses broke our connection," Melia continued.

"No, I don't think so."

"Then you're just ignoring me?"

"Like I said, maybe we don't want to talk to you."

"I'm going to Tyrannis."

That got Melusine's attention. "Just going to fly on over?"

"I'm going to the marketplace to find a healer–someone who can brew an antidote for Mother's curse."

If anyone in Faerie could concoct a potion to counteract their mother's curses, it would be a muannaye. "Already tired of flying?" Melusine tried to sound bored.

"Not for me, for Plantine."

Melusine looked at her sister from beneath her eyelashes. "Was that your idea or Tatou's?"

"If Plantine refuses to leave the tree house, who is going to kiss her? If our spells worked, so did hers. I can't wait around for her to fade to dust."

"How noble of you." Melusine couldn't bring herself to ask for a cure, too. Maybe Melia would get one for her anyway. What was she thinking? She'd already made up her mind.

"I know you're upset," Melia said.

"Why would I be upset?" Melusine's tail splashed a wallop of river water at her sister. Melia ducked, but she was still soaked. *How did I do that?* Melusine wondered. She shrugged–it had felt good.

"How could I know what Mother would do?" Melia asked.

"For all I know, you plotted this whole thing with her. You've always wanted to fly. And here you are, every night, a magnificent black eagle."

"No matter what you tell yourself, I was trying to do the right thing."

Melusine's tail churned the water. Her sister took a step back.

"I'm leaving Illialei in the morning," Melusine said. "I'm going to the mortal world to marry Raymond. He's agreed to a simple ceremony. No family."

"Melusine–"

"He promised me he's not going to break his troth."

"Father promised–"

Melusine's tail smashed a torrent of water in her sister's direction.

Melia reached the opposite shore. "I was hoping you'd wait until I got back from Tyrannis, that you'd keep an eye on Plantine while I'm gone."

"Not a chance." Melusine's tail writhed beneath the surface. "Our little sister can take care of herself just fine."

17. Plantine's Seduction

Plantine stared at the carved door cut into the oak's massive trunk. It led to the subterranean room where her mother practiced black magic. It was always locked, but this morning it stood open–just a crack.

Since Melusine and Melia had left, their mother had changed. She'd stopped crying at night, which Plantine found odd. But she'd also stopped getting dressed and wearing her boots. She wandered through the tree house in loose nightgowns, her feet bare and golden hair in disarray, Malachi underfoot. Sometimes she went from window to window as if she expected a visitor, but no one ever came–except Marguerite. Her mother's only friend brought tea, honey, and some food from Bryndale. Pressina barely ate.

Plantine understood why her sisters refused to forgive their mother. She understood why they'd moved out of the tree house. But Plantine couldn't abandon her mother, even after what she'd done, or what she'd said about it being her fault that her father had broken his faerie troth.

Even before her father's death, Plantine had possessed a secret pleasure for tragic stories, which she'd indulged during her frequent trips to the Grand Library. These days her mother cut a haunting figure who filled Plantine's heart with just the right amount of angst. With her pale skin and dark smudges beneath her eyes, Pressina exhibited a vulnerability her youngest daughter found breathtaking. The essence of her mother's wound seeped into Plantine's psyche, and she embraced it.

What bitter wrong had planted the seed that made Pressina who she was? Plantine yearned for the truth.

She'd experimented with conversation long before Elynus had died. Her mother had often brushed her off; she was busy with this or that. But now, confronted with her youngest daughter's inexplicable devotion, Pressina would gaze at her as if seeing her for the first time. One time she touched Plantine's cheek and apologized. They'd wept together–healing tears.

Plantine held her hand out in front of her. The skin on the back was thinning. It wasn't her imagination–she was fading.

A black hole of fear erupted within her. She slowly rotated her wrist. The fading wasn't as apparent on her palm. She dropped her hand. Her mother's spell had changed the rules of Plantine's life, especially the unspoken ones. Like, Never enter Pressina's study. It wasn't so much that she wanted to challenge her mother, but she needed to *know* her. Plantine trembled as she eased closer to the door. Did she dare follow the stairs down to her mother's underground chamber? If it made Pressina angry, what else could she do? Plantine was already dying.

She placed her hand on the door and listened. Utter quiet. She pulled the door open and descended the steps down to her mother's study.

Pressina was collapsed over a large table. Plantine rushed across the room and placed a hand on her mother's shoulder. Pressina didn't move. Malachi, curled up on a stack of parchment, hissed. Plantine tried to pet the creature, but it showed its tiny fangs. She dropped her hand.

A number of chests were stacked on the floor around her mother's chair. Several of them stood open. Parchment littered the table. Plantine's entire body tingled. They were letters from her father–hundreds, perhaps thousands of them. She squeezed her mother's shoulder. "I had no idea," she whispered.

Pressina lifted her head. "We've lost everything."

Plantine's brow creased.

"The queen has won." Pressina said the word queen with such hostility. Plantine struggled for an appropriate sentiment. Her mother reached for Plantine's hand. "I should have told you. I should have told all of you."

"Tell me now."

Pressina wept as she told her youngest daughter how she'd fled to the mortal world, how meeting Elynus had changed everything for her, how she'd finally hoped for justice, and what her disgraceful return to Illialei with her daughters had truly meant.

When she confided the rest of her story, Plantine choked. A red cloud filled her mind. She stared into her mother's lilac eyes. "How could you keep this from us?"

"I had to protect you. What good would it have done for you to know the truth?"

Plantine bit her lip.

"We'll live humiliated and disgraced for the rest of our lives," Pressina said.

"No." Plantine's rage felt safer directed away from her mother. "No, this isn't over. Not yet."

"You can't tell your sisters," Pressina said.

She patted her mother's hand. Plantine and her sisters weren't speaking.

"Queen Olivia's decree makes speaking the truth a crime in Illialei," Pressina said. "Anyone who talks about these things will be banished to the mortal world, forever. Do you understand me?"

Plantine closed and opened her eyes, an exaggerated movement, a slow acknowledgment. It was the only thing she could manage. The truth had left her in a daze.

"If you ever get a chance to make things right, you must take it," her mother said. "Do you understand? You must take it."

Plantine gazed into her mother's lilac eyes and shivered.

When Pressina left the study, Malachi trotted behind her.

Alone with her father's letters, Plantine's heart swelled. She ran her fingertips over one parchment, then another. She took her place in her mother's chair. A sense of destiny infused her. She closed her eyes and spread her fingers, gathering the loose parchments into a single mass. As she shuffled through them, sliding one over and another under, she hummed.

Her fingers settled upon a parchment. She opened her eyes and gazed upon it. Her father's penmanship was exquisite, each mark a bold stroke.

To be so close to him—her eyes watered with joyous tears.

It took her days, but Plantine read and filed every single letter.

✧✧✧

"She's not feeling well," Pressina said.

Tuck stood at the front door of the tree house. He held a bouquet of daffodils and a book. He pushed the gifts into Pressina's hands. "Will you give these to her?"

Plantine pressed her back flat against the wall; her heart raced. She wanted to see him, to share the terrible secret her mother had divulged, but what if someone overheard? Banishment to the mortal world would be intolerable—perhaps life-threatening—to any creature from the enchanted world. Plantine couldn't risk putting Tuck in that kind of danger. Once he saw her, he would know she held a secret. If he pressed, she'd be unable to lie to him.

Seeing Tuck would have to wait.

Pressina shut the door. Plantine listened to his footsteps fade down the stairs that spiraled the oak's trunk. Her mother pushed the tree elf's gifts into her hands. "He's very attentive." Her distaste for her daughter's suitor was clear in her tone.

"He means well."

Pressina raised an eyebrow but said nothing else.

Plantine went to the kitchen to fill a vase with water.

Years ago, an old wood elf had delivered and installed a contraption that collected dew from the oak's leaves. It had taken more than a moon cycle for the reservoir's bowl to fill. Once Plantine and her sisters had tasted the refreshing drink, they'd stopped laughing at the strange device and vine tubing that crawled from it. An added bonus, the water kept wildflowers fresh for weeks.

Plantine took the vase to her room and threw the book on her bed. She lay down beside it.

"Every day, you're getting stronger within," the voice whispered.

Plantine could hardly contain her excitement. *"Father? Is that you, Father?"*

"Such a loyal daughter," the voice said.

She burst into tears. *"I'm so sorry, Father. We—I never meant for you to drown. The spell ... I don't know what happened. I don't know why it didn't work. I tried so hard."*

Silence.

"Father, you forgive me, don't you?"

An image of a silver bowl, covered with jewels, flashed through Plantine's mind. *"Find this. Bring it to me, and all will be forgiven,"* the voice said.

Plantine wiped her eyes. She slid from her bed, landing with her knees on the floor. Her father reached to her from beyond the grave. He offered her an opportunity to make amends. *"Yes, of course, Father."*

"It is the door."

"The door to what?"

A sword with a shimmering blue blade exploded in her mind's eye. *"This is the key."*

"Tell me where they are, Father."

"You must find them. That is the task before you."

Plantine hugged herself. She'd seen sketches of the same basin and sword in his letters to her mother. *"I will, Father. I'll find them, and bring them to you."*

"Then I will give you this."

An image of herself seated on a granite throne filled her mind. Her hand flew to her chest. Desire pulsed through her veins. A ravenous hunger swallowed her heart. She opened her eyes. Her father was gone.

But he needed her help.

Plantine's fading worsened. When her father visited, it escalated. Hair fell from her head, and she was left with intolerable headaches. A strange malaise possessed her, and her refusal to leave the tree house made it impossible to do the one thing her father had asked of her–find the basin and the sword.

For the first time in her young life, uncertainty plagued Plantine. If she ventured beyond her self-imposed prison, the gossips of Illialei would make sure Tuck found out about her condition. Who knew what he would do? She feared it would be something that might jeopardize her father's visits. There had to be another way to find the sword and basin.

She asked Pressina to teach her scrying. The only thing it showed her was an ocean of water and a forest of trees. Were they clues she couldn't comprehend, or was she just a failure?

Most nights, she paced her room rather than sleep.

She took to biting her nails–a bad habit of Melia's. At least she hadn't begun to stutter.

How much time did she have?

She reread every word her father had written about Umbra.

Melia had been wrong. Her mother and father had been right. Umbra must incarnate. To be the vessel, to seize the throne, to determine the outcome of the battle between Dark and Light.

Plantine turned the matter over and over in her mind.

Could she do it? Did she dare?

During one of his visits, her father showed her the book that he'd written, *The Book of Umbra*. A muannaye had it. Lord Zachariah Goring.

How to get her hands on it?

18. The Mugnnai Valley Marketplace

Using every bit of self-control she could summon, Sevondi pressed her hands against the small iron table before her. It wasn't enough. She called upon the memory of her aunts and the long line of black witches who had come before her. That helped.

Pogo stood in the middle of her shop, kneading his wool hat with stubby fingers. She wanted to strangle him–or worse–but the troll had served her lineage for generations. Her deceased aunts would be horrified if their niece spelled–or otherwise harmed–one who had served them with such devotion.

Sevondi's right eyebrow twitched. Slightly higher than the left, it was a significant imperfection for a muannaye and betrayed her mixed bloodlines. "Tell me–once more–how you let it slip away."

"Moog serves Lord Goring–"

"Your twin." Sevondi still couldn't fathom how Zachariah had won the troll's loyalty. It was true, Moog had never served her family as his brother had, but still, shouldn't family bonds count for something?

"Aye." Pogo continued the third recounting of his failed mission. "My brother received news of Elynus' death first."

"Then, it's true? His daughters murdered him?"

He twisted the wool cap in his hands. "Aye, they drowned him, ma'am."

Sevondi stood up. The depravity of mortals never ceased to amaze her. The thought calmed her, briefly, until she remembered Zachariah possessed *The Book of Umbra*, and hadn't bothered to send word.

Her lover betrayed her. "Elynus and Zachariah would never have learned about the sword and basin if I hadn't told them," she said. "Now he intends to incarnate Umbra without me? How? He is a muannaye. He can't bear Umbra's energy. It will kill him."

Sevondi crossed her arms and glared at the troll. Her great-great-grandfather had been a powerful sorcerer from Kyrakkos. His blood in her veins might allow her to contain Umbra's consciousness–it was a risk worth taking.

Walking toward the front of her shop, she gave Pogo a jolt with an exaggerated sway of her hips. He stumbled and dropped his hat but didn't lose his balance. She hoped her aunts would appreciate her restraint. Beyond the canvas flaps of her shop, the market was slow.

"It might not be as bad as you think," the troll said.

"You defend Zachariah?"

"The sword has left Idonne, ma'am."

Sevondi whirled around. "You're sure of this?"

"There is word from Typhos. A young priest defended a mage from the Hidden City in the matter of a gambling debt. The sword he drew had an unmistakable blue sheen. They sail to Faerie as we speak. My source has no doubt the blade is Koldis, and the priest is a thief."

Sevondi flipped the sign hanging over the shop's entrance to *Closed* and pulled the drapes. She swept past Pogo, who stood well clear of her, and re-settled in the chair at her iron table. She knew Anton, the head priest of the Order of the Idonnai. That one of his own had stolen the blade from beneath his nose must enrage him.

She laughed. "This is good news."

The troll gave her an encouraging nod.

She rubbed the copper bracelets that circled her biceps. "Does Moog know?" Sevondi pointed at Pogo. "Don't let him gain that sword before we do. That, I couldn't forgive." With an extended finger, she drew the line she would cross–despite the memory of her aunts–in the air. "Do you understand?"

The troll returned the wool hat to his head and jammed his hands into the pockets of his shapeless trousers.

"Does the thieving priest sail to Tyrannis or Illialei?" Sevondi asked.

A lovely mortal, with long dark hair and eyes the color of deep blue sea, poked her head into Sevondi's shop. "Excuse me. Are you the dragonwitch?"

"Can you not read?" Sevondi demanded. "We're closed."

The girl continued her halting entrance. A shoulder, followed by one bare foot, slipped through the closed awning of Sevondi's storefront.

"I came to the market to find a h-healer." The girl hesitated.

Sevondi could see her cheeks flush in the dim light. An indigo stain marked her forehead.

"I couldn't help but notice the advertisement out front. And then I heard voices. You're a dragon-w-witch?"

"The Dragonwitch," Sevondi corrected her. She took great pride that she was the only dragonwitch. None of her aunts, not even the powerful Imelda, could summon the beasts Sevondi called at whim.

Yet something about the girl made Sevondi curious. A sweet smell emanated from her. She rose and moved toward her, swishing her long skirts, flipping the long dark hair she wore unplaited, all the while holding the girl's gaze.

At Sevondi's approach, the girl stilled. "You draw the p-protective shields?" she asked.

Sevondi sniffed. The girl pulled back.

"You're mortal," Sevondi said, "but there's more to you than that, isn't there? And what is that mark on your forehead?"

The girl's eyes darted in Pogo's direction. "D-does it make a difference?"

Sevondi was not in a generous mood. Thoughts of Zachariah's treachery, and plans of how she might best him, consumed her. The concentration required for shield work was beyond her.

"The shields are intricate. They draw on the power of the blood, and I would need to balance the energy of any shield with that tattoo." Sevondi indicated the blue spot with a nod of her head. "So, yes, it makes a difference. But, you'll have to come back. Today isn't a good day. What are you?" She reached for a strand of the girl's long hair and held it beneath her nose. "You smell of Illialei, and yet, there's something else." Short for a muannaye, she stood on her tiptoes and peered behind the girl. "You have no wings, but there is such a strong smell of *bird* about you."

The girl jerked her head. "If you won't help me, I won't waste any more of your time."

"Do you hear that, Pogo? She barges into my closed shop, then becomes incensed that I refuse her." Sevondi flicked her fingers toward the market. "Run along, then. Go find your healer. Protective shields are for those in grave danger. I sense nothing dark about you."

"I have v-visions. They frighten m-me," the girl answered back.

"Pogo, sh-she's sc-scared by what she s-sees." Her curiosity aroused again, Sevondi reached with her hand to press her palm against the girl's forehead.

The girl pulled back. She was gone.

Sevondi sighed. Creatures of all kinds came to the Muannai Valley Marketplace. Although the girl intrigued her, she wasn't the most curious she'd ever seen.

She returned her attention to Pogo. "And what of the basin? Is there any news about the bowl?"

"It's believed to be in Faerie."

"But how is that possible when no one has seen or heard of it in all these years?"

"Most have forgotten its existence, ma'am."

"You must locate it, Pogo. Do you hear me? I promised Imelda on her deathbed that I would incarnate Umbra." Sevondi brushed aside her other promise, the one to Isadora–that she wouldn't incarnate Umbra. "If Zachariah doesn't wish to share my destiny, I won't allow him to rob me of it. Whatever it takes, I must have the sword and that bowl."

"We'll get them."

The troll's assurance soothed her; she cooed, "You've been faithful all these years."

"Aye, you and your family have always paid generously for my service."

"When I'm the embodied Umbra, sitting on the throne of the stronghold of Calashai, I'll make sure you want for nothing."

Pogo bowed and took his leave.

Absorbed with thoughts of Umbra's incarnation, Sevondi had already forgotten the girl.

19. In the Shadow of the Ruadain

Melia soared across the Nuada–an endless sea of dry grass. For several days, the seven peaks of the Ruadain had been her target, but now, she angled for the highest and most northern one. With every beat of her wings, the mountain filled more of her view, finally transforming into the sheer wall of dirt and rock, brush and tree, lording over the plains before her.

To the east, dawn threatened.

She needed to find a nesting place before she tumbled from the sky. Slowing her speed, she scanned the terrain. A rocky crown circled the mountain's base. She aimed for that. Minutes after she'd landed on a bed of dense pine needles, the sun crossed the horizon line and she reverted to her half-faerie form. Perfect timing.

She padded through the thin forest that jutted from broken stone. A high ledge drew her attention. By grabbing roots, and digging her fingers and toes into barely visible cracks in the stone wall, she pulled herself up the mountain's craggy face.

Her reward was a large abandoned nest. What a wonderful place to curl up and sleep away the day. Before she closed her eyes, Melia plucked a tuft of feathers from the tightly woven sticks.

Eagles.

✧✧✧

"Melia." Plantine's voice called to her like a dream. *"Melia, I need your help."* The message was so faint. *"Melia, please!"*

She opened her eyes. *"Plantine?"*

"Will you help me?"

The request elicited a slow smile. Melia had feared Plantine would never speak to her again. *"Yes, of course."*

"I need to find ... some ... things."

"As soon as I get back to Illialei."

"Where are you?"

"In Tyrannis."

Silence.

Desperate not to lose their tenuous connection, Melia tried to explain. *"I came to–"* She stopped.

At the marketplace, the spell casters and potion makers Melia had spoken to claimed that the remedy Pressina had woven into the original black magic was the only one. However, a muannai who'd overheard Melia's dilemma had recommended she consult the troll, Embril. She might be able to concoct a poultice to leech the agent of Plantine's fading from her body. But the troll's shop in the market was closed. She spent every spring and summer in Aldaine and had left for the city during the last moon cycle.

What if Embril was as at a loss to break her mother's spell as the rest of the healers? It would be cruel to fill Plantine with hope then take it away.

"What do you need me to find?" Melia asked.

"Never mind."

"Plantine, I want to help you."

"You've already done enough."

Melia swallowed pebbles of guilt. While Pressina's dark spell had proved a blessing for her, Plantine and Melusine had paid too dearly for their part in Elynus' death. *"Can it wait a few days? I've almost reached Aldaine."*

"Please, don't cut your adventure short on my account."

Melia could reach Aldaine by morning, but that would add at least two days to her return. Maybe Plantine couldn't wait two more days. *"Plantine?"*

Cold silence.

Melia could return to Aldaine after she helped Plantine. She would look forward to the trip. The muannai were fascinating, and the rugged beauty of Faerie's northern country appealed to her. The deep forest, green valley, and open plains that swept to the towering crags of the Ruadain were so different from the light-filled woods, lush floral meadows, and rounded mounds that were called mountains in Illialei.

In the meantime, if she could coax her little sister from the tree house, it would be such a relief to see her. Her mind made up, Melia settled back into the nest to sleep for the rest of the day.

Boom! Boom! Boom!

Melia jolted awake.

Boom! Boom! Boom!

She peered over the edge of the nest at the deserted ledge and sparse forest. As far as she could see, no one and nothing moved, yet the rocks cradling the nest trembled.

Boom! Boom! Boom!

Perhaps a storm rolled in from the sea, invisible to her, on the mountain's north side. She searched for the approach of dark clouds, but overhead, the grey-washed sky was flat and serene–and innocent of the crashing that shook the mountainside.

Boom! Boom! Boom!

Her pulse galloped. What was going on?

As quietly as possible, she eased out of her bed of sticks and debris. Hunched over, she followed the ledge that circled the mountain.

Boom! Boom! Boom!

Clang! Clang! Clang!

She froze. Amidst the thunderous rumble and sounds of metal crashing against metal, voices yelled and smoke drifted from below. Melia flattened her belly against the ground and crawled toward the rock wall that shielded her view. It was less than half her height. When she reached it, she slowly inched up onto her hands and knees.

The haze from a dozen enormous fires made the ghastly scene waver. Hundreds of muannai swarmed, ant-like, around the base of the mountain, forging crude weapons. Melia dropped her head and almost smashed her nose against the ground. A big whiff of dirt had her wheezing. Her eyes watered as she pinched her nose and backed away. Around the curve, she panted against the wall of the mountain.

Boom! Boom! Boom!

Several of the muannai beat enormous drums. The rest shouted back and forth while they smelted metal in the flames, or hammered orange bright shards in the Ruadain's shadow. Melia wiped her nose and wrapped her arms around her waist. Her heart continued to pound against her ribcage.

Boom! Boom! Boom!

If she could hear what they were saying, maybe she could understand what they were doing. She crawled back toward the short wall.

In the valley, at the marketplace, Melia had been dazzled by the tall, lean, wingless muannai. Their bronze complexions with shades which varied from dark to light; the way they dressed to show off their muscular bodies–even the females favored slacks fitted to their sleek limbs; their plaited hair pinned high on their heads with ornate combs of wood, shell, and metal, created a mystique that had made it difficult for Melia not to stare.

She chewed on her thumbnail. The muannai at the base of the mountain dressed in black from head-to-toe. Uniforms. Not one wore the deep-colored shirts with ruffles running down the front that had made the marketplace a kaleidoscope of color.

Desperate to know more about the strange army below, she crawled back to the wall. With her ear pressed against the grey shale, she strained to hear, but every word remained unintelligible. She raised her head. Although the boom of the drums had stopped, the shouts still remained unclear. However, this time she noticed the scorched ground that marked the perimeter where the muannai worked. They'd burnt a large swath of the Balyudor. Melia's stomach churned with anger. The wanton destruction of the forest's beauty sickened her.

She scooted backward, her butt on the ground, her hands scattering pine needles. In her eagle form, she could fly among them, and they'd never suspect she was eavesdropping.

The sun would set soon.

The moon rose in the east, casting a silver glow upon the face of the mountain. Melia surveyed the muannai camp below. With her eagle vision, every detail became clear. Although most of them were male, there were a few females scattered among them. Like their male counterparts, they wore tight black pants, black leather boots, and unadorned black shirts. Grease and dirt smudged their faces, and exposed arms and hands. The long plaits of their hair were tied back into thick ponytails. Some picked at their meals, others lay sprawled on blankets spread on the ground. A few gathered beneath a tree, the only one still standing in their midst. All the rest had been chopped down.

Melia flew toward it.

"Good day's work."

"Lord Goring will be pleased."

Where had she heard that name before?

"How will he know?"

"He knows everything that happens in the Ruadain."

"Reckon he'll come down the mountain and shower us with gold for our effort?"

"He will after he incarnates Umbra."

Her breath caught. Lord Goring had been her father's partner, the one who'd petitioned for the investigation into Elynus' death. Now, he wanted to incarnate Umbra?

"Sorry, if I don't put a lot of faith in Goring's grand promises."

"If you don't believe him, why are you here?"

"You joined."

"You don't just tag along with the cult of Umbra."

The conversation hollowed Melia's stomach. Her mother had been right. She and her sisters had stopped nothing. Not Umbra's incarnation, and not war. An eerie chill traveled from the crown of her head to the length of her tail feathers.

"What are we going to do when we finish here?"

"Follow orders."

"Be good little soldiers, eh?"

The second muannai whispered. "Between you and me, I think Goring's got his eye on the stronghold of Calashai."

"What? The regency?"

"As a start."

"The grey faerie is popular."

"Why do you think we're building an arsenal?

"Elendah is committed to peace. We won't win any friends by strong arming her."

"Maybe force won't be necessary. I've heard Goring and her are tight. You know, wedding bells, share the crown and all. I'm thinking the weapons are for what comes after."

"After what?"

"After Lord Goring becomes regent, he'll want to expand his power, and that means more for all of us, know what I'm saying."

Melia's belly knotted. Elendah, the grey faerie of Aldaine, was the regent of the stronghold of Calashai and the only grey faerie in the realm. Someone needed to warn her that Lord Goring and his cult of Umbra intended to spread war across Faerie.

After she helped Plantine, Melia would find Tatou. Maybe the pixie could compose a message to Elendah, and they could devise a way for Melia to deliver it when she came back to Aldaine.

20. Falling

The hard knock of a tree branch jolted Melia awake.

She was falling–again. She must have nodded off.

The last thing she remembered was gripping the oak's highest branch with her talons as she waited for the world to wake up. Now, bark scraped her fingers as leaves, slick with dew, slipped from her grasp. Her teeth ground together, and her stomach flipped as she ricocheted downward. Momentum would shoot her straight through the tree house's thatched roof.

She attempted a telepathic warning to Plantine, but her concentration ended when her backside crashed into another branch. She catapulted forward like a rag doll. Her fingers grabbed air. Och! Her head snapped back. A warm feeling spread from the base of her skull down her spine.

She hung, suspended upside down, her ankle wedged in a crook between the tree trunk and a branch as round as a wine barrel. This was a first. She craned her neck to see how close she'd come to slamming into the roof. Too close. When she extended her arm she could almost touch it.

If she could just pull herself up. Again, she swiped air. The branches on either side were too far away, and she didn't have the strength to draw her torso up to reach the one above.

Why hadn't Plantine moved out of the tree house and away from their mother?

Thoughts of Pressina added to the anger spiking Melia's mind. What her mother had done to Plantine and Melusine was inexcusable. Unforgivable. And unbelievable.

Melia closed her eyes as if that could wipe away her last memory of Melusine–defeated and humiliated–hiding her serpent's tail in the Nyssalei. She wondered if she could have done more to stop her older sister from marrying Raymond. Probably not. The realization didn't make her feel less guilty.

Blaming Plantine for hiding out in the tree house wasn't going to erase her guilt either.

Cool air brushed Melia's hair into her face. She fingered a lock and pressed it to her nose. Did she really smell like *bird*?

No one other than the dragonwitch had told her that–not even Tatou, and her best friend would have said something if she'd noticed.

Melia dropped the strands, but not before she detected a distinct whiff of ... damp feathers. After the cool nights in Tyrannis, Illialei's warm weather had left her sticky. She'd splashed in the river before landing in the oak.

So what if she smelled like bird? Flying was worth it.

Melia took a deep breath and refocused. Blood rushed to her head. Every effort to twist her ankle free proved futile. She wasn't going anywhere without help. *"Plantine!"*

"Melia?"

Barely a whisper. *"I'm stuck outside, hanging upside down in the oak."*

Movement flickered in the corner of Melia's eye. The window to her sister's bedroom, the highest one in the tree house, cracked open. A flutter of white, accompanied by a soft tap-tapping, crossed the roof in Melia's direction.

Plantine's silent judgment washed over her. *"You shouldn't have come here."*

"You asked me to help you."

"We should have met somewhere else."

"You never leave the tree house."

Long silence. *"We could have met at Pebble Rock."*

"Sorry, I didn't think of that."

"You can't stay here. Mother is furious with you."

"Then help me get down, and we'll go someplace we can talk."

Plantine edged closer. *"How did you end up like this?"*

"I fell asleep while I was waiting for the sun to rise."

As an eagle, Melia flew all night, every night. Flying intoxicated her. Perched high in the bough of a tree, at the end of a long flight, she often dozed off. She'd wake up, already changed back into her faerie form, tumbling through air and tree limbs. Sometimes, she'd catch a branch and climb the rest of the way down. Her new collection of bruises seemed a small price to pay for the flight she'd always craved, but this was the first time she'd ever gotten stuck.

"What do you want me to do?"

"Help me reach that branch." Melia indicated the one overhead with her chin.

Plantine moved behind her. Her palms exerted a gentle pressure against Melia's back. Melia's body swayed, but nowhere near high enough to reach her target.

"Push harder."

"I've lost a lot of strength."

"Try."

Plantine shoved Melia's shoulder blades. Melia stretched her arms and fingers. It took several tries before she could reach the limb overhead. Now she swung in a U shape, her ankle still twisted at an odd angle. She wiggled it again. *"Can you push my heel through?"*

Plantine ducked beneath the oak's branches and balanced on her tiptoes. Her arms shook with effort, but Melia's ankle didn't budge.

"Help me swing up higher onto this branch."

Plantine let out a loud breath as she crossed back beneath her sister.

"Good morning, girls."

Melia's body tensed. Her eyes darted from side to side as she listened for Pressina's approaching footsteps. Two bare feet entered her peripheral vision. Her mother wasn't wearing her boots.

"Mother–" Plantine began.

"Let me help your sister."

Melia flinched as her mother's firm hands flattened against her back.

Like Melusine, Pressina was stronger than her slim frame suggested. With her help, Melia was able to wrap her arms around the branch she hung from. She twisted her head to see her mother and sister.

Two pale wraiths with disheveled hair and dark smudges beneath their eyes stared back. Although her mother's unkempt state shocked her, Plantine's disintegration was worse. Three bands of white streaked her sister's gold hair, the blue had washed from her eyes, and the skin on the back of her hands appeared translucent.

Melia looked away at the same time Pressina gave her another push. Disoriented, Melia rolled over the oak's knotty limb. The tree let go of her foot and she somersaulted through the air.

Plantine yelped as Melia smashed face-first into a thatch-covered beam. A stake of pain drove into her forehead; a stab of heat pierced her ankle. She bit her tongue to keep from crying out.

"Are you all right?" Pressina hurried over.

Melia pushed her mother's hand away. "I'm fine."

Her mother stood up. "Plantine, leave me alone with your sister."

Melia's heart pounded as she struggled to stand. *"Meet me at Pebble Rock,"* she told Plantine telepathically. She thought she saw her sister nod before she slipped inside the tree house.

"Did you hurt your foot?" Pressina asked.

Melia faced her mother.

Pressina's lilac eyes, two shards of purpled glass, contradicted the honeyed tone of her voice. She was trying to glamour her.

Melia moved sideways. A sharp burn stung her ankle. She kept her eyes down. A less obvious attempt to fend off her mother's glamour was more than she could handle this morning.

"You shouldn't bother your sister," Pressina said.

Melia glanced up. The intensity of her mother's eyes had burnt out. It was a small victory. "Are you her jailer now?"

Her mother frowned. "Plantine isn't feeling well."

"And whose fault is that?"

"I'm glad you brought up the question of blame."

Melia swallowed hard.

"You let me believe what happened at Ashleam Bay was Melusine's idea," her mother said.

Melia's stomach hollowed.

"But it was you."

Minute convulsions trembled through Melia's body.

"Plantine is dying, and Melusine will never return. And you"–Pressina crossed her arms tightly as if to restrain a desire to hit her daughter– "you murdered your own father."

Melia's defenses suffocated in her throat. Her mother was never going to accept that it had been an accident.

Pressina stared beyond her into the Sylvan Forest. Melia followed her line of sight, but all she could see were giant grey-green trees, swimming in a sea of wind-brushed fern. "You need to leave," her mother said. "You're not welcome here."

The hard words echoed through Melia like infinite stones falling down an endless well. "I didn't come here to see you," she clarified.

"I want you to leave your sister alone."

"I was trying to help her."

"Is that why you went to Tyrannis, to fetch her a cure?"

Melia hated that her mother knew her as well as she did. "Yes."

Her mother looked at Melia's empty hands. "It appears your trip was unsuccessful."

"Don't you care that she's going to die?"

"She's not going to die."

"Have you looked in a mirror lately? You both look like ghosts."

Pressina's gold hair flew wild in the breeze blowing in from the west. Tears welled in her eyes.

For a brief instant, Melia thought they might overcome the chasm widening between them. She reached out to comfort her mother, or to urge her to say more, she couldn't say which, but Pressina's head shot up before Melia's hand could touch hers. Her mother's lilac eyes had steeled into the strange color that gave her glamour such power.

The wind gusted. The oak's leaves rustled in concert with the trees in the forest behind them. Any possibility for rapprochement passed.

Melia took another step back. The searing pain in her ankle drew her attention away from the gutting of her heart. "It wasn't Plantine's fault that

Father broke his troth." She couldn't stem the anger she'd carried since her mother had blamed her sister for their father's mistake. "What did you expect? That he would be the single mortal in history to honor his faerie vow?"

"Leave. Now," Pressina said.

"Gladly." Melia hobbled toward the open window.

Her mother's arm snaked out. She grabbed Melia's bicep. Her fingernails pinched. "Watch out."

A dark feeling shot up Melia's spine. Did her mother mean to practice more black magic on her?

"Marguerite overheard a troll asking after Elynus' daughters at the Hive."

Melia pulled her arm away. It was a strange warning. Trolls didn't cross the Maeldun Bridge. Her mother had probably misunderstood Marguerite. She was careless when it came to listening to others. Not that it mattered, Melia had no intention of returning to the Hive. She doubted her sisters did either.

"I'll be sh-sure to st-stay away from there."

Pressina's stony silence ended their conversation.

Although her ankle spiked and burned every time she put weight on it, Melia forced herself to limp through thc tree house and out the front door without a backward glance.

✧ ✧ ✧

Melia headed straight to the enchanted gardens.

Cutting through the pixies' kingdom was worth the risk: It would shorten her route to Pebble Rock, heal her ankle, cool her temper, and maybe, she could corral Tatou.

When Melia reached the gardens' stone perimeter, she whistled. Years ago, she and her friend had agreed upon a tune to identify themselves.

No reply.

Melia looked at the sun chasing the sky. It was much later than she'd realized. She whistled again.

Still no answer.

Although all pixies called the gardens home, Tatou did little else than sleep there. She'd probably left for the day. Melia looked down at her ankle. It was huge. She didn't know how much longer Plantine would wait for her. Maybe the pixies wouldn't notice her trespass.

The half-faerie vaulted over the stone perimeter as best she could to land on her good foot in a flood of pale, yellow trumpets. She sucked in the luscious scent of honeysuckle, crossed her fingers, and hobbled on.

The enchanted gardens magnetized joy, more so than anywhere else in the Whole. No one and nothing entered the pixies' domain without benefiting from its ambrosial ethers, or paying for their good effect. Hot waves of emotion Melia had struggled to control only moments before dissolved. She tested her foot. It was still tender but no more painful spikes.

"Who goes there?"

Melia groaned and pulled up short. Lying wouldn't help. She turned around to face her interrogator.

A dimpled male pixie twittered toward her. His hands were poised between his lips.

"Please d-don't call your friends," she said.

If he whistled, dozens of pixies would surround her in an instant, wiping her concerns and sorrows from her conscious mind. The glamour of one pixie might be thrown off, but when there were dozens, it became impossible. She'd be forced to while away the hours, a happy prisoner until her captors saw fit to escort her to the enchanted gate and release her from their spell.

"Do you want to dance?" he asked.

Another pixie emerged from the leaves of a giant willow. "And sing?"

Four more followed. They filled in a ring around her.

Maybe they'd let her pass if they thought she'd entered the gardens with permission. "I was looking for Tatou."

"What do you want with that silly excuse for a pixie?" a black-haired boy with legs as long as a spider's shouted.

"Yeah, what do you want with her?" another jeered.

"I n-need her help."

"We'll help you," the dimpled pixie shouted.

A blonde landed on the hedge of flowering lavender next to Melia. "We'll help you forget everything you've ever remembered. Hey, wait.

Aren't you Pressina's daughter?"

"Y-yes."

The blond pixie turned to her friends. "She's the half-faerie–the one who murdered her father because he wouldn't help her destroy Illialei and kill us all." She lighted from her perch and fluttered in front of Melia's face. Her brown eyes blazed as she drew her fingers to her lips.

Melia pleaded once more.

A shrill pop burst from the pixie's tiny body. The freshness of the air intensified. Dozens more pixies swarmed into view. They filled in the circle around Melia.

Involuntarily, she drew a deeper breath. The morning shimmered around her. She was transported to a glorious day in her past, running carefree through an iridescent wave of blooms in an emerald sea of leaf and grass to escape her chores and lessons.

She and her sisters hadn't accidentally killed their father; their mother hadn't cursed them; Melusine hadn't fled the Realm of Faerie to marry Raymond; and an army of threatening muannai wasn't gathering and swearing its allegiance to Umbra in the shadows of the Ruadain.

Melia pressed her forefingers against her thumbs and exhaled the air in her lungs–a sweet trick Tatou had taught her to clear her head–but pixie glamour was potent in the gardens. The numbers swarming around her made it overwhelming. The present receded. All she wanted to do was sing.

The pixies cheered.

21. Pebble Rock

Plantine wore a circular path of flattened grass in front of the large grey boulder known as Pebble Rock.

Where was Melia?

She paused her stride long enough to focus her mind. *"Melia! What is taking you so long?"*

A faint sound of singing intruded. She sent her telepathic call again. More song. Plantine walked to the back side of Pebble Rock. She lowered herself onto the bench formed by a natural cleft in the stone.

She sent another message. Yes, the connection was weak, but Melia should be close by. And why all the singing? The only thing between the tree house and Pebble Rock was the enchanted gardens.

Plantine jumped to her feet and ran toward the enchanted gate. Gasping for breath, she peered through the gate's ornate lattice. A thousand shades of green, quilted with varicolored blooms, hid the revelers, but their unmistakable bursts of song confirmed the pixies held a captive.

She stamped her foot on the graveled walkway. "Oh!" Tatou was the only one who might persuade the mischievous faeries to let Melia go before they'd finished their fun.

Plantine hurried back to the rock. It stood at the edge of the Sylvan Forest. Using the birdsong Tuck had taught her, she whistled as many different cries for help as she could remember. Cardinals, orioles, swallows, a mocking bird, and an owl flocked toward her.

"My sister is being held by the pixies. Tatou–you know Tatou?"

The birds chirped and the owl hooted in the affirmative.

"Please, find her and tell her to meet me–Plantine–at the enchanted gate without delay."

The birds scattered in all directions. She walked back to the gate. The anger she felt toward Melia for dragging her to the mortal world to kill their father hadn't abated, but if her sister could help find the sword and the basin, she might forgive her. After all, Melia had spent years running wild with Tatou and knew her way around Illialei better than anyone. As an eagle, she was becoming familiar with Tyrannis as well. Who better to find the things Father needed?

Plantine reminded herself to take care with her thoughts around her sister. She needed to protect her mother and the secret they now shared. Who knew what Melia would do if she found out? Probably violate Queen Olivia's decree, without a thought to the consequences, and get them all banished to the mortal world.

At the gate, raucous singing mixed with the heat of the late morning sun. Plantine sat down to wait. The scent of grass and the perfume of flowers wafted on a breeze from the sea.

Plantine loved Illialei. She closed her eyes and imagined herself seated on the Cathedral Palace throne as the queen of the Realm of Faerie.

"Plantine!"

She wiped the sleep from her eyes and pushed herself up. How long had she dozed? The sun overhead told her almost an hour.

Tatou fluttered before her, her mouth frozen in a tiny O.

Plantine brushed her hair behind her ears and slipped her hands into the pockets of her dress. "It's only Mother's spell. I'm fine."

Tatou blinked in rapid succession.

Plantine ignored her obvious dismay. "The pixies captured Melia."

"Do you know how long they've had her?"

"Almost two hours," Plantine said.

"When did she get back from Tyrannis?"

"Early this morning."

Tatou nodded in the direction of the rousing chorus belting through the foliage. "Do you want to come with me?"

"Mmmm. Maybe I'll wait."

Tatou slipped through the enchanted gate and disappeared into the gardens' abundant greenery. Shortly after, a sharp whistle pierced Plantine's ears. She raised her hands to protect them, but when no other sound was forthcoming, she dropped her arms and gripped the gate's lacy metal. The singing stopped; the dull buzzing of bees took its place.

She thought she heard voices but couldn't make out the words. She shifted her weight from foot to foot. Maybe she should have gone with Tatou.

A few minutes later, Melia emerged with a huge smile on her face. Tatou perched on her shoulder. At least two dozen pixies followed at a distance.

When Melia reached the gate, a blond pixie yelled, "She won't be thinking about killing us any time soon!"

Plantine frowned. Even she had to admit, the rumors about Melia had spun out of control since their father had drowned.

"She's still a little dippy," Tatou said.

Melia threw out her arms and spiraled in a tight circle. "Dippy?" she snorted.

Tatou hopped from her shoulder and threw Plantine a knowing glance. "Back to Pebble Rock?"

"Yes," Plantine said.

Melia shifted between a melodic hum and a lilting song the entire way. When they reached the rock, Plantine returned to its natural bench. Melia bobbed and twirled for a few more minutes before spilling onto the grass in a relaxed heap. Tatou landed next to Plantine.

Melia stared at them for so long, Plantine feared her sister remained trapped in a pixie haze. "Can't you do something?" she whispered to Tatou.

Melia giggled. "I'm afraid I've got bad news from Tyrannis, little sister."

Plantine braced herself. "What is it?"

Melia's countenance turned serious. She got up onto her hands and knees. "After I left the muannai valley, I flew to–"

"Did you cross the Maeldun Bridge?" Plantine had seen pictures of the enormous iron and chain structure, spanning the Undine River between the Sylvan Forest in the south and the Balyudor's deep woods in the north. Tuck had told her it was an in-between place when he'd found her staring at an illustrated plate in one of the library's geography books.

He'd leaned over her shoulder. She'd felt his breath on her hair. "Strange things happen in in-between places, especially at in-between times," he'd said.

"In-between times?" She already knew the in-between times were twilight and daybreak, but she'd wanted him to remain close.

"Hey! Are you listening?" Melia asked.

Plantine returned to the present. "I'm sorry. My thoughts drifted."

Melia's gaze intensified, as if she were trying to read her mind. Plantine reinforced her mental shield by imagining a locked door.

Either Melia had given up on her mental trespass, or she'd finally collected her wits. "Yes, I crossed the bridge," she finally answered. "It's very big and black."

"What about the muannai valley? Did you go there?"

"Yes, I went to the marketplace and saw a lot of muannai."

"Are the dark faeries as remarkable as they say?"

"Yes."

Plantine stiffened. She'd never considered the female muannai her rivals. "Tell me about them."

If her path carried her across the Maeldun Bridge, and Plantine had an inkling it might, she needed to be prepared. The Albiana ruled Illialei, but she'd read in one of her father's letters that with Umbra's power, the queen of the Realm of Faerie could rule Illialei and Tyrannis.

By her description of the muannai, Plantine could tell Melia was quite enamored of the wingless dark faeries. "Then, they're more beautiful than the faeries of flower and field?" she asked.

Melia squeezed onto the bench next to Tatou. "It's hard to compare them. The muannai are exotic, but I found them easier to talk to." She paused. "Except for one."

"Which one?" Plantine asked.

"The dragonwitch."

"You met her?" Tatou piped up.

"Who's that?" Plantine asked.

"Nandana told me about her. She's kind of an illustrator too."

"Did she help you?" the pixie asked.

"No."

"Why not?"

"Isn't that mark on your forehead enough?" Plantine pushed into her sister's mind, encountered a dark tangle of thought, and retreated. Maybe it wasn't a good idea to invade her sister's mind uninvited this morning, and yet, a wanderlust possessed her. "I want to see everything you saw." Passing mental images to each other had been something they'd done as children.

"Tatou, do you mind?" Melia asked.

"By all means." The pixie swept her arms toward the two half-faeries. "Pretend I'm not here."

"Tatou, please," Plantine pleaded. "It won't take long, will it?"

The pixie snapped her wings. "Go ahead."

Melia shared scenes from her trip with her sister, one by one.

The sights thrilled and delighted Plantine until they reached a healer's shop. "Why did you stop there?"

Melia confessed she'd gone to Tyrannis to find a cure for Plantine's fading.

Plantine's throat constricted. "But the shop is closed. It's covered in dust."

Melia opened her eyes. "She's in Aldaine. That's why I crossed the Nuada."

Plantine had studied maps of Tyrannis. The Nuada was a vast prairie, located between the valley in the south, the deep woods in the west, and the mountains in the north. The great city of Aldaine nestled on the northernmost peak of the mountain range.

Pictures of that sparkling city, overlooking the Great White Sea, and its crowning jewel, the stronghold of Calashai, had always drawn Plantine. She could stare at them for hours.

Elendah, the grey faerie of Aldaine, sat on the stronghold's throne as regent. A granite throne. "Her presence keeps war at bay," Tuck had told her once when they'd discussed the battle between Dark and Light.

Plantine shivered as Melia continued.

"I reached the southern rim of the Ruadain right before dawn and needed a nap. That was where I was when you contacted me."

Plantine listened intently as her sister told her about the drums, the fires, and the hundreds of muannai forging weapons at the base of the mountain.

"They have a leader. It's the same muannai who worked with Father and demanded the investigation into his death." Melia chewed on one of her fingernails. "I can't remember his name."

"Oh dear," Tatou said. "Is it Lord Zachariah Goring?"

Melia's eyes brightened with recognition. "Yes."

That name. Something niggled deep inside Plantine. A colorless cloud enveloped her. She drifted.

The scent of saltwater and tobacco. A leather-bound book, centered in candlelight, within her grasp. Her father watching from the shadows, but not only her father.

The hidden figure encourages her with a shimmering sword and a gem-studded basin, an ivory flower and a granite throne.

A ruby eye stares.

Bells toll.

Hushed words shake her soul, "You have but to reach."

A black rose revealed, its velvet unfurled. Plantine extends her fingers.

A black wolf snarls.

She pulls back her hand. "Father, forgive me, but I cannot."

He is gone.

The absence suffocates.

Time and space collapse around her.

The mist blackens.

She fights to orient her body.

A faint echo ripples through the drowning fog. Someone calls her name.

Melia?

No.

A pixie's voice penetrates the thick swathe of darkness.

Melia's arms circled Plantine's chest, heaving her up. She'd slipped to the ground. Tatou hovered close by. The coolness of the stone bench supported the backs of Plantine's legs. Melia waved her hand in front of her face and snapped her fingers. Plantine scooted herself farther away, flattening her back against the stone behind her.

"You fainted," Melia said.

Plantine rubbed her arms. "It's nothing."

"It didn't look like nothing."

It was hard for Plantine to look her sister in the eye and lie outright.

"Has anything like this ever happened to you before?"

There had been a time when Plantine had trusted Melia. "Sometimes, Father's ghost comes. He's grown stronger in death."

Her sister took a step back.

"Sometimes a black wolf comes with him."

Melia looked as though she'd come across one of the dead chipmunks Malachi occasionally left for their mother on the tree house doorstep.

Plantine's eyes watered. "Do you think Umbra is as bad as Nandana told you he was?"

"How can you even ask that?"

Plantine flinched. She'd always believed Melia to be more courageous than either herself or Melusine. "What if Mother and Father were right? What if Umbra must incarnate?" What was she doing? Melia didn't understand.

Her sister shook her. Plantine offered no resistance.

"I won't listen to you–or anyone else–champion Umbra," Melia said. "Have you been shielding your thoughts the way Melusine taught us?"

Melia would never understand how much Plantine cherished every connection she shared with their father, or that she didn't want to shield herself from him. "I've been getting terrible headaches. Everything drains me. I'm afraid the fading is accelerating." She pulled a fistful of silver-white strands from her head. "I need a cure."

Melia crouched on the ground before her. "I'll fly to Aldaine and find that healer. But I won't go until I know you'll be safe while I'm gone. Tell me more about these visits from Father."

Plantine rubbed her temples. She didn't have to tell Melia everything.

Only the parts about the sword and the basin. And the book. Yes, best to start with that. "Father wrote a book. It's called *The Book of Umbra*."

"I don't believe this," Melia murmured.

Before she could stop herself, Plantine's words poured out in a torrent. "I need to find it for him. There's also a sword and a basin. I need to find them, too."

"How do you know about these things?"

"He shows them to me when he visits."

"He's sending you pictures of all these things?"

Plantine detected the panic in her sister's voice. She shouldn't have asked for her help.

"Are you certain these images are coming from Father?" Melia asked.

"Of course. You haven't heard from him, then?"

"No."

A keen tremor suffused Plantine. For all her sister's strong beliefs about right and wrong, Melia comprehended nothing.

"Have you heard from Melusine?" Melia asked.

"Not a word." Plantine was beginning to understand. Her sisters were irrelevant. Their father had chosen her as his agent.

"Have you discussed any of this with Tuck?" Tatou asked.

Plantine dug her toe into the ground.

"Maybe Aldous and Tuck–"

Plantine jumped to her feet. "No!"

"What if–" Melia turned away. "Did you hear that?"

Plantine listened. "The wind in the forest?"

Melia pointed toward the undergrowth, thick with weeds and shadow. "There."

"It was probably a deer," Plantine said.

"Maybe." Melia didn't look satisfied, but she pressed her fingers to her brow as if she tried to remember what they'd been talking about. Plantine stared at the blue spot between her sister's eyebrows. It was rather pretty, like a blue ornament.

"What if it's not Father who's contacting you?" Melia whispered.

"What do you mean?"

"Nandana told me Umbra absorbs the residue of soul embers–their ashes. Father was obsessed with the incarnation. What if that obsession created a soul ember when he died?"

Plantine stared at Melia. The seductive whisper didn't belong to her father.

"What if Umbra absorbed the ash of his soul and his ability to penetrate our minds?"

Plantine swayed; her sister steadied her.

"You're getting so weak," Melia said.

"I'm fine."

"You're not."

"Let's go to the library," Tatou said.

"What good will that do?" Melia asked.

"No," Plantine said.

"We need help," the pixie insisted. "We need to understand what's happening with Plantine–why she's fainting and receiving requests to find these specific things–"

"I'm fainting because of Mother's spell," Plantine said.

"It would be good for you to see Tuck," Tatou said.

"No, I need to get back to the tree house," Plantine insisted.

Melia and Tatou exchanged glances.

"Why?" Melia asked.

"I have things to do."

"What? Find these things for Umbra? He's the one contacting you, not Father's ghost."

Plantine had to get away from them. "I need to check on Mother. I'm sure your visit this morning upset her." She gathered her skirts and ran.

22. On the Way to the Grand Library

Melia and Tatou stood beneath the towering magnolias that shaded the enchanted gardens' north wall. They watched Plantine disappear through the fragrant grove, her sheer, white gown rippling behind her like so many butterfly wings as the forest swallowed her whole.

"Should you go after her?" Tatou asked.

"No," Melia grumbled.

The pixie darted through the air, her gossamer wings catching the sunlight dappling through the trees. "Do you really think Umbra is reaching for her?"

"I don't know, but if Umbra absorbed the ashes of Father's soul, he could have absorbed his ability to penetrate our minds. And what about Mother? I've never seen her like she was the afternoon she cursed us–or this morning. Some dark force possesses her. What if…"

Tatou, twirling in graceful arcs, stopped spinning. Her wings drooped. "What?"

"What if Umbra reached my mother? That afternoon, before she cursed us, Melusine told Mother we'd stopped the coming war. Mother told us we were fools, and she was right."

The pixie puckered her lips and pulled them with her fingers. "I can't believe the muannai would turn against the grey faerie."

"Not all of them, only the ones following Lord Goring–the cult of Umbra. And it's not certain. The muannai who said that was only guessing."

"Even so, it's cause for concern. Elendah is thought to be the grey sentinel."

Melia's brow wrinkled.

"The prophecy," Tatou said.

As soon as she'd crossed the river into Tyrannis, Melia had pushed the troubling verses from her mind.

"As long as the grey faerie watches over the Realm of Faerie, no war will come to its shores," Tatou said.

"I don't remember the prophecy saying anything about that."

"'Beware. Cunning will test the grey sentinel's shield'."

Melia tossed her hair over her shoulder. "See, that's why I don't like prophecies. Who would ever figure it meant that?"

"It's an interpretation."

Melia rolled her eyes. "But the grey faerie is in Tyrannis. How can she keep war from coming to Illialei?"

"The realm hasn't always been divided. The north was once called the Dark Lands and Illialei was called the Territory of Light. As regent of the stronghold of Calashai, Elendah keeps the power of the Albiana in check."

"First my father, and now you," Melia said. "What is wrong with the Albiana? I thought they were beloved rulers."

"Melia, there are things you don't know."

"Obviously." She walked to the tree line and kneeled to examine the ground. "Do you see this?" She pointed to a patch of exposed dirt. The faint imprint of a heel was visible. "A boot left those marks. Besides my mother, who wears boots in Illialei?"

"You think someone has been spying on us?" Tatou asked.

Melia followed the short trail of scuffed leaves until it disappeared.

"Mother warned me about a troll asking after Elynus' daughters in the Bryndale market. I didn't believe her."

The pixie landed on her shoulder. "Trolls don't cross the Maeldun Bridge."

"That's what I thought. Now I'm not so sure. But, then again, that's an awfully big boot for a troll."

Tatou repositioned herself in front of Melia's face, so the half-faerie couldn't see anything but her. "Let's go to the library. I want you to talk to Aldous. He knows your mother, and he knew your father."

"You're being very mysterious."

"I'm sorry, but we shouldn't be talking about these things here, especially if someone is spying on you."

Tatou was nervous–or was it fear? Melia had never seen her friend afraid before.

"Fine," Melia said. "We need to get moving if we're going to make it before dusk."

The pixie zoomed ahead. Climbing High Hill would be the most direct route to the Cathedral Palace. Tatou flew in that direction.

✧✧✧

They were almost to the palace when the red-leafed maples and flowering cherry trees on either side of the road grew hazy.

Melia jerked her head from side to side to clear her vision.

The column of sunflowers bisecting the glassy boulevard wavered. Each bloom had appeared sharp-cut mere seconds ago. Everything blurred as an opaque mist dropped behind her eyes. The mist deepened, closing out every bit of light like a heavy curtain. She staggered with her hands in front of her.

"Tatou." Melia spun and lost her balance. Down on the ground, she rubbed her eyes. "I can't see."

"Stop fighting," a gruff voice snarled.

"Tatou?"

"We won't hurt you," the same rough voice barked.

"Then why must you blindfold me?" Plantine's nervous voice wove its way through Melia's consciousness. She pushed up on her eyelids. They were open, but everything she saw was black. Rough hands pressed against

her head, a strip of light tore at the darkness. Cold metal pressed against her lips.

"Drink," the voice growled.

Melia gagged and spit until the liquid touched her tongue. It tasted of fresh-cut grass and roses with a hint of lemon. She stopped resisting.

It felt as if her head was being submerged under water. Her thoughts, trapped in some vague place, became incoherent. She tried to press her hands in the dirt and push herself up, but her elbows buckled. She slipped back into the crush of sunflowers behind her.

Light hit her irises. The world around her returned. Above her, yellow-orange petals danced with every clumsy effort to right herself. The scent of damp ground and green, woody stems enveloped her. "Incredible," Melia murmured.

Tatou followed her into the clump of towering blossoms. "Are you all right?"

Melia plucked an enormous sunflower and wagged it in front of her friend's face. "Have you ever seen anything so incredible?"

"Every day," the pixie said.

"But it's never been like this! The golden petals, their creamy texture"–Melia buried her nose in the sunflower–"the tangy bouquet."

Tatou tugged on Melia's hand. "Sit." She flew behind the half-faerie and pressed on her shoulders. "Up," the pixie said. "We need to get to the library before you shift. I want you to meet Aldous as a faerie, not an eagle."

Melia laughed.

Tatou reached into her pocket.

Before she knew it, Melia was coughing, spluttering, and covered in pixie dust. Her dreamy ecstasy receded. She wrestled herself away from the sunflowers and tried to stand up. "Och!" She clutched her forehead. Pain radiated from every bone in her skull. She staggered and tripped, then landed on her knees.

Tatou hovered so close to her face, the faint airflow from her quivering wings brushed the half-faerie's eyelashes. "What is going on?"

The image that flashed through Melia's mind was unclear, but its meaning wasn't. "Something dreadful has happened to Plantine."

"Something dreadful has happened to you too."

"No." Melia rubbed her forehead with the fingers of both hands. "But I've never shared an experience like that with one of my sisters. We've always sent messages or pictures. But this time I was there. I felt what Plantine felt. I heard what she heard. I drank what she drank."

Tatou frowned.

"At first, everything was black, then I realized she was blindfolded. Someone was forcing her to drink something." Melia traced her lower lip, searching for a residual drop. "It was the most delicious thing I've ever tasted."

"And what Plantine drank affected you," Tatou said.

The more Melia considered what had just happened, the more disturbing it became. She jumped up and rubbed her arms to get her shivering under control.

"Is she hurt?"

"Nych. The voice said they wouldn't harm her. But who would blindfold her? And why? I saw nothing to show me where she was. Nothing." Melia held out her hand. The pixie settled in her upturned palm. "We need to find her."

"You can cover more ground as an eagle. Your vision will be better. We're almost to the library," Tatou said.

Melia considered the sun.

"The palace is around the bend. We've come all this way. Why don't we make sure you're all right before we go off on a wild search for Plantine?"

Melia wanted to argue with her, but her mind remained fuzzy around the edges. There was something she could do, but she couldn't recall what it was. She searched her friend's eyes, then she remembered. "I can contact Plantine."

"Maybe that's not such a good idea."

"I can find out where they've taken her." Melia dropped Tatou on the ground, then settled cross-legged beside her. She closed her eyes and concentrated on opening the place in her mind where she could connect with her sister.

"Wait!" Tatou shouted.

Melia pulled her attention inward and focused on Plantine. It was easy to bring to mind the impression of her sister that morning, running away from her, her white gown fluttering into the forest. *"Plantine."* Her sister was so close, Melia could reach out and touch her back. She put out her hand.

Plantine ran deeper into the woods.

Melia followed the music of her laughter and a fragrant trail of night jasmine–a scent she'd never associated with her sister before. *"Plantine, wait!"*

Her sister evaporated.

Melia raced through the trees. *"Plantine!"* she screamed.

The forest floor writhed beneath her feet. A swirling vortex of black space opened where solid ground had been only moments before. Melia's hands clutched at snakelike vines dripping from ancient trees. This was not the Sylvan Forest.

She screamed louder as her body stretched taut. The loam sucked at her feet and ankles. Her hands pulled harder on the vines. The tug-of-war wrenched her shoulders from their sockets. *"Help!"*

The force that had found her was stronger than either of her sisters or her father, as it seized possession of her inner world. She tried to disconnect, but it wouldn't let go. *"Plantine!"* she cried one more time.

"She's mine."

The sheer force of the assertion jarred Melia's bones. *"No!"* The single word fragmented in a gale force that whipped the trees, threatening to rip the vines from her grip. The cycloning winds turned icy. Her teeth chattered.

"Come and get her," the dark voice challenged.

"You can count on that," Melia whispered. Her father had never been able to affect the weather, or transport her consciousness to another dimension. One of her hands slipped.

"You're not strong enough."

The black earth sucked her deeper. Sinister laughter reverberated through the inky air.

A tiny voice reached through the shrieking winds. *"Melia!"*

Melia's second hand slipped. The black muck reached her shoulders. She was going to die, buried beneath oozing filth.

"Melia, come back," the bell-like voice sounded so familiar.

"No one can help you, half-faerie," the dark voice bellowed.

Half-faerie? She strained with her arms and her legs, but the mud was consuming her. A spark of light floated into view. *"Tatou."*

The malignant owner of the dark voice hovered as the black mire drained away.

Melia slumped against the exposed roots of a gnarled tree. Her heart pounded in her ears. The spark of light pushed back the drowning blackness. Melia reached for it. The star pulsated inches from the tips of her outstretched fingers. It wouldn't let her hold it, but its glow gave her hope. The weight of her body fell away as the light drew her up toward the sky. Melia's arms became wings. She soared above the tree line. Fresh wind hit her face.

"Do not cross this threshold so lightly again."

The warning hit Melia like a hammer driving a stake. She almost fell to the ground. The natural world returned around her.

"What happened?" Tatou asked.

Melia lay stretched out on the grassy road, spent. Her friend buzzed in a frantic figure eight above her face. Tatou had saved her. Melia followed the pixie's circuit for several minutes. She refused to say Umbra's name. "I'm not sure." But it had been him.

Tatou was full of questions. The ordeal had left Melia smashed inside. What was worse, she'd gleaned no information to help her find Plantine and was terrified of trying to contact her again.

The sun fell from the sky.

How long had she been trapped in some inner chamber, tormented by Umbra?

"Let's go to the library," Tatou said.

Melia forced herself to get up and walk.

23. The Elves

Around the next bend, the Cathedral Palace glistened, a luminous fortress of white. Emerald and sapphire banners fluttered from the turrets–the colors of the Albiana. Melia heaved a sigh of relief. The striking image of light made the threat of Umbra seem far-fetched.

They crossed the palace's white drawbridge. As Melia's hand brushed the golden handrails, her gaze followed the shimmering fish darting below in the well-stocked moat. Then she remembered Plantine, and her body stiffened. She had no reason to doubt the telepathic vision she'd received. Her sister had been kidnapped. But why, and by whom?

Beyond the drawbridge, the palace gates were attended to the east and west by brownies. Short–the tallest reached Melia's shoulder–and ruddy-faced, they stood erect. They held bantam shields bearing the insignia of the sapphire lily against their breasts. Miniature blades hung at their sides. Posted four rows long and two rows deep, they wore livery of blue, green, white, and gold.

Tatou flitted right and left, acknowledging the miniature guardians. Any other day, Melia would have mimicked the pixie's salute, but today she hurried to keep up.

Sunlight cast long shadows across the palace lawn; inside, the torches were not yet lit. Everything looked grey. Melia's footsteps echoed off stone walls as she followed the small halo of Tatou's radiance through dim passageways.

"It's so quiet," Melia said.

"All the faeries are gone," her friend whispered. "Queen Luisa and her entourage have retreated to the Summer Palace. Each year her visits grow longer."

"What is the point of calling it the Summer Palace when the weather never changes in Illialei?"

"Things were different when the palace was named."

"Sounds as though a lot of things used to be different," Melia said. Tatou didn't respond. "Why does Luisa stay there? With everyone gone, it's like a tomb in here."

"She's convalescing."

"From what?"

"Years ago, she visited the mortal world. She returned ... worn down is the best way to describe it. Some believe she's never fully recovered."

"Luisa visited the mortal world?"

"It was her nineteenth birthday. She was wild back then. Her mother, Queen Olivia, couldn't control her. People avoid talking about it," Tatou said.

"I wish they would avoid talking about me." Melia was still trying to brush off the nasty accusation made by the pixies in the enchanted gardens that morning.

"I wish they wouldn't talk about you, either," Tatou said.

"Have you ever been to the Summer Palace?" Melia asked.

"Yes."

"I haven't." Melia could count, on one hand, how many times she'd entered the Cathedral Palace. Pressina harbored a grudge against Queen Luisa. Her mother had never delved into the root of her bitterness, but when Luisa had celebrated her daughters tenth birthday, proclaiming Lilliane the future queen of Illialei as was the custom, Pressina had refused to attend the declaration ceremony. She forbade her daughters from attending as well. However, Melia and her sisters wouldn't have dreamed of missing the celebration. Everyone in Illialei had been invited, and they weren't going to be the only ones to miss it.

They never regretted their decision. Queen Luisa had lavished every expense, and their mother had never found out they'd gone. Scurrying through the maze of halls now, a smile brushed Melia's lips. She missed those days when she and her sisters had trusted one another.

When they reached the library's two tall burnished doors, Melia paused to catch her breath. She'd never been inside. This was Plantine's world.

"Come on," Tatou said.

Melia squared her shoulders and pressed her hand against one of the doors. Even though it was made of heavy brass, it gave way with the slightest push. Inside, the library smelled of orange wax.

Tatou whizzed by the side of her head. "Follow me."

Melia's eyes drank in the portraits, tapestries, and maps that cluttered the walls. Her bare feet sank into plush rugs. She understood why Plantine came here. Although it was peaceful, the promise of fantastical stories hung in the air. "Where are we going?"

"To the west wing." Tatou pointed to the small window they'd just passed. "At the end of the day, when the sun is just so in the frame, Aldous settles in his favorite chair with Basil for afternoon tea."

"Basil?"

"The library's cat."

The pixie rounded a corner and flitted down a short, wide aisle. Beyond a sitting area of mismatched but colorful sofas and chairs, a bright fire burned in a large stone fireplace.

"If we're lucky, there'll be enough tea for us." Tatou regarded Melia. "There's a big grass stain"–the pixie flitted closer–"right there."

"Have you forgotten about Plantine?"

"No, I haven't. But you don't have to look like a drowned water rat the first time you meet Aldous. Head Librarian is a prestigious position. Besides, it's not dusk yet, and I could use a bite to eat before we start flying all over Faerie."

Melia glanced down at her long summer coat. In addition to the spot her friend had pointed out, the hem was tattered, and one of the sleeves had a small rip.

"Take it off," Tatou ordered.

The sleeveless dress Melia wore beneath left her bruised arms exposed. She swatted at one of the larger stains on the jacket. "No."

"Do you have something to tie back your hair?"

Melia searched her pockets and found a frayed navy ribbon. She stood, stone-faced, while Tatou tugged her thick brown hair into a ponytail. She couldn't believe the elves would care about her appearance. Nevertheless, she let her friend brush a few loose strands of hair from her face and pat her cheeks.

The pixie yanked on Melia's jacket collar. "That will have to do."

A huge shadowy figure rose against the far wall. "Ahem, I say, is someone there?"

"It's Tatou. I'm with a friend."

"Splendid," the same deep, full voice said as the oldest wood elf Melia had ever seen shuffled into view.

Most wood elves lived long lives, but this one was a fossil. Snow-white hair puffed from both sides of his head, and bushy white eyebrows hung over his spectacles. His appearance reminded Melia more of an owl than a wood elf. She half-expected him to hoot when he opened his mouth.

He wore a blue plaid bathrobe over what looked like pajamas as he scuffed along in a pair of faded blue slippers. Not nearly as stocky as most wood elves, he was hunched over around the edges. Melia looked behind him for the creature who'd spoken.

"My favorite pixie," the old elf said.

If he'd not been standing right in front of her, Melia wouldn't have believed the full, rich baritone belonged to him.

"Aldous, this is Melia, Plantine's sister," Tatou said.

She should have guessed the old elf was the palace librarian.

His eyes twinkled as he motioned toward a long, low table behind him. "You two are right on time for tea. Please, join us. There's plenty more where that came from."

The scent of warm sour-drop biscuits–one of the few non-sweet treats popular in Illialei–woke up Melia's empty stomach, but dusk, and her change, were coming soon. There would be no time to benefit from the elf's hospitality. She grimaced. It would be a nice furry rabbit for her tonight.

Tatou was deep into the social niceties with the elf. Melia was trying to interrupt their conversation when she noticed an old ginger cat settled on one of the overstuffed sofas. Basil?

Inquisitive was the word Melia would have chosen to describe his expression. Before she could absorb the ramification of the cat's presence –or its attentions toward her–a voice she'd heard somewhere before called out, "Tatou."

When Tuck came from behind a wall of cabinets, Tatou and Aldous fell silent. Once again, Melia thought he looked more like a dark-headed Huron Knight than any elf she'd ever seen.

He shook her hand with a firm grip. "I've missed your sister's visits to the library," he said. "How is she?"

"Not good. She's been kidnapped."

24. Lord Zachariah Goring

Tuck's hands shook. His face, flushed only seconds before, drained to white. He became more agitated as Melia described her telepathic exchange with Plantine. "We must find out where they've taken her."

"She was frightened," Melia said, "and the effects of our mother's curse is rendering her more fragile each day. I don't know how long she can last on her own."

Everyone turned to Aldous as if his advanced age or position as head librarian endowed him with knowledge beyond their grasp.

"I was afraid something like this might happen," he said.

His statement rattled Melia.

"Why?" she and Tuck asked at the same time.

Aldous shuffled toward a faded wing chair and collapsed into the seat. "All this talk of Umbra, Umbra, Umbra." He pressed his fingers against his lips. He opened his mouth as if to speak, then stopped himself.

"What?" Tuck echoed Melia's frustration.

The old elf rubbed the knuckles of his left hand with the fingers of his right. He stared into the distance. "Tuck, you'll be relieved of your duties at the library until she's safe."

The muscles in Melia's leg twitched. She backed away. She never wanted others to see her change. She searched for a place to shield herself from their view.

"The troll your mother warned you about," Tatou said.

As soon as the words were out of the pixie's mouth, Melia could have kicked herself. The gruff voice from Plantine's vision and the boot prints at Pebble Rock dovetailed with her mother's warning of a troll–or something worse–from Tyrannis.

Melia didn't realize she'd stopped moving until she saw the elves and Tatou staring at her. It was too late to hide. The air around her vibrated as her body reshaped itself into the form of a large black eagle. It only took seconds.

"YEEEEEEEOOOOOOOOOOOW!"

She'd forgotten about Basil.

He flew through the air as if spring-loaded. Coming straight at Melia, the cat howled like a banshee. However, unlike the wailing women so named, he seemed intent upon much more than foretelling her eminent demise.

Tuck dove at the meteor of ginger fur shooting through the air. The library cat eluded the tackle. Basil's eyes were on fire with lust for his prey –her. She recognized the appetite. It motivated her to move.

It usually took a few minutes to get her bearings, find her balance, and create enough momentum to lift her body from the ground, but she didn't have a few minutes. She stretched her wings and flapped, succeeding in a few awkward forward hops.

When Basil lunged, she flattened her belly against the thick carpet. The movement was enough to remove her as the bull's-eye. She searched the room for a high point and saw a bookcase several yards away. To her keen hearing, the light brush of Basil's paws against the library's floor thundered a warning. The cat's determined breaths assured her he'd positioned himself to pounce. She swept her wings wide and lifted from the ground.

"Watch out!" Tatou cried out.

Basil landed on Melia's back with a screech. She had to applaud his daring. Not many creatures his size would have taken her on. She'd eaten raccoons larger than him for dinner. Melia rolled her body mid-flight, hoping to offload her unwelcome passenger. The cat succeeded in digging the claws of his front paws deeper into the back of her neck. She squawked as the sharp points dug into the skin beneath her feathers, but she kept rising.

Aldous shambled toward them. He waved his arms wildly over his head. "Basil, you mustn't attack the guests."

Back on his feet, Tuck closed in from behind. *Only a few more feet to safety*, Melia told herself, certain the cat would slip. She soared. The cat's weight had no effect on her orientation; as an eagle, she was that big and strong.

The cat clung to her neck, his hind paws dangling in the air. When she landed on top of the bookcase, he growled.

"Let go," Melia crackled in bird talk.

Basil's growl intensified.

They were too high for the elves to reach them. Stupid cat! She'd rip him apart with her talons.

"Basil!"

The cat's head jerked.

Tuck voiced a calm authority. "You're hurting Plantine's sister."

Basil stopped his incessant growling; a sheepish look stole over his face. It seemed Plantine carried weight with the library feline, and Melia didn't even think her sister liked cats. Basil retracted his claws. Unappeased, Melia dipped her head and leaned in for a good peck. The pale pink triangle of the cat's nose made the perfect target.

Basil screeched.

She spread her wings to their full span. "If I ever catch you slinking through the palace gardens alone–"

"Melia!" Tatou squeaked.

Chastened, she glowered at the orange fluff ball but didn't retract her wings. Basil slid down the bookcase in their shadow, glaring the entire way. Tuck scooped up the cat.

Tatou spiraled through the air and settled on the tree elf's broad shoulder. "Thank you."

The puncture wounds in Melia's neck smarted. She directed one more squawk at the cat Tuck squeezed in his arms. Its orange hair straightened as if it were a short-quilled porcupine.

They'd barely had time to recover from Basil's charge when loud sobbing burst forth from the direction of the library's exterior doors. Melia froze as the wailing drew near; the sound was all too familiar.

Aldous seemed equally perturbed to see who'd arrived. "Pressina."

"You were right," her mother said. "I should have listened to you long ago."

Melia perched on the bookcase, alert and listening.

Pressina wrung her hands. "My youngest daughter is gone. They came to the tree house. They took her by force. Can you believe it? By force!"

"Who?" Aldous, Tuck, and Tatou asked in a chorus.

Pressina managed to keep her sobbing at full throttle as they crowded around her. She choked between gasps and hiccups. "That damn troll from Tyrannis. He came into my home with a group of thugs–muannai, I think. Yes, they were muannai. I'm sure of it."

The old elf reached for Pressina's hand. "Come, sit with us."

Before letting him take hold of it, she twisted the jewels on her fingers for maximum effect.

Aldous led her mother to the collection of mismatched sofas and chairs. She settled there, groping her rings without pause.

Melia thought she might be overdoing it–just a tad.

Nobody noticed the fire turning to coals and the long shadows in the library's many corners as night descended. Grateful for the shroud of twilight, Melia watched from atop the bookcase.

The old elf looked stiff settled on the sofa beside Pressina. "Do you have any idea where they've taken her?"

Tuck stood taut as though he were a soldier instead of a librarian. Tatou flitted above their heads.

"It must have been Zachariah."

Melia's heart skipped a beat.

Tatou froze midair.

The tree elf's eyes widened. "Are you certain?"

Pressina wailed.

Aldous waited for her exaggerated weeping to subside while Tuck stared at a spot over Pressina's head. The tree elf's stony expression hinted that her copious tears left him unmoved.

Finally, calm enough to speak, she leaned into Aldous. "Elynus collaborated with him."

The head librarian shook his head as he pressed her hand. "Pressina, where is the book now?"

She answered with more weeping.

Although Melia had a million questions about *The Book of Umbra*, she wished to avoid her mother. Their encounter earlier had been enough for one day. She remained silent and still.

Pressina's cries continued. Aldous produced a blue silk square. As her mother wiped her nose, she turned her lilac eyes in Melia's direction.

The tick-tock of the library's clocks became deafening as the seconds clicked by. When her mother twirled the hanky and patted Aldous' knee, Melia knew the shadows had kept her safe.

"Elynus knew his life was in danger, although not from his daughters." Pressina's sniffles escalated into another round of hysterics.

The head librarian's expression was unreadable as he patted her hand. Melia hoped he didn't believe that she and her sisters had murdered their father.

Finally, Pressina took a deep breath and made a show of collecting herself. "He feared that the work would be incomplete, or that his research would get lost. He often wrote to Lord Goring as both a resource and a precaution. The muannaye was as passionate about the work as Elynus."

"What a surprise," Tuck muttered under his breath.

Pressina ignored him, training her enormous lilac eyes on Aldous. "My husband thought he would be a safe ally for his ambitions. Since Lord Goring can't travel to the mortal world ..." Her voice trailed off as she wrung the handkerchief. If it had been a living thing, it wouldn't have survived the assault.

After several minutes, Aldous prodded her. Melia had the distinct feeling that if Plantine hadn't been in danger, Pressina would never have revealed the next bit of information to a living soul.

"Elynus told Lord Goring about ..."

Aldous waited. Her mother obviously didn't want to confess what her father had revealed to the muannaye.

Pressina gave a faint, twisted smile. "Elynus wrote to Zachariah of his ability to communicate telepathically with his daughters. And"–she hesitated a moment–"he assigned an envoy to travel to Faerie upon his death, with a letter of instructions and the book. The messenger was to give the package to Lord Goring and no other."

Aldous dropped Pressina's hands and ran his fingers through the white puffs on either side of his ears. "Plantine is in grave danger."

"After Elynus' death, I tried to contact the muannaye, but I've received no correspondence in return. Nothing until today. Goring sent those muannai to kidnap my daughter. I'm sure of it. He'll use her as a puppet if no one stops him."

Melia struggled to put all the pieces together.

"I fear you're right," Aldous said. "Let me see what we can do."

"It's too late!" Pressina shot up, her body stiffening into a sharp line as she glared at Tuck. He returned her withering look. She cast a long shadow across Tatou. The pixie inched away. "Don't you understand? Everything is always too late. My husband had to die before Luisa would lift a finger, and when she finally did, that investigation was a farce." Pressina turned to Aldous. "Tell me. How do three girls accidentally drown their father?" She gave him no time to answer before she went on another tear. "And where is my sister, now? Indulging herself at the Summer Palace while the world falls apart around her!"

The old elf got up and faced Pressina with his full height, which wasn't much more than when he'd been sitting. "We knew this day would come."

Melia was impressed. No one stood up to her mother; if her beauty didn't overwhelm them, her anger did.

"But what did you do to stop it?"

"Pressina–" He reached out to calm her.

She backed away. "No! No one in this wretched palace has ever done anything to help me. It was foolish of me to think anything would be different now!" She turned and almost tripped over her long skirt before she stormed away.

No one made an effort to stop her. The tree elf glared at her retreating back. Tatou settled on his shoulder while Aldous crumpled into his wing chair. Silence filled the library.

Unanswered questions flooded Melia's mind. Why had her mother come to Aldous about Plantine? What had she expected him to do? Had the old elf warned her Plantine might be kidnapped? Obviously, he'd heard of *The Book of Umbra*. How did her mortal father know Lord Goring, a muannaye? Why had he entrusted his life work to him? And to what purpose had he revealed the supersensory connection he shared with his daughters?

Her mother had a sister?

Tuck and Aldous argued below. Melia's questions fizzled. Only one needed to be answered tonight. Where was Plantine? Everything else would have to wait.

Melia searched the room for Basil. She spotted the cat, perched sphinx-like on a table at the far end of the sitting area, his golden eyes fastened upon her.

"Tatou, the cat," she cawed.

"Melia." Aldous' voice boomed, despite his exhausted physical posture. It seemed forgetfulness, and not protectiveness, had kept him from revealing her presence.

She wasn't going to hold that against him.

Tuck hurried toward Basil. The cat didn't look pleased when the elf grabbed him again and held on tight, but he didn't squirm for his freedom either.

"I must find Plantine!" Melia cawed.

"If she was taken under Goring's orders, you'll need help," Aldous said.

He removed a tapered candle from a wooden box and shuffled toward the fading fire. When the candle's flame flickered, he headed down one of the wide aisles that fanned out from the sitting area. Everyone followed. Tuck kept Basil in a firm embrace. Melia and Tatou flew behind them.

At the end of the aisle, Tuck took the candle from Aldous with his free hand and pushed it into a sconce on the wall. The old elf rummaged through the contents of a broad, flat cabinet. Haphazard sheets of parchment blew away like dry leaves as he searched the drawer's contents. After several tense moments, he grasped a large document.

Satisfied, he shuffled across the foyer. It didn't take long to discern that the page he'd laid across the table was a map of Faerie. Tracing the Nyssalei River from its mouth at the Great White Sea, his finger paused south of the river's fork, close to the Maeldun Bridge. Tapping northwest with his finger, he found the Veiled Tavern. After rubbing his eyebrow with his other hand, he shook his head. "Gumf may have information, but the tavern is dangerous. Among other issues, there are too many foreigners and unsavory types to eavesdrop." His finger slid east. "There."

"The Balyudor?" Tuck asked. "We'll lose weeks searching that gloomy labyrinth."

"No." The head librarian mouthed a name as his finger tapped the map. "Her cottage is right there, at the edge of the woods."

The tree elf seemed to know who Aldous was talking about.

"More than Gumf, she is the eyes and ears of Tyrannis. She'll know where Lord Goring intends to take Plantine." Aldous turned to Melia. "The muannaye has a mansion in Aldaine. It sits above the cloud line, between the city and the stronghold of Calashai. I suspect he'll take her there, but let's be sure."

"Whose cottage?" Melia asked.

"Shh!" Tatou said.

"But I don't know who he's talking about, do you?"

The pixie's expression was strained.

Tuck frowned.

"You said there were things Aldous could tell me," Melia said.

"Not now. You're going to get us in trouble." Tatou exchanged glances with the librarian. He nodded. "I'll tell you later," she said.

Melia ruffled her feathers. Secrets piled up around her. "Why can't you tell me now?"

Tatou wheeled around and slapped her hands against her hips. "Because I can't."

Pixies were known for their flaring tempers, but Melia had never been at the receiving end of Tatou's. "What's wrong? Did an ant crawl up your petal skirt?"

Her friend threw her arms in the air and turned to Aldous. "She's as stubborn as a dairy cow. She won't listen to anything anyone says. She's always been this way, but she's worse when she's an eagle." She glared at Melia.

The temptation to swallow her friend whole jolted Melia out of her black moment.

Aldous came around the table and stood between them. "Melia, there are many things Pressina, or perhaps I, should have told you before tonight." His command of the eagle's tongue was fluent. "But now, the hours tick by, and your sister is in grave danger. I doubt anyone can save her tonight, but we can obtain information that will make her rescue possible. You can fly to the Balyudor and return to the library by dawn. Will you do this for your sister?"

How could she say no?

He turned to Tatou and continued his eloquent appeal in eagle. "As for you, little one, perhaps a sense of guilt for what we've withheld from Melia –more than censure for her persistence–provokes your temper. Hmm?"

Melia appreciated the librarian's defense. She puffed out her chest. "What if the person who lives in the cottage can't speak the tongue of eagles?"

The old elf reached his hand into the pocket of his plaid bath robe. "That won't be the problem."

"Then, what will be?" Melia asked.

"Her prickly nature," he said. "She'll need to be encouraged to give you the information we need."

"You expect her to use force?" Tuck interrupted.

Aldous gave his head an adamant shake. "Nych. Charm her." He pointed to Tatou. "You're the best one to do that. You've flown with Melia before?"

"Yes."

"Good. Just remember, whatever happens, no pixie dust." He again mouthed two words Melia couldn't understand "... and pixie dust are an unpredictable combination–one we wish to avoid." He peered at Melia and Tatou over the top of his glasses. "The two of you can work together tonight?"

Melia checked with her friend before they nodded their agreement.

"But they're strangers to–" Tuck mouthed a word. Melia presumed it was the person's name. "What if she won't let them in?"

"I've thought of that." The old elf pulled the object he'd been fiddling with from his pocket and laid it on the table. It was a simple beaded bracelet of rose-colored quartz. "She'll recognize this. It has meaning to her."

"What meaning?" Tuck asked.

"That's not important. It should be enough to get them in the front door. The rest is up to them. When they return in the morning, we'll use whatever information they've gathered to plan Plantine's rescue." Aldous had been speaking in eagle. He rubbed the back of his neck and reverted to the common tongue. "And I'll find a way to explain some things to Melia that she should have been told long ago."

Tatou and Tuck looked worried. Very worried.

25. The Spring Faerie

Tatou fingered the bracelet Aldous had entrusted them with. She wore it looped around her neck. "Don't even ask," she said. "I'll tell you when we cross the river."

Melia wanted to refuse to move until her friend told her who lived in the cottage, but it was getting late, and they had a long flight ahead of them. She needed a clear head to navigate. That meant putting all her questions aside. She cocked her head to indicate she wouldn't argue.

Appeased, Tatou shimmied across her feathers to straddle her back. The pixie's arms circled Melia's neck, her legs cinched Melia's upper torso above her wings. Even with the heavy beads, her friend was an easy passenger to carry.

The cool night air cleared Melia's head as the wind's current swept away Tatou's initial efforts at conversation. Melia welcomed the silence. She concentrated on flying. The enchanted world's waxing moons lit the way.

Aiming toward the Balyudor, she scanned for movement below. To the southwest, an out-of-season fog rolled across Southend Pier. The grey-white clouds extended inland. The tree house roof jutted from them. The city of Bryndale, nestled between the mists and the Footing Fields, was sleepy and dark. Candlelight flickered in a few windows.

To the northwest, beyond the enchanted gardens and Sylvan Forest, the iron columns of the Maeldun Bridge stretched into the night sky. Melia veered in that direction, to make sure no one traveled that route.

A hare bounded across the fields. She dove in a tight spiral. Tatou's hands squeezed as they shot toward the creature. It never had a chance. One quick rip with her beak, and the small creature fell silent. Like pulling an apple from a tree, or ripping a strawberry from a garden patch–except it wasn't. Killing was always a strange experience. The simple, practical matter of obtaining food as an eagle repulsed her half-faerie self–ever present but submerged within. Yet she'd never been able to override the instinct. It was part of her mother's curse. The one thing that mitigated the pleasure of flight. Now Tatou had witnessed her savagery.

Melia swept upwards, carrying the carcass in her talons.

The Nyssalei lay ahead. Melia searched for ships, west to the Great White Sea, and east, where it forked into two mighty rivers. The Undine snaked through Tyrannis, while the Nyssalei curved back around Illialei.

Six long shadows rocked gently along the muannai valley docks, large boats bringing merchandise and trade from the rest of the enchanted world. Nothing unusual about that, it was a busy harbor, and all the ships were anchored. If Plantine's kidnappers had sailed from Illialei that afternoon, they couldn't have reached the valley port yet.

Beyond the bridge and rivers lay the Balyudor. An entire army could have marched beneath its roof of leaves and vines, and Melia would have been blind to their movements. Aldous was right, they needed eyes and ears close to the ground.

Melia took measure of the width and breadth of the Balyudor. If the scale of Aldous' map was accurate, their destination was close. She descended.

When the ground was near, she let the hare drop, finishing the flight with as gentle a landing as possible for the benefit of her passenger.

"That was tremendous." Tatou scrambled from her back to the thick floor of forest leaves. "Scary when you swooped for that jackrabbit–and disgusting." She stuck out her tongue. "But I've never felt the wind like that on my face, and I was sure, if you'd flown a bit higher, I could have touched the moons."

Melia responded with excited chirping as she hopped toward dinner. She was thrilled her friend didn't hold her natural appetite against her.

"Slow down, I can't understand a word you're saying," Tatou said.

A snarl ripped from behind one of the trees. Melia froze halfway between Tatou and the dead hare, craning her head sideways. Two feet away, Tatou cowered. The faint glow emanating from her wings shouted, Here I am! Melia took one hop back in the direction of her friend. The beast growled again.

If the thing was hungry, maybe leaving the hare would be a worthwhile sacrifice. Melia hopped from foot to foot.

An enormous shadow lunged overhead. It didn't want her dinner.

Melia flapped her wings and swooped to snatch Tatou with her talons. She didn't have to hear her friend scream to know she hurt her, but Melia couldn't let go. The dark shadow paced and growled beneath them.

A loud crack, as though a wooden door had slammed, drew Melia's attention. There was a faint light ahead. Aldous had said there was only one cottage in the Balyudor, and it belonged to his friend. Melia flew toward the visible glow. The beast raced beneath them, leaping and swiping at Tatou.

Melia veered around trees and rope-like vines swinging from the branches. Although there were far too many close calls, she managed to keep Tatou out of their pursuer's grasp. When she broke into a small clearing, Melia almost crashed into the steepled roof of a yellow, A-frame house.

Their hunter, an enormous black wolf, circled the yard below, slobbering and pawing the dirt. Chickens rustled in an open pen. A plump goat, tied to a post, bleated. The wolf ignored the animals, its icy howl shattering the quiet night. Melia's talons pushed deeper into Tatou's flesh. She couldn't risk losing hold of her friend.

The smell of the pixie's blood mixed with the smell of barnyard animals. The wolf snarled and leapt.

A short, stout figure tiptoed around the corner of the house. Melia could distinguish a patterned kerchief, tied beneath a strong-willed chin, and a rather large, hooked nose. Knobby hands white-knuckled a large, iron skillet. The wolf, focused on her and Tatou, didn't ever see its attacker.

"Bull's-eye."

A loud crunch resounded through the yard. The wolf collapsed into the dirt. Melia lowered her friend to the ground.

Their skillet-wielding savior whirled around, shaking her weapon high in the air. "And what kind of fools are you? I have half-a-mind to knock some sense into your pretty little heads." She reached Tatou and crossed her arms. Still gripping the skillet in one hand, she leaned over and frowned. "A pixie in Tyrannis? What's the world coming to?"

Tatou struggled to stand, but Melia had torn one of her wings. Off balance, her friend stumbled. The stout figure dropped the skillet and tried to pick up the pixie.

Tatou shrank from her hands.

Melia spread her wings into a shield. "Thank you for saving us from the wolf."

The stout figure leaned over to pick up her skillet. "You're welcome, I suppose."

Melia inclined her head in the direction of the wolf, still passed out cold. "What are you going to do when it wakes up?"

The wizened figure turned beady eyes on her. "Don't you worry. I'd never assume to count on the two of you for help." She wagged a crooked finger back and forth between Melia and Tatou. "Nych, you two"–she settled her hands on her hips with the skillet sticking out to one side –"were good for bait, not much else."

"Bait?" Melia asked.

The old dwarf–or whatever she was–turned on her heels. "That wolf wanted the both of you. He didn't even see me. Your pixie's hurt pretty badly," she hollered as she disappeared around the corner of the house.

The top lobe of Tatou's right wing was torn, and some blood congealed on her right shoulder where Melia's talons had shredded her skin. In her eagle form, there wasn't much she could do to ease her friend's pain. "I'm so sorry," she whispered.

"You saved my life."

"We need to get you inside that cottage."

The short, squat figure careened around the side of the little house with a bundle of rope. She walked straight to the wolf and bound its forelegs. "Got you now," she muttered. "You and your friends slinking around these woods at night. Some folks don't like it." She jerked hard on the rope, twisting it into a fancy knot. Then she grunted and shuffled over to work on its hind legs.

"Where is Aldous' friend?" Melia asked Tatou. "Do you think this dwarf will let us go inside?"

The pixie giggled, then winced.

"This is funny?"

Tatou pointed at the creature trussing the wolf as if it were a roasting chicken. "That's her."

It was hard to believe the gnarled creature was the eyes and ears of Tyrannis. "Are you sure?"

"Spring faeries are different."

"Spring faerie?" Melia asked. "She doesn't have any wings."

"Shh," Tatou said. "She's the only one left. Her name is Flora."

"Why such a big secret?"

"Queen Uriel's decree," Tatou said. "You can't talk about spring faeries, or say Flora's name in Illialei."

Melia sifted through the Albiana monarchy. Queen Olivia was Luisa's mother, Queen Uriel was Olivia's. "I don't understand." She watched the creature bind another coil of rope around the wolf's snout.

When the spring faerie was finished, she gave the wolf a swift kick in the rump with her tiny booted foot. Straightening her kerchief and wiping her brow, she walked toward Melia and Tatou. "Are you two going to stand there all night or come inside for milk and cookies?"

Melia flapped her wings. She didn't dare pick up her friend, and the spring faerie had already disappeared around the corner of her house. "Wait here," Melia told Tatou.

Just when Melia turned to follow the spring faerie, Flora returned with a wooden box. She set it down next to Tatou. The box was padded with a clean but frayed pillow. Flora reached her twisted hands toward the pixie. "There, there. If you can pop into my hands, love, we'll carry you inside like a little queen on a throne."

Tatou whimpered her pain as she crawled into the faerie's hands. Flora slipped her onto the pillow with a gentleness that belied her earlier display of gruff strength. Melia followed them around the house, across a wooden porch, and through a back door.

Flora headed toward a table surrounded by four chairs on one side of the room. A black cat sat upon it, in the middle of a stack of books, a loaf of bread, and a bowl of apples. Like Flora, she seemed most interested in Tatou, but Melia wasn't taking any chances. She perched on top of a chest that was pushed against the wall.

Braided rugs covered wooden floors which were worn but swept clean. Knickknacks filled a few scattered shelves. The smell of ginger, and something just-baked, lingered in the air. A kettle hung over a fireplace in the center of the back wall.

Flora made room for Tatou's box on the table. She instructed the pixie to lie on her stomach, then poked at her wings and shoulders.

Melia craned her head at Flora's loud clucking sounds. "How bad is it?"

"Let's put it this way, she won't be flying anywhere else with you tonight."

Melia forgot about the cat and glided down to the table. "But we have to go back to Illialei."

"Not this one. Not tonight." Flora wheezed as she waddled toward the fireplace. "She's got a dislocated shoulder, severe bruising of the upper body, a deep puncture in her neck, and one torn wing. I can mend her, but she'll need bed rest for a few days."

Melia turned around and met a serene, unblinking gaze. The cat appeared equal parts disinterested and unimpressed with her.

"That's Bella," Flora said. "Takes a bit more than a flower faerie shifted into an eagle to get the hair on the back of her neck to stand up."

Melia found the spring faerie's ability to see through her eagle form disconcerting. She hopped back toward Tatou.

"Don't you bother her." Flora filled the kettle with water from a pitcher on the counter. She reached into some cabinets and pulled down several tins and a glass jar. Herbs. She crumbled a mixture from the containers into a small bowl and pounded them with a pestle.

Gingersnaps sat upon one of the windowsills, cooling. Melia was hungry, but sweets were never her favorite thing to eat. As an eagle, the warm rounds looked even less appealing. Flora misunderstood her curious stare and brought the plate to the table. "You'll like these. They're the best." She grinned and ran back toward the fire where the water boiled.

Melia stepped away from the offering, disappointed.

The spring faerie returned to the table with full hands. She managed several bowls, a pair of scissors, and a skein of cottony fabric. She snipped away the blood-stained petals of Tatou's dress. When she found the rose-quartz beads that hung around Tatou's neck, her face transformed into a grimace. "Thieves!"

"Nych. Nych," Melia squawked.

Flora shot into the corner and grabbed a broom. When she came at Melia, her eyes glinted with fury. Melia beat her wings, preparing a counterattack.

"It was Aldous," Tatou squeaked.

"What have you done with him?" the spring faerie shouted. "I should have known! Who else but thieves and bandits would dare wander the Balyudor at night unprotected?" She swung her broom, missing Melia by mere inches. From the corner of her eye, Melia saw Bella crouch.

Tatou pulled herself up and gripped at the side of her box. "Aldous gave us the beads to show you as an introduction."

Flora continued to circle beneath Melia. "How do I know you're not lying?" She swung out again with the broom.

The bristles came down on Melia's left wing. Irate, she spun in the air. Her eyes darted between Bella and Flora. Black rage fueled her predatory nature. She could take out Flora's eye or deliver a death gash to the cat's neck. It would make a decent meal, but Flora would be on her in an instant with that broom. She glowered and screeched as the room narrowed. All she could see were Flora's beady eyes. Whatever influence had restrained her instincts for killing Basil in the Grand Library evaporated.

"Melia!"

She craned her head to the right. Tatou clung to the side of her wooden box. Tears streamed down the pixie's face. Melia's thoughts jumbled, diluting the black haze within. A mighty force smashed her to the ground.

"Why did you do that?" Tatou shouted.

Lying dazed on the floor, with her talons clawing air, Melia wondered what she'd done.

"Flora, I'm talking to you!"

Melia opened her eyes to Bella's intent stare. The black fur of the cat's face was inches from hers. In her peripheral vision, she thought she saw

Flora, broom still in hand, snicker.

Melia tried to roll over on her belly. At first she thought her left wing had been crushed because the pain was excruciating, but nothing cracked or flopped. She managed to rotate halfway, but momentum returned her to her back.

Flora shuffled in her direction. For a minute, Melia feared a powerful kick from her tiny boot. Instead the spring faerie leaned over and squinted in her face. "How do I know you didn't steal that bracelet from Aldous?"

"Because if we'd stolen it from him, we wouldn't have brought it to you!" Tatou said.

Flora rocked back on her heels. "It's been a long time since anyone from Illialei has wanted anything to do with me."

No doubt.

The spring faerie wanted to examine the damage she'd inflicted. Melia pulled away. Aldous had been far too generous when he'd described her as prickly.

"Let me set you on the table and make sure your wing's not broken," Flora cooed.

The sudden shift in her personality made Melia's head spin, but somewhere between treating Tatou's wounds and making a salve for Melia's wing–Flora had bruised a tendon when she'd smashed her with the broom–Melia's feelings toward the spring faerie softened. A deep sorrow surfaced in Flora's eyes whenever she wasn't bustling around her kitchen, or tending their injuries.

Minutes later, Melia stood on the table. Flora sat in one of her tiny chairs with her chin resting in her hands, a glum expression on her face. They both watched Tatou slumbering in the box between them. The spring faerie had given the pixie a sleeping draught.

Aware she lacked her friend's charm, Melia wracked her brain for a way to ask for the help she needed. Her eyes settled on the rose beads. "Aldous told us you know more about what goes on in Tyrannis than anyone."

Flora dropped her hands from beneath her chin and slipped them into the pocket of her wrinkled apron. The long sleeved red-patterned dress she wore beneath the buttery-colored apron clashed with the kerchief on her head. The dress was a kaleidoscope of brick tones, the kerchief a crimson plaid. It was a strange outfit. "Aldous said that about me?"

"Yes." It was hard for Melia to believe the rumpled old creature sitting across the table was a faerie of any kind.

"Is he still a handsome devil?"

Handsome and devil weren't the two words that came to mind when Melia thought of the palace librarian.

Flora waved her hand in the air. "No need to answer that, I'm sure he is." She was blushing.

Melia was glad she wasn't in her faerie form. She might have giggled, and then Flora might have boxed her. "Why don't you visit him?" she asked. Flora's wrinkled face soured, but Melia forged ahead. "You could travel to the palace library and see Aldous yourself."

Not a happy face.

"After Tatou mends."

The spring faerie's features blossomed into a full-blown grimace.

"Not a good idea?" Melia guessed.

"I'll die before I ever set foot in that treacherous Cathedral Palace again, I will."

"All right," Melia croaked.

Flora snorted and crossed her arms over her heaving bosom. "Those Albianas! Daughters of Light–bah!"

Melia was tempted to ask her about Queen Uriel's decree, but the spring faerie was so unpredictable, she might get out her broom again. Melia tried to steer the conversation to Plantine and Lord Goring.

"My sister has been kidnapped. That's why we're here. That's why Aldous gave us the bracelet. He said you could help us."

Flora's eyes narrowed to slits. She clasped her hands together and rested them on the table. "He overestimates my abilities. I wouldn't be knowing a thing about anyone being kidnapped, missy."

"But Aldous says you know everything that goes on in Tyrannis."

"As I said, he gives me far too much credit."

"Surely, you've heard something about a troll and group of muannai who crossed the Maeldun Bridge?"

"Nothing."

"Do you know Lord Goring? My mother thinks he's the one

responsible."

Flora showed the palms of her hands. "Then go bother him."

"I have no idea where to find him, or why he took her in the first place. My sister's not well. I need to rescue her."

"Aren't you the hero?" Flora said in a rather nasty tone.

Although Melia squawked every word in eagle, the spring faerie continued to address her in the common tongue. "Why won't you help me?"

Flora snatched up the beads and rubbed them between her fingers. "I came to Tyrannis for good reason. Aldous–and everyone else worth their salt in Illialei–knows that. I'd appreciate you reminding him that I'm not one of Queen Luisa's poppets."

"But this has nothing to do with the queen. It's about my sister. Please."

"I had a sister once," Flora said.

"Then you understand how important this is to me."

"There's something that's very important to me, too."

"What is it?"

The spring faerie's face darkened. "I want to see Illialei burn."

Melia pulled her head back into her neck and searched the spring faerie's eyes for a hint that she was clairvoyant, that she knew about her visions somehow.

"Wh-why?"

Flora glared back at her, eyes on fire. "You really don't know, do you?"

"They wouldn't even tell me your name," Melia admitted.

The spring faerie relaxed back into her chair. "Things are changing in Faerie," she said. "The Albiana are going to get their due." She sounded like Melia's father. "Rescuing your sister won't stop what's coming." Now she sounded like Melia's mother.

"What do you mean?" Melia asked.

Flora wrestled with something on the tip of her tongue. She needed motivation to reveal her secrets.

Melia searched the room. Her gaze settled on a stunning silver bowl on one of the knickknack shelves. Among the worn wood and collection of dull stone carvings, it dazzled like a golden egg. diamonds, emeralds, and sapphires encrusted its rim. The silver it was forged from rippled with a mysterious force.

26. Secrets

Flora almost knocked over her chair. "What are you doing?"

The damn eagle was perched on the shelf in front of the dwarf basin. It spread its wings to keep her from it.

The spring faerie jumped up and down. Her booted feet rattled the hardwood floors. "I knew it! Bella, do something!"

The cat opened one eye but otherwise remained immobile.

"What do you know?" the stupid bird cawed.

"You snuck over here in the dead of night to steal it!"

"It's beautiful. Must be worth a lot of gold."

"I'd never sell it," the spring faerie said.

Flora tried to reach around the bird and grab the basin, but its wingspan was almost the length of her height. Even with one wing injured, the bird had no trouble blocking her.

"Where did you get it?" the eagle asked.

Flora considered her broom, or maybe the skillet. She didn't think Aldous knew about the basin, but what if he did? After everything she'd been through, could he betray her? "Did Aldous send you for it?"

"No, he told me you could help me find my sister. But if you won't help me, then I'll take it."

The eagle had finally got her attention.

Although it had been a long time since Flora had carried weapons, not many creatures stood up to her. She studied the blue-black feathers and determined gaze of the one who challenged her now.

Drip. Drip. Drip.

A glimmer of warmth reached the outermost shell of her frozen heart. The black eagle was much more than a flower faerie who had shifted her form; she was a warrior–one who didn't know she could fight yet.

Flora rubbed her chest as if circulation could alleviate the memories that had shattered her heart into icy shards. Oh, if she kept to herself and gave all her attention to Bella, her goat, the chickens, and her garden; if she made enough soap to trade with Gumf and the muannai at the marketplace; if she baked blueberry pie–or ginger cookies–every single day, the chill didn't bite so hard. But Flora had to admit it never went away.

It never would.

She sighed. The genocide of the spring faeries, the great warrior race of Illialei, was seared into her flesh and bones. They'd questioned Uriel Albiana's right to reign, and had paid dearly. Flora had no doubt, she would hear the cries of their burning on her death bed. She deserved as much. She hadn't saved a single one of them.

Flora lunged for the basin one more time. Gazing into its mysterious eye was all she had left. She wasn't going to lose it. The eagle fended her off. Maybe if she gave the bird what it wanted, it would go away and leave her alone. "Everything was just fine until your stinking sister had to go and get herself kidnapped."

The spring faerie marched over to the kitchen counter, picked up a pitcher, then headed out the back door. She returned and slammed the pitcher down on the table with such force water sloshed over its rim. When she was sure she had the eagle's attention, she pressed her hands flat on the wood surface. "I'm going to help you. But don't you dare breathe a word of what you're about to see to anyone. Got that?"

"Yes," the eagle said.

Flora assumed it was lying. She folded her arms across her chest. "I've got friends you don't want to meet. If you cross me, I'll make sure you never see your sniveling excuse for a sister alive again. Got that?"

"Yes."

That sounded a bit more sincere. "All right then. Bring me the bowl."

The eagle gripped the bowl's rim with its talons. It was light, even with all the jewels circling its edges. The eagle still dropped it. The basin made a loud bang and careened on its side.

Flora retrieved the rolling disc herself. "Dwarf metalwork is the finest in the enchanted world–damn near indestructible." The spring faerie placed the bowl in front of her, then filled it with water from the pitcher. She stared at her reflection. When had she gotten so old and square-looking? She tugged at the knot of her kerchief beneath her chin and tried not to think of her youth–when she'd gotten up every morning at dawn to train in the Footing Fields with her kin.

"How is this going to help me find Plantine?" the eagle asked.

Flora ignored the question.

The bird ruffled its feathers and paced the width of the table. With each step its talons rapped against the wood.

"Would it be too much for you to keep still?" Flora steeled her mind. Umbra always tried to seize her inner world as soon as the eye opened. She never let him. The battle was their shared ritual, the price she paid to use the basin's magic. Flora dreaded it as much as she welcomed it. It kept her mind sharp. But she couldn't deny, of late, that every time she used the basin, Umbra grew stronger.

Flora pushed everything else out of her mind and stared into the bowl. A mist rose from the water's placid surface. It smelled of wood and rosemary. "Would you look at that?"

The eagle pulled back. The bowl had shown the bird's reflection as a young faerie with pale skin, deep blue eyes, dark brown hair, and a strange mark on her forehead. The bird eyed Flora questioningly.

"It shows us things, not always what we expect," she said.

Flora returned her attention to the vapors rising from the bowl. It was as if the water boiled, but the water's surface remained still. A mist that smelled of forest herbs wreathed them. She nodded forward, her nose almost touching the water. The misty vapors turned from stone-white to cloudy-grey to smoky-charcoal.

The eye opened.

There was little light in the scene it showed. Two shadowed figures spoke. Sometimes Flora could hear. She turned her head, placing one ear close to the water. She strained to listen.

"She's agreed to marry you?" The rough voice sounded as though it belonged to a troll.

"Yes, she believes it's what Elynus would want. When will we reach the stronghold?"

Flora peered down at the basin. A muannaye towered over a troll. She recognized Lord Zachariah Goring. A mast was behind them, its sails open and full. They stood on the deck of a ship at sea.

She turned her head and tried to hear more. Nothing.

The spring faerie gazed into the bowl. The image whirled away. Another one appeared. A female with waist-length hair lay on a bed. Although the girl's eyes were closed, white gems sparkled on her earlobes. A low-cut gown exposed a matching necklace that draped her breast. The dress' velvet bodice rose and lowered in a steady rhythm. Definitely asleep.

Curious. The girl clutched a crystal vial in her hand. Flora searched for more clues. A fur blanket covered the bed, but the floor of the room was rough wood. Flora sensed a rocking motion as the source of light–unseen by her–swayed.

A ship's cabin.

She observed the girl once more. There was something familiar about her face. Flora searched her memories and gasped.

The jarring realization broke the basin's trance.

Across from her, the eagle shivered. Flora jumped from her chair and rounded the table. She touched its feathers. They were freezing.

Umbra.

He'd gone after the bird, and it was losing the battle. She held the back of the eagle's neck with her thumb and forefinger and shook hard. "Snap out of it!"

The bird was dazed.

Flora started a fire and filled the kettle with water. She placed several smooth stones close to the flames and soaked a cloth in the warmed water. She wiped down the eagle's wings until they didn't feel like ice. She wrapped the hot stones in dry rags to make a nest. She helped the eagle settle into it. She didn't stop her ministrations until the bird returned her gaze. When the bird twitched its wings and squawked, Flora returned to her chair.

The mist had evaporated. The bowl sat empty of liquid. The pixie slumbered in her wooden box. Bella slept, curled in a furry ball, on one of the braided rugs.

The cottage was safe. Umbra was gone.

"I'm better, now," the eagle said. "Thank you."

It seemed afraid. "What did you say your mother's name was?" Flora asked.

"I didn't, but it's Pressina."

Flora stroked her long chin with her thumb and forefinger. "I didn't realize."

"Does it make a difference?"

"It explains why the muannaye snatched your sister."

"What do you mean?" the eagle asked.

"You don't know, do you?"

The bird hopped from foot to foot, silent.

Flora wasn't surprised Pressina had never shared her legacy of heartbreak and injustice with her daughters. "No, your mother never would have told you."

"I don't know what you're talking about."

Flora sighed. "I don't suppose you do. Queen Olivia's decree."

"I've lived in Illialei almost my entire life, and I've never heard of any decrees until tonight. First Uriel's–"

The blood drained from the spring faerie's face. She took the bowl back to the counter, wiped it off, and replaced it where it belonged on the shelf. Her hands shook the entire time.

She returned to her small kitchen and took two metal cups and one small plate from her tiny cupboard. She dipped them into a wooden pail. She set the plate on the ground. Milk for Bella. She brought the two filled cups to the table and pushed one in the eagle's direction. The tremor in her hands had stopped. Just the thought of eating helped. "Can't have cookies without fresh goat milk."

Flora reached toward the plate of gingersnaps. When both her hands were full, she stacked the nine cookies she'd retrieved into three small columns in front of her. She didn't speak until she'd eaten every last crumb and drained her cup and the eagle's. Apparently, the eagle didn't care for goat's milk. Or cookies.

Flora released a burp as she wiped the corners of her mouth. "You're welcome to go outside and rustle up something more to your tastes."

"You haven't told me about my sister."

Flora crossed her arms. "No, I haven't."

The eagle waited.

"Umbra got you, didn't he?" Flora asked.

The eagle flapped its wings.

Flora shifted back in her chair. "I'm still stronger than him. But you and your sister are a different matter altogether. For you the basin is dangerous. I'd never peer into its waters again if I were you."

The eagle indicated the bowl with its beak. "How did you come to have this?"

Flora would never forget that day. It had changed her life. "I found it while I was foraging for herbs, at the base of the Ruadain. Stumbled right over it, half-buried in the dirt. I've kept it safe all these years. And no one needs to know I have it."

"How did you know it was magic?" the eagle asked.

"It was obvious to me that it was dwarf-made. And most things dwarves forge have some magic in them. Like I said, morc than half of it was deep in the ground the day I found it. It was filthy. I took it to the beach for a good rinsing. The waters of the Great White Sea showed me its power for seeing. No other water opens the eye. The well behind my house is deep. It reaches a water table fed by the sea. I can use the basin's eye whenever I want."

"What do you see?" the eagle asked.

"These days, I usually see Umbra first, but not tonight. He went after you, didn't he?"

The bird bowed its head.

"I can use the basin's magic with no ill-consequence, but you'd be wise to forget you've ever seen it," Flora said.

"I will, if you help me find my sister. Did you see her?"

Whatever had happened when the bird stared into the basin had left it shaken. But it wasn't going to confide in her. Flora pointed at the bowl.

She wanted to be sure. "This will be our secret."

The eagle nodded.

Flora rubbed her mouth. That time she believed the bird. "All right. Your sister is on a ship. She's asleep in one of the cabins, but she's not tied up. Are you sure she was kidnapped?"

"Yes."

"She's being treated quite well for a captive. She wore a gown. Jewels dripped from her ears and neck." Flora tugged at her earlobe. "She's going to marry the muannaye."

"That's not possible," the eagle said. "You didn't see my sister."

Flora shrugged. "Looks the same as Pressina when she was young."

The eagle flinched.

"Your sister is sleeping peacefully. She's not worried about returning home."

"They've drugged her, given her some potion," the eagle said.

"She held a crystal vial in her hand, that's true."

"Where are they taking her?"

There was only one stronghold in Faerie. "The stronghold of Calashai."

"But why there?"

"For the wedding?"

The eagle hopped in an agitated circle. "Why is the basin dangerous to me and my sister?"

Flora pushed herself away from the table, so that her chair rocked on two legs. The eagle deserved to know the secret the cowards of Illialei kept for their queen. "The Albiana blood that runs in your veins makes you vulnerable to Umbra."

The bird stopped moving. "You're mistaken." Flora pressed her lips together as the eagle came toward her. "I'm no Albiana."

"Queen Luisa went to the mortal world," Flora said. "She was just a princess then. When she didn't return, Queen Olivia–"

"Lukas Skai left Queen Olivia after Luisa was born." It was one of the few facts of Illialei's history Melia retained from her half-hearted studies at the Bryndale school. Probably because she'd always found the lack of kings in Faerie curious. "She had no consort, no one to father another a child."

Flora shrugged. "Olivia has had plenty of lovers."

The bird crashed around her cottage in reckless flight. Flora covered her head with her arms. The pixie rolled over on her pillow but didn't wake up.

The eagle returned to the table. "You're lying."

"The Albiana bury their secrets deep in decrees and silence."

The eagle flapped its wings.

"It's true that her father has never been named, but your mother was raised as the throne's heir until her seventeenth birthday. By all accounts, she was a dutiful daughter, faithful to her mother in every way. But when Luisa returned from the mortal world, Olivia made her decision. Pressina would never sit on the throne. The creatures of Illialei were very obliging when it came to forgetting Queen Olivia had ever had a second daughter. Because–"

"There's always been only one daughter and heir to the throne." The eagle choked over the words.

"Your mother felt betrayed. When she left the palace, she made it clear she'd never forgive her mother–or her sister. Queen Olivia issued her decree: No one in Illialei was to ever speak of Pressina–or her descendants –as Albiana again. None of you exist."

Flora watched the bird. She wasn't going to bring up the sapphire lily unless it asked.

27. Interrogation

The walls of Flora's cottage closed in on Melia. Black rage incinerated her veins. She needed fresh air. She needed to fly.

Outside the cottage, she bounced from branch to branch. Under the canopy of the Balyudor's leafy ceiling, it was the time of night when even creatures that wandered under the cover of darkness slept. Against that deep silence, every movement Melia made cracked like thunder.

She tried to find a calm place in the storm of her mind, but there was none. From what Flora had said, the truth of her bloodline was common knowledge in Illialei–even though nobody talked about it. To her.

Flashes of memory cascaded through her: the odd look, the quick whisper, and the sudden silences. She'd always attributed them to her being a half-faerie with no wings, but now, the occasional solicitous deference, or appreciated and undeserved respect also fit. She pieced the images together as though they were beads on a string and made them whole.

Everyone knew.

Is that why Verbena accused her of plotting with her father? Because of Queen Olivia's decree? Did the flower faerie believe she sought revenge? Was the silencing of their Albiana bloodline the crime her father had referred to?

It was a betrayal, but it wasn't worthy of war.

Thoughts collided in Melia's head. Hours ago, she'd comprehended the place of refuge the library had become for Plantine among the elves, now she felt betrayed by them–and Tatou.

Everyone knew ... except for Melia and her sisters. Queen Olivia's decree didn't matter. They should have told her.

And what about her mother?

Melia began to understand the circumstances that drove her, but it didn't quell her fury. Blackness seethed within. There were too many secrets.

Her eagle belly interrupted with demands for food. When was the last time she'd eaten? She couldn't remember past the hare she'd dropped for the wolf that had chased her and Tatou into Flora's yard.

Plantine's strange admission at Pebble Rock bubbled up from the cauldron of mire boiling within her. It hadn't made much sense at the time, but now Melia wondered. Did the black wolf bound in Flora's yard have any connection to the one her sister had seen with her father's ghost? To Umbra? And what about the basin? Plantine hadn't described it, but what if the bowl Flora wanted kept secret was the same one their father wanted Plantine to find?

Melia never wanted to get near that bowl again. The encounter she'd had in its smoky haze had been worse than the one she'd had on the way to the Cathedral Palace. Umbra had made it clear he was going after her sister, and there was nothing she could do to stop him.

But she had to.

Melia peered at the cottage through the trees. Flora thought Tatou would be strong enough to fly in two or three days.

She couldn't sit around that long and do nothing.

Plantine sailed on a ship to the stronghold of Calashai. The stronghold was in Aldaine. Much too far to reach by morning.

Her chances of finding the ship at sea were worse.

Besides, what could she do alone? Peck out an army of muannai's eyes?

Dawn was close. The elves, specifically Tuck, waited at the Grand Library. He loved Plantine, and if anything Flora had said were true, Melia would need his help to save her sister.

She needed to return to Illialei.

The Cathedral Palace came into view just as the physical spasms that preceded Melia's transformation from eagle to faerie began. She took one last look east before her descent. The fog that had shrouded Southend Pier and the rest of Illialei's coastline the past night had lifted. Radiant dawn glistened across the Great White Sea.

An unsettling realization distracted Melia as she tossed head over heels into the grass.

Plantine sailed on a ship.

Last night, Melia had searched the rivers and the coves along the Granite Cliffs for vessels, but it had never occurred to her that Plantine's kidnappers would have been so bold as to dock in the harbor at Illialei.

She stood up. Her arm and shoulder tender. She massaged them while she scanned the western horizon. It was a waste of time. If the ship Plantine was on still sailed in Illialei's waters, it was out of sight from where she stood, land-locked. She pounded her fist against her forehead. If she'd searched the shoreline last night, Plantine might already be back at the tree house–safe.

A ferocious rumble in her stomach reminded her she needed more food. Although she'd snatched a fish from the Undine's waters on her flight home, she felt faint, as though she might pass out.

The palace orchard was straight ahead. She stalked toward the thick grove of trees.

After harvesting a couple of the golden fruits, she settled on a silky patch of grass. The apples were crisp, tart, and enormous. She ate them too fast. With her stomach full, her eyelids grew heavy.

Plantine's voice jerked her awake. *"Melia, are you there?"*

"Yes," Melia replied in her mind.

"Good," Plantine said. *"I need your help."*

"I'm going to find you," Melia assured her.

"There's no danger."

"But you were kidnapped."

"Don't worry. They've given me a healing drink to stop the fading until I reach the stronghold of Calashai. I'm going to be married and sit on the stronghold's throne."

Melia's whole body stiffened. *"What about Tuck?"*

No response.

Melia tried to recall what else Flora had told her she'd seen in the basin. She'd no sooner thought of the bowl than her sister seized upon it.

"Thank you," Plantine said. *"I knew you'd help me find it."*

Melia's mind shrank from her sister's unexpected appreciation, but she'd woken too late to the danger. Plantine probed her mind with a tender precision Melia couldn't deflect. Her head throbbed as Flora's tiny yellow cottage, with its steepled roof and windows trimmed in green, blazed in her mind. A sensation that bordered between pleasure and pain consumed her. She needed to slam the door of her mind shut but found herself unable to do so.

"Stop fighting me," Plantine murmured.

How was her little sister doing it? She invaded Melia's mind with a dexterity their father had never achieved and Melusine had only dreamed of.

Halfway between sleep and wakefulness, Melia struggled to reach full consciousness. She tried to bring forth pictures of the apple trees surrounding her, the fields in the distance, the sun climbing high in the sky above her. Each image washed away beneath Plantine's gentle but persistent onslaught.

"Show it to me, show it to me, show it to me."

Her sister's words became an invading hum, infiltrating every nook and cranny of Melia's mind. Where had her sister garnered the strength for such an assault? Yesterday morning she'd hardly been able to maintain their silent connection.

Melia pressed her hands to her head as Plantine's relentless penetration continued. The intricate design of the basin's jewels and the luster of its silver metal burned in her mind. There was no doubt her sister had received the picture, exquisite in its detail.

"Thank you. I must go, but when you find the sword..."

An inner silence descended. Melia clamped down on her mind, but it was too late. Flora and Tatou were in grave danger.

She jumped to her feet and raced toward the palace.

28. The Priest from Idonne

An odd stove-like box sat outside the library doors. Strange. It hadn't been there the day before. Melia leaned over to smell burning wood chips mingled with a floral perfume. Tatou would have been able to identify the precise ingredients if she were there.

But she wasn't.

The pixie was far away–in danger–and it was Melia's fault. If she could only shift into an eagle at will. Frustrated with her limitations, the half-faerie considered her options. There weren't many. Even riding the fastest horse, it would take more than a day to reach Flora's cottage.

Better to fly hard when the sun set.

Melia hurried through the library doors. Endless rows of shelves and haphazard aisles created a deserted maze that offered no clue as to the direction she should go. Her concern for Tatou and Flora only increased her agitation and decreased her ability to think clearly. She attempted to retrace the same route the pixie had taken the day before, but she heard nothing, and no one came to greet her. When a large white rat startled her, they both jumped. It scurried away. Distracted as she watched it disappear into the shadows, she stubbed her toe on the leg of a wooden table. Objects collapsed like dominoes. A large globe rolled into a crystal obelisk, which knocked a wooden box off the table's edge, sending a shower of metal coins exploding everywhere. The floor quaked beneath her. Bookshelves rattled. Melia reached out with both hands to steady the tall cases. A heavy book slammed down on her big toe. She yelped. The pain was excruciating. Before she could pick up the book, an enormous clove-colored tiger bounded into view. It raced straight toward her. Melia blinked. It wasn't her imagination. She turned to run and twisted over her tender toe. Her tailbone hit the floor first. The palms of her hand smashed down next, jamming her wrists.

The giant cat leapt.

Melia closed her eyes and screamed.

The tiger landed above her, boxing her in with an enormous chest and four menacing paws. If she hadn't believed the large cat was real, its animal heat and fur against her arms and legs proved it wasn't some hallucination. She convulsed and screamed again.

The beast lifted its head and roared.

Her mind blanked.

"Sinjiin, that's enough."

"It's Melia. Call that thing off of her." She recognized Tuck's voice.

Aldous huffed and puffed. "Is she all right?"

A young man with dark, tousled hair walked toward her. He grabbed the scruff of the tiger's neck and pulled the great cat away from her.

Nandana's mark blazed. Melia's heart thundered. She stared at his green eyes, his cheeks bronzed by the sun. She rubbed her eyes. Nothing exploded or burned or died. This wasn't a vision either. He was real.

Standing alert, he scratched behind the tiger's ear with one hand. A brown cloak draped over his shoulders. It was the same one he wore in her visions.

He stared at her.

The thump of her heart threatened to deafen her. She didn't know whether to run or shout. She wished she could fly back to Flora's cottage and yell to Tatou, He's here! She itched to prove his presence, to touch him, but she couldn't will a single finger to move. So she remained on the library floor, while Nandana's mark burned a hole in her forehead.

She didn't even know his name.

"You're shaking," Tuck said.

It was true, her arms and legs jittered. She tried to stand up, but her arms and legs wouldn't work.

Aldous peered from around the tree elf. "Oh dear, she's as white as a saucer of milk. Boys, carry her over to one of the sofas. We must get some tea and honey in her."

Tuck lifted her ankles.

The stranger slid his hands under her shoulders. "Ready?" he asked.

The physical contact was so reviving, Melia melted into the sensation.

"Are you ready?" he asked again.

Her neck and shoulders tightened. What if she stuttered? She managed a stiff nod. His face was so close to hers, she closed her eyes to create some emotional distance.

He lifted her as though she were weightless. When they started walking, he ordered Tuck to slow down, Aldous to move that table, and Sinjiin to stay out of the way.

It was all an incredible dream. She was distraught by her encounters with Umbra, Flora, Plantine, and the tiger. When she opened her eyes, he'd be gone.

The warmth from Nandana's mark spread, it pulsed through her body. She recalled the Illustrator's words: Like you, he lives in a world where he feels like he doesn't belong.

Melia opened one eye. His chin was so close to hers, she could smell his sweat and a hint of the sea. He watched ahead, navigating the library's aisles. When he returned her gaze and smiled, her heart stopped.

"Are you all right?" he asked.

His voice came in through her ears but settled in her belly. The sound of it filled an emptiness she didn't even know existed. Her own laughter came out soft, unexpected. It seemed to satisfy him that nothing terrible was wrong with her.

The crackle of burning logs and smell of wood smoke let her know they'd arrived in the library's west wing. They settled her onto a sofa. When his hands were gone, Melia placed hers over her chest and took several deep breaths.

She watched him walk away through half-open eyes. Aldous produced a cool cloth for her forehead and directed Tuck to prepare a cup of chamomile tea with a generous portion of honey.

"She looks like she's seen a ghost," the stranger said.

Melia absorbed the sound of his voice. It was really him.

He stood to the side, ramrod straight, with feet spread wide and hands behind his back. His brown cloak covered most of his height. He wore high leather boots. Melia remembered the light in Melusine's eyes when she'd first described Raymond. She began to understand.

The young man returned Melia's stare. Her cheeks tingled. She turned to Aldous and Tuck. They saw him, too. They heard him speak, too. She looked back at her stranger. His eyes were the shifting colors of green in the forest on a summer day.

The warmth radiating from Melia's forehead persisted. She pressed her fingers against Nandana's mark. The warmth transferred to her fingers. She pressed the palm of her hand flat against her skin. Images of him from her visions flashed through her mind. She dropped her hand. The mental pictures faded, and her stomach fluttered.

How was he here? Where was he from? Each question spilled over the next like water tripping over rocks. What was his name? She pushed her palm back against her forehead. The images from her visions returned. The same warm feelings rushed through her veins, and the beat of her heart found the same steady rhythm. Two more times she returned her palm to her forehead.

Aldous shuffled toward her. "Melia, are you all right? Did you hit your head?"

She smiled. Even for a half-faerie living in the enchanted world, the emerald-eyed stranger's appearance was an unfathomable thing.

The old elf relieved the younger one of the cup of tea he'd prepared. "Tuck, help her sit up."

When they had her sitting, Aldous handed the cup to her. When she could hold it without her hands shaking, she risked speaking. "Where is the tiger?"

The stranger pointed to the furry, clove-colored mound curled at his feet. Her hand jiggled and she spilled a bit of tea.

"Sinjiin won't hurt you," he said. "He detained you earlier because you were eavesdropping."

"Detained?" Her temper flared. "He lunged at me."

The tiger stretched its enormous legs. Sharp claws the length of Melia's fingers extended from the pads on its feet. No wonder Basil was nowhere to be found.

"The tiger's hearing is acute. When he heard you running away, he meant to stop you."

She recalled the loud crash of objects falling when she'd stubbed her toe. The tiger's hearing wasn't that acute. "I wasn't eavesdropping. I was lost."

"In the library?"

"It's only the second time she's been here," Tuck said.

"Unlike you, Ryder, Melia doesn't live in a world of books," Aldous said.

His name was Ryder.

"Then I owe you my most sincere apology," he said. "The things I must discuss with your friends"–he indicated the librarian and his apprentice –"are sensitive in nature. If Sinjiin was overzealous, it was on my account. He looks after me."

The tiger growled as if he resented the last claim.

Perhaps it was her nerves, but the tiger's protest struck Melia as funny. She giggled. "If I'd known he was so caring, perhaps I wouldn't have been so petrified when he landed on top of me."

"Sinjiin is a mage from the Hidden City," Ryder whispered. "He travels as a tiger to conceal his identity."

The most powerful mages in the enchanted world dwelled in the Hidden City. They seldom ventured beyond its mystical borders. Their magic was so strong, they feared being targeted for abduction or coercion. Melia wondered what had drawn the tiger from its safe haven. Her gaze returned to the oversized cat. "Then, he must be a giant."

"Physical transformation often reflects the size of the heart," Ryder said.

The large cat rested its majestic head on its paws. Melia's regard seemed to please him. She wondered if his animal instincts could sense her body becoming calm.

"Are you feeling better?" Ryder asked.

"Yes, the tea has helped." It was a lie. The sweet drink had upset her stomach. Something else had calmed her. *Him.*

Ryder's eyes darkened to the deepest shade of forest green. Had he hoped she might admit the truth? She couldn't. The mere thought of confessing his unique effect on her tied her tongue in knots.

Aldous dropped into his wing chair. "The two of you"–he pointed to Ryder and Melia–"have common interests."

Her heart leapt. Nandana was right. Ryder had been called to her. She sat on her hands to restrain herself from returning her palms to her forehead as she fixed her gaze on the old wood elf. Maybe he could shed some light on the mysterious connection that had brought her and Ryder together this morning.

"Ryder is from Idonne," Aldous said.

The Idonnic Prophecy. Melia set her cup and saucer down on the low table before her. That couldn't be good news, no matter how much the mark on her forehead tingled.

"He's a member of the Order of the Idonnai, and I believe his arrival on our shores is most fortuitous."

Not if he believed the prophecy.

The tiger lifted his head and made a sound between a grunt and roar.

"He disagrees?" Melia asked.

Ryder's face reddened. "What I must discuss with the librarian is confidential. So if you've recovered from your scare, I'll come back later to speak to the elves."

Melia's heart careened. He didn't know her or recognize her. He had no idea they searched for the same answers. Maybe they didn't. Maybe Nandana was wrong and the mark meant nothing.

Aldous motioned to Ryder, who remained standing like a statue beyond the sofa and chairs. "There is no need for secrets between those present. Please, sit. Hear what Melia has to say. You'll soon realize your concerns are the same." The old elf looked at her. "Where is Tatou?"

How could she have forgotten? "They're in trouble," Melia said.

"Who?" Ryder asked.

Tuck bolted from his seat. "What news do you have of Plantine?"

Melia couldn't help but wonder if the tree elf's wiry build owed anything to his inability to sit still for any length of time. "I'm not certain about my sister, but if we don't set out for the Balyudor soon, whoever seeks the basin will hurt Tatou, and maybe, Flora."

Ryder's eyes fired with attention. "You've found Isolt's magical basin? The one forged by Haff and Gweff in the depths of the Ruadain?"

Flora hadn't mentioned Isolt–or Haff or Gweff, but how many magical basins forged by dwarves could there be in Faerie? Melia nodded.

"Where is it?" he asked.

Melia would have told him anything, but she looked to Aldous for direction.

"You may speak freely," the elf said.

Melia recounted the past night's events. Ryder interrupted her with questions about Flora; he seemed to find it hard to believe that she possessed the basin. When Melia arrived at the point where she and Flora peered into the bowl, she skipped over her own encounter with Umbra and told them what the spring faerie had seen.

"That can't be true," Tuck said.

Melia winced. She'd hoped to pull him aside and explain her sister's abrupt marriage plans in private.

The tree elf's face flushed red. "I know that's not what she wants."

Melia recalled the effect of the drink she'd shared with Plantine in her vision. "You're right. They're giving her a potion. It strengthens her disintegrating body while it alters her mind. We must stop the wedding. If vows are spoken ..."

Every court in the enchanted world viewed the breaking of any sacred vow harshly–and the vows of matrimony were considered the most sacred. If Plantine exchanged an oath of marriage with the muannaye, there would be no remedy. Whatever tender feelings flourished between Tuck and Plantine would be off-limits for eternity. Tuck would be as guilty as her sister if he pursued her. But after Plantine's interrogation in the apple orchard that morning, Melia had to think of Tatou and Flora first.

She turned to Aldous. "I'm afraid my sister's going to tell the muannaye that Flora has the basin." She covered her mouth with her hands. By speaking the spring faerie's name in Illialei, she'd violated Uriel's decree. "What's going to happen?"

Aldous looked puzzled.

"I said–" Melia mouthed Flora's name.

"Ah. Not to worry. We've cast a protective barrier over the library. Only those welcome can enter. Anyone unwelcome will lose interest in our thousands of books this morning and wander away with no recall. It should hold for a while. We filled the kiln with plenty of incense to insure enough time to discuss the things which must not be discussed in Illialei this morning. So please, continue."

Relief flooded Melia's body, but she couldn't remember what she'd been talking about.

"You were telling us about Flora and the basin," Aldous prompted.

Melia searched their grim faces. "She keeps it out in the open for anyone who enters her cottage to see. We must bring her"–it still didn't feel safe to say Flora's name–"the spring faerie, Tatou, and the bowl to Illialei."

"A spring faerie lives?" Ryder asked. "I thought they all burned when Queen Uriel proclaimed eternal summer over the lands she ruled."

Melia's chest squeezed. "What?"

Aldous rubbed the palm of his hand against his forehead as though it would never stop hurting. Everything pleasant drained from his face. "One survived. Her name is Flora. Most spring faeries never traveled to the mortal world, but she was always"–he paused, searching for the right way to describe her–"unusual. When Uriel made the decision to banish springtime from Illialei, being on the other side was the only thing that saved her."

Sinjiin's keening roar carried the heaviness Melia struggled to absorb.

"By the time the cries of her kin, burning alive in the fields, reached her in the mortal world, there was nothing Flora could do. She returned in time to bury the dead, but left Illialei soon after," Aldous said.

Melia's arms stretched at her side like two clubs with curled fists. Until last night, she'd never heard of the spring faeries or their murder. No one ever talked about it. The memory of her father's words chilled her to the bone. There are no innocents in Illialei. She looked from Aldous to Tuck. She thought of Nandana and Tatou. Everyone knew, but no one said anything. No one did anything. This was worse than what Queen Olivia had done to her mother. Much worse. Melia's stomach revolted. No wonder Flora wanted Illialei to burn.

"She's lived for years isolated in the Balyudor," Aldous said. "And she's no friend to the Albiana. She won't return to Illialei, or allow the basin to be brought here."

"You're right." Melia's skin crawled. Uriel was her great-grandmother.

29. Nandana's Mark

Ryder sensed Melia's distress. He wanted to comfort her, but wasn't sure how. Other than the time he'd spent with Shilda, he knew little about females. And Melia was very different from the Idonnic herbalist who had been like a mother to him.

It wasn't only the blue mark on her forehead, which was a few shades darker than her eyes flickering between worry and hope. Something compelled him to gaze at her. It was the same thing that made him yearn to be near her, and made him never want to leave her side. Then it dawned on him.

The thing that had burned in his heart, the thing that had pushed his hand, made up his mind, and pulled him across the Great White Sea from Idonne, had been Melia.

It didn't make sense, but he'd come to Faerie because of her.

Stealing Koldis from the Idonnic Library archives; saving the mage–lying like a striped fur boulder beside him; risking everything to stop Umbra's incarnation; they were all excuses for something he'd been unable to explain.

Until now.

Ryder had never seen a creature as graceful, or as mysterious, or as vulnerable as the one seated between the elves. He sensed the great burden around her, and remembered his childhood dreams of being a hero.

He would be her hero.

He would help her save her friend and the spring faerie. Her sister too.

Aldous pointed to Melia and Ryder. "You two must work together."

Yes, finding the basin and safeguarding it, along with the sword, would have to wait. "When do we leave to save your friend and the spring faerie?" he asked.

Melia's eyes brightened. He'd said the right thing.

"What about Plantine?" Tuck asked.

Ryder pushed his cloak aside and settled his hand on Koldis' hilt. Touching the blade fortified his resolve. "I don't understand why this muannaye kidnapped her. If he wants Isolt's basin, then he must also want to incarnate Umbra. Flower faeries can't contain Umbra's consciousness. There are few who can. It would have made more sense if he'd kidnapped the queen or the princess. Their Albiana blood has the strength to contain the dark master."

"If only things were so simple." Aldous directed Tuck to a cabinet. "Bring me the family tree. The Albiana bloodlines are not as pure as they once were."

Melia flinched with Aldous' use of the word *pure*. Ryder wondered what nerve the elf had struck. Tuck returned with a large scroll which he handed to the head librarian. The old elf spread it on the low table. Ryder sat down next to Melia.

His body had never been more aware of someone beside him. She leaned forward with her crossed arms settled on her knees. He mirrored her posture and stared at the parchment that held her attention.

The name *Albiana* was scrawled across the top of the page. The same hand had inked a series of lines connecting one name after another. Gwyneth was the first name at the top of the diagram. For three generations, the diagram showed a clear line of succession. Gwyneth had given birth to Ava, who had given birth to Uriel, who had given birth to Olivia. After Olivia the diagram branched. She had two daughters–Luisa and Pressina.

Following this alteration, the diagram became even more complicated, for the family tree showed Luisa had two daughters as well–Gabriela and Lilliane. The names Melusine, Melia, and Plantine indicated they were the daughters of Pressina. Gabriela had a daughter named Lola.

The only other item of note was the tiny letter M by the names of each of Pressina's daughters, and Luisa's first daughter and her granddaughter. Ryder was astounded.

Melia was a half-faerie with Albiana and mortal blood.

"Flora told me last night," she said.

"You didn't know?" Ryder asked.

"Olivia's decree prohibits the population of Illialei from recognizing or speaking of Pressina–or her descendants–as Albiana," Aldous said.

Another Albiana decree. No wonder Melia looked as if she wanted to be anywhere but here. Ryder gave her what he hoped was a kind look. Maybe one day he could share his own confused lineage with her.

Aldous settled back in his chair, pressing the tips of his fingers against one another. "The Order has long imposed separate spheres of knowledge. I assume Anton has continued with this discipline?"

Ryder nodded.

"Who is Anton?" Melia asked.

"The head of the order, and Ryder's mentor," Aldous replied. "Have you heard of the Idonnic Library, Melia?"

"Not the library, only the prophecy," she said.

Ryder flinched. The prophecy was popular in the enchanted world, but he had no intention of encouraging the propaganda that Umbra's incarnation could bring anything but despair. He said nothing.

"Ah, the prophecy," Aldous said. "I suppose you heard about it in school."

Her already pale skin bleached to white. She nodded. The reaction increased Ryder's interest in her. If she disagreed with the prophecy, Aldous was correct. They had much in common. Ryder remained silent, preferring that the librarian explain the world he sought to be free of.

"The priesthood is an elite race of scholars," the old elf continued. "They chronicle and record the history and future of the enchanted and mortal worlds."

"The future as they see it, without interference," Ryder said.

"The Order is founded on a fundamental principle of observation. They record. They don't intervene," Aldous said.

"They're cowards." Ryder appreciated the slight upward curve of Melia's lips.

"Perhaps, but it's not our place to judge. Their chronicles of the past, as well as their prophecies of the future, are invaluable, and not to be questioned," Aldous said.

Melia squirmed as the old elf defended the priests. Ryder could guess her thoughts. Long-winded discussions aren't going to save my friends. "There's more than one prophecy?" she asked.

"The one about Umbra's incarnation is the most famous," Aldous replied.

"And the least reliable," Ryder growled. "I've studied Umbra and his history–"

"Then, you must know a lot about him," Melia said.

"Yes," he said. "I know enough not to believe in a fool's hope that his incarnation will have some benefit."

"There are many who feel as you do," Aldous said.

The more Ryder let his gaze wander in Melia's direction, the more her physical presence affected him. Her movements were so graceful, spirited, yet natural. Like a flower opening to the sun.

"What you didn't learn," the old elf addressed Ryder, "or were not privy to during your studies, was the evolution of the Albiana family tree. As you can see from this diagram, through Queen Luisa and Pressina, the Albiana blood has been mixed with mortal. These–pardon the expression, Melia–*halves* are believed to be the preferred vessels for Umbra's incarnation."

Ryder flattened his lips in dismal understanding. Although Anton had shared much of his exhaustive knowledge about the Albiana with him, he hadn't shared this. As long as the sword was in Faerie, and the location of the basin unknown, Melia and her sister weren't safe. Instinctively, he reached for her hand. When she let him hold it, his heart boomed in his chest. Her eyes met his gaze, then fell away. He held on to her hand.

"It's always been believed the dark master would shun a pureblood Albiana because a pureblood could rein him to her will." Aldous said. "But an Albiana with mortal blood–"

"Would be more susceptible to his domination," Tuck interjected, "yet still be strong enough to contain the strength of his consciousness."

As an expert on Umbra, Ryder understood the dark master's power to seduce and corrupt. A vessel with mixed blood would be a wild card, uncontrollable and unpredictable.

Aldous turned to Melia. "I suspect Lord Goring intends to complete the work your father began."

"They are among those who believe that when the battle between Dark and Light begins, the old laws will die, and the one who sits on the Cathedral Palace throne will fall," Tuck said.

"Elynus convinced himself the death of the old laws would throw open the doors between the mortal and enchanted worlds, the doors locked to him," Aldous said. "Now, Lord Zachariah Goring–a muannaye who can't travel to the mortal world because no muannaye can–foolishly believes the same."

"But we don't think that's what's going to happen," Tuck said. "We think, when Umbra incarnates, all the doors between the enchanted and mortal worlds are going to close, as the prophecy predicts."

"There's much arguing about that in Idonne," Ryder said.

Melia shrank back into the sofa. Although he didn't want to let go, Ryder let her hand slip from his. Her chin quivered. "Everything is starting to make sense," she said.

"Get her another cup of chamomile tea," Aldous ordered his apprentice. "She looks a bit peaked."

"Could I have one without honey?" she whispered.

Tuck made her a second cup. When he brought it to her, she thanked him, but didn't lift her bowed head, even when the head librarian addressed her directly.

"Now that your father has died," Aldous said, "the telepathic link you shared with him will make targets of you and your sisters. If Umbra absorbed the ashes from your father's soul, it will be easier for him to seek you out and influence you, with or without the basin. Elynus was unwise in trusting this information to Goring, who gave him much aid in his research through the years. It's no surprise he came for Plantine first. She's the weakest."

Melia brushed her eyes with the back of her hand.

Tuck kicked a bookcase.

"How so?" Ryder asked.

Aldous exhaled a weary sigh. "When the daughters locked their father in a sea cave, they threatened to keep him there unless he promised to not incarnate Umbra."

Good for them, Ryder thought.

Melia's teacup rattled against the saucer.

"They didn't know there was a well in the cave fed by seawater," the old elf said. "When the tides rose, he drowned. It was a tragic accident."

Ryder looked sideways at Melia, lost in her teacup. "I'm sorry you lost your father in such a disturbing way."

She bobbed her chin but continued to gaze at the carpet.

"To punish their participation," Aldous said, "their mother placed curses upon them. The curse she placed on Plantine has caused her physical disintegration."

Ryder stared at the head librarian in disbelief. What kind of mother could exact that kind of revenge on her child? His heart pounded in his chest.

"If that wasn't enough, Elynus left *The Book of Umbra* to Goring upon his death," Aldous continued. "All the muannaye needs now is the basin and the sword. If he can get his hands on those, I fear he'll waste no time attempting the incarnation of Umbra's consciousness into Plantine's body."

Ryder's jaw tightened. He'd been a fool to bring Koldis to Faerie.

"In her weakened condition," the head librarian said, "I fear Plantine will be unable to fight Umbra's darkness. His consciousness will either annihilate her, or she will become a savage queen, darker than any have ever imagined." The old elf looked at Melia. "Please don't misunderstand me, your sister is lovely, but all creatures have bits of ambition, unbridled anger, or the like within. Umbra amplifies such darkness in those who've had contact with him."

"I won't let him possess my sister," Melia's voice shook.

Adrenaline pumped through Ryder's body. "And you shouldn't. After we rescue your friend and the spring faerie, we'll secure the basin. Without the basin, there can be no incarnation." He didn't mention Koldis. Finding out the sword was within reach could only add to her fears.

"Then we must leave for the Balyudor at once," Melia said.

Finally, she raised her head and held his gaze. The blue pools of her eyes drew him in until it felt as though their souls touched. He made a silent promise to do everything in his power to help her.

The precise moment he stated the wordless vow, the intriguing mark on her forehead evaporated.

Not trusting what he'd just seen, he leaned closer. The blue spot had vanished without a trace.

Aldous' eyes grew twice their size behind his glasses.

"Where did it go?" Tuck asked.

It seemed beyond explanation.

Melia touched the space between her eyebrows. "It's gone? Are you sure?"

"Yes," Ryder said.

She shook her head. "Nandana didn't tell me that would happen."

"Who's Nandana?" he asked.

"The Illustrator. She–" Melia stopped. "Never mind."

Ryder didn't press, although he was aware that Tuck and Aldous watched them both with great curiosity.

30. The End of the Beginning

Melia woke suddenly, twined in silk sheets. She sat up and rubbed drowsy eyes as she struggled to get her bearings. The scent of roses wafted through an open window. A delicate gown caressed her skin with every move. She swung her legs over the side of a high bed. Beneath her feet, luxurious rugs crisscrossed a tile floor. The lattice path led to the other side of the room where a vanity, embossed with gold-leaf, disappeared in the shadows beyond a wall of mirrors.

She approached her reflection. The indigo spot was indeed gone, her forehead bare. She pressed her palm against her skin. Nothing. It had faded yesterday afternoon when she'd met Ryder.

He was the one.

Now what?

Nandana had told her that she had a path to follow. That the mark would call someone to her. Someone who came from a world where he didn't belong. Someone who searched for the same answers she did.

Now Ryder was here in Faerie. He'd come from Idonne to help her.

It was almost too much too believe.

She looked at her forehead once more. The spot between her eyebrows remained inert. Now that the mark was gone, she missed it.

She examined her reflection more carefully. Her height, alabaster skin, and thick hair hinted at her ancestry. Most faeries weren't as tall as the Albiana. She and Melusine had always towered over the faeries of flower and field. Plantine, more petite than either of her older sisters, had blended more easily. Melia stared at her hands. Most faeries couldn't hold a pixie as easily as she held Tatou, but her palms and fingers were long. She'd never given it much thought.

She touched her lips.

She hadn't stuttered once yesterday. She'd hardly been able to speak when the tiger had jumped on her, but when she'd opened her mouth, her words had been whole.

She never tripped over her words when Tatou was with her, but yesterday her friend had been far away.

She retreated from the mirror. Her reflection doubled and tripled, then split into an infinite number between more mirrors hanging from each of the room's walls.

Her life would have been different if she'd been raised in the palace as Queen Luisa's niece and Olivia's granddaughter, but the queens of Illialei had denied her existence. The awareness made her uncomfortable, and brought the first taste of her mother's bitterness.

It also set her free.

The invisible cloud of lies that had followed Melia, every day since she'd come to Faerie as a child, was gone. A nascent self-confidence remained. She knew the truth of who she was, and could speak without twisting over her tongue.

She padded to an open window. Below, thousands of roses bloomed in the late morning sun. She thought of Flora, and a deep sympathy stirred within her. What kind of evil banished springtime? Guilt followed. By allowing Plantine to ferret out the location of the basin, she'd betrayed her promise to the spring faerie.

The palace walls closed in on her.

How had she managed such deep sleep in the monument to Queen Uriel's crimes? She'd never slept through her shift into an eagle before. She remembered Aldous encouraging a final cup of tea, no doubt laced with something stronger than chamomile. Then she'd been escorted here, to this room.

Her sleep had been peaceful, but now, she itched to get out of the palace. Every luxurious detail served a façade of dazzling beauty. An effect so breathtaking, it had long since silenced any claims of justice for Flora's kin.

The knowledge that Queen Uriel's blood ran through Melia's veins only increased her distress.

Through the window, the sun climbed in the sky. Tonight she would travel with Ryder, Sinjiin, and Tuck to the Balyudor. She'd wanted to leave last night, but Aldous had insisted she'd needed to rest. He'd assigned Ryder and Tuck the task of packing supplies. If their travels took them all the way to Aldaine, it would be a long trip.

Melia could fly, and Sinjiin could run with Ryder on his back, but the tiger couldn't carry the tree elf, too. Aldous had promised Tuck the fastest horse in the palace stables. Even so, traveling over land, it would take too long to reach Flora's cottage.

Her thoughts returned to the priest. Ryder. She brushed her lips with her fingers. How would his lips feel pressed against hers?

She flattened her hands against her thighs. What was she thinking? Kissing him risked undoing her mother's spell. Losing her ability to fly. Her stomach knotted as she clasped her hands. When he'd held hers yesterday in the library, it had felt so natural.

Melia's gaze returned to the mirror. Her reflection showed a dark silhouette against a backdrop of light. The contrast frightened her. That the mix of Albiana and mortal blood pumping through her heart made her more desirable to Umbra sickened her.

But he'd chosen Plantine because she was weak. Melia took a step back, out of the interior shadows and into a ray of sunlight filtering through the window. Maybe Umbra wasn't as strong as everyone claimed.

The thought didn't make her encounters with him–or the secrets she'd learned about the Albiana–any less disturbing. Had her father known about the death of the spring faeries?

If he had ...

Melia's world tilted. She'd been furious in Achill when he'd refused to listen to her, but had she listened to him?

There are no innocents in Illialei.

Yet bringing war to the faeries and elves and brownies for the Albianas' crimes? That couldn't be right either. Could it?

She had to get out of the palace.

✧ ✧ ✧

Melia followed the hall to a flight of wide marble stairs. She hurried down the stairwell. It led to a door. The strong smell of hay and horses greeted her when she shoved it open. A covered walkway led to the stables. Uniformed brownies milled about. The silhouette of High Hill was visible beyond the high-ceiling stone barn. Melia moved with a determined stride. It was time to visit Nandana.

Someone called her name. She turned her head.

It was *him*.

Ryder crossed the corral on a magnificent black horse. Melia smiled. She couldn't help herself.

"Where are you going?" he asked.

"To visit a friend before we leave."

"Does your friend live anywhere near the Nyssalei?"

Her heart raced. "The eastern shores are closer to the palace, but her shop is close enough to the river's western shores."

Ryder pointed to Sinjiin, pacing in the fields on the other side of the corral. "He'd love to bathe."

Melia leaned against the fence. "He'll scare the faeries." She thought of Verbena and laughed.

"You think that's funny?" he teased.

"I do."

"Would you care to ride him?"

"The horse?" Melia asked.

"No, Sinjiin. Aldous asked me to choose the fastest mount for Tuck. This is Zephyr." Ryder combed the horse's mane with his fingers. "I need to take him for a run. See if he can keep up with the tiger."

Her body tingled with excitement. "The horse won't be afraid of him?"

"Watch." He whistled. Sinjiin lifted his head and ran. He leapt over the high fence of the corral, then skidded to a stop a good distance from Zephyr. The tiger lowered his head and walked toward the horse. Ryder whispered soothing words the entire time. When the horse nosed the large cat, Melia was speechless. "Ready to go?" he asked.

Melia nodded toward Sinjiin. "You're sure it's all right with him?"

"Can you carry her?" Ryder asked the tiger.

Sinjiin met Melia's gaze and lowered his belly to the ground.

"He's waiting," Ryder said.

Melia climbed the fence and walked over to the big cat. His golden eyes twinkled, otherwise, he remained still.

"Wrap your legs around his belly and lean over his back. Grab the scruff of his neck with both hands and hold it tight. He's fast."

Ryder called to one of the brownies. The corral's gate swung open. He kneed Zephyr and the horse sprang forward.

Once they were out of the corral, Sinjiin circled wide and took the lead.

"How do I guide him?" Melia called back to Ryder.

"He can smell the river."

Ryder's words mingled with the wind as Sinjiin tore across the fields, leaving screaming brownies and hysterical faeries in his wake.

It was another kind of flight.

✧ ✧ ✧

Melia pushed open the blistered blue gate. Ryder tethered Zephyr's reins to the fence and followed behind her.

They'd left Sinjiin splashing in the western Nyssalei, roaring and creating havoc. Normally the most deserted stretch of river, a crowd of elves and faeries had raced from Bryndale to witness the spectacle of the tiger's bath.

The gossips would be talking about it for weeks to come.

In contrast to the circus they'd left behind, Nandana's empty porch and the roses trailing through the Illustrator's yard looked sad. The flowers drooped, brown tinged their petals, and the colored building beyond the yard seemed faded and tired. Melia's steps were heavy as she walked the rocky steps to the shop's front door.

Too much had changed in five moon cycles.

The anger she'd felt at the Cathedral Palace resurfaced. There was so much Nandana hadn't told her. Melia wanted to know why.

"I hoped you'd come." The Illustrator opened the door before the half-faerie could knock. Half-filled chests covered the front room's floor and sofa. "I've been packing."

The room and the studio beyond were empty of cats. "Where are–"

Nandana pointed to the half-faerie's forehead and nodded toward Ryder. "He came."

Melia flushed. The woman cleared a place for them to sit as Melia introduced them.

"Coffee?" Nandana asked.

"Yes," Ryder said before Melia could decline.

The Illustrator disappeared.

"She was expecting me?" he asked.

"It's complicated."

Ryder pointed to her forehead. "The mark that disappeared?"

"You don't seem surprised."

"I–"

Before he could finish, Nandana swept into the room. "He answered the Call." She carried a tray with a full pot of coffee, three cups, and a plate of chocolates.

"I did feel a pull," Ryder said. "But I must admit, I didn't recognize the source."

"You're aware of Umbra?" Nandana asked him.

"Very much so," he said.

The woman pointed to Melia. "She's the one."

The muscles in Ryder's neck corded. "If there's any truth to the prophecy, and that's more than I'm willing to concede, I hoped it might be her sister."

"I don't think so. Plantine is weak," Nandana said.

He pushed the hair from his forehead. "You would condemn Melia to carry that burden?"

The woman poured the coffee. "Nothing is ever certain until it happens, but I marked Melia with the Call, and here you are."

"It was a test?" Melia asked.

"More a means of discernment. Tell her," Nandana said to Ryder.

"There are two schools of thought when it comes to Umbra," he said. "The first is to prevent the incarnation. The basin and sword can't be destroyed. The magic–and the evil within them–are too strong. But they can be safeguarded. If the portal is never opened, Umbra will remain forever in the Void." He stopped.

"There is a second thought," Nandana prompted him.

Ryder frowned.

The way they interacted unnerved Melia. It was as if they'd already met. "What is the second thought?" she asked.

"That Umbra must incarnate," he said. "That someone must bear the burden of his darkness and have the strength to integrate it with their own light."

Melia set down her cup of coffee. Nausea gripped her stomach. They stared at her. She stood up. "No." Her body shook. "It won't be me."

"Melia, please sit down," Nandana said.

She shook her head. "We have to save Tatou and the spring faerie. We're returning to Tyrannis tonight."

"Then you've met Flora?" Nandana asked.

Melia glared at her, then at the door and out the window. "Now you defy Uriel's decree–after you and everyone else in Illialei have buried that horror in silence for years?"

"Indulging in anger about a past no one has the power to change will only cloud your judgment. Our greatest hope lies in the future, focus your energy there." The woman's voice was soft, but each word she spoke was clear. "Your eyes are fresh with youth, and your heart is pure. That is your strength. Hold to it."

Melia turned to Ryder. "Do you believe any of this?"

"I've never wanted to believe that Umbra must incarnate," he said. "The darkness of his consciousness is so vast that it would be too great a burden for any single person to bear."

"That is why you've been called," Nandana spoke to him, but she walked toward Melia. She took the half-faerie's hands in hers. "The great spiritual battle looms. Your destiny approaches. Flora was once a brilliant warrior.

Learn everything you can from her, but cling to Ryder. Cling to your heart."

The woman had lost her mind. She'd never incarnate Umbra. "You're wrong about all this–about me ... us," Melia whispered.

"Perhaps," Nandana said. "But my work here is done. I'm leaving Illialei."

This wasn't the conversation Melia had come to have with the Illustrator. Panic squeezed her heart. The sun would set soon. They must return to the Cathedral Palace before it did. "Where will you go?"

"To Azyllai." Nandana winked. "I've always fancied meeting the gods."

31. At Sea

Plantine collected her thoughts as she stared at the blank parchment on the desk before her. Around her, the ship creaked as it rocked in the sea. How quickly her fortunes had changed. If she'd listened to Melia and Tatou, and gone to the palace library to see Aldous and Tuck, she wouldn't be here.

A black shadow fell across her heart. She couldn't afford to think about the tree elf. Not now, when all her dreams were on the verge of coming true. No, she'd made her decision, and it would require her to cut Tuck out of her heart, out of her mind, and out of her life.

Her heart quivered as she reached for the quill pen. A deep and unfamiliar sorrow fought a great battle with the anticipation growing within. The pain must be buried; all sweet memories of her time with Tuck, banished. It was the only way to move forward and lay claim to the future that called her.

She made a conscious effort to still her hand before she began writing.

Dearest Mother,

I'm sorry if I scared you yesterday. I threw quite a fit when the muannai came for me. It's true they were callous and rough, especially that troll (his name is Moog). I had no idea they came at the behest of Lord Zachariah Goring. I suspect that comes as a shock to you as well. But that is not the end of the surprise. Lord Goring wishes to marry me.

* * *

A tear dropped onto the page. Plantine blinked. Was she crying? She wiped her eyes with the back of her hand and heaved a great sob. Why were both parts of her so strong? Marrying the muannaye was the only way to achieve justice for her mother ... her father ... and herself. There was no place for Tuck–or her love for him–in Tyrannis. She must put him behind her.

She would–with determination and resolve.

Plantine dried her eyes and resumed writing.

I admit, it was a forceful proposal, but I believe Father would want me to continue his work, and this marriage will be the vehicle to achieve that.

Regardless, I seek your blessing for the union.

Plantine nodded. Her mother would agree. This was her chance to make things right. Her jaw steeled.

As I write this, we sail to Tyrannis. Your support would mean more than you can imagine. Melia warned me the muannai women are fierce rivals for our beauty. But I'll not let them win.

Would you please join us in Aldaine for the wedding? Do not delay, things are moving quickly.

Mother, have hope. This is the opportunity you bid me take.

Your most faithful daughter,

Plantine

She creased the parchment into thirds and held the stub of sealing wax in the candle's flame until it softened. When the letter was ready, she let it sit on the desk as she slipped a hand into her pocket. When her fingers curled around the cool crystal, she calmed. Pulling the vial from the thick folds of her dress, she tugged on its cap. The dropper popped out. She placed three drops on the tip of her tongue. A reviving current flowed from the interior of her mouth to the top of her head, it traveled down her throat and settled in her belly. From there, it coursed through her limbs and into her hands and feet.

She examined her palms. They were no longer translucent. She tugged on her hair. No strands came free. The elixir cured her mother's curse–as long as she took the medicine regularly.

Yesterday, she'd taken the potion four times. Plantine brushed away the awareness that today it had taken twice as many doses to keep her disintegration at bay. Wondering if Tuck's kiss could have cured her served no purpose, either. Scoffing at the mere idea of true love, she slipped the vial back into her pocket, gathered her shawl, and headed to the ship's deck.

The sun slipped toward the horizon. It would be night soon. Plantine clutched the letter beneath her shawl as she searched for Zachariah. There, near the stern. He'd promised to have the letter sent to her mother by messenger hawk as soon as it was written. He'd told her to find him. With head held high, Plantine began the long walk toward him, past the gritty sailors who smelled of sea and piss. A handful made up the crew who'd pawed her and *escorted* her from the tree house. She ignored their bold glances as she maintained her purposeful stride.

Zachariah was deep in conversation with the troll. They didn't see Plantine. She slowed down and veered toward the railing. When she was close enough, she stopped. Pretending that she stared at the sea, she strained to hear their conversation. It was impossible to decipher anything but a few words here and there.

Plantine shifted her gaze until the muannaye entered her vision. He was striking, and she took pleasure in studying him–her betrothed.

He stood impossibly tall, his dark hair pulled into a ponytail. The grey at his temples only made him appear sophisticated. He favored snow-white shirts with ruffles, and vests that accented his broad shoulders and slim torso. He towered over Moog, yet their familiarity spoke of a trusted relationship.

She took another step closer to the pair. In the midst of their heated discussion, her approach went unnoticed. Plantine brushed away strands of hair the wind blew about her face. She fiddled with the silk shawl Zachariah had gifted her with only this morning.

When she'd given him the information she'd gleaned from Melia's mind about the basin, his attitude toward her had transformed. Until then he'd treated her as a child, but now he understood her value. She leaned over the ship's rail and twisted her body in the direction of her fiancé and his confidante.

They bandied about the name of a dragonwitch in the muannai valley. Several of the ship's crew burst into song; the revelry created gaps in the conversation. Plantine couldn't hear the witch's name.

She took a step closer. They spoke of the basin. And the wolves. Plantine shivered. They always spoke of the wolves.

"Darling." Zachariah had spied her. He cut short his exchange with Moog and strode toward her. A possessive hand dropped onto her shoulder. Plantine smiled. Zachariah's brown eyes sparked. The troll offered a half-hearted bow and wandered off.

Plantine handed her betrothed the letter. "I'm sure my mother's worried about me. It would mean so much to me to set her mind at ease."

He snapped his fingers. A crewman came running. The muannaye gave instructions for the letter's delivery and the young male ran off, eager to win his superior's approval. A frisson of satisfaction cut through Plantine's remaining doubt.

Above all else, she craved power.

32. Black Wolves

Black pushed the last orange-red stripe from the western sky. Melia, waiting alone in the shadow of the palace walls, shifted into an eagle. As soon as she ascended into the dark moon night, her beak pointed toward the Balyudor's deep woods, a strange sensation gripped her. A blue spark blossomed into the image of a magnificent flower in her mind's eye. Although she'd only seen the sapphire lily once, Melia recognized its distinctive indigo petals.

The need to visit the lily overwhelmed her.

She slowed the beating of her wings and tried to shake the compulsion to fly toward Lake Vivientiana. The urge only became more insistent.

Melia landed on the branch of an apple tree. The more she tried to push the image of the flower away, the brighter it burned in her mind, tugging her will away from warning Tatou and Flora.

She tried to fly north once more. A heavy weight dragged her down, as though her feathers had turned to stone. She needed to see the sapphire lily–tonight–before she left for Tyrannis. When she relented and pivoted in the direction of the lake, the unseen resistance fell away.

With zero moonlight to guide her, the world below was a yawning abyss. Eagle instinct guided her flight. Light emanating from the Summer Palace became visible first. Soon she heard the spray shooting from the fountain in the lake's center. The image of the flower never wavered, and her curiosity mounted as she neared her destination.

She looped in a graceful arc toward the sound of water licking the shore to land with a soft crinch when her claws hit sand.

The smell of water saturated the air. Following the shoreline, she picked up a fresh, sweet scent which became steadily stronger. The light from the smaller palace no longer illuminated the beach. She flapped her wings and took a few more long bounces into the blackness. Her beak hit something fibrous.

The sapphire lily towered over her. She took a deep pull of its perfume. Then another. Her agitation calmed. A sweetness infused her blood. Her heart swelled. Her dark moon visions, Umbra–and Nandana's alarming declaration–no longer seemed threatening. An awareness of life's mystery, of her place in the Whole, of being exonerated in her father's death, swept over Melia. Elynus had not been wrong; the Albiana were tyrants; Flora's kin deserved justice; the events that would deliver it had been set in motion. A belief that all would be well, that everything would unfold toward a triumphant future, assuaged the doubts which often consumed Melia's confidence. She savored the revelation, allowing it to fill her.

After taking one last drag of the flower's intoxicating perfume, she launched into the black night.

✧ ✧ ✧

Melia flew across the river toward Flora's yellow cottage. She pumped her wings. Faster, faster.

A bright light loomed ahead. The scent of burnt wood hung in the air. Dark plumes crowned a horde of flames licking the night sky.

Melia's broken promise to the spring faerie burned like a hot coal in the back of her throat. She'd never meant to reveal that Flora kept the magic basin in her home, but Plantine's telepathic probing had been relentless. Melia tried not to think about what had made her sister so strong. She tried to believe it was as Plantine had told her: Lord Goring was giving her a potion. But only two days ago, she'd seemed near death, physically disintegrating according to their mother's spell. It was getting harder to ignore her concern that Umbra had reached her little sister, and that he was giving her strength.

The burning sensation in Melia's throat spread to her stomach. The hope bequeathed by the sapphire lily receded as panic besieged her.

Cutting a sweeping arc, she descended through the leafy roof of the Balyudor to investigate.

Smoke suffocated the woods. Her eyes watered, and she struggled to breathe. A stench filled the air. Tatou. Melia's heart pounded.

Stunning silence blanketed the random clicks, rustles, and calls that crescendoed in the first hours after nightfall. Melia kept quiet too, searching through the blinding film that turned the dark moon night even blacker. Soot and fumes thickened as she flew toward the small cottage in the clearing. A wicked howl slashed the deadly calm. Her heart missed a beat. She fluttered to the nearest branch. An answering howl was echoed by a third, a fourth, and then a fifth spine-shivering cry into the night.

She let go of the branch and entered the smoldering haze. Ash burned her eyes and coated her wings. She flew blindly. The sound of voices arguing was the only thing that hinted she'd reached the clearing.

She choked and wheezed. All that remained of the spring faerie's quaint home and split-rail fence was blackened stumps. For a brief second, Melia thought she'd entered one of her visions. Then she heard Flora. In the middle of that black hole, the spring faerie wrestled with a figure more than twice her size.

"Go find your own stinking treasure," she yelled at the top of her lungs. "This is mine!"

Flora and the tall figure pushed and pulled the basin between them. "You little shit." The spring faerie jumped on one of her opponent's feet with both of hers.

He grunted.

"You're going to pay for burning my home!"

A fist came down like a club on the patterned kerchief covering the spring faerie's head. She staggered and fell without releasing her edge of the basin's rim. The hulking figure dragged her through the burning yard.

Flora kicked and squealed. Melia angled her body. Eagle instincts propelled her as she bore down on her target, two slits in a black mask. The towering thief released the basin. He threw up his hands to guard his eyes. She jabbed at the exposed skin on the back of his hands with her beak. He yowled and retreated. She flapped and pecked air, forcing him take more steps backward.

The masked brute turned and ran as Flora wrapped her arms around the basin and rolled to one side.

Melia took a victory lap in the sky.

Flora was on her knees; an arrow sliced the air, inches from her ear. She dove back into the hot dirt, her stout shape hiding the basin from view.

Several black wolves circled the perimeter, snuffling and growling. Their black pelts blended with the night. Two broke away from the pack and slunk toward the spring faerie. Aghast at the scene playing out beneath her, Melia screeched a warning.

The next arrow clipped her tail feathers. She searched for the archers. A solid wall of twisted trees protected them.

"Save yourself!" Melia's shrill cry split the air. She zigzagged right to left, shot up, and then plummeted in a crazy dance. Arrow after arrow whizzed by her.

Flora ran across her incinerated yard, the silver basin clutched to her heaving chest. One of the wolves raced behind her. The hulking black beast leapt. The spring faerie spun around, holding the bowl in front of her as though it were a shield. The wolf smacked its snout into the dwarf metal, whimpered, and slunk aside.

A downpour of arrows kept Melia away. The second wolf circled wide to creep behind Flora. Melia screeched again. The fanged hound sprang and landed on the spring faerie's shoulders. She fell face-first into the steaming earth. The basin skittered off to the side. Melia plunged after it. Flora's bloodcurdling scream paralyzed her. She wheeled. Two dark streaks emerged on the back of Flora's patterned dress. Melia fluttered down. The black wolf paced as if it were a demon guard. All hope of finding Tatou alive perished in Melia's heart.

A second muannaye came from nowhere. She'd seen that black uniform before. It was the same one the muannai who'd forged weapons in the southern Ruadain wore. These muannai were members of the cult of Umbra. She couldn't let them win.

Melia dove for the basin. The muannaye jerked the silver bowl from her grasp just as her talons scratched its rim. Another hailstorm of arrows showered her. The black figure disappeared with Flora's treasure into the forest's depths.

"You tell Zachariah he's a coward. You tell him I said he's a fool and a coward," Flora bellowed at the top of her lungs. "You tell him this isn't finished."

Melia shrieked into the night beside her.

Nothing answered. The muannai and wolves were gone.

Flora lay in the clearing, her vehement threats now gut-wrenching sobs.

An airless shroud compressed Melia's heart. Her trip to Lake Vivientiana had been an indulgence. Standing before the sapphire lily had filled her with a fleeting, unfathomable comfort, but at what cost? If she'd ignored the flower's summon, she might have saved Flora's home–and the basin. She wished she could dissolve into the smoke and ashes clogging the air. A darker dread pulsed through her as she began to search franticly for Tatou.

The pixie was nowhere.

A pain she'd never felt before knifed Melia's heart. She couldn't catch her breath. The hope from her brief encounter with the lily was forgotten.

She redoubled her effort to find her friend. How could she have let this happen?

Melia flinched at the sight of each small corpse. Not one of Flora's chickens had survived. Beyond the clearing, a goat bleated. With a leaden shuffle, Melia followed the sound through a wall of dense, crooked trees.

When the animal fell silent, Melia called out.

"Over here," Tatou chirped in perfect eagle.

Melia's heart rocketed.

The pixie hid in a patch of long grass near a tiny stream with Flora's goat.

The half-faerie burrowed her eagle head against Tatou's stomach. The pixie smoothed Melia's feathers with her free hand. Her wounded arm still rested in a sling, and bandages crisscrossed her back and chest. "We're safe," the pixie said. "What about you?"

"Now that I know you're alive, I'm fine." Melia's body softened–from the crown of her head down to her last tail feather–until she remembered the spring faerie. "But Flora's injured."

The goat staggered to its feet. Its backside and hind legs were burned raw. It bleated its awkwardness and discomfort.

"What happened?" Melia asked.

Tatou flitted over to the goat and tried to sooth it. "Clover was the hero. The first whiff of smoke and she carried me here by the water. She went back for Flora, but Flora wanted to put out the fire and find out who'd started it. Clover stayed with her as long as she could, but Flora was crazed. She wouldn't leave her cottage. Not even as it burned to the ground around her. Clover finally gave up and came to wait with me."

An eerie silence descended upon the trio as they walked back through the woods. When they reached the scorched clearing, Flora was gone. Dizzying awareness choked Melia. She should never have left her alone. This was too much like the burning of the spring faeries. Melia crossed the yard and cawed her name.

Tatou and Clover waited in stunned silence at the edge of the burn site. From the opposite side of the yard, Melia heard a noise that sounded like the spring faerie grunting. She'd managed to crawl beyond the torched perimeter. Digging beneath the leaves that layered the forest floor, she scratched for root beetles.

"Grind them up for a poultice," Flora wheezed on her hands and knees. She pinched the insects between swollen fingers and dropped them in the pocket of the apron still tied around her waist. "Good for burns, any open wound," she said as she continued her work.

Melia didn't try to stop her. She sensed the contact with the unburnt ground soothed her.

When Flora finished, she pushed herself back to sit facing Melia with her legs straight out in front of her. "Well, black eagle," she said. "Look what helping you got me. Another burning. Whoever you told about the basin didn't waste any time coming for it."

The truth gouged Melia's stomach. Uriel Albiana had banned springtime forever in Illialei, killing all the spring faeries but one–Flora. Now Melia, Uriel's granddaughter, was responsible for the incineration of Flora's rebuilt life.

"Plantine pried the information from my mind." What a limp excuse. "There was nothing I could do ..." Melia stopped trying to defend herself.

"Shouldn't have let you see it," Flora said.

They sat without saying anything for a long moment.

"Back there, were you talking about Lord Goring?" Melia asked.

Flora snorted. "Full of himself muannaye." She crossed her arms over her chest. "Frustrated he can't cross to the mortal world. He'll do anything to see Umbra incarnated. Thinks the incarnation will change everything. It will, only not in the way he predicts."

"You think he's responsible for this?" Melia asked.

It was the third time she'd heard the muannaye's name in almost as many days. Now, Flora blamed him for the arson of her home and the theft of the basin. Things weren't looking good for Plantine.

"That would be the one," Flora said. "Lord Zachariah Goring. There's a mouthful for you. Acts like he's descended from royal bloodlines with claims to the Calashai's throne. When it comes to the muannaye, there are no royal bloodlines. Until now, I've looked the other way when it came to his foolishness. But burning down my home and siccing his wolves on me ... you mark my words, he's made an enemy of me, and I'll make him pay."

Melia shredded twigs and leaves with her talons. Lord Goring was the monster Plantine would marry if Melia didn't save her. "We were on our way to warn you," she said. "Aldous' apprentice, a priest from Idonne, and a mage from the Hidden City are crossing the Maeldun Bridge tonight. I flew ahead of them."

"A priest from Idonne? I didn't expect that," Flora said.

Melia craved any insight she could gain on the mysterious Ryder. "What do you mean?"

The spring faerie waved her hand. "It doesn't matter. You're too late with your warnings, anyway."

Melia couldn't argue. Brilliant orange coals consumed every last bit of Flora's home. By dawn, nothing but white ash would remain. "You need someone to dress the cuts on your back ... and the burns on your face. Is there anyone I can fetch for you?"

Flora shrugged her shoulders. "I've plenty of chits to call in."

Melia had heard that trolls lived in caves beneath some of the large boulders scattered throughout the Balyudor. She'd also heard female trolls were fleet of foot, and that they were the most skilled healers in Faerie.

In the distance, wolves howled. The ping-pong of their cries convinced

Melia they relayed a message. But to whom? And what was the message? She couldn't come up with an answer, and Flora offered nothing.

"I'll follow you back to the clearing," Melia cawed.

Flora pushed herself up to her feet. Melia's affection for the grumpy faerie grew as she watched her fight against the pain of her wounds. She wished there was something she could do to help her, but she wasn't a healer, and Flora was much too large to ride on her back.

"Where will you go?" Melia asked.

Flora remained silent, her face grim.

"I can't leave you here alone," the half-faerie said.

Bella, Flora's cat, had yet to show itself. And for all her heroics, Clover didn't seem to be adequate company.

"Your friend's better than when you left her," Flora said, "but she still can't fly with you. If she wants her wing to heal properly, she'll need to stay with Clover and me at least one more night."

"But where will you go?"

They reached the blackened clearing where Clover and Tatou waited. Flora whipped around. "The Veiled Tavern."

Located in the heart of the Balyudor, the tavern was infamous throughout the enchanted world. The decision didn't thrill Melia, but she couldn't offer a better meeting place. Flora waddled across her yard, away from the half-faerie. Clover followed after her.

Melia would have to meet them at the inn tomorrow. She hopped over to Tatou to explain. "*He* is here in Faerie–and Nandana's mark is gone."

The mysterious blue smudge had only been visible when she was in her half-faerie form, but the pixie still searched Melia's feathered head as if she might see something that confirmed the claim. "Just like that, it's gone?" Tatou gazed beyond the edge of the burn site. "Is he here?"

"No, but when I arrived at the library this morning, he was there, with a tiger that almost ate me because it thought I was eavesdropping."

"What?"

"After we talked awhile, the mark went away."

"Just because you talked with him?" Tatou said.

"I think so. No one could believe it. Aldous and Tuck were there when it happened, too."

"They saw it disappear?"

"Yes, so did he. His name is Ryder. I've got to meet him at the Maeldun Bridge."

"Not without me," Tatou said.

"You're not ready to fly. You're still healing."

The pixie stamped her foot. "How can you leave me again?"

"It's just one more night."

Tatou looked across the yard. "Oh no."

Against the light from the fire's embers, Flora cradled something inert in her arms. Bella, her black cat.

Melia's throat constricted. She couldn't fathom an adequate gesture of comfort.

"We have to go to her," Tatou said.

As the friends made the long, slow trek across Flora's incinerated yard, Melia was sure the weight of her heart would break open her chest. When they reached the spring faerie, Tatou fluttered up to perch on her shoulder.

Flora didn't push her away.

33. Koldis

Ryder glared into the Balyudor.

He stood with his shoulder against the single straight tree trunk in sight. The dark moon night crawled toward a charcoal-grey dawn, but the slow growing light failed to penetrate the tangled wall of trees, vines, leaves, and undergrowth before him. He turned back to the dying fire. Its orange embers glowed. A beacon for the black eagle. It shouldn't have taken Melia all night to warn her friends.

Worry lodged in his jaw. The concern he'd struggled with most of the night returned: Nandana's prediction that Melia would incarnate Umbra. Had the dark entity reached the Illustrator and influenced her somehow? Why else would she place such a burden on Melia–or on anyone?

He gripped Koldis' hilt. He'd never let Melia do it. It would destroy her.

A few feet away, Tuck sprawled like a bag of stones on a pallet on the ground. Zephyr slept against the tree elf, back-to-back. Ryder stared at the pair, mystified. The eerie howls punctuating the night had failed to wake either of them.

Fury inched up Ryder's spine. Like the priests in the Order of the Idonnai, Tuck valued reading–studying, words–and apparently, sleeping–above all else. It galled the young priest.

Words, after all, were easy to twist.

He picked up a stick, walked over to the lingering coals, and stirred the ashes. His own efforts to sleep had proved futile, and Sinjiin had never considered rest. While Ryder had searched for a spot free from overhanging leaves and branches to build the fire, the tiger had disappeared into the woods to hunt for wolves.

Sinjiin should have returned by now, too.

Ryder let the stick fall from his hand. He couldn't wait idle any longer. He stepped forward to rouse the elf.

A rustle of leaves filled the quiet of breaking dawn. He turned his head.

The black eagle perched on a low tree branch. She was alive.

Their eyes met. Her wings unfolded. There was a crack of blue-black feathers and she was gone.

He searched the small clearing. Had it been an illusion?

He walked toward the tree and almost collided with her when she emerged wearing the same clothes she'd had on the day before–a simple dress and tattered jacket. She might as well have donned a regal gown of silk. The grace of her half-faerie, half-mortal self heightened the beauty of everything around her. Before, the thick mess of woods had writhed with wickedness. In her presence, the jade of the tree leaves and the wisdom of ancient bark showed itself.

He restrained the impulse to embrace her. She seemed skittish as she twisted her fingers. When she gazed into his eyes, he saw the shadow of some fresh inner wound. "What happened?"

Her bottom lip quivered. "Flora–"

"Tell me," he said.

She looked away. "Muannai and black wolves attacked her. They burned her home and stole the basin. It's my fault."

Ryder stared at the ground. Sinjiin had warned him against bringing Koldis to Faerie. Now the basin, Ormrun, had slipped from his grasp. "Are Flora and your friend all right?" he asked.

"Yes, but Flora has serious wounds. She kept Tatou safe, but my friend still isn't strong enough to fly with me. They're headed to the Veiled Tavern now. Have you heard of it?"

"Of course."

"We must meet them there today."

"It can't be far from here. You must be exhausted. Try to get some rest."

"I can't."

Ryder didn't insist. He understood.

"Where's Sinjiin?" she asked.

"Hunting wolves."

"I hope he finds them."

He nodded, appreciating the fierce sentiment. "They don't have the sword," Ryder said. "The sword is the key to the portal. Without it, your sister is safe, and Lord Goring's ambitions are only that."

"How do you know they don't have it?"

Ryder had purchased a plain casement for the blade after his encounter with Captain Tom of the Lucky Seahorse. Simple in appearance, it kept the sword's blue shimmer concealed.

"You don't know," Melia said.

He hated to admit he was a thief.

As her eyes darted around the clearing and back to him, she chewed on one of her fingernails. She was afraid for her sister. If he told her he carried Koldis, the certainty that the muannaye didn't have it might calm her. He didn't have to admit he'd stolen it, or that he was a fugitive.

Her eyebrows raised. She pulled her finger from her mouth and pointed. "Your ... blade ..."

His fingers, resting on the hilt, had eased the sword from its sheath. A thin strip of luminescent blue metal protruded. He shoved it down and gripped her arm to pull her away from the still sleeping Tuck.

"You have it, and you've kept it secret from me? From everyone?" Melia asked. "Why?"

"I told you, after we rescue your sister, I'm going to take it, with the basin, to the Isle of Minnanon."

"But you don't have the basin," she said.

He refused to blame her and her sister for that. "I'll get it."

"But how did you get the sword?" Her words shook. "And why did you bring it to Faerie? At least handle it with more care, and don't put it on display for anyone who has eyes to see."

Her tumble of questions and lecturing tone poked at him. "I've kept it safe without your help."

Their eyes locked. He wanted her to trust him. He opened his mouth–

The ground shook. Branches cracked. Birds shot into the sky. The enormous clove-colored tiger leapt between them, swung his head, and roared.

Zephyr whinnied. Tuck jerked awake. The elf and horse were on their feet.

A blur of air pushed Ryder back. The tiger's enormous torso resized as his stripes and fur evaporated. Four limbs morphed into arms and legs, paws became hands and feet. A lemon-colored turban and male countenance elongated from the tiger's face as a slight masculine body, clothed in red pantaloons and a black vest, emerged. Ryder had witnessed the transformation many times, but it remained startling.

Melia's eyes widened.

"Turnskins," the mage said.

Ryder crossed his arms. "I should have guessed."

"What are turnskins?" Melia asked.

"They're not wolves," Sinjiin said.

"But I saw them," she said. "Huge and fierce. One ripped open Flora's back with its claws."

"They're muannai. Am I right?" Ryder asked.

The mage nodded.

"There are draughts that simulate the changes you experience by enchantment and Sinjiin produces at will," Ryder continued. "The potions allow a creature to shift into an altered form for a period of time. But the essence of the change is only a mask, so when a turnskin speaks in their animal shape, there is always a slight perversion to their tone." Ryder looked at Sinjiin. "The pitch of those howls was higher than any wolf I've ever heard. Where are they going?"

"They twist through the Balyudor with the speed of a whip," Sinjiin said. "One tires and the next one takes its place. I've never seen anything like it. I followed the trail but never caught up with them. When I cornered two, after they'd handed the basin off, they were sick with exhaustion. They'd already resumed their muannaye forms, and it was easy enough to make them talk. They're relaying the basin to Aldaine under Lord Goring's command. They're taking it to the stronghold of Calashai."

"How did they get it?" Tuck demanded. He leaned on a plain walking staff Aldous had pressed upon him during their last moments in the palace library.

Melia held up her hands as if to calm him down. "Tatou is safe, but these turnskins burned Flora's home to the ground before I could warn her of the danger. She's wounded. We've got to meet her and Tatou at the Veiled Tavern today. But the basin ..." She looked to Sinjiin.

"The turnskins are making use of a little-known pass which circles the western Ruadain," the mage said. "It's steep and treacherous, but it's the most direct route up the mountains. There's no way to overtake them."

Tuck turned, kicking up dried leaves and dirt. When he stopped next to a crooked ficus tree, Ryder expected him to sag against it. Rather, he punched the trunk with all his might. The elf shook his hand. "The news goes from bad to worse."

Ryder walked over and put a hand on his shoulder. "This isn't over. Now that Melia's friends are safe, we can rescue Plantine and retrieve the basin."

The elf pushed his hand away. "While Goring is five steps ahead of us."

The priest stamped out the fire. "You're right. There's no time to waste. We'll ride on Sinjiin's back," he said to Melia.

She looked around as if searching for other options. There weren't any. She nodded, but didn't meet his eyes. Was she still upset about Koldis? He searched her silence, but her face gave away nothing.

Sinjiin, having resumed his tiger form, waited for them.

Melia's hand brushed his arm; his breath caught. Her hair smelled like wildflowers.

He made a second silent vow. Umbra would never touch her.

34. Dark Moon Vision

Melia suppressed a shiver of anticipation when Ryder held out his hand. Sinjiin lay on the ground beside her. Ryder's grip tightened, helping her to balance as she straddled the tiger's wide, muscled girth. Once she was settled, Ryder positioned himself in front of her. There was nothing to hold on to but him. She hesitated before resting her palms on his hips.

As Sinjiin raised his forelegs, she swayed backward. When the tiger stretched his hind legs to their full height, the gap she'd been careful to maintain between her chest and Ryder's back collapsed. She pressed her teeth against her bottom lip.

"Ready?" he asked.

The warmth of his back against her chest softened her anger over the sword. Physical contact with him soothed her. Another thing she'd never experienced with anyone before. "Yes."

Sinjiin entered the thickness of the Balyudor, his pad so silent Melia could hear herself breathe. Behind them, Tuck whispered to Zephyr. The thud-clop of the horse's hooves settled into a predictable rhythm as they wove between thick vines that swung overhead and twisted roots which surfaced like knotted webs from the dried leaves layering the ground.

No one spoke. The buzz of insects, croak of frogs, and twitter of birds rose around them. Melia struggled to keep her eyes open in the wood's dim light. When she let her cheek rest against Ryder's back, the smell of him–grass, sweat, and smoke–filled her. She let her arms circle his waist.

When he didn't say anything, her lips curved upwards. Her anger had fled. For a moment, she felt as if nothing bad could ever happen. She sank into the precious reprieve.

Her thoughts wandered. Did Tuck know Ryder carried Koldis? She doubted he or Aldous would have approved of the priest bringing the sword to Tyrannis.

Thinking about the sword made her nervous. She was so sleepy. If Plantine probed for its whereabouts, she'd have little defense against her.

Melia forced herself to stay awake as the forest of wrinkled bark marched by, but images of black soil smoking in the night haunted her.

She'd never wished to harm her father ... her sisters ... or Flora.

Nandana had told her that her path would be difficult, but she'd never warned her about leaving a trail of destruction in her wake. Ryder was supposed to help her, but he hadn't even been there last night when Flora was attacked. Besides, he'd brought Koldis to Faerie and told no one.

Her body stiffened, pulling away from his. Just because he'd answered the call of Nandana's mark didn't mean he was trustworthy. Or capable. She needed to be more guarded with her feelings.

She needed Tatou to help her sort things out.

Late in the afternoon, when the dense undergrowth gave way to an opening carpeted with springy grass, a cold sweat broke over her. A thick layer of clouds created a dismal backwash that did nothing to make the Veiled Tavern–squatting like a fat brown toad on a green blanket–appear more inviting.

"We'll be several hours. You should get some rest," Ryder said.

Melia's sensibilities chafed under his authoritative tone, but the small resentment couldn't explain the tension crawling up the back of her neck. The entire day, dread of entering the mysterious tavern had vied with the anticipation of reuniting with Tatou and Flora. She swore under her breath.

"What's wrong?" Ryder asked.

"Everything," she said. "We've lost the basin because I couldn't stop Plantine from stealing its location from my mind. Now, I know exactly where Koldis is"–she pushed her chin in the direction of his hip–"and I can barely keep my eyes open. The Veiled Tavern is the last place I need to be."

"I'm sorry," Ryder said. "I should have told you about the sword, sooner. I only–"

"You don't trust me," she said.

"It isn't that."

They reached the stone path which divided the tavern's pristine yard in half. Sinjiin stopped.

Melia scowled at the oblong wooden structure sitting in the middle of the lawn. "When we were young, the wood elves told us stories about this place," she said. "No matter how many guests arrive each night, the inn always has the perfect number of bedchambers."

"Did they tell you about the dreams?" Ryder slid from the tiger's back, bowed to her, and held out his hand.

"Yes. That's why I'm frightened to go inside."

"Ah," Ryder said.

A wave of warm air hit them as Sinjiin blurred into his mage form.

"You're wise to be wary of the Veil," them mage said. "For those who wish to keep their secrets, it's not safe to sleep inside."

"But we're all tired." Ryder pointed to Melia. "Look at her. She needs rest before we push on to Aldaine."

Sinjiin indicated the tavern's backyard. "There's the perfect place to nap after lunch."

The deep green grass did looked heavenly. "You think it will be safe to sleep there?" Melia asked.

"Whatever mysterious essence unlocks the dreamer's mind is contained within the Veil's walls," Sinjiin said. "So, yes, if you nap outside, you should be safe from your sister. And whoever else might probe your innermost sanctums."

Melia dropped her gaze from Sinjiin's dark eyes, no longer golden in his mage form. She could feel Ryder watching, too. She hadn't told either of them about her encounters with Umbra.

Maybe she'd been too quick to judge Ryder about the sword.

"But enough talk." The mage clapped his hands. "I could eat five wolves, and I've heard the Veil's chefs are some of the finest in the enchanted world."

Tuck, who'd lagged farther and farther behind them the entire afternoon, arrived.

Melia wanted to stay outside a little while longer. "I'll lead Zephyr to the stables."

Ryder's eyes searched hers. "Are you sure?"

Tuck handed Melia the reins. When the priest seared him with a pointed look, the elf ignored him. He unlashed his walking staff from the pack on the horse's back.

Sinjiin headed toward the inn's engraved wooden doors. Perhaps feeling rebuffed, Ryder turned on his heels to follow.

As the priest disappeared into the Veil's darkened interior, an unfamiliar emptiness hollowed Melia's heart. She was used to being alone, and yet, holding on to Ryder during the trip through the woods had been comforting.

Zephyr nuzzled her cheek; she rubbed the horse's nose.

"Can you believe he doesn't speak birdsong?" Tuck shook his head. "He's a priest from Idonne."

Melia's heart drummed in her ears. "Maybe learning to wield–" She swallowed her words.

Ryder had told them in the palace library that he'd skipped his classes in the priesthood's aviary to train with the Idonnai Guard. Although it meant he couldn't understand her when she was an eagle, she admired his priorities. After all, unless she was in her eagle form, she didn't speak birdsong, either.

"You wouldn't understand," Melia said. She only wished Ryder had told her about Koldis sooner. It had been such a shock, seeing the sword hanging from his belt.

"No, I guess not," Tuck said.

He followed her as she led the horse around the side of the building. She wished he wouldn't.

Deep in thought, Melia tripped over nothing when the dark moon vision possessed her inner eye.

✧ ✧ ✧

The world blisters around me. A living beast, the fire rejects nothing in its path. Deafening cracks fragment thick beams of wood into malevolent skewers; horses rear and gallop, out of control they throw themselves into danger. The storm of terror spins me in its wake. Dizzy, I clutch at myself, while men I've never seen in Faerie wield swords and heave axes.

The ground is slick. I trip and slide. My wrists slam against the ground. My face is inches from Tuck's. He's facedown, spread eagle in a dark pool. His walking staff–split into jagged spears–lies by his side.

I scream.

"Melia." Ryder's voice reaches through my horror.

I can't see him. My voice won't hush. I swear my throat is bloody.

"Melia!"

Tatou hovered inches from her face. Ryder, Flora, and Tuck stood in a circle around her. Spooked, Zephyr showed the white of his eyes.

"You were screaming," Tatou said. "We heard you inside the tavern."

Melia wanted to take heart that she'd experienced no pleasure in the vision, but when she saw the dwarves, trolls, and muannai gathered on the Veil's wide veranda, their eyes saucered with questions, she wanted to tear across the plush lawn, and lose herself in a feral existence that had nothing to do with Umbra or Plantine, the basin or the sword, her mother or her father–

Ryder reached for her hand. "You're shaking."

She shoved both her hands deep in the pocket of her summer coat.

He dropped his arm. "What happened?"

"Not with all these people staring," she whispered.

"Tuck, tell them to go back inside. Tell them she saw something that frightened her, a mouse."

The elf's mouth pressed into a slash of contempt, but he didn't argue.

"Thank you," Melia said.

The green of Ryder's eyes deepened.

"Sometimes ..." She searched for words as Tatou's familiar weight settled on her shoulder.

A gangly, oversized dwarf hurried in their direction. "What happened?" he yelled to Flora.

The spring faerie shifted to stand in front of Melia, hands on her hips.

"She's getting ready to tell us."

The half-faerie's confidence evaporated.

"It was Umbra, wasn't it?" Flora asked.

The tension in the tight group mounted.

"No ... why would you think that?" Melia asked.

Flora held her gaze. An ill-fitted dress hung like a sack over her short, square body. Its sleeves ended at her elbows. Cloth bandages protruded to her wrists. The burns on her face were covered with a salve that made her cheeks shine.

Beyond their small group, Tuck's efforts to shoo the gawkers inside had failed.

The large dwarf crossed his arms. "Are you Pressina's daughter? You look just like her."

It was a question Melia could answer. "Yes."

The oddly-proportioned creature–his arms were longer than his legs–held out his hand. She had to offer hers. He pumped it up and down. "I'm Gumf, the Veiled Tavern's proprietor. I've always had a soft place in my heart for your mother, and I'm pleased to hear the news of your sister's wedding agrees with her. Pressina is sailing to Aldaine as we speak. That must be where you folks are headed, yes? Sister of the bride? Come inside. Tell me all about it." He waved his hands as if he were a mad conductor. "Show's over! "

The crowd murmured and whispered among themselves as they filed back inside the tavern. Flora waddled behind everyone.

Melia's legs wouldn't move. Tatou remained on her shoulder. Ryder had never left her side. "My mother will get to Aldaine before we do," she said. "And so will the basin. Plantine is doomed."

"Elendah, the grey faerie lives." Tatou stroked the side of her friend's head. "As long she sits on the stronghold of Calashai's throne, Plantine will be safe. Umbra can't incarnate."

Melia tugged on a strand of hair. "I only wanted to stop these visions and I thought ... my father is dead. Melusine has exiled herself to the mortal world, and my mother rushes to Aldaine to serve Plantine up to a monster with a thick slice of wedding cake. Why did I ever think I could stop Umbra's incarnation?"

"Because you can," Ryder said.

She searched his eyes. She had the impulse to touch him. He didn't stop her when she raised her hand. She brushed his cheekbone with the tips of her fingers. A current ran through her.

He pressed his hand against hers, holding it against his cheek. Her breath caught. The feel of his palm against the back of her hand was hot. If it were anyone else, she would have jerked away. But Ryder's touch melted her defenses.

Tatou coughed.

Ryder dropped his hand.

Melia pulled away to brush a hair from her face, as if that's why she'd raised her hand in the first place.

"Lunch?" the pixie asked.

The moment of tenderness dispersed.

35. The Veiled Tavern

Melia found herself blinking as her eyes adjusted to the tavern's dusky interior. The smell of fresh-baked bread and other delicious scents made her mouth water. The Veil's chefs–dwarves who'd parlayed their skills for crafting metal into the preparation of tasty food–were legendary, and she was hungry.

Ryder led them through a paneled hall into the marble-walled foyer. Tatou remained on Melia's shoulder.

In the cavernous main room, enormous logs crackled in four fireplaces, drying the damp from the end-of-summer chill. The nearest hearth was brick. The one on the tavern's back wall was carved from white stone. On the third wall, to Melia's right, a stark iron grill covered the fire. In that section there were no tables, only wood bays to play the game of stones. A number of trolls crowded one of the compartments, drinking and shoving one another for a chance to roll the engraved rocks. They weren't much taller than Flora.

The fourth fireplace was cut from smooth, black marble. Several muannai smoked slender pipes in leather booths that flanked the dark retable. There, the largest fleet of dwarves scurried at the beck and call of the wingless dark faeries.

She wondered if Lord Goring had ever come to the Veil. Maybe Gumf knew him. Maybe they were friends. But that seemed unlikely, since Flora had chosen the tavern as her refuge. Melia didn't believe the spring faerie would have come here if she didn't trust its proprietor.

They passed a long bar that dominated the room's center. Muannai, dwarves, and trolls jostled one another for bitters, wine, and bar stools. An army of dwarves with full hands and stained aprons ran back and forth from the kitchen.

Everyone stared.

Sick of feeling self-conscious, Melia held her head high. Her visions, the weight of her guilt–nothing about her life was their business.

One by one, the patrons returned to their drinks and meals.

"He's handsome," Tatou whispered. She was talking about the priest.

"Yes," Melia said, "but the sword he carries is Koldis."

Her friend's hands pressed deeper into her shoulders. "Does Plantine know?"

"Not yet," Melia whispered. "And I'm not going to tell her."

The Veil's proprietor sat with Tuck, Sinjiin, and Flora at a rectangular table flanked by two rough-hewn benches. Silverware and napkins were set on a white tablecloth. Three carafes filled with a dark amethyst liquid waited in its center.

Melia almost tripped over Tuck's walking staff. "Why do you have to bring that thing with you everywhere?" she asked. "You don't need it to walk."

"You'll see."

His cryptic response annoyed her as much as his complaint that Ryder had never learned birdsong. "When?"

Before the elf could answer, Gumf stood up–carafe in hand. "The finest blackberry wine in Faerie." The dwarf didn't ask who wanted a drink before he filled each crystal goblet–including a thimble-sized one for Tatou–to the rim.

Flora downed hers with a single gulp. When she caught the half-faerie staring, she covered her mouth with her hand and whispered, "The best blackberry wine is in the cellars of the stronghold of Calashai, but this is pretty good."

Melia disliked the blueberry wine and honey mead popular in Illialei, but her mouth was dry. She took a sip of the wine. Ripe blackberries and a light bitter aftertaste exploded on her tongue. She took another swallow. The cool liquid set her at ease, silencing her fears of the Veil.

Flora grinned as Melia drained her glass.

Gumf refilled it and raised his goblet in a toast. "To the sister of the bride."

Melia choked. Wine burned her nose. Ryder jumped up. She waved him to sit back down. When she could speak, she asked Gumf, "Then you've heard from my mother, directly?"

"This morning." The dwarf sat with his elbows on the table, rubbing his knuckles. He wore a wrinkled white shirt. His jowls spilled over the collar. His lips were too thick. "She sent a messenger hawk. Asked me to watch out for you."

The half-faerie reached for her glass and took another huge swig.

"Don't drink so fast." Tatou yanked a strand of her hair. "Remember the ylandria."

Melia was so appalled to learn that her mother was spying on her she hardly registered her friend's scolding. "Flora, what do you think about Lord Goring marrying my sister?"

"It's not my concern."

Melia set her goblet down hard. Purple blotches splashed onto the tablecloth. "Lord Goring isn't your concern?"

Flora's eyes–which shifted between an earthy brown and intense black, depending on her mood–darkened. "Who he's marrying, or who he's not marrying, isn't my concern."

"Plantine isn't going to marry him," Tuck said. "She's not in love with him."

The spring faerie raised her hand toward the tree elf. "See. You've got nothing to worry about. Has anyone told Sevondi about the wedding? That's what I want to know."

Melia scrambled. Where had she heard that name before?

Gumf drew his hand down the side of his face. "Why do you always have to look for trouble, Flora?"

She pointed to her bandages. "Look at me, and tell me that I'm the one who's stirring up trouble."

"Goring didn't burn down your house," he said.

Flora threw her napkin on the table. "I see he's bought you too."

"You weren't a target. What happened last night was an accident. Some careless muannaye smoking woodvine in the Balyudor."

Two slanted lines of snarled grey hair slashed the spring faerie's forehead. "Careless? That's what you think!"

The odd-shaped dwarf tilted his head to the side. "Haven't I done everything I could to help you and your friend?" He indicated Tatou. "Didn't I call for Nivea the second you arrived?"

"Who's Nivea?" Melia asked.

"The best healer in Tyrannis," Gumf said.

"Good, but not the best," Flora said.

"The best," the proprietor said.

"I'm the best," Flora said. "Embril is the second best. Then Nivea. She's a troll, so is Embril. But I don't hold that against them."

The Veil's proprietor raised his long, lumpy arm to point at Tatou and Flora. "Results speak for themselves."

"Yes, it's a good thing I brought those root beetles along." Flora tapped the table. "Let's see who you send for the next time you're in need." The spring faerie covered her mouth with a gnarled hand. "It won't be Nivea," she said to Melia and Tatou.

The half-faerie kept her mouth closed, but a few giggles tickled the back of her throat as Gumf shifted around and made his bench creak. He came to rest with his arms over his chest. "I told you, I'm going to help you rebuild your home."

"I don't need your pity." Flora pressed her hands flat on the table. "I need a killing potion. I'm sure Sevondi will oblige when she hears about her lover's plans to marry this one's sister." She raised her eyebrows and tilted her head toward Melia. "Sevondi and Lord Goring were going to be married. At least, that's what Sevondi thought."

Melia put together the name and face of the muannaye who'd refused to help her. Sevondi was the dragonwitch in the Muannai Valley Marketplace, the one who could draw protective shields.

She couldn't believe Plantine's kidnapper and the dragonwitch had been lovers.

"Any news of her whereabouts?" Flora asked Gumf.

He waved her off.

"I'd place my bet on the Muudron Stone," the spring faerie said. "If anyone asked me."

The dwarf shook his head, but shock flecked his eyes. He turned away from Flora and their pointed banter stopped.

"What's the Muudron Stone?" Melia asked.

"Sorcerers and witches used to sail all the way from Kyrakkos to practice black magic there," Tatou said. "But that was ages ago."

"It's east of here," Flora said. "A stage of crumbling rock. Sevondi thrives on drama."

"You know her?" Melia asked.

"I stop by her shop on my trips to the valley. She likes to think she knows the best places to scavenge ingredients for spells. Herbs, bird eggs, snake skins, roots and such. She doesn't."

"Do you do spells?" Melia asked.

Flora looked at Tatou and then the ceiling.

"Spring faeries don't need magic," Tatou said. "They're very connected to the Whole, more than the rest of us."

Flora sipped her wine.

"Then why do you need to find Sevondi?" Melia asked.

"Because I need a killing potion."

"Why can't you make one yourself?"

"It's not my specialty, although maybe I should learn."

The arrival of lunch ended Flora's limited patience with Melia's questions. Loaves of bread, bowls of soup, tarts stuffed with grilled meat, and platters piled high with sautéed greens and onions covered the table. Not a drop of honey.

Melia was ecstatic. She reached to fill her plate. While they stuffed themselves, she tried to untangle the Tyrannis alliances. Gumf and Flora were old friends, but the dwarf wasn't about to stand up to Lord Goring. Or Pressina. She snuck glances across the table. The spring faerie was up to something.

The sound of her sister's name drew Melia's attention to Tuck. He was telling Sinjiin, Gumf, and Ryder something about her.

"One afternoon, Plantine was feeling mischievous. She'd been studying an intricate pattern of hand movements that promised to mesmerize the most resistant subject. After she put Basil, the library cat, into a sleep so deep we feared he'd never wake up, Aldous and I refused to let her practice on us."

Melia wondered if this had happened before or after her sister's failed spell at Ashleam Bay. Probably before.

"She went in search of a subject who would prove more of a challenge than the cat. After all, he's old, and napping is his natural state. Even if it's usually easy to wake him." Tuck chuckled. His glass was empty. The wine must have loosened his tongue; he rarely spoke so much. "A delicious smell hung in the halls outside the palace kitchen. Plantine wanted to sample what the cooks were making. She waltzed into the kitchen. One of the cook's assistants shooed her out. Plantine danced her hands, drawing a complicated picture of circles and lines with her fingers. I managed to slide a chair behind the old field faerie before her knees collapsed. Plantine laughed out loud and all the other cooks came running. She couldn't stop laughing. It sounded like bells."

Melia knew the sound Tuck described. From the day she was born, whenever Plantine encountered something that amused her, that peal of delight would fill the air. There had been none of that when Plantine had interrogated Melia in the apple orchard. Her sister had been seductive, relentless, irresistible, and dangerous. Melia set her napkin on the table. What if Plantine found her here at the Veil, drunk on blackberry wine?

Tuck had stopped talking. Everyone watched Melia. "Please, continue," she said, preferring the elf's memories to hers.

"That's all," Tuck said.

"Then it's time to plan our trip," Ryder said. "And Plantine's rescue."

The black caterpillars above Gumf's eyes crawled toward the ceiling. "Perhaps she doesn't wish to be rescued."

Melia tried to shake the wine's dullness from her brain.

"Pressina is very pleased about the wedding," the dwarf said.

The half-faerie twisted on her bench.

"You remind me of her," he said to Melia.

Were those tears welling in his eyes? Melia searched the faces of her companions, desperate for someone to intervene.

"Your hair is darker than Pressina's," he continued. "But the planes of your face, and the shape of your eyes; they're the same."

She pressed her lips together. She didn't know how much more of this she could listen to.

"Your mother was here once." A dreamy look passed over the dwarf's eyes. "For five memorable days she enchanted us all."

Melia couldn't recall her mother ever being enchanting. Beautiful, yes. Enchanting, no.

"I found her, lost in the Balyudor," Flora said.

"She's never been to Tyrannis," Melia said.

Gumf looked askance at Flora.

"She was a mess," the spring faerie said, "wandering in circles through the woods. When she told me she was an Albiana, I brought her to the Veil. Gumf collects strays."

Melia's head and shoulders jerked back as Flora's words hit her.

"That's what you are," the spring faerie continued. "That's what all the Albiana are. Strays." She didn't look at Melia as she spoke. She stared at the table. "Illialei, the Realm of Faerie, isn't your home."

Gumf's fists slammed the table. Every empty glass and saucer bounced or rattled. "Flora!"

"Gwyneth Albiana may not have been born in the Realm of Faerie, but it became her home," Ryder said. "It's the rightful home of her descendants."

Sinjiin dragged a finger across his throat, indicating for the young priest to be quiet.

"I'll not listen to you defend them." The spring faerie folded her napkin once and set it down. She stood up, brushing the wrinkles from her sack-like dress.

When she walked away, Sinjiin hurried after her. "Flora–wait!"

Melia gripped the table. She stared at the purple spots staining the white cloth. It felt as though someone had cut out her heart, tied a rope around it, and thrown it out to sea.

Tatou's light touch stroked the back of her hand. Melia couldn't look at her. She couldn't move. Her gaze found the flames in the fireplace. She thought she could hear the cries of the spring faeries as they burned. The gate of her heart clanged shut. The few moments of allowing it to breathe had been a mistake.

"It's hard for Flora to care about you," Tatou said.

"Why?" Melia asked.

"Caring for someone with Albiana blood–again–opens wounds that have never healed for her."

Melia didn't move her head, but she let her eyes leave the fireplace to search her friend's face. "Again?"

"All the spring faeries loved Gwyneth Albiana for bringing the sapphire lily to the Realm of Faerie. They were the ones who first understood the lily's power," Tatou said.

"And they knew how to make it grow." Gumf leaned away from the table and rested his hands on his ample belly. "You've never seen anything until you've seen a field of sapphire lilies."

Melia's brows pushed together. "But there's only one flower."

Tatou looked at the others. "Who wants to tell her the story?"

Ryder and Tuck turned to the Veil's proprietor.

"It's been a long time since I've told that one." Gumf called a dwarf to clean the empty saucers and platters from the table. "Bring us some water."

After he took a few sips, he began.

36. A Field of Lilies

"Most of us think it was the gods of Azyllai who gave Gwyneth the lily's seed and sent her to the Realm of Faerie," Gumf said. "She never said as much, but when she arrived on the shores of Lake Vivientiana in that gossamer bubble, there was a lot of speculation. She carried the seed in a jeweled box, and she wouldn't let herself be distracted until it was planted. She was a gardener through and through.

"We're all gardeners here in Faerie, but only the spring faeries rivaled Gwyneth's ability to make things rooted in the ground thrive." The dwarf cleared his throat. "Every spring faerie is born knowing the power of the unwritten things in life. They were the first to suspect the sapphire lily's beauty extended well beyond the flower's appearance.

"Everything in Faerie feeds the mortal world in some way or another. Each of our lives"–he pointed to everyone sitting around the table–"and every living thing in the enchanted world, fuels mortal imagination and dreams. Without us, the mortal world would wither, because the mortal mind would die."

As Melia listened, every moment she'd spent on Lake Vivientiana's shores returned. The schzzzzz of the lake's fountain, the gentle lapping of the water against the shore, her claws crunching through the grit of sand. Even the flower's scent–something like fresh berries mashed with basil and honey–came back to her.

"Gwyneth revered the flower," he continued. "Every morning and evening she nurtured the plant. Her devotion endeared her to the spring faeries, and their fondness for her grew into an obsession with the lily. After her daughter, Ava, was born, and the lily gave its first bloom, it became rare to find Gwyneth alone with the flower. One or two spring faeries always accompanied her visits.

"As Ava grew older, Gwyneth bestowed the honor of tending to the lily on the spring faeries. She still visited the plant daily, but she allowed the spring faeries to care for it. With her blessing, they seeded new plants. By the time Ava ascended the throne, a field of sapphire lilies bloomed on the southwest shores of Lake Vivientiana. And though the spring faeries were warriors, the field of lilies was their greatest glory."

Melia's heart raced. The story Gumf told resonated with the pull she'd felt to go to the lily before she'd left Illialei. Her body had pulsed with the need.

The dwarf took another drink of water. "It's no surprise the spring faeries grasped the lily's true purpose before anyone else did."

Melia scooted forward to the edge of her seat. "What was that?"

"The bloom of each lily holds the good deeds we've not yet done. The ones we carry in our heart. Millions of them."

A dreamy flutter rose in Melia's chest. She rested her elbows on the table and propped her chin in her hands. "But there is only one flower now. What happened to the field?"

Gumf scrubbed his forehead with his palm. "When Gwyneth passed into the Unknown Beyond, Ava took the throne. She was a fragile queen, with all her mother's heart, but none of her mother's strength. Her daughter, Uriel, refused to spend time with the lily. Gardening in the mud, dirtying her gowns, was beneath her.

"As Ava aged, the spring faeries feared Uriel's reign. They whispered among themselves, What kind of queen would she be without the influence of the lily's perfume?" The dwarf released a heavy sigh. "When Ava died, the spring faeries demanded an audience with their new queen. If Uriel wouldn't assume the single task demanded of her bloodline, they would challenge her right to sit on the Cathedral Palace throne."

Melia held her breath. Why had her mother never hinted at the mystery that saturated their lives?

"But no one anticipated the horror of Uriel's temper. Nor did they realize she'd harnessed a dark power forming in the Void–Umbra," Gumf said.

An icy knowing stiffened Melia's spine.

"The spring faeries challenged a great enemy with no preparation. They were right about the sapphire lily, but they were wrong about the Albiana. The lily didn't bestow any power upon the line of queens, it only tempered the great power for magic inherent in their blood. The contingent of spring faeries had barely left the throne room when Uriel conjured her black spell. By the time they reached the apple orchard, it was done–springtime forever banished from Illialei."

Melia gasped. Memories flushed up. Her mother descending to her occult room deep in the trunk of the oak tree. Plantine holed up in the palace library studying spells and potions. Her mother calling forth shimmering prisons and cursing her daughters.

"Flora was in the mortal world. She reached Illialei by sunset, but all her kin were already dead. The field of lilies burned with them. Only a handful of flowers survived. No one had the courage to stand with Flora against such a powerful queen, so she left Illialei."

"She needs to return," Tuck said.

Everyone looked at him.

"It has to be said. Umbra is the black in the heart of man that doesn't die with his mortal body. The desire to do good, flourishing in the mortal heart, is the natural counterbalancing force. The field of sapphire lilies must bloom again. Otherwise, we're all lost, not only mortals and their world."

"And Flora is the only one who can do this?" Melia asked.

Tuck threw his napkin on the table. "Elves have been trying in secret to seed new plants. Every effort fails."

"I flew to Lake Vivientiana last night," Melia said. Everyone stared at her. "It's why ... I couldn't leave Illialei without seeing the lily. If I hadn't gone–"

"You couldn't have stopped last night's attack," Tatou said. "There were too many of them."

"There were only two," Melia whispered.

"No," Tatou said. "You're forgetting about the archers. When Clover took me to the stream, the woods were thick with them. If you'd arrived earlier, they would have killed you."

"They'll do worse to Plantine if we don't reach her in time," Tuck said.

"What's worse than death?" Tatou snipped.

"No one died last night," Tuck said.

"Flora's cat did!" The pixie's wings trembled. "Don't worry about your precious Plantine, Lord Goring needs her. He won't let anything happen to her."

Melia raised her eyebrows at the force of her friend's challenge.

"What?" Tatou asked. "Does he think Plantine is the only one in danger?"

Tuck pushed away from the table. "That's not what I meant."

"Then what did you mean?" Tatou charged across the table to stand in front of him. "Those wolves would have swallowed me whole last night if Clover hadn't had the good sense to hide me. Did you see the wounds on Flora's back, or notice the burns on her face? And Bella is dead! We've all been injured trying to help Plantine."

The elf raised his hands. "I'm sorry, you're right. I'm thinking only of Melia's sister because I know how vulnerable she is from her mother's curse."

Tatou's pixie temper soared. "Not too vulnerable to locate the basin and send–"

Gumf slammed the table with the palms of his hand. "Stop it, both of you."

The tree elf and the pixie's expressions remained heated.

"You're all on edge," the Veil's proprietor said. As if on cue, three dwarves appeared by his side. "Let them take you to your rooms. Bathe and get some rest. You can continue your journey in the morning."

No one moved.

He waved his sausage fingers in the air. "Go on. Pressina asked me to offer help with your travels. I'll have some provisions packed for the lot of you, and provide another horse to keep Zephyr company on the trail. They'll be saddled and ready to leave at dawn."

Although Tatou couldn't wait to bathe, Melia refused to go to the room Gumf had provided for them. Her friend left her standing on the tavern's wide back porch with Ryder. It was almost sunset.

"You can't take the sword to Aldaine," Melia said. "It's far too dangerous."

Ryder's hand went to the blade's hilt. "What would you have me do with it?"

"You should have left it wherever you found it."

"The sword was on display in the library archive for all to see, and with little protection. I could never have left it there," he said. "There are too many in the enchanted world who know the blade's purpose. They were already circling, waiting for the right moment to snatch it from beneath the order's nose."

"You could have left it in Illialei with Aldous."

"So the queen could seize it?"

"Aldous would have hidden it, and not told a soul he had it in his possession," she said.

"He wouldn't have to. Did you hear what Gumf said about the sapphire lily? Queen Luisa doesn't tend the flower. For all we know, she's as corrupt as Uriel. No, I wouldn't leave Koldis within her grasp."

Twilight turned the Veiled Tavern's spongy grass from bright green to mossy grey. When Melia changed into an eagle, they wouldn't be able to communicate. "I would say leave it here, but Gumf would probably send it as a wedding gift to Aldaine."

"I concede the danger in carrying it with me. It would be equally dangerous to leave it here, or anywhere else. It won't be safe until it's in the hands of the Grey Council."

Tremors in her arms and legs warned Melia she would change soon. She hated for anyone to see that, especially him. She reached for Ryder's hand and squeezed it. "I can't spend the night inside the tavern. You understand."

He nodded, but didn't look too happy about it.

"I'll be back before dawn." She ran toward the trees edging the lawn's perimeter. "Maybe I'll think of something by then. Flying clears my head," she yelled over her shoulder.

The sensations of transmogrification jolted her body. Once it began, the change came fast, similar to Sinjiin's. Her nose and toes stretched into a beak and talons. Her feathers absorbed her sleeveless dress and summer jacket. At dawn, she always resumed her half-faerie form fully-clothed. It was better than naked, but it would have been nice if her dress had been washed, or the holes in her jacket repaired.

Clover, Flora's goat, grazed nearby. A thick bandage covered her rump. She watched the half-faerie shift with alert brown eyes. When Melia stood in the grass as an eagle, the goat batted her eyelashes in recognition.

Melia hoped the priest hadn't watched her transformation. She circled around and was relieved to see the porch was empty.

But one more question festered.

She landed on the porch's wood rail and perched upon it until a troll flung the back door open. Flying over his head, she entered the tavern's interior. All the cooks stared as she flapped by. Beyond the kitchen, she kept to the shadows along the wall. She found the Veil's proprietor stationed at a mahogany table in the foyer. When she landed on its shiny surface, the dwarf waved his arms.

"It's me," Melia shouted in eagle.

Gumf's arms fell to his side. "I'll be. I'd heard Pressina cast a spell upon you girls after Elynus died, but I had no idea she'd become so skilled. I'd never guess you were anything but an eagle, and a magnificent one at that. How wide is your wing span?"

Melia stretched her wings their full eight feet.

He wagged his head. "Pressina outdid herself."

She tried not to think about Melusine slithering through the dirt as a dragon-winged serpent every Sunday. Or the eerie glow of Plantine's eyes as their blue faded with the rest of her. "What did my mother do when Flora brought her here?" Melia had been dying to ask the question all afternoon.

"Lovely faerie, your mother," he said. "One of the loveliest I've ever known. I gave her the finest room in the inn. Everyone here adored her."

Melia tried to reconcile that image with the recluse who had raised her. "Why did she leave?"

Gumf threaded his fingers across his knuckles. "It was the vision. It upset her. That's why she left us."

"What did she see?"

He crossed one arm over his chest. He covered his mouth with his other hand.

Melia had to know. "Tell me."

Gumf dropped the hand from his mouth. "She saw the spring faeries burn. She felt the fire on her skin. She ran to the Undine to quench the flames. No one could stop her, although we tried. She was crazed with the horror of what she witnessed. I understand that's when she slipped into the mortal world. It was easier to cross over in those days. I heard she fell in love with your father soon after."

Melia stared at the dwarf. It was impossible to imagine the Pressina she knew sitting at the Veil's bar throwing back blackberry wine, or tormented by a vision of genocide, but Gumf seemed sincere.

For the first time in her life, Melia realized she didn't know her mother at all.

37. The Lasimas Diamond

Ryder found Sinjiin and Flora leaning against one of the wood bays where the Veil's patrons, mostly trolls, played stones. Sinjiin drank a mug of bitters. The spring faerie stood sullen, her hands in her pockets. Uncertain how to approach her after his words had caused her to storm off, he decided to go with something basic. "I'm sorry I upset you earlier."

Flora looked him up and down. "I'm too old for lectures about anything."

Ryder offered a half-bow. He met her stern gaze as he straightened. "You're right. It wasn't my place."

Flora dug her hands deeper into her apron pocket.

Sinjiin slapped him on the back. "A round of stones, my friend?"

Ryder had watched the game a few times, but never played. Gambling was high on the long list of activities the Order of Idonnai disapproved of, and Melia's abrupt departure hadn't left him in the mood to test his luck. "Pass."

Flora bucked her head up. "I'll take you on."

Sinjiin's teeth gleamed. Ryder followed them to the head of the bay. This he had to see.

After bickering over a few points–which line to stand behind (there were three levels, and Flora insisted they use the one farthest from the target), the number of stones to be thrown in each round (between five and nine, Flora demanded seven), and how much each round would be worth (Flora refused to even consider gold)–Sinjiin rolled the die to see who would go first. The mage won and went to the tray hanging from the side of the bay to select his seven rocks.

Flora waved down a dwarf and ordered a pint of bitters. Sinjiin missed all six targets. The spring faerie's face became one huge grin. When it was her turn, she shoved her half-empty mug into Ryder's hands and sauntered to the tray of engraved stones.

She took her time with her choices, dropping them one by one into the pocket of her apron. Preparing her first toss, she positioned the toe of her left boot with the line they'd agreed to throw from. She took one of the rocks from her pocket, pulled back her arm, and heaved the small stone into the highest valued target.

Sinjiin's eyes goggled. Flora killed him in the first round.

Before long a crowd of trolls pushed against Ryder. The spring faerie made a spectacle of herself with each toss but always hit her target. Now the trolls were placing bets on her win. Ryder enjoyed watching her play. Despite her theatrics, her technique was solid. She wasn't winning because of luck.

At the end of the fourth round, Flora made what looked to be an impossible shot. Sinjiin's mouth fell open.

The game was almost over when Gumf pushed his way through the crowd. "You two"–he pointed to Ryder and Flora–"come with me."

"Not until I've won," the spring faerie said.

Sinjiin waved his mug. "Go on. Victory is yours."

"Then pay up," she said.

The mage reached into the recesses of his red pantaloons and pulled out ten silver coins. It was twice as much as they'd agreed to play for. He shoved them all into Flora's outstretched palm, curling her fingers over the small pile.

She jerked her hand away to count each one, but even in the amber light, Ryder could see her brown eyes twinkle. He looked at Sinjiin. The mage hummed. It was the same tune the sailor's sang on the Lucky Seahorse when the sky was clear. Ryder understood. The mage had restored something more important than Flora's home. He'd revived the core of who she was—a warrior who won.

Gumf led the priest and the spring faerie through a labyrinth of halls. He ushered them into a private room and closed the door. A few candles sputtered in iron sconces. There were no windows.

The dwarf walked toward the single table filling the room. In its center were a pair of brown leather gloves and a wood box marked with ciphers. Gumf drew up one of the chairs and indicated they should sit too. "Funny you asked about Sevondi this afternoon," he said to Flora.

"And why is that?" she asked.

"One of my stable boys overheard a troll talking about her only a little while ago."

"It's funny what you can hear when you're eavesdropping. What did the troll say?"

Gumf ignored the dig and the question. He turned to Ryder. "That sword you're carrying"—he pointed to Koldis—"it wouldn't happen to be the one Lord Goring's looking for, would it?"

Ryder resisted the impulse to rest his hand on the sword's casement.

"Here we go," Flora said. "How much is he paying you to deliver it?"

The muscles in the dwarf's face twitched. Again, he ignored her provocation and focused on the priest. "You care for Pressina's daughter a great deal, don't you?

Ryder straightened his back against the chair. "Yes."

"I thought so. When we were outside—after she'd been screaming and scared everyone in the tavern to death—"

Ryder's jaw locked.

"—it was admirable the way you were so patient with her and calmed her down. Her mother told me she has these fits. Always scares everyone—"

"What do you want?"

Gumf held up his palms. "I think we can come to an agreement that will benefit us all."

The dwarf's head bobbed up and down like the donkeys Ryder had fed in Idonne as a boy. The priest raised his chin. A familiar corkscrew pressured his gut. The Veil's proprietor was good, but Anton, his mentor and the head of the Order of the Idonnai, was better when it came to maneuvering the emotions of others.

The priest intended to maintain enough goodwill for the dwarf to lead them back through the maze of halls to the tavern's main room. "I'm listening," he said.

The Veil's proprietor reached for the ciphered box. He opened the lid. A saffron orb, the size of a small melon, rested on a plum-colored silk cloth.

"One of the Rykkiel," Ryder said.

Across the table, Flora's eyes widened.

"You recognize it."

"Yes, Anton possesses the Bellissimas."

"They're the seven largest diamonds in existence, mined from the depths of the highest mountain in Azyllai," Gumf said. "Each one is a different color and imbued with a unique magical property." He struggled with the leather gloves. "The Bellissimas shields its bearer from evil's sight. Is that correct?"

"Yes," Ryder said.

Gumf stroked the yellow globe with his gloved hand. "The Tasimas transports its bearer to a destination they visualize in their mind."

Flora had almost crawled across the table to get a better look. "How long does it take?"

Gumf snapped his fingers. "You could be at the stronghold like that."

"Then we'll wait until morning, when Melia can join us," Ryder said.

The dwarf returned the Tasimas to the box. He pulled off the leather gloves and laid them on the table. "Pressina told me how set her middle daughter is against Umbra's incarnation."

Ryder forced himself to listen to the dwarf's entreaty.

"Let's be honest, here, among ourselves. Umbra can't be stopped; the incarnation will happen; it's only a matter of time. Elynus trusted Lord Goring with *The Book of Umbra*. Now we see how much wisdom he showed in that choice. Goring has chosen the druid's daughter to fulfill his legacy."

Flora snorted.

The dwarf ignored her, again. "And risked Sevondi's wrath."

The spring faerie's eyes narrowed. "She's waiting for us, isn't she? Sevondi's planning to ambush us on the way to Aldaine and take the sword.

That's what your trolls overheard, isn't it? You want the priest to take Koldis to Goring tonight, so she can't cause him any more trouble."

The dwarf's slack mouth and shifty eyes confirmed her words.

Ryder needed something to drink, a glass of water. There wasn't one. "How does she know I have the sword? For that matter, how do you know?"

Gumf pulled out a square of parchment. It crinkled as he flattened it on the table. It was the same Wanted notice the captain of the Lucky Seahorse had used to extort Ryder and Sinjiin for gold when they'd sailed from Typhos to Faerie.

"I don't want any trouble," the dwarf said. "You care for the girl. There's no reason to send you back to Idonne in chains. Take the sword to Lord Goring tonight, and there'll be no need to order your arrest."

"If anyone's going to be arrested, it should be the muannai who killed Bella and burned down my house," Flora said.

Gumf rubbed his palms against his temples. "If we help Goring, things will be much better for all of us once Umbra incarnates–and he will incarnate."

"If I understand what you said earlier," Ryder said, "the diamond is useless to me. I've never been to the stronghold. I won't be able to visualize it."

The dwarf pointed to the spring faerie. "She has."

Ryder stood up. "I've heard enough."

Flora reached for the Tasimas.

The priest lunged to stop her.

38. The Dragonwitch

Faerie's two moons remained black. It was the second dark moon night in the cycle. One more before the moons showed themselves as twin slivers of light.

In her half-faerie form or as an eagle in the mortal world, Melia would have been blind, but as an eagle by enchantment, her sight remained sharp. She flew east, beyond the Balyudor toward the valley.

The wind on her feathered face cleared the haze of the Veil from her head. It seemed as if the tavern had bewitched her, but it was probably only the residual effects of the blackberry wine.

She took advantage of the empty skies to practice her spirals and dives. Minute alterations in her wing position made breathtaking changes in the arc of her spins and the speed of her dives. Focused on precision, she refused to dwell on Plantine, her mother, the basin, the sword, or Lord Goring.

Thoughts of Ryder and the sapphire lily were harder to push away. He always defended her and assumed the best of her. If he could see one of her visions, would he still believe in her?

Melia tried to imagine what he would think if he could see the images of dead faeries, mangled pixies, and drowned mermaids that haunted her.

She nose-dived, pulling out of the descent seconds before her beak jammed into the ground.

When Nandana had predicted Melia was destined to incarnate Umbra, Melia had refused to listen. Ryder had argued against the claim as well, and who would know better than him? He'd studied Umbra as a priest in Idonne, and he believed the vast darkness of Umbra's consciousness would be too great a burden for any single person to bear. He also doubted any hope offered by the prophecy. Yet, when Melia had breathed deeply of the sapphire lily's perfume, a confident peace had enveloped her; the constant fear fueled by her grisly visions had dissolved.

Still, Nandana must be wrong. Melia would never incarnate Umbra. Not even if a field of sapphire lilies bloomed.

A light danced below. She coasted into a descent.

A small fire burned on a stone floor. It illuminated a semicircle of pillars that stood upright on an elevated stage. Steps spiraled around the platform of what appeared to be an ancient temple. She'd been flying east. Was this place the Muudron Stone?

Melia whorled down and landed in a copse of trees to the left of the formation. From her vantage point, she saw cracks and chips in the boulders of the columns. The steps were worn with the passage of time and of use. Although it stood in ruins, the outdoor temple looked holy in the flicker of firelight.

She was about to fly to the Muudron's center when a shadow caught her attention. The fire maker? She peered through the leaves. He paced between the columns. She searched for a way to get closer without being observed.

Clumps of trees ringed the amphitheater, but she risked exposure flying between them. The high grass offered the best camouflage. She cocked her head to listen for anything that might want to eat her. There were only insects scratching and chittering in the field, and the whisper of a stream nearby. She fluttered to the ground and slipped through the tall blades of grass.

Several yards from the stage she saw the troll. He watched the south as he paced. He looked harmless enough with his wool cap pulled down over his forehead. Most of the trolls playing stones in the bays at the Veiled Tavern had worn similar caps. His heavy boots clacked against the rocks with every step. He shoved his hands into his pockets only to pull them out again. He wrapped his arms around his chest and sighed. He couldn't stand still.

Melia needed to return to the tavern, but an inner twinge made her hesitate. The troll hunkered down to throw a few more sticks on the fire.

Minutes ticked by. Melia gouged the dirt with her talons.

The troll returned to the pillar's dark shadows.

She straightened her wings and eased back through the long grass. She'd wasted enough time spying on the unremarkable subject.

The ground trembled. Something large and fast slammed the steppes.

Three enormous black shadows plunged onto the stone stage. A female muannaye straddled one of them, riding bareback. Long, dark hair flew behind her. When the wolves–were they turnskins?–came to a halt, the muannaye vaulted to the oblong dais at the Muudron's center. Firelight bathed her form as she circled the animals, laughing. Her exhilarating energy was infectious.

Melia parted the long grass with her beak and stared.

The figure was slight for a muannaye, standing barely taller than a field faerie. She had no fear of the beasts, encouraging them to nuzzle her back and shoulders as she stroked their fur with slender fingers and delivered tender kisses to their snouts. When one of the wild dogs licked her face, she pushed it away with a playful slap. "Pogo!"

The troll edged from the shadows. He stopped, maintaining a distance between himself and the wolves. "Over here."

Melia stared, unbelieving. Muannai were known for their exquisite, physical perfection, but this one's right eyebrow sat a good half-inch higher upon her brow bone than the left. It was the dragonwitch from the marketplace. Sevondi's single flaw made her distinct. Melia's heart raced. How could Flora have known she would be here, at the Muudron Stone?

"Come closer, they won't bite," the muannaye teased the troll.

"I'm fine over here."

"All right, boys." Sevondi cuffed one of the turnskins before leaning to whisper something in its ear. The mournful howl that followed sent a shiver up Melia's spine. The muannaye slapped its rump. "Off with you."

The three wolves leapt together from the stone floor to vanish into the night. Sevondi crouched before the troll, her movements languid. "What did you learn at the Veiled Tavern? Anything useful?"

Pogo pulled the wool cap from his forehead and worried it with stubby fingers. "He's here."

"You're sure?"

"My source saw him this afternoon with Gumf. He's got the sword with him."

Melia's heart pelted. Ryder. She needed to warn him.

Sevondi laughed. "What a fool. But such a useful fool, nych?"

Melia hugged her wings closer to her body. She strained to listen to every word.

"He's not alone," the troll continued.

"Who's with him?"

"A mage from the Hidden City who travels as a tiger."

"Interesting, any others?"

"An elf from Illialei and the sister of the bride."

Sevondi scowled.

The troll was the one who'd been in Sevondi's shop when Melia had asked the dragonwitch about drawing the protective markings to ward off evil. He didn't mention Tatou or Flora. His spy must have seen them after the spring faerie had left the table, and Tatou's size made her easy to overlook.

"Their plans?" the muannaye asked.

"They're headed to the stronghold of Calashai to rescue the half-faerie. They'll leave the Veil in the morning."

"Then we must be prepared," Sevondi said.

The veins of Melia's throat pulsed. How did the troll know so much about them? Had Gumf betrayed them? No, the dwarf wouldn't endanger her after he'd promised Pressina to help them. His fondness for her mother was embarrassing, but it was genuine. There were so many trolls and dwarves coming in and out of the Veil, Pogo could have paid any of them to eavesdrop.

Sevondi paced. Most muannaye wore slim pants and high boots, even the females, but not her. She wore a sleeveless blouse even though the night was cool. Her billowy skirt touched her calves, and she wore sandals.

Muannai seldom wore jewelry, but everything about Sevondi was atypical. Metal bands wrapped both her biceps and right forearm. Intricate patterns traced her arms and legs; a crescent moon and small star marked one of her temples.

She didn't look like someone who would be happy to be replaced at the altar. If what Flora had told them today was true–maybe she hadn't been. The scene playing out on the stone stage didn't look promising for Plantine. Maybe Goring didn't intend to marry her sister after all. Melia hoped. Then what kind of game was he playing?

"I wonder if Zachariah knows they're coming. What do you think?" she asked the troll.

Pogo shrugged.

"I'm in no mood to warn him."

A gash split open the night sky. Blinding light eclipsed Sevondi and the troll. A bowed over figure spilled from the tear and rolled onto the Muudron's stage. The thing wrestled with something it held in its arms.

"Get off me, you oversized oaf!"

A wool cloak snapped against the pavement as the bulky figure rolled back and forth. Ryder. The cape billowed behind the priest, leaving the sheath of his sword visible in the zigzagging light.

Two booted feet kicked against his grip. Flora.

Where had they come from?

Thunder boomed as the slash of light closed. Sevondi and Pogo stared, their mouths open. Ryder and Flora continued to wrestle, oblivious of their audience.

She had to protect Koldis. Melia flew toward them. "Flora! Ryder, the sword!"

The priest had managed to pin the spring faerie to the ground by throwing one of his long legs over her two short ones. Gasping for breath, he had an arm against her chest, between her neck and ample bosom. With the bandage on her chin and the salve on her cheeks, her face shined like a macabre mask.

Melia circled her companions. Flora gripped a round gemstone in her gnarled fingers.

"Melia?" Ryder asked.

Sevondi edged over to the ensnarled pair. Melia widened her circle and flapped her wings harder. Ryder let go of Flora.

The spring faerie winced as she righted herself. "The Tasimas works," she said.

Sevondi stared at the yellow stone in the spring faerie's hands. "My friend, this is impressive, even for you."

Flora acknowledged the muannaye's compliment with a tilt of her head. "I don't have much time, and I need a potion."

Ryder's face was a mask of disbelief. "You stole the Rykkiel to get a potion?"

Flora sniffed. "Borrowed. I borrowed the Rykkiel to get a potion. Someone needed to test it, don't you think?"

The priest's eyes burst with indignation while Sevondi's blazed with hunger. "Did you say 'Rykkiel'?"

The spring faerie fumbled to cover the ball with her apron. "It's nothing."

"When I heard about the fire," the muannaye said, "I feared the worst, but I can see you're all right."

"Yes, I'll be fine. But I need a killing potion."

Ryder glared at the spring faerie. Sevondi circled them, but kept her gaze on him. "For him?"

Flora glanced at the priest towering over her. "He's annoying, but no need to put him to death for it. No, I need one for your kind, a muannaye."

"Do I know her?" Sevondi asked.

"Him," Flora said.

"Who is it?"

"You know who ordered my home burned."

The muannaye's lips curled. She gave a single shake of her head.

"Your lover," the spring faerie said.

Sevondi's eyes turned black. "That is not funny. Not even from you."

Flora attempted to stand. The yellow ball slipped from her grasp and rolled across the uneven stone tiles. Sevondi snapped her fingers and pointed in the orb's direction. Pogo ran after it, but Melia reached the ball first. She hovered above it, using her eight-foot wingspan to keep the troll at bay. Unfortunately, the gemstone was too slick to grip with her talons.

Pogo took a step closer.

She screeched as loud as she could.

The troll covered his ears and backed away.

Melia observed the Rykkiel, wondering how it worked.

Sevondi motioned for Pogo to hold his ground.

Melia screeched again. This time she used her highest pitch.

The troll returned his hands to his ears.

Melia feinted in his direction.

He moved back a few more feet.

"You must want to kill Goring yourself," Flora said.

Sevondi squinted. "He surrounds himself with bodyguards–his cult. You won't get near him."

"Maybe not," the spring faerie said. "But if I do, I'm going to be ready."

"Why are you allying with these fools?" Sevondi swished her finger between Ryder and Melia. "I'm the one who can make the Albiana pay for what they did to your people. That's all you care about. That's all you've ever cared about. Help me incarnate Umbra."

"No."

Sevondi pushed her face into Flora's. "You had Ormrun all these years." The muannaye lifted her hands to reach for the spring faerie's throat.

Melia dove between them before circling back to the Rykkiel with her talons extended. The troll, distracted by Sevondi and Flora, had missed his opportunity. Relieved, Melia remained in high alert. She wouldn't leave the yellow globe unguarded again.

Flora put her hands on her broad hips, showing the bandages on her forearms.

The dragonwitch's eyes narrowed. "Something about you has changed."

Flora dug her hands into her apron pocket. Her fingers groped. Melia recognized the chink of coins. "I can pay for the potion."

"Nambrial is hard to cultivate, even for a spring faerie," Sevondi said.

Flora held her bandaged chin in one hand. "I've never tried to grow any. Are you sure it's deadly?"

"It's all in the proportions," the muannaye said. "The herb is delicate, and the amount for each batch varies. It will be trial and error even for you. There are much easier ways to end a life."

Ryder marched between them. He leaned over Flora. "We're going back to the Veil, now!"

"Fine. I'm ready. Thank you, Sevondi. I'm sure I can make it work."

The dragonwitch ignored Flora's pleasantries, her eyes were glued to the priest.

Melia's stomach moiled. Ryder stomped like a wild horse toward her and the Rykkiel.

Sevondi raised her hands, palms up, fingers spread. She stretched one arm toward Ryder and the other toward the nearest grove of trees.

Leaves rustled and branches snapped and popped. A dark mass ballooned against the skyline. The shape sparked and imploded before bursting against the dark moon night like a molten egg.

Melia ducked, but her gaze never left the creature unfolding in the sky. It was magnificent. Marvelous. The most incredible thing she'd ever seen.

Enormous wings canopied the Muudron Stone. Blue-green scales glistened. An ear-splitting roar shattered the valley. The creature lunged at the priest with knife-like claws.

A dragon.

Melia's heart pounded in her throat as she mimicked its every movement: spreading her wings, arching her neck, thrusting her head forward. She opened her beak–and cawed. The dragon spewed purple-orange flames across the sky.

Ryder unsheathed Koldis; a shimmery blue streak lit the heavens. He parried with the monster several minutes before Melia realized he battled an illusion. She tried to tell him, but he couldn't understand her.

Sevondi murmured a single unintelligible word. Her hands sucked the dragon from the night; the creature's energy exploded through her fingertips. Bolts of blue lightning sprayed Ryder with a ghastly liquid that hardened in seconds. He stood like a statue, encased in stone with the sword held high.

Melia deflated.

The blade shimmered, untainted by the foul substance.

The dragonwitch moved toward it.

"Flora, help us!" Melia abandoned the Rykkiel and flew at Sevondi, certain she could rip the eyes from that beautiful face.

The dragonwitch thrust her hands at Melia. More blue lightning erupted from her fingertips. The same slick liquid that had saturated Ryder coated Melia's feathers. An unbearable stench gagged her. The heavy goop didn't harden, but the weight of it forced her to land on the stone dais.

Melia tried to fling the foul liquid from her wings. It dribbled into her eyes, blinding her and burning her pupils. It seeped into her beak, making her choke, but it didn't harden.

Sevondi eased the sword from the priest's grasp.

Unable to bear the heavy liquid's weight, Melia curled onto her back. Useless with her talons clawing the air, she searched for the yellow globe. Flora and the troll tussled at the edge of the stage.

Melia turned toward Ryder. Fury shot from his eyes. Where was Sevondi?

"Melia! Melia!" Flora cried.

She hobbled in the direction of the spring faerie's calls. Pogo lay flattened behind her. Flora's bandage dangled from her chin. The spring faerie knelt over the yellow globe. "Sit on my shoulder. It will carry us back to the Veil."

The strain of shuffling along with the liquid mortar coating her wings had drained her. "What about Ryder?"

"He's not going anywhere until sunlight melts Sevondi's spell. That will be about midday tomorrow."

Melia hesitated.

"Now!" Flora gripped Melia's wing.

"But the sword–"

Time and space smashed around them.

39. The Statue of the Myydron Stone

Ryder's body was sheathed in granite; his hand, reaching for the trees, was empty.

There had been a dragon.

He'd seen its fiery breath with his own eyes. He'd felt the heat blister his skin. He'd heard the beast's deafening roar. He'd drawn Koldis to slay it.

But the dragon hadn't been real. It had been an illusion, a spell.

Where was Melia?

He attempted to turn his head. His eyes shifted left to right. The stone mask pressed against his face. He stared at the pillars of crumbling rock. They were all he could see. At least he could breathe.

Where had everyone gone?

He tried to pull his arm to his side. He tried to kick his leg. He could hardly expand his chest; the hardened mortar squeezed his musculature as if it were a vise. Yet his raised arm felt weary. It ached.

What kind of foul spell had the muannaye cast upon him?

If the witch had hurt Melia–

He pressed his lips together, the extent of movement he was capable of behind his granite mask.

If she was in danger–

He could do nothing.

Ryder released his frustration with a guttural roar from the bottom of his feet; the muffled sound deafened him, but went nowhere.

Blessed Idonne, he hated this country where nothing was what it seemed, and everything that could possibly go wrong did.

As a boy, reading book after book in the halls of Idonne's sacred library, frustration had consumed him. Every tale's hero had been lacking in some regard. Ryder had been confident that, given the chance, he'd win where others had failed.

This was worse than all the storybooks put together. He'd practically given the sword away.

Where was Melia? Had the witch turned her into a stone eagle?

And what about the damned spring faerie?

How dare she take the Tasimas as if it were hers? If they were in Idonne, she could be charged with theft, reckless action, something, but he knew of no courts in Faerie.

When Gumf found out Sevondi had Koldis, he'd be furious as well. Ryder had no doubt, the dwarf would find some way to shift the blame to him and find Flora innocent, even though she'd been the one to take advantage of the diamond. Those two had a tight bond.

He strained to listen. The stone covering his ears muted every sound. He thought he heard a voice murmur behind him. He slowed his breathing. Its raspy echoes silenced.

The witch who'd cast the spell on him appeared in his peripheral vision. She'd cinched Koldis in her leather belt. The incandescent blue blade shimmered against her hip and thigh in the moonlight. The sight sickened him as she sauntered toward him.

"Pogo, look. The hero from Idonne. He's come to the Realm of Faerie to stop Umbra's incarnation. But wait, look what he's brought me."

She pulled the blade from her belt in a single stroke. Holding the luminescent sword with two hands high above her head, she undulated in the firelight.

Ryder's blood made a deafening sound in his ears.

She continued to taunt him. "You failed. I'm going to incarnate Umbra and become the most powerful queen the Realm of Faerie has ever seen."

A troll entered Ryder's field of vision. The short creature leaned against one of the Muudron's columns.

"They're going to come back for him," he said.

The witch frowned at the troll. "Not right away."

"They'll bring the mage. He won't fall for your tricks."

She shoved the sword back into the makeshift scabbard of her belt. "Fine."

"I'm only looking after your interests. That's my job."

"Thank you, dear Pogo," she said, but her tone wasn't grateful. She placed two of her fingers between her lips and whistled. Each blow sounded more piercing than the one before it.

Finally, two black turnskins leapt up on the stone platform. They sniffed at Ryder. When they howled and flattened their ears, the muannaye soothed them. "Ready to ride to Aldaine?" she asked the troll.

"Sevondi–"

"You were in such a hurry to leave."

He walked with a slight limp. "My brother, Moog, lives in Aldaine. He'll be more useful to you there than me."

"Fine. Enlist him to our cause, but you will still accompany me."

"I hate the city."

The muannaye leaned over the troll. "That stupid half-faerie will not steal my birthright."

Ryder struggled to make sense of what he'd heard. Her birthright? She was a muannaye. A muannaye couldn't contain Umbra's embodied consciousness. That was why Lord Goring had kidnapped Melia's sister in the first place. If he could have incarnated the dark master himself, he wouldn't have bothered with the half-faerie.

"What about Lord Goring?" the troll asked.

"Not your concern."

"Look what he did to Flora. Burnt her home to the ground–"

"Nych. Don't talk to me about her. She hid that basin for years. Now she has one of the Rykkiel." The witch paced. "I'll use a killing potion on her."

Ryder could only dream.

"You can't storm the stronghold alone," the troll whined.

"Are you sure Goring will take the basin there?"

"It's the most likely place. Moog has told me he maintains a suite of rooms in the north tower. And Elendah will never allow you to roam the stronghold unescorted."

"Elendah's days are numbered."

The troll pulled the wool cap from his head and rubbed his hand over a rather large lump. "Flora banged me up pretty good. It's a long way to Aldaine. I'm not sure I'm up for the trip."

"If you'd gotten the Rykkiel, fool, the trip would be easy."

The troll jammed his hat back on his head. "Lord Goring's not going to let you have your way on this, either. He's convinced Pressina's daughter will make a better queen."

"For him," Sevondi hissed. "But I don't intend to let this opportunity slip by!"

The troll shook his head.

"When I sit on the stronghold's throne as the embodied Umbra, you'll want for nothing. Enlist your brother's aid when we get to Aldaine, and he won't either."

She slapped her thigh. One of the turnskins lowered its belly to the ground. Sevondi helped Pogo clamber onto its back before positioning herself behind him. When she whistled again, the wild dog carried them north; the second one ran at its heels.

Ryder mulled over what he'd heard.

In his studies of Umbra, he'd come across an obscure branch of knowledge once. It regarded a lineage of black witches in Tyrannis. A muannaye had mixed blood with a powerful sorcerer from Kyrakkos to conceive a daughter–Regina. There had been some conjecture that a female descendant from that line might be able to contain Umbra's consciousness.

Ryder swore under his breath.

The possibility alone was a catastrophe.

He had to get the sword back.

Blessed Idonne, the granite tightened around his arm like a tourniquet–around his head, his neck, his chest, his legs, and even his feet.

Around him, the valley was quiet. Dawn must be close. He closed his eyes and prayed to the gods of Azyllai for the first time since he was a child.

40. Flora's Plan

Melia banged over Flora onto an unyielding curve. It felt as though someone had shoved her through a wall of wind. She smelled skunks and mushrooms. They were in the woods, and she was wedged against an enormous tree root.

It was quiet, except for the spring faerie's panting.

Melia pushed herself away from the root and onto a blanket of leaves. She tested her talons against the ground and craned her neck from side-to-side. She rose and spread her wings. All there.

Flora crawled away from her, reaching out with one hand and then the other.

The yellow globe nested in another web of roots. Flora was aiming in the wrong direction.

"What is that thing?" Melia asked.

"The Tasimas. It's one of the Rykkiel. It will take you wherever you want to go." Flora spoke in the tongue of eagles. The language sounded like ancient wisdom coming from her lips.

Melia's despair lifted. "Will it take me to Aldaine?"

"It will take all of us there if you'll help me find it," Flora continued to speak in eagle.

"Tatou, Tuck, Sinjiin–"

"I said, all of us. Are you hard of hearing?"

Melia kept her eyes on the diamond. "Where are we?"

"Close to the Veiled Tavern."

"Why not at the tavern?"

Flora halted her crawling. "Because I knew you'd ask a thousand questions and demand answers to every single one of them."

Melia blinked. She'd never imagined the spring faerie had given her much thought. "Why did you take Koldis to Sevondi?"

"I didn't."

Flora recounted the private meeting with Gumf and Ryder earlier that night.

Melia couldn't keep still. "Did Ryder agree to take the sword to Lord Goring?"

"Of course not."

Melia's heart seized upon Flora's assertion. She would never have believed the spring faerie could trust the priest after he'd defended the Albianas' right to call Illialei their home.

She stepped closer to Flora. The burns on the spring faerie's face were healing, otherwise she looked the same. But Sevondi had said she was changed. The dragonwitch was right. Maybe it didn't show on the outside, but something inside Flora had woken up.

"Are you listening?" the spring faerie asked.

"Yes."

"You need to pay attention."

Melia's pulse quickened, heightening all her senses. She stretched her neck toward Flora. "Okay."

"While Ryder and Gumf jabbered back and forth, I came up with a plan, but I needed to make sure the Tasimas worked the way Gumf said it did. The dwarf can be tricky sometimes. You can't believe every word that comes out of his mouth. And I needed that killing potion–"

"But you didn't get it."

"I got what I needed. I can grow the Nambrial in Aldaine. If I have any problems brewing it, Embril's there. She'll help me."

A storm of questions seethed inside Melia, but she kept her beak shut. As much as she wanted answers, she also wanted Flora to keep talking.

"When I saw the chance to take the Tasimas, I didn't think the priest would act as fast as he did. Good reflexes, that one. We'll pick him up on the way to the stronghold."

"But what about the sword? It's gone and we have nothing."

"That's why we need to get to the stronghold as soon as possible–to assess Goring's army, strategize, and prepare for Sevondi's arrival. You don't lose one battle and give up, you regroup and make a better a plan."

Melia scratched at the floor of leaves. Flora was so altered she seemed like a stranger. "Why are you helping me?"

"That's not the right question," Flora said. "You've got a lot to learn–you and the priest. I'm not sure I've got enough time or energy to train you. Maybe I'll enlist Sinjiin ..." The spring faerie speared Melia with her eyes. "The right question is: Who are you?"

"Me?" Melia inched backward.

"You're the first Albiana since Ava died to hear the sapphire lily's call."

Effervescent waves coursed through Melia's body.

"Tatou told me," the spring faerie said.

Melia's heart stopped beating. "Aren't you furious? I could have warned you in time. Your house wouldn't have burned to the ground–"

Flora waved her quiet. "War isn't pretty. And make no mistake, the battle between Dark and Light is upon us. But it's far from over. And for the first time since my people died, I can imagine springtime returning to Illialei."

"But–"

"Enough with counting every mistake over and over again. That Sevondi took the sword does complicate things, but nothing's happened yet that we can't overcome. Now, are you ready to save your fool of a sister and help me stop Goring once and for all?"

"Yes."

"Thank goodness, dawn is almost here."

Flora sketched out her plan.

Melia pointed out the Tasimas before she flew back to the Veiled Tavern.

✧ ✧ ✧

Melia watched the Veil's front porch.

Flora's predictions were correct. Gumf's trolls patrolled the large yard.

Sinjiin lounged on the porch, his eyes alert. Tatou lay on her belly, balanced on the tiger's back. Tuck leaned against the porch railing, his walking staff loose in his hands.

The Balyudor's leafy ceiling filtered the first ray of dawn as Melia shifted into her faerie form. Her clothes were ruined and the stench of Sevondi's spell remained strong as her bare feet padded through the soft, slick grass.

Tatou flew toward her. "Where have you been?"

"Long flight. I needed to clear my head."

Her friend came to an abrupt halt midair. "What's that smell?"

"I could use a bath," Melia said.

Gumf appeared on the front porch. "And some new clothes." He snapped his fingers. Two dwarves came from the interior. The Veil's proprietor issued an order. The dwarves disappeared.

When Melia reached the porch, Gumf covered his nose with his hand. The trolls gave her a wide berth. Sinjiin came up and sniffed her. The big cat mewled.

"What did you get into?" the dwarf asked.

Melia was grateful Flora had coached her. "A chicken coop in the valley. I guess I got greedy. One of the children woke up. Before I knew it, it was raining rotten eggs."

Gumf didn't even glance at Melia as she told her story. He watched the yard and the woods with his arms locked across his chest. "Best to stay away from domesticated animals and stick with what's wild."

"I've learned my lesson."

"We were supposed to leave at dawn," Tuck said.

"I'm sorry. I'll be quick with my bath."

The elf shook his head. "Your friend, the priest, was arrested last night."

Tatou shrugged with her hands held wide.

Flora had warned Melia to keep everything she said brief. "For what?"

Gumf held out a square of parchment.

She unfolded it.

"He stole Koldis from the Order of the Idonnai," Tuck fumed.

Melia pretended the news knocked the wind out of her, that she was lightheaded with disbelief. She reached for one of the columns that supported the porch's roof. She let herself sway against it.

"I still can't believe it," Tatou said.

"They came for him in the dead of night," Gumf said. "Took him in chains. I've never seen anyone in Tyrannis in chains before."

Melia goggled at the dwarf's outrageous show. She made her's equally convincing. "I feel so betrayed," she said.

Sinjiin roared.

Gumf held out his hand for the parchment. "I assume you'll want to leave as soon possible. The horses are ready, and we've packed plenty of food for the trip across the plains."

✧ ✧ ✧

Melia forced herself to frown all the way to Tatou's room. When she closed the door, she slid down it and laughed so hard she felt a pang in her side.

"You're hysterical," Tatou said. "When the dwarves bring your bath, I'll ask them to bring you some lemon verbena tea."

Melia couldn't stop laughing. Maybe Tatou was right and some of it was her nerves. When she could take a full breath, she told her friend what had really happened.

Tatou plucked at her skirt. "I believed Gumf. Every word. What a story, Ryder arrested and taken away in chains."

"There is that Wanted notice," Melia said. "It's real."

Tiny spasms jerked the pixie's wings. "Gumf told us Flora was so angry she left with Nivea last night."

"He believes he's helping my mother," Melia said. "But we have the Tasimas. We'll be in Aldaine before nightfall."

The pixie settled on the bed's thick cover. Melia couldn't help but notice how delicious the puffy blanket looked. She wished she had the time to crawl under it and fall asleep.

"What are we going to tell Tuck? And Sinjiin?" Tatou asked.

"Nothing. We'll ride away from the Veil, the way we planned. Flora's not that far. She'll tell Tuck about the sword with Sinjiin there, to make sure he doesn't do anything crazy when he finds out. Then we'll go back to the Muudron Stone for Ryder. I hope he's all right. Flora said Sevondi's spell melts in daylight."

Tatou's shoulders slumped.

"What's wrong?" Melia asked.

"I believed the worst about both of them."

The half-faerie rose to comfort her friend. Tatou held up her hand and pinched her nose. Melia stopped.

"Yesterday afternoon, after lunch, I told Flora about the sapphire lily calling you," Tatou said. "Her face lit up. But then, when she wasn't here this morning, I believed she'd abandoned us."

"There's no way you could have known Gumf was lying," Melia said.

"Would you have believed him?"

Melia hated to think she would have. "Yes."

Tatou sat a little straighter.

"I need to tell you something else," Melia said.

"What?"

"It's something Nandana told me when Ryder and I went to visit her."

Tatou waited with round eyes.

"She said I'm the one who's destined to incarnate Umbra."

The pixie gasped.

"And now, Flora believes springtime can return to Illialei because I heard the sapphire lily's call."

Tatou's eyes opened even wider. "Oh dear," was all the pixie managed before two dwarves knocked on the door, carrying a wooden tub filled with steaming water.

✧ ✧ ✧

Melia soaked in hot water scented with cinnamon oil. It had taken four basinfuls to get the stink and grease of Sevondi's spell off her.

She closed her eyes.

Her sister's melodious voice seeped into her brain. *"Melia, where are you?"*

Melia gripped the sides of the wooden tub and pulled herself upright. *"Plantine?"*

"We're at the stronghold of Calashai. I'm waiting for an audience with the grey faerie. You have to come for my wedding. I want to have at least one of my sisters with me, and Melusine ..."

"Plantine, you can't marry the muannaye. He's a monster."

"You've never even met him."

"I know what he did to Flora."

"Who is Flora? Never mind. I'm not going to listen to your gossip—"

"He sent his turnskins to her cottage in the Balyudor. They burned down her house. They killed her cat."

"Turnskins? What are you talking about? That's impossible. He's been with me the entire time—"

"Since he kidnapped you? Plantine—"

"I'm not going to listen to you make false accusations."

Melia tried to think of another way to alert her sister to the enormous mistake she was about to make.

"Are they still drugging you?" Melia held out the hope that drugs or some spelled potion, not Umbra's influence, made Plantine determined to ruin her life.

"I'm not being drugged."

Melia remembered how woozy—and blissful—she'd felt after she'd shared the potion with Plantine through their telepathic vision. *"What about the potion they forced you to drink?"*

"It's a tonic." Plantine paused. *"The one you flew to Tyrannis to find, but couldn't."*

Och, the barb hit home.

"Goring's healer is wonderful. She brewed a remedy to stop me from fading, and it's working. I feel stronger than ever."

That was obvious. *"Then he hasn't kissed you?"* True love's first kiss would stop Plantine's disintegration. She wouldn't need a tonic to make her whole. Could Goring's kiss do that?

She repeated the question. When Plantine didn't answer, Melia realized how much she'd enjoyed being away from her sisters. No one to ignore her, make fun of her, or tell lies about her. It was an unsettling awareness; she should have missed them terribly, awfully, but she didn't. She hadn't even tried to find Melusine in the mortal world. She hadn't even thought about it.

"Melia, the ceremony is going to rival any celebration at the Cathedral Palace. You can't miss it."

"What about Tuck?"

"I. Am not. Going to talk. About him."

Or. The basin. *"He's here, Plantine. He's coming for you,"* Melia said.

"Don't you dare bring him here."

"Plantine–"

"Have you heard nothing I've said? I'm going to marry Lord Goring. I'm going to sit beside him on the Calashai's throne. Tuck doesn't need to see that ..." Her voice softened. *"I don't want him to see that ..."* Her voice broke.

"Then don't–"

A penetrating chill gripped Melia. She couldn't lose their connection. *"I'll come to the wedding. Tell me where to find you when we reach Aldaine."*

An angry silence echoed through her. *"Promise me you won't ruin my wedding."*

If there was any chance for Melia to break the illusion that seized Plantine's mind, she'd need to be standing in front of her. *"I promise. Nothing upsetting."* What a lie. Plantine would be furious when they showed up with Tuck.

"A suite is being prepared for me at the stronghold. I'm told it's charming, with a private courtyard and a fountain."

Melia shivered. The water in the tub had turned cold. She stood up and reached for one of the thick towels folded nearby. *"We'll be there soon."* Her final words drifted into nothingness.

Plantine had already closed her mind without probing about the sword. Not that it mattered.

Melia didn't know where it was anymore.

Growing up in between Melusine and Plantine, Melia had always felt plain. Now she saw something different in the mirror.

She turned in a circle. The copper-colored blouse with ruffles rippling down its front and formfitting brown pants were striking. The short burgundy jacket cinched her waist and flared over her slim hips. But what she really loved were the soft leather boots that laced her calves and hugged her feet like supple gloves. Used to going barefoot, she'd refused them. But the troll had shoved them back into her hands.

"It's cold in Aldaine," he'd said, keeping his hands jammed deep in his pockets. "And rocky."

They felt like skin.

The fine clothes were a welcome but hard to accept gift from someone who was ready to send her across Tyrannis with a pack of bold-faced lies.

Knock. Knock.

She opened the door. The same troll who'd delivered her clothes stood in the hallway. His eyes widened when he saw her; his tongue tripped over his words. "It's t-time."

She followed him through the Veil's winding halls.

Tuck, Tatou, and Sinjiin waited with Gumf on the wide porch. When they saw her, their eyes registered surprise.

"Melia?" Tuck asked.

Tatou landed on her shoulder. "And everyone always said Melusine was the pretty one."

Melia couldn't stop her smile.

Gumf bounced on his toes. It seemed he couldn't wait to be rid of them. "Is everyone ready?"

One by one, they nodded.

The Veil's proprietor didn't escort them to the stables.

41. Distrust

Tuck held out his hand. "Give me the Tasimas."

Melia had searched every drawer, shelf, crack, and cranny in Tatou's room at the Veil for something to carry the large diamond in. When she could find nothing else, she'd settled on a pillowcase.

Flora held it now as if it were a bag of dried beans behind her back.

Sinjiin crouched off to the side in the distance between them.

Flora squinted at the tree elf. "We're going to Aldaine together."

"We don't need to get the priest," Tuck said. "He's wanted throughout the enchanted world for stealing Koldis. Each of you"–he pointed to them one by one with his staff–"saw the Wanted notice. Gumf's lies don't change the fact that he's a criminal."

"How dare you?" Melia marched over to Tuck. "You don't know anything about it. No one protected the sword in Idonne's library. He took it to keep it safe from those who would incarnate Umbra for their own gain."

The elf sneered. "Now you sound like your father's daughter. Twisting the facts into an excuse to do what you want. Who would incarnate Umbra, except for their own gain?"

She wanted to grab his stupid stick and smash it in two. The only reason she didn't was because Aldous had given it to him. "Leave my father out of this."

Tuck stood toe-to-toe with her. A head taller than she was, he looked down at her. "The official investigation may have found you innocent, but Plantine told me you wanted your father dead."

Her chin trembled. The lie hurt worse than the one Melusine had told about her—that she conspired with her father to destroy Illialei.

"Sh-she t-told you that?"

Tuck's jaw shaped into a hard line. "It's no wonder you and Ryder are close. A thief and a murderer throwing in their common lot."

Sinjiin lunged. He brushed Tuck hard enough to knock him to the ground, but not hard enough to do the elf any real harm.

Tuck sprang back to his feet. He rallied to face the tiger in a crouch. "Who knows what your crime is?"

Sinjiin had stalked away, but now he padded back toward the elf.

Tuck held his ground.

The pair circled. Tuck cut and lunged at the tiger. Throwing himself on Sinjiin's back, he grabbed the tiger's throat. When the cat had enough of Tuck's chokehold, he rose on his hind legs and threw him off.

The elf rolled to the ground and jumped back to his feet. Sweat stained the back of his shirt and plastered his hair to his forehead. He held up his fists.

Sinjiin, three times Tuck's size, roared in his face.

The elf's eyes bulged; he took a step back.

Sinjiin nosed him.

Tuck took another step back.

The tiger toyed with his prey.

Tuck circled the big cat. With his head dropped into his shoulders, he rammed Sinjiin's side with all his strength.

The tiger didn't budge.

Tuck grunted, his face the color of an apple.

Sinjiin dropped to his belly as the elf charged.

Tuck flipped over the tiger's back and ate a face full of dirt. He rolled over and stared at the ceiling of branches overhead.

Tatou sprinkled him with pixie dust. "Stop fighting."

Sinjiin curled on the ground and proceeded to clean his claws with his sharp teeth.

Tuck pushed himself up. His hair was full of leaves. He wiped the dirt from his knees and walked over to his staff. He shook the stick at them. "I want to use Hermes' Wand," he said. "On all of you."

Flora rolled her eyes. "How long is that going to take?"

Melia rested against a boulder with Tatou on her shoulder. "What's he talking about?"

Tatou cupped her hands around the half-faerie's ear. "His walking staff is a wand that discerns the truth."

Melia studied the dull rod. "How?"

"If you tell a lie while you're holding it in your hand, it will radiate light, illuminating the darkness cast by intentional deception."

Melia's body still quivered from Tuck's insults. "It looks like a piece of firewood," she said. "He better be careful someone doesn't burn it."

Her friend swatted the side of her head. "Aldous treasures it. I'm surprised he loaned it to Tuck."

The idea of a lie detector made Melia curious. After all the lies that had been told about her, she itched to test it. But Tuck already stood in front of Flora. The spring faerie had volunteered to go first.

"Hold the wand. I'll ask you a question," he said.

Flora's tiny boot tapped the dirt.

"Did you use the Tasimas to take Koldis to Sevondi?"

"No."

Tuck watched the wand. Nothing happened.

"Are you sure?" Tuck asked.

"Yes."

"Is your palm pressed against the wood?"

Flora exhaled a loud breath "Yes."

"Are you the only spring faerie who survived the burning?"

Flora threw the wand on the ground. "Next."

Tuck leaned over to pick it up.

The rest of them had drawn lots. It was Tatou's turn. She hovered next to the wand.

"Place at least one of your palms on it," Tuck said.

The pixie's wings fluttered as she pressed both her hands against the stick. She winked at Melia.

"Are you keeping any secrets from me?"

"That's not a fair question," Flora said. "It's too broad. Reword it."

Tuck gave an exasperated sigh. "Are you keeping any secrets about Umbra?"

Tatou pulled her hands off the wand. "That's not very specific either."

Melia paced. She shouldn't have told Tatou what Nandana had said.

Tuck pushed out his jaw. "Do you know anything about the sword, or the basin, or *The Book of Umbra* that you haven't told me?"

Tatou squeezed the wand. "No."

"Next," Flora said.

Melia wiped her palms on her pants. Tuck pushed the wand toward her. She let it slide between her fingers.

"Hold it tighter," Tuck said.

Melia pretended the wand was the tree elf's neck and squeezed it as hard as she could.

"Does Plantine love the muannaye, Lord Zachariah Goring?"

"No."

"Are you going to Aldaine to help me stop the wedding?"

"Yes."

"Did you mean to kill your father?"

"That's enough," Flora said.

Melia held Tuck's gaze. Her heart banged in her chest. "No."

Tuck stared at the wand. It remained as dull as ever. He swallowed hard. "I'm sorry."

Melia gave a minute shake of her head. "I accept your apology."

Sinjiin morphed into his mage form. He gave Tuck a toothy grin as he took the wand.

"Can Ryder be trusted to help us?" Tuck asked.

"Yes," the mage said.

The elf cleared his throat. "I'm sorry for doubting everyone. I'm ready to go to Aldaine now. With all of you."

Melia wanted to see the wand light up, but they needed to get to the priest. She'd have to wait for another time to tell an intentional lie and see if it worked.

Tuck unleashed Zephyr while Melia untied the reins of the other horse.

The elf pointed the pair toward the Veil before swatting Zephyr on the rump. The horses trotted off.

Everyone gathered around Flora who held the Tasimas wrapped in the pillowcase. As soon as she made direct contact with the diamond, it would whisk her–and whoever was in physical contact with her–through the dimensions.

Melia had almost forgotten. "Plantine is at the stronghold." Everyone stared at her. "She contacted me at the tavern when I was bathing."

Tuck came around the others. "Is she all right?"

Melia could see the hunger in his eyes for news of her sister. She tried not to look at the wand. Maybe testing it wasn't such a good idea.

"She's as fine as can be expected."

She wasn't about to share the details of her telepathic conversation with Plantine. Tuck needed to be there for her sister when they arrived at the stronghold. He might be the only one who could reach her. If he knew Plantine refused to talk about him, much less see him, would he abandon her? Melia couldn't take that risk.

"I told her we'd be there soon. How well do you know the Calashai?" she asked Flora. "Is there a suite of rooms with a courtyard and a fountain? She kept talking about that."

Flora rubbed her unruly eyebrows with a crooked finger. "I can probably land us someplace close to it. After we pick up the priest."

The half-faerie winced. "Of course."

Tatou pursed her lips.

Melia knew what she was thinking. True love's first kiss would save Plantine. It would also stop Melia from shifting into an eagle.

A future where she could never fly looked bleak. That made her feelings for Ryder complicated. There were moments it was easier to forget he existed.

42. Reunited

Ryder sensed a slight give in the stone skin. He fought against the casing with his shoulders, elbows, and thighs, but his rocky prison held firm. It was maddening. He'd become one of those ridiculous storybook heroes. Bumbling and blindsided, he'd been defeated by the first witch who'd crossed his path.

Except he wasn't defeated, yet. He'd get the sword and basin back. Somehow.

As the sun climbed in the sky, liquid trickled down the back of his neck. A foul stench suffocated him. A horse he couldn't see whinnied and snorted; the sound came from the side of the stage.

"Is someone there?" Ryder yelled.

He tasted his lips and spat. He turned his head. He eased it up and down.

The stone sheath was melting in the sunlight.

He wiggled the fingers of his hand, the one that had been raised all night. He couldn't spread them, but they curved. He pulled down on his arm, hard. There was a dull crack as his body launched forward.

He smashed facedown on the stage with his arm stretched above his head and his torso still locked in stone. He strained to turn his neck before slamming his shoulders against the rock platform.

Worn out from his efforts, he panted. Sticky liquid soaked his armpits.

His back burned with heat.

When his cloak felt soaked with the dissolving spell, he pressed the stage away with his sword arm. His body lifted with the thrust.

Finally.

A shell of soggy granite armor, a mold of his chest, remained beneath him. Ryder scrambled to his feet.

He gagged. The odor was nauseating. He had to find water–a river, a lake, a pool–anything to wash the blue-grey stench from his body.

Overhead the sun closed upon its zenith.

Staggering and overwhelmed by the rank smell, Ryder ran in the direction he'd heard the horse cry earlier.

Marshy grass sucked at his boots. The water-soaked ground led him to a stream. He dove into its small bed, twisting and scrubbing. The dense blue-grey liquid flooded the small body of water. He snatched up long blades of grass and rubbed them against his cheeks and hair.

He walked farther upstream where the water was still clear and tore off his cloak and the rest of his clothes. He submerged them in the water before banging them with the largest rock he could find. He grabbed more grass and scrubbed himself raw.

Satisfied he'd done the best he could with the resources he had, he wrung his clothes dry. If he laid them out on one of the nearby boulders, they'd dry in the sun.

The troll had said the others would return for him.

He'd give them a day before he went to find them.

"My goodness. What have we here?"

Ryder jumped up, startled. He'd fallen asleep in the long grass. He scrambled toward the boulder where his clothes dried in the sun. "Stop staring," he said.

The spring faerie stood a few feet away, her arms akimbo, a wide grin plastered across her face. "At such a fine specimen of masculinity?" she chortled. "Wouldn't dream of it."

Ryder seethed. Raised in the priesthood, he'd had limited interaction with females. He certainly wasn't used to parading before them without his clothes.

"I found him," Flora yelled.

Ryder tripped and spun in circles while trying to get his legs in his pants and his feet in his boots. Everything still smelled. He heard the elves and felt Sinjiin coming toward him. The ground quaked as the tiger bounded through the sea of grass.

The priest struggled with the buttons of his shirt as he turned around. Tatou rode the tiger's back. Ryder searched for Melia.

Was that her, wearing high boots and a dark red jacket? At first glance, he thought she was a muannaye, but her skin was too pale. Then he recognized her deep blue eyes, the ones that hinted of the mystery at the bottom of the ocean.

She offered a tentative smile.

A sensation of light spread through his chest.

She looked ... confident, striking. He wanted to run to her and take her in his arms, but years of restraining his emotions made following through with such an open display of affection too awkward. His body remained immobile, but his gaze never left her face.

"I'm sorry we left you behind last night, but Flora"–she emphasized the spring faerie's name–"insisted it was pointless to retrieve you before noon. She told us it would take the sun that long to melt the granite. We saw the spell's remains at the Muudron Stone."

"Smelled it too." The pixie pinched her nose.

Ryder had forgotten the stench as soon as he'd seen Melia. Thank the gods of Azyllai he hadn't thrown himself at the half-faerie and crushed her in its stink.

Sinjiin nuzzled Ryder's palm. The priest reached down to scratch behind the tiger's ears. The big cat pulled back.

"What?" Ryder asked him.

When the tiger roared, he understood his friend needed to tell him something in private. The others hung back, repelled by the foul odor. Ryder waved them farther away. "Wait for us at the stone. We won't be long."

After Tuck–eager to reach Plantine–hurried everyone away, Sinjiin morphed into his mage form.

"Then it's true? You've lost Koldis to a witch?"

The priest dropped his head. "It was a trick. The dragon was an illusion. I drew my sword before I realized the trap she'd set."

Sinjiin frowned. "A dragon came from nowhere, and you believed?"

"You weren't there. You didn't feel the heat of its fiery breath burn your skin."

The mage shook his head as he walked over to a short bush. He began plucking its flowers.

"You've never been deceived by an illusion?" Ryder asked. "Besides, if that damned spring faerie hadn't–"

"Never hide your failings behind the mistakes of others," the mage roared. "It's bad enough you didn't tell me the whole truth in Typhos. If I'd known you sought Isolt's basin, I might not have–"

Ryder–stunned by the mage's anger–laughed. "Let me save your life?"

Sinjiin paused to rub his chin. "Exactly. The string of bad luck that has hounded us since we arrived on these shores isn't a coincidence. That basin is dangerous–it has a mind of its own. It killed one dark lord from the Hidden City eons ago. I'm not eager for it to kill another. You're not in Idonne now. You no longer deal with words on a page. Every action you take has great consequence."

"Don't you think I know that?" Ryder asked. "I'm the one who broke my vow, and I'll be the one who stands trial in Idonne if the priesthood ever drags me back there."

"Don't be such a martyr. I've already told you how to defend yourself if you're ever imprisoned for breaking your Oath of Non-Interference. That isn't what I'm speaking of."

Ryder towered over his friend. "Then what are you talking about?"

Sinjiin shook the wild bouquet in his hands. "You don't respect the magical things you seek, or the foes who take them from you."

The priest rounded on him like an angry bull. "Is this how you seek release from your debt? By lecturing me!"

Sinjiin didn't flinch. "You dream of being a hero, a great adventurer, but you have much to learn. If you want to capture these powerful objects, you're going to have to discipline your heart as much as you discipline your body."

Red-faced, Ryder backed down. "I didn't think she'd cast a spell."

"No, you didn't think. You only raced in, sword held high."

"And where were you? Passed out, snoring in front of a fire?"

Sinjiin resumed his harvesting of the small white flowers. "Gumf didn't invite me to your meeting with Flora. Perhaps you should have let her take the Tasimas."

Ryder threw his hands in the air and stomped toward the boulder where his cloak dried in the sun. When he grabbed the brown wool, he gagged. He threw the cloak down and turned back to Sinjiin. "The dragonwitch might be capable of incarnating Umbra," he said.

Sinjiin shoved the bunch of tiny white flowers into Ryder's hands. "By the gods of Azyllai, could things get any worse?"

"What do you want me to do with these?" Ryder asked.

"Eat them. They'll disperse the lingering stench of the witch's spell."

43. The Stronghold of Calashai

The next time the Tasimas shoved them through the wind wall of time and space, they arrived in a knot, on a grass lawn bound by grey stones. Melia's arms and legs snarled with those of her traveling companions. Flora knocked the half-faerie's chin with the diamond; the warmth and heaviness of Sinjiin's paw, his claws retracted, pressed against her back; an elbow–Tuck's?–jabbed her stomach. Hermes' Wand rolled down an incline. The elf crawled after it.

Melia righted herself, but not before she ended up with a mouthful of Ryder's knee. She massaged her jaw. It seemed the more passengers the Rykkiel carried, the more tangled they became. Her senses still reeling, she oriented herself.

They'd landed in a large courtyard. A fountain shot a single plume into the sky. Symmetrical diamond-shaped walkways radiated from the geyser. Farther away, a number of muannaye gathered around a massive black iron gate and guardhouse. Four marched in their direction.

A stone fortress stared down upon them.

The stronghold of Calashai? Compared to the Cathedral Palace, it looked dull. And this wasn't Plantine's suite, although it was a courtyard, and there was a fountain.

Overhead grey clouds blanketed the heavens. Four corner towers pushed beyond the thick shield, their stony crowns invisible. One of them must be the bell tower Tatou had told her about.

A strong gust of wind whipped Melia's hair into her face. She shivered, grateful for her boots and jacket. The tang of salt filled the air. She cocked her head and listened. Waves crashed in the distance. The Great White Sea.

Flora still gripped the Tasimas between gnarled fingers. Tatou dug the pillowcase out of the spring faerie's apron and held it open. Flora dropped the diamond in, twisted the makeshift bag closed, then slung it over her shoulder.

Melia considered Ryder. Since they'd left him alone with Sinjiin by the stream, he seemed different. Constrained. Had Sinjiin chastised him for losing the sword? Her feelings for the priest swung back and forth like the switching tail of a spirited horse. She wanted to get to know him better; she was afraid of what would happen if she did.

The four muannaye approached. There would be no time to sort through her mixed-up feelings for him anytime soon. The guards rested their hands on the hilts of their swords, but none wore the head-to-toe black of the cult of Umbra. Melia's body relaxed.

Two of the muannaye had fallow-colored skin, the complexion of the others was chocolate. All four wore their hair in long, dark plaits that hung beyond their shoulders. Their fitted attire accented the slim musculature beneath it. One had eyes the color of a clear sky. He watched their every move.

"We're peaceful–"

"We're here to see–"

Melia and Ryder spoke together.

Flora, shorter than everyone but the pixie, elbowed her way to the front. "We're guests of Elendah."

Two of the muannaye smirked at one another with raised eyebrows.

The spring faerie continued in her usual gruff manner. "My name is Flora. These are my"–she pointed her thumb at the rest of the group –"friends. Tell the grey faerie we're here."

"We've received no word that the stronghold's regent is expecting such strange visitors," one of the muannaye answered.

Flora stamped one of her boots. "Who said anything about strange?"

"Even in Aldaine, falling from the sky is not–" The muannai's eyes met again.

"Usual," the second one finished the first one's sentence.

The other two guards flanked the small group although no one drew any weapons. Their eyes kept returning to Tatou, sitting cross-legged on Sinjiin's back. Beneath the layer of clouds, she looked like a little ball of sunlight. Or maybe they were concerned with the tiger, who stood regal beside Ryder on four paws.

"We don't have any weapons," the priest said.

Melia cringed at the reminder.

Four pairs of eyes searched their bodies. The heat from their stares swept Melia from head to toe. She tightened inside, but held her head high.

"Wait here," the first one said.

Flora fiddled in one of her pockets. "We will not." She pulled out her hand. The muannaye leaned forward. She stuck out a fist, almost grazing his nose. He pulled back. A silver band embedded with a deep blue stone encircled one of Flora's fingers. Melia didn't care much for jewels, but the ring was exquisite in its simplicity.

The spring faerie wagged her finger under the muannaye's nose. "This ring proves I'm Elendah's friend. So, mister guard, you take us inside, or there'll be hell to pay for you."

The muannaye straightened and whispered with his counterparts. "Follow us," he ordered. He led them toward the stronghold with the other three guards ringed around them.

"It's not necessary to treat us as criminals," Flora muttered.

No one answered her complaint.

Wind roared in their faces as they walked along one of the stone pathways.

From a distance the stronghold gleamed without color. Up close, gold and copper streaked the grey stone. They passed through a series of columns and arches. Melia's heart sank. Black-clad muannai lined the stronghold's exterior walls. There were too many to count.

The group entered an unobtrusive doorway. When they crossed the threshold, darkness enveloped them. The muannaye who led them hardly paused to let their eyes adjust. Melia's boots touched soundless on the smooth tile, but she heard voices and movement.

Where was Plantine? Did she dare risk telepathic communication?

When they turned a corner, a dim hall bustled with muannai, trolls, and dwarves who whispered and watched as they passed.

"It's so busy," Tatou said. "I'd always imagined the stronghold as tranquil."

The muannaye leading them slowed his pace. "Preparations for a wedding are in progress. When the celebration is over, the halls of the Calashai will return to their usual calm and quiet."

Melia's stomach clenched. Goring wasted no time. She stole a glance at Tuck. Even in the shadows, his face looked green. Ryder gripped her elbow as if to offer his support. His awareness of how much the wedding disturbed her touched her. It also reminded her of why she'd come to the stronghold–to find Plantine and put an end to her sister's bridal charade.

To be sure the muannaye spoke of the same wedding she intended to ruin, Melia asked, "Who are the lucky bride and groom?"

"Lord Goring and–"

One of the muannai trailing them snickered. "Some no-name half-faerie from Illialei."

Heat raced through Melia's body. "That would be my sister."

The muannaye who led the way stopped and turned. He appraised them with new eyes. "Your sister? We were told to expect you, but not so soon. These are your friends?"

Melia nodded.

He gestured to one of the muannaye as the other two withdrew. Bowing, he introduced himself. "I'm Yrrick, and I'm at your service." He made a sharp turn to move in the direction opposite of the one he'd been leading them.

Flora glared at Melia. "Oh, now, thanks to your fool of a sister, we get the royal treatment."

They rounded a corner, and welcome light spilled from one of the rooms ahead. Melia's breath caught when she saw more cult members–motionless shadows–observing everyone who walked by. She rubbed the knots in the back of her neck.

Yrrick led them into a bright hall. Hundreds of tapering candles danced within bronze wall sconces. Among the candles, huge canvases painted with fields of daisies hung alongside long mirrors in elaborate frames on pale golden walls.

Butterflies flitted among low, gleaming tables and luxurious loungers with sumptuous pumpkin-colored pillows. Two black marble fireplaces mirrored each other from opposite ends of the room. Both contained roaring fires. The scent of night jasmine, the flower of Tyrannis, filled the air.

The room felt like a wild meadow contained within four walls.

Yrrick made another sweeping bow. "This is the Welcoming Hall. Please, make yourselves comfortable."

He was gone before Melia could ask if he went to retrieve Plantine.

Sinjiin padded the length of the room. Tatou alighted from his back to examine the paintings. Melia's hand flew to her mouth when her friend disappeared into one of the frames. She rushed over to the picture. Tatou pirouetted among the daisies. Melia's lips parted; her spontaneous laughter eased the tension in the back of her neck. The stronghold's fortress-like façade belied a magical interior.

She looked for the others.

Tuck and Ryder–locked in a spirited discussion in the corner–seemed oblivious to the magic in the paintings. At one point Ryder gripped the tree elf's shoulders and shook him. Although she would have loved to know what they were arguing about, the threat of Tuck shoving the wand into her hand and asking some question about Plantine kept her away.

Flora sat on one of the sofas, straightening her kerchief and smoothing her wrinkled dress.

Sinjiin joined Melia. He remained outside the canvas with her, but his gentle roar showed he appreciated the enchanted picture too.

"It's amazing," she said.

Sinjiin surveyed the hall. Other than their group, it was empty. He shifted into his mage form. "The stronghold is an extension of Elendah herself, it embodies her consciousness," he said.

"Then she's different from the Albiana queens," Melia observed. "To appear so plain from a distance, yet have such a remarkable interior ..."

"Elendah's story is fascinating," Sinjiin said. "Do you know it?"

"No."

"She was a foundling, adrift in the Great White Sea. A seagull rescued her and carried her to Faerie. An old woman no one had ever seen in these parts before cared for her. When Elendah was nineteen, her caretaker vanished. She was left alone, the sole grey faerie in these lands."

"How lonely," Melia said.

"For years, she wandered the barren shores of Tyrannis and the Ruadain," Sinjiin continued. "When she climbed this mountain, she fell in love with its proximity to the sea. Over time, the stronghold built itself around her, brick by brick, stone by stone. There's not a stonecutter, bricklayer, or mason in the entire Whole who will lay claim to the work."

"I had no idea the grey faerie's magic was so powerful," Melia said.

Sinjiin tapped his chest. "Not magic, desire."

"I don't understand."

"The magic of powerful desire doesn't require props, or potions, or even spells–rabbit's tails, turtle's feet, a raven's beak–all are unnecessary. When the power that emanates from within us is strong enough, it flows outward. The ability to manifest what is inside ourselves, into the material world, is the greatest magic of all." Sinjiin spread his arms wide. "The stronghold of Calashai is Elendah's skin."

More questions formed in Melia's mind, but before she could put them into words, the mage blurred into his tiger form and padded away. Something about the dragon at the Muudron Stone danced on the edge of the half-faerie's awareness. Perhaps it had to do with desire. In the same way Elendah had longed for an unusual and spectacular home, Melia longed for the brilliant power and ferocity of the fiery beast she'd seen ignite the night skies. If nothing else, it would be a sensational way to confront Verbena–and the rest of Illialei's gossips.

When a female muannaye entered the hall alone, a wave of

disappointment carried Melia's dreams of dragon-ness away. She'd hoped her sister would come.

Although slight in build, the female muannaye stood as tall as Ryder. Her light brown hair was plaited and piled high upon her head. Simple wooden combs held the braids in place. The hairstyle was identical to the one favored by the females in the valley. However, unlike those muannai, who wore the kind of slacks and boots Gumf had given Melia, this one wore a simple cornflower blue gown that clung to her hips, and slippers. "Greetings. I'm Chloe."

"Where is Elendah?" Flora asked.

"She's indisposed," the muannaye answered.

Flora didn't ask any more questions, but her eyes flattened into dark slits as Chloe served lavender tea and flat cakes with lemon cream. Famished, Melia stuffed herself as graciously as possible while pressing for news of her sister.

Apparently, Goring was Aldaine's most eligible bachelor, and his whirlwind courtship of Plantine was the subject of much scorching gossip in the halls of the Calashai and the tea rooms in Aldaine.

The conversation was awkward, but Melia forced herself to receive the muannaye's excited recitations with appropriately placed oohs and ahs. Flora offered bracing looks over the rim of her tea cup. Tuck squirmed but remained stoic.

Ryder, who'd remained seated and silent while everyone ate, stood up. "May I see the north tower?"

Chloe's hands jerked. The serving platter slipped and the leftovers spilled onto the ground. She knelt to clean them up. "I'm sorry. What a mess I've made."

Melia tried to discern whether the muannaye was scared, or if the dropped tray had been a calculated diversion. It was hard to say, but her patience was at its end. "Can you take me to my sister?"

"Of course." Chloe seemed eager to leave Ryder in the Welcoming Hall.

"Tatou, will you come with me?" Melia asked.

The pixie landed on her shoulder. Flora grunted. Melia acted as if she didn't hear her. The spring faerie wanted to kill Lord Goring. What would

Plantine do if Flora blurted out her intentions? Melia didn't want Flora seized by the menacing watchers dressed in black.

The spring faerie increased the volume of her guttural promptings until it sounded as though they stood in a barnyard.

When they became impossible to ignore, Melia relented. "Do you want to join us?"

Flora wiped the crumbs from her mouth with the back of her hand and jumped from the sofa. She heaved the pillowcase with the Tasimas across her back.

Chloe stared at the faerie's odd-looking sack.

Melia gritted her teeth.

44. Pixie Dust

Chloe led them through a monotonous maze of grey stone corridors. She stopped at a rounded wooden door where a cult of Umbra member stood guard. She flirted with him before knocking.

Melia chewed on a fingernail.

When Plantine didn't answer Chloe's loud knock, the muannaye cracked the door.

Antsy, Melia pushed past her. Tatou remained on her shoulder; they gasped at the same time. Her sister's suite enshrined a garden that rivaled the pixies' enchanted one in Illialei. In the foyer, blooming flowers climbed the walls–in the front room they overflowed low tables and overstuffed chairs. Melia's boots sank into soft grass. Stupefied, she listened. Birdsong streamed from the adjoining room.

The melody of Plantine's voice sang with the birds. "Who's there?"

Melia followed the sound.

Trees, rooted deep in the ground, extended beyond the ceiling, their tops invisible. Yellow warblers chattered and swooped. A small sparkling stream spilled its way round an enormous bed.

Now Melia understood Tatou's fascination with Elendah; she wished to meet the grey faerie as well.

Plantine ran toward them. "Melia! Tatou!" She stopped in front of Flora. "Who's this?"

"The last spring faerie alive," Flora answered, her voice tart.

Plantine looked at her sister, her eyes round with disbelief. "She's a spring faerie?"

Flora waddled past them, disappearing into the foliage.

"Yes, and she's ... special," Melia said.

Despite her gruff ways, Flora had done nothing but stand by Melia. She'd been the one who had told her the truth when everyone else in Illialei –including her own mother–had kept their Albiana blood secret. And Flora believed that when Melia heard the sapphire lily's call it meant something: the hope that springtime might return to Illialei.

Melia looked at her sister. She didn't trust her enough to tell her about the lily, but she did need to tell her about their Albiana blood, and the danger from Umbra because of it.

"I thought all the spring faeries died," Plantine murmured.

"As you can see, Flora's very much alive," Tatou said.

"You know about the genocide of the spring faeries?" Melia asked.

Plantine shrugged. "The *Old Texts* gloss over that period in Illialei's history, but there are other sources if you're looking."

Regardless of Uriel's decree, Melia couldn't imagine keeping such a crime secret. "You never said anything about it."

"Did you ever ask? No, you've always made fun of my love of books."

"You're right." Melia tilted her head.

Plantine hugged her. "It's not your fault that you don't have a head for the important things in life." She laughed and dragged Melia and Tatou toward the bed.

Flora stood in front of an armoire on the other side of the room. She'd taken the pillowcase that held the Rykkiel from her shoulder. It looked as though she was searching for a place to hide it.

Plantine clapped her hands. They were no longer translucent. She blossomed with vitality. The fading of their mother's spell had fallen away. "I'm so glad you're here!"

Melia began, "Plantine, are you sure–"

"Don't," her sister commanded.

Melia looked to Tatou for help.

"You need to see Tuck," the pixie said.

Her sister's face contorted. "I've put him behind me."

"He loves you," Melia said.

Plantine pouted with a bored expression. "Many love me."

Melia searched her sister's eyes. She'd always been ambitious, but never vain or haughty.

"Tuck is not your past," Tatou chirped.

Plantine sneered. "I'm an Albiana. Don't you think a common tree elf is beneath me?"

Every nerve in Melia sparked. "Who told you about our mixed blood?"

Plantine studied her fingernails.

"Did you read it in a book?" Melia asked.

"No."

"How long have you known?"

"What difference does it make?"

"I've never seen you this ... brittle," Melia said.

Her sister scoffed. "I'm the same as I've always been, only older, and I understand if I'm to wed, it must be to someone who is worthy of my troth."

Those sounded like their mother's words, not Plantine's. "You've had knights and warriors cross oceans for you. Goring worked for Father."

"He did not work for Father. They collaborated. And, he's the most desirable bachelor in Faerie."

"So I've heard," Melia said. "But he kidnapped you."

Plantine's lip curled. "That was a misunderstanding."

Melia grasped for something to break through to her sister. "Is he a turnskin? Does he change into a black wolf? Do you even know?"

Plantine pressed her hands to her ears. "If the only reason you came to the Calashai was to ruin my wedding, I want you to leave. Now!"

Flora stood by the side of the bed, her long, hooked nose peering over the mattress. "What about Sevondi?"

"Who?" Plantine asked.

"Goring's lover," the spring faerie said.

Melia held her breath.

Flora scrunched her nose. "Zachariah is a rascal. The way I see things, once you two lovebirds say your vows, he'll still be slipping off for a bit of her. She's a wild thing–least that's what they say in the valley."

Plantine paled to white. "You little liar! Melia, take this–whatever she is –out of my suite."

"Where should I take her?" Melia asked.

Flora held up her hand. "These are nice rooms. There's plenty of space to share."

Plantine glared at Melia. "Get her out of here."

Tatou reached into her pocket. Pixie dust. Melia nodded. Tatou blew a handful of powdery sparkles into the air. A colorful shower rained over Plantine and the spring faerie.

A sob caught in Flora's throat. It escalated into uncontrollable hiccoughing and howling. Aldous had warned them about spring faeries and pixie dust, but he hadn't offered any specifics.

Plantine brushed the shimmery powder from her nose and face. "What is wrong with her?" The pixie spell had left her unfazed.

Melia tried not to think of Umbra lurking behind the beautiful mask of her sister's face. "We'll take her out of your way," she said.

"Yes, you will."

Melia put her arm around Flora's shoulder. She tried to get her to stand up, so she could guide her from the bedroom, but the spring faerie writhed from her grasp as though she were an overwrought child. She pounded the dirt with her hands and fists. "Life's not fair." Flora moaned. "I hate Uriel Albiana! Torture and excruciating pain are too good for the lot of them!"

Plantine's countenance transformed. She gazed down at the weeping Flora with curiosity. She kneeled, stroking the spring faerie's kerchief-covered head. Maybe the dust's effect had been delayed. She rubbed Flora's shoulders. "Poor thing. So sad. Let it all out."

Melia looked at Tatou. The pixie shrugged.

Plantine whispered in Flora's ear, "Uriel was very bad. I don't trust that nasty Luisa either. She shouldn't be queen."

Melia's stomach tightened.

Tatou motioned her aside. "We need to let Flora have her cry."

"Did you hear Plantine? The stronghold's throne is not enough for her. She's strategizing for the one at the Cathedral Palace as well."

"She wants to be the Queen of the Realm of Faerie," Tatou whispered, although Plantine was so engrossed with Flora's grief, she wouldn't have heard the pixie if she'd yelled.

"I fear she'll become a tyrant," Melia said.

"Maybe Tuck can reach her."

"She'll never agree to meet him."

"We have to convince her that seeing him is the right thing to do," Tatou said.

Chloe stood in the door-frame. "May I enter?"

Plantine ignored the muannaye as she helped Flora into the enormous bed that took up much of the bedchamber.

Chloe hesitated before she spoke. "Yrrick has announced a dinner party. Lord Goring wishes to welcome his bride's sister and her traveling companions to the stronghold."

Dread echoed in the hollow of Melia's chest.

Plantine rushed from Flora's side. "Who else came with you?"

"A priest from Idonne"–Melia paused–"his pet tiger, and a tree elf." They'd left Sinjiin in the Welcoming Hall in his tiger form. If he wanted Chloe–or anyone else at the Calashai–to know he was a mage, he could tell –or show–them himself.

Plantine's eyes glinted with dark temper. "A tree elf?"

"Yes," Melia said.

Plantine turned away from the servant. She pressed her palms together and closed her eyes. "Thank you, Chloe. You may leave us now."

The muannaye curtseyed and departed.

"I told you not to bring him here!" Plantine exclaimed.

Tatou darted toward her.

"If you throw any more pixie dust on me, I'll have you locked up," Plantine warned.

The pixie hovered in front of Plantine's face with her hand in her pocket.

Melia held her breath. It was the last dark moon night in the cycle, and it looked as though it was going to be a long one.

45. A Dinner Party

Lord Goring sat at the head of an oval table covered with a red and white checked tablecloth. His elbows were on the table, and he clasped his hands in a single fist. His shoulder-length hair, pulled back in a ponytail, with silver-grey streaks at the temples gave him a sophisticated air. Two gold earrings hung from his earlobes. His brown eyes, flecked with gold, observed everyone and everything around him with a curiosity he made no effort to conceal. The thinness of his upper lip–contrasted with the fullness of the bottom one–bestowed his narrow face with cruelty.

Plantine sat to his right. The chair to his left was empty. Sinjiin preferred his meals raw and had declined their host's invitation to dine.

Melia, flanked by Ryder and Flora, sat across from the muannaye. Tatou hovered between Plantine and Flora. After making clear her disappointment that Elendah would not be joining them, the pixie fell silent.

None of the other wedding guests at the stronghold had been invited to this early dinner. It was a private party for the sister of the bride and her friends. Melia wondered who had influenced the meal's timing. If it had been after sunset, she would have had to decline and hunt with Sinjiin.

She hated to admit the food was delicious.

Two female trolls darted around the table, delivering bowls of red and purple lettuce drenched in a sour and tangy dressing, platters of corn-on-the-cob grilled in the husk, pan-fried greens with onions, brown beans baked until they were soft, and enormous mushrooms sautéed in butter and wine. Melia passed on the golden bread which was crunchy on the outside but gritty on the inside. Cornbread.

The main course was some kind of meat–brisket roasted in a spicy sauce. Lord Goring called it barbecue. Tatou, Tuck, and Flora wouldn't touch it, but Melia nibbled on her serving when she thought no one was watching. Ryder and Goring ate quite a bit of it, washing it down with a drink called beer which Melia didn't care for at all.

Everything about the meal paid homage to the mortal world–the muannaye was clearly a fan. But it was impossible to relax, even though Goring worked hard as a host. Cult members watched everything from the room's corners like omniscient black statues. Two more stood at the door.

"Will you be returning to Idonne?" Goring asked Ryder.

"Not for a while."

The muannaye nodded. "I understand the order doesn't take breaking the Oath of Non-Interference lightly."

Ryder set down his fork. "You're right, they don't."

"I've never met anyone who's done it before. Tell me, how does it feel to be such a rebel?"

"Perhaps it would have felt more rebellious if I were a full-blooded Idonnai, but I'm not."

Goring's eyes narrowed. "Of course, you're not. The Idonnai look like scarecrows. Tall, light skin, light hair, and all of them are thin as rails. But you're like a bull. You must have felt out of place with your dark hair and green eyes."

"I did."

Goring nodded. "Then would you say it was more a rejection of a false identity than a rebellion against–who is the head of the order these days–Anton?"

"Yes," Ryder said.

The muannaye rubbed his jaw. "To be honest, I don't understand those priests, either. All that commitment to recording and chronicling and documenting. They never do anything."

Ryder laughed. "Exactly."

Goring called one of the trolls. "Bring him more beer."

The muannaye's natural charm slithered through every crack in Melia's psychological armor. She tried to hate him, but he was fascinating to watch and listen to. He turned his attention to Flora.

Her face was a mask. The only evidence of the grieving faerie the pixie dust had called forth earlier was a touch of pink rimming her eyelids. The inscrutable warrior Melia had encountered in the woods near the tavern had returned.

Melia was beginning to understand the roles Flora played, and how she used them to disarm those around her. You'd never have guessed by the way she bantered with the muannaye now, that he'd ordered her house burned, stolen her most prized possession, and been responsible for Bella's death.

Or that Flora's primary purpose for being at the Calashai was vengeance.

"One day the muannai will be as free to travel between the mortal and enchanted worlds as the rest of you are. That's my dream," Goring said.

"No, they won't," Flora said.

"Ah. You can foresee the future. Is that a special talent spring faeries possess?"

"Anyone can read the times, compare them with the winds of change, and draw their own conclusion."

"Now, you're a poet."

"Flattery doesn't become you, Zachariah. Umbra's incarnation will close the ancient doors. It won't open new ones."

Goring twisted the cuff of his fitted white shirt. "And you know this, how?"

"The Whole is self-protecting, and Umbra is mortal ash. Everything about him is dead to the mortal world. Incarnated or not, it will repel him."

"Then why bother?"

"No one argues that the Whole is out-of-balance, or that something must be done."

Goring prodded her. "Least of all you."

Flora's eyes flashed. "Least of all me."

The muannaye leaned back in his chair. "The truth is that none of us here at this table, or anywhere in the Whole, know what new age Umbra's incarnation will usher in."

The spring faerie raised her glass of beer. "But we can all agree that it will be a new one."

Goring picked up his glass to match her toast. "To the advent of a new age, a springtime in history."

Words rarely impressed Melia, but even she had to concede the muannaye's eloquent exchange with Flora dazzled.

The spring faerie dabbed her napkin to her lips.

Tuck sat next to Ryder, and for the first time since he'd left Illialei, the tree elf didn't carry Hermes' Wand. He hadn't said a single word the entire meal, or eaten much, but he did keep trying to catch Plantine's eye.

Every time Goring caught the elf looking at his fiancé, he squeezed her shoulder, offered her a bite of food from his plate, or whispered something in her ear that made her blush.

Plantine offered stiff smiles but stared at her food as if she were a puppet. It set Melia on edge.

When dinner was finally over and the trolls had cleared the tables, Tuck finally spoke. "Plantine, did you get the book I left for you at the tree house with your mother?"

She offered a mechanical nod. "Yes."

"Did you read it?"

Plantine pressed her lips together. When she looked at Tuck, her bottom lip quivered. "I haven't had time."

Goring rubbed her arm. "Preparing for the wedding is keeping both of us busy."

Tuck snorted.

Goring cocked his head.

Everyone in the room held their breath.

The muannaye took his time rising from his chair. He didn't hurry when he reached for the thing wedged into the shortened scabbard he wore on the side of his belt. He laid it on the table and then placed his large hands, palms flat, on either side of it, so the shiny black thing was between them. He shifted the weight of his body to his arms and hands.

"Have you ever seen one of these?" he asked Tuck.

The tree elf lips formed a gash as he angled his chin.

"It's called a Glock gen-three nineteen," the muannaye said. "If I were to pick it up, aim it at any living thing, and pull this trigger"–he pointed to a small lever–"I could kill that thing with one shot."

Everyone but Tuck instinctively shifted back in their seats.

Goring's eyes ripped into the tree elf. "Guns are dangerous toys, but I'm quite taken with them." He pointed to the black statues in the corners of the room. "I give them to all my friends."

He shifted his gaze to Ryder. "Think about that the next time you want to visit the north tower."

46. Restraint

The next morning Melia and Tatou followed Yrrick through the Calashai's winding halls.

Flora remained in Plantine's suite, snacking on leftovers from breakfast. Plantine was still asleep. Melia doubted there would be anything left for her sister to eat when she woke up. The spring faerie had a hearty appetite.

"I need to fortify myself. I've got a lot of work to do today," the spring faerie had muttered. "I'm going to find some Nambrial seeds, and do some research on those Glocks."

When Melia had offered to help, Flora waved her off. "I do my best work alone."

The half-faerie was too off-kilter to argue. Saving Plantine was turning out to be more challenging than she'd ever dreamed it would be.

"How was your first night at the stronghold?" Yrrick asked.

Tatou coughed. Goring's display of the gun had upset the pixie the most.

"We'd hoped to see Elendah," Melia said. "We were disappointed she wasn't at dinner."

Yrrick nodded his head. "She's hard to find these days. Lord Goring has convinced her that her life is in danger."

Tatou flew faster to draw even with him. "Is it?"

He shrugged. "Lord Goring says a lot of things that may or may not be true."

Melia raised her eyebrows. "You don't trust him?"

Yrrick stopped. "He's the one who would benefit most from Elendah's death."

"What about Umbra?" Tatou asked.

Yrrick pointed to the horizon. "Without an agent to do his bidding, he's as much of a threat to the grey faerie's life as those storm clouds blowing in from the sea."

When they reached an arched doorway, he pointed north. "The stairs are there, at the edge of the cliff. They lead directly to the inlet. Your friends left earlier, but if you hurry, I think you'll be able to catch them."

Melia inhaled deep breaths of salt-drenched air as she crossed the lawn. A ray of sunlight shot through the gathering clouds. Far below, the Great White Sea crashed against unrelenting cliffs. The sound was invigorating. More clouds blew in from the sea. By the time she reached the stone staircase carved in the side of the mountain, a thick fog swirled around them. Melia could see a few arm lengths in front of her, but that was all.

The pixie sat in her familiar spot on her friend's shoulder. "Do you think it's safe?" Tatou asked, as Melia balanced on uneven steps.

The half-faerie was determined to make it down to the ocean. "I want to see Ryder and Sinjiin. Tuck, too. I want to know what they did last night."

After Goring's dinner party, the muannaye's friends had escorted them to their respective rooms. Even though no one had told Melia that she couldn't fly, she'd stayed all night with Flora and Tatou in Plantine's suite. Her sister had gushed over the muannaye until Melia had gone cross-eyed.

"He'd never kill anyone," she'd said.

Right.

"He just likes to wave that thing around and make threats–like in the movies."

Whatever those were.

Plantine refused to hear a single word about Tuck.

Watching her sister push love away upset Melia, but wasn't she doing the same thing with Ryder? Melia couldn't force Plantine to face her feelings about Tuck, but she could at least try to talk with the priest about her feelings for him.

"Your mother will be here soon," Tatou said.

Gumf hadn't lied about that. Pressina sailed to Tyrannis as they spoke. "Yes, all of a sudden she's eager to marry Plantine off. I'm dying to know what inspired her change of heart," Melia said. "Probably doesn't want to miss her youngest daughter's rise to power." The half-faerie swayed. The steps were narrow, and there was nothing to hang onto as they descended.

"Be careful," Tatou said.

Melia focused on the precarious stairway.

When they heard voices, the pixie flew ahead into a shroud of white mist.

By the time Melia's boots crunched sand, the sky ahead was clear. Ryder and Tuck stood on a large shelf of rock overhanging the sea. The priest's cloak–a grey one someone at the stronghold must have given him after he'd abandoned his ruined one at the Muudron Stone–billowed behind him. Tuck leaned on the wand. Sinjiin lounged beside them. Tatou flitted between a pair of seagulls, giggling.

Melia's heart expanded. Against the intense grey light of the sun, ocean spray glistened like diamonds. It was a magnificent scene. She'd remember it forever–

If her sister didn't become an evil queen and destroy the Whole.

Ryder's face lit up when he saw her.

Melia's heart leapt.

"Are you all right?" he asked.

"I'm fine, I think. Can we walk?"

He took her arm. His touch evoked the same feelings it always did. Nothing bad could happen when he was close.

Yet, so many things already had.

She stopped to face him. Not sure how to begin, she plunged ahead. "You answered Nandana's call."

"Yes."

Her heart thumped so loudly in her chest, she feared he could hear it. "Why? Why would you leave your home for something so uncertain?"

"I'm an orphan, abandoned at the priesthood's gate when I was an infant. The priests raised me, but they were never my family. There was a loving couple, Garrick and Shilda, who looked after me as best they could.

But Idonne was never my heart's home. It never will be."

"What was that like–growing up without knowing who your mother and father were?"

"I don't know anything different."

Melia wondered if it was worse than being banished by the mother who raised you. "The place I grew up isn't my home anymore, either."

"We have that in common, searching for the place we belong." He rested his hands on her shoulders.

They gazed into each other's eyes. He leaned forward. Her hand flew to her mouth as she pulled away. The priest's cheeks turned a bright shade of red. He released her. His hands fell to his sides.

An icy gust pushed them farther apart.

Melia's stiff body refused to yield. The sound of her mother weeping behind a locked door in the tree house haunted her, as did her father's cries before he'd drowned in Ashleam Bay. People who fell in love got their hearts broken–or worse. "Please understand," she said. "Things that are good never last in my world."

"Your past isn't your future."

"You say that with such confidence. How do you know?"

"Nothing in my past prepared me for you," he said. "Yet here we are."

She brushed her hair from her eyes. Why had she thought she could have this conversation? "Yes, but–" If he kissed her now, she'd never fly again. She clasped her elbows and took another uneven step back. What was she doing? They needed to focus on why they'd come to the stronghold. "Ormrun and Koldis are on their way to Aldaine. The basin might already be here."

Ryder moved toward her. "I promised you I'd take the basin and sword to the Grey Council."

"You have to find them first–and then keep hold of them."

"Sinjiin and I have a plan," he said.

"I hope it's better than the one that brought the blade to Faerie in the first place."

He didn't defend himself.

"I'm sorry, but if we don't do something soon, my sister will pledge herself to someone she doesn't love for eternity."

A shadow crossed his face.

Melia turned to the sea's horizon. It felt like the only safe place to look. Ryder pivoted, reflecting her withdrawal.

She rubbed her forehead and told herself it didn't matter that his eyes were as green as the forest on a summer day, or that he only saw what was good in her.

A lone seagull flew overhead.

She watched the grey-blue bird spiral and coast.

He waited.

Melia didn't know how to explain what flying meant to her. Or how to confess the guilt she carried over her sister's curses. "We need to stop the wedding," she said.

He turned away, silent.

As Ryder walked back to the ledge where the others were, Melia's boots dragged in the sand behind him.

✧ ✧ ✧

Tatou sat on Sinjiin's back, her favorite new perch.

Melia glimpsed the hope in her friend's eyes as she and Ryder approached. When Melia shook her head, hot wetness filled her eyes.

"What did Plantine say after dinner?" Tuck asked. "Is she ready to cancel the wedding?"

Melia couldn't open her mouth. Pushing Ryder away had left her more confused and burdened, not less. She pleaded to Tatou with her eyes.

The pixie flitted to Tuck's shoulder. "I'm sorry. Not yet."

Melia watched Ryder in her peripheral vision. She wished he would give her some sign that he understood how hard everything was for her, but he focused on her friend.

"She drinks a potion Embril makes for her. It's stopped her from fading –as you saw last night, she looks more beautiful than ever–but it leaves her confused," Tatou said.

"About what?" Tuck asked.

"About Lord Goring," the pixie answered.

The elf gripped the wand so tight his knuckles turned white. "I'll kill him."

Sinjiin bounded up on all fours and roared. The wind warmed around him. He blurred into his mage form. "Didn't you learn anything last night? The cult of Umbra will not let you near him."

"I'll find a way."

The mage shook his head. "Did you notice anything else?"

Tuck shrugged. "He flaunts his role as Elendah's advisor, and the rest of the muannai fawn over him."

"The grey faerie's absence from such a dinner for Plantine's sister indicates the muannaye's power in the stronghold."

Anger coiled in Melia's stomach as she recalled Goring's arrogance.

"Each one of us must watch our step and take care with our words in the Calashai's halls." Sinjiin said. "Goring tests our sentiments. His spies are everywhere. If he detects we're here to obstruct his ambitions, none of us will be safe. And there'll be no one to help Plantine, and no one to secure the basin and the sword–which let's not forget–is also why we're here. We must play our roles as well as he plays his."

"I'm not here to play games," Tuck said.

"Don't forget Pressina will be here soon," Tatou said.

Tuck pounded the wand against the rock. "I need to see Plantine before she arrives."

Sinjiin eyed him. "I agree, and you two"–the mage pointed to Melia and Tatou–"must arrange the meeting."

"That will be more difficult than it sounds," Melia said. "Have you noticed, Goring's army is everywhere?"

"Then be clever. Make it look as though it's an accident, but make it happen."

He pointed to Tuck. "Please, remain calm. Don't give Goring a reason to imprison you. Or worse."

"Elendah is the stronghold's regent. Goring has no authority in its halls," the elf said.

"Don't be so sure about what he can or can't do. Until we see Elendah, and judge the soundness of her mind and body for ourselves, we must tread with caution."

"Caution has gotten us into this mess," Tuck shouted.

"No, carelessness"–the mage gave Ryder a pointed look–"has gotten us here."

Melia bit her bottom lip. Her heart went out to the priest. She'd pushed him away, and now Sinjiin lectured him.

"What are you going to do?" Tuck asked the mage.

"We're going to investigate the north tower," Ryder said. "Goring is guarding something up there. We're going to find out what it is."

Apprehension pricked Melia's chest. "Please, be careful."

He didn't acknowledge her words.

47. Caught

Ryder pressed his back against the stone wall as he listened for the echo of boots to fade. A drop of salty sweat trickled from his brow. It burned his eye, but he didn't wipe it away.

He was squeezed into one of the alcoves spaced along the stronghold's halls. He gripped a knife stolen from the kitchen. It was sharp enough, but it was no match for a gun.

Goring's patrols crawled through the corridors like ants. Whatever the muannaye guarded in the north tower, he wasn't taking any chances on it being discovered or taken.

Ryder suspected it was the basin. Perhaps *The Book of Umbra*.

When the hall fell silent, Ryder wiped his eyes and peered down the hall. Sinjiin's furry head showed itself from the alcove across from him. The tiger nodded.

They slipped from their hiding places. Neither said a word.

For the hundredth time Ryder wished they could have used the Tasimas, but neither of them had been to the north tower before.

He pushed down the clawing frustration that twisted his stomach since Melia had dismissed him on the beach. Nandana's mark had called him to her. He'd crossed the Great White Sea to answer that call. Yet she denied the significance.

Her mother's ship would arrive in Tyrannis soon. The tree elf blamed

Pressina for Plantine's situation, but after last night's dinner, Ryder doubted that was the case. Her stony indifference showed a willfulness neither Tuck nor Melia cared to acknowledge. She was going to marry Lord Goring because she wanted to, not because she was a puppet.

He kept his observations to himself, though. Melia and Tuck seemed to want to believe that Plantine was being manipulated. Nothing he said was going to change their minds. Instead, he and Sinjiin had agreed to focus on regaining the basin and the sword. Preventing Umbra's incarnation was the most important thing to him again.

More boots marched toward them. Sinjiin slunk into the nearest alcove. Ryder squeezed into the one across from the tiger.

One of the muannai sniffed the air like a dog. "What's that smell?"

From the corner of his eye, Ryder could see the tip of black boots.

The muannaye sniffed again. "The scent of a stranger lingers in these halls. Bring Alrick. Tell him to come as a turnskin."

Boots banged against the stone floor.

Ryder heard the flick of a match. The scent of woodvine curled beneath his nose.

Blessed Idonne. This was worse than the Muudron Stone.

Click.

The muannai stood in front of him with a gun leveled at Ryder in one hand and a smoke in the other.

The priest's heart thundered in his chest.

Click.

Sinjiin charged.

The muannaye screamed.

The gun clattered across the stone floor. Ryder hurried to pick it up. He caught up with Sinjiin, who dragged the unconscious muannaye by one foot. The tiger head-butted the body into one of the alcoves. It flopped like a fish, refusing to stay hidden.

An eerie howl bounced from the stone walls. Another followed.

They released the body and ran, away from the turnskins and the north tower. The corridors became a confusing maze. Panting and drenched in sweat, they stared at the body. They'd made a circle. The high-pitched howling gained on them.

They raced in the opposite direction. They reached a stairwell and climbed to its height. They burst onto the stronghold's ramparts. They ran the narrow gauntlet until they reached a high-ceilinged vestibule framing an enormous door. Ryder heaved his weight against it. The door remained steadfast.

The sea gleamed beyond the parapets. They'd found the north tower.

Ryder turned.

A pack of turnskins slobbered and showed their sharp teeth.

Sinjiin roared.

Ryder waved his knife and aimed the gun. He slid his finger over the firing lever Goring had shown them last night.

The turnskins advanced inch by inch.

Ryder pulled the trigger.

Click. Nothing happened.

A corded black net dropped from the ceiling.

Sinjiin fought and roared as Ryder hacked the web with his knife. The blade nicked the steel-like cables, nothing more. Three of the dogs pulled an outer line with their strong jaws. The priest lost his footing. The knife and useless gun clattered beyond his reach as the net pulled tight around them.

Goring paced. "I'm disappointed. I thought we'd reached an understanding at dinner. I wouldn't ship you back to Idonne, and you'd stay away from the north tower."

A pair of metal cuffs wrenched Ryder's hands behind his back. The length of chain between the manacles circling his ankles barely allowed him to hobble. "I made no promises."

Goring stroked his chin. "Not directly, that's true. But then, you don't put much stock in promises. Or vows. Or oaths, do you?"

Ryder forced his face into a calm mask.

The muannaye turned to Sinjiin. The tiger fought the rope that muzzled and bound him. "My bride-to-be hates cats. Did you know that?" Goring pulled the Glock from his holster and aimed at Sinjiin with the palm of one hand over the top of the gun and the finger of his other hand on the trigger.

Ryder threw himself across his friend.

Click. Click.

Goring sighed. "Why don't they ever work the way they do in the movies?"

Blessed Idonne, the muannaye was mad.

"Take them to the dungeons. I'll send word to Anton I've got his boy."

Ryder kicked over the bucket of filthy water the guards had left behind. It reeked of piss. Everything about the stronghold's dungeons was foul. Half of the sputtering torches had blown out as they'd paraded by. No one bothered to relight them. Living things scratched and skittered down the slime-covered walls.

Sinjiin lay trussed on a pile of moldy straw, observing him.

Ryder paced the small space. His bare feet squished a jellylike substance, making him want to retch. The cult had stolen his boots and cloak. He threw himself at the bars of the cell's door. They jangled. His shoulder throbbed."We're the only prisoners in this hole," Ryder said. "They can bury us alive down here. Who would know?" He shuffled over to Sinjiin. Working blind, with his manacled hands behind him, he tried to loosen the rope that muzzled his friend. It was impossible. He shuffled back to the wall-to-wall grill in front of their cell. He didn't see any guards. "The knots are too tight. I can't untie them. Shift into your mage form and you can slip out of them."

The tiger growled.

Ryder searched the corridor again. "I told you, we're alone."

The tiger morphed into his slim male body. The ropes that bound him fell away. "We need to think," he said.

"About what?" Ryder asked.

"The Tasimas."

"If we think about it hard enough, will it come to us?"

"You forget I'm a mage from the Hidden City."

"You can call the Rykkiel to us?"

"No." Sinjiin retrieved the bucket Ryder had kicked over and made it into a seat. "That would be impossible, but there is something I can do. Be quiet. I must prepare myself."

48. An Unexpected Ally

Melia followed Chloe to the illusionary meadows of the Welcoming Hall. The large room was dark. None of the candles were lit. A few embers glowed in the marble fireplaces, but neither Ryder, Sinjiin, nor Tuck were there. A swathe of butterflies, wings folded in camouflage, blanketed one of the sofas. Nothing else moved in the long shadows.

When Chloe turned to leave, Melia grabbed her arm. "I was supposed to meet my friends here."

The muannaye pulled away from the half-faerie's grasp and brushed her sleeve. "Perhaps they've been detained."

Melia tilted her head. "By who?"

Chloe waved to someone passing by in the corridor. "I don't know."

"Please escort me to their rooms. I'll never find them on my own."

The muannaye fiddled with one of the wooden combs in her hair.

Melia wished Flora was with her. She'd assail Chloe's evasions with a tart comment. "I need to see my friends."

"I don't know where they are."

Melia pulled herself up to her full height. "Take me to my friend's rooms."

Chloe threw her arms down by her side. "Follow me."

The muannaye's icy demeanor worried Melia. She hurried after her. Chloe led her to a kitchen twice the size of the one in the Cathedral Palace.

Melia couldn't count the number of dwarves and trolls scurrying about the cavernous space. Yrrick stood in the middle, shouting orders.

The acolyte gave Yrrick the slightest bob of her head. "She wants to see her friends."

As Chloe made a hasty exit, Yrrick scanned a menu a dwarf had handed him. "Tuck went down to the inlet."

She had no time for a game of questions. "Why?"

Yrrick waved off a troll. "He seemed upset. Maybe he went to clear his head."

She believed that. Evidence of the impending wedding confronted them at every turn, and after lunch, Plantine had eluded a meeting they'd set up near the fountain in the stronghold's main courtyard. Tuck had thrashed the ground with Hermes' Wand. Melia had been surprised when the stick didn't splinter or break.

"Where are Ryder and Sinjiin?" she asked.

Yrrick gave her a probing gaze.

"Well?"

He nodded to a dwarf before he pulled her out of the kitchen. He lead her down two long, empty halls to a darkened recess. He shoved her into the cramped space, scanning the corridor before he joined her.

"What's wrong?" she asked.

"Your friends are in trouble."

"What kind of trouble?

"They went nosing around the north tower. Would you know why they did that?"

Melia's heart beat like a wild bird in a cage. "Are they there now?"

Yrrick snorted as he took a step back to scan the hall again. "No one's up there now except for Goring and his army."

"What about Elendah? We haven't seen her since we arrived at the Calashai. Every time my friend tries to schedule an audience with her, she receives a dismissal."

Yrrick searched her eyes. "The Calashai's become a sticky web."

"What do you mean?" she asked.

"The long-legged spider's tales of intrigue have convinced Elendah his army must remain in the stronghold after the wedding."

"You're talking about Goring?"

Yrrick nodded. "These days, Elendah doesn't listen to anyone else."

"And you're telling me this–because?"

"You fidget and look away whenever Goring's name is mentioned. I'm loyal to the grey faerie. Her blindness to the muannaye's grab for power infuriates her most devoted acolytes."

"Then why doesn't someone do something about it?"

"Those closest to her say she acts strange. That a haze envelopes her mind."

Melia wanted to know more, but the sun would set soon. "Where are Ryder and the tiger?"

"In the dungeons."

Her voice rose sharply, "What are they doing there?"

"Shh. If Goring finds out I've told you, we'll be joining them."

"I need to see them."

"They're not allowed visitors," he whispered.

She felt the twitches that warned her change was coming. "I won't abandon them. Where are the dungeons?"

"You'll never find them on your own."

Melia gripped his arm. "Tell me where they are!"

He looked at her hand. "They're beneath the stables, but you don't understand the danger."

She was out of time. "I'm beginning to."

"Your sister's wedding ..." he hesitated.

"Yes?"

"I wouldn't let any sister of mine marry that traitor."

"I'm going to stop her."

"If I can help–"

"How can I find you?" she asked, already running down the hall.

"Ask around the kitchen or the guardhouse, but watch your back. Those still pledged to Elendah's regency dwindle by the day."

Melia's muscles contracted as she searched for a window.

The stables were easy to find, but the Calashai's west wall was solid stone. She flew; she hopped. She pecked at every crack until her beak ached.

Nothing.

Perched in an enormous redwood tree overlooking a brightly lit courtyard, Melia sorted through her options.

Carriages squeaked and groaned as glamorous muannai and foreigners wearing exotic gowns and cloaks exited their plush interiors. Horses with plumed headdresses snorted and stamped, their copper shoes clacking against the courtyard's stone walkways. A small army of trolls shouted among themselves as they drove the empty carriages and horses to the stables.

Snippets of gossip fueled the dark undercurrents swirling through the night air.

"Do you think he's in love?"

"Zachariah? Hardly."

"What about Sevondi?"

"The dragonwitch?"

"They made such a striking pair."

"She can't be pleased."

"Perhaps they're plotting together? Something deliciously wicked."

"It's no secret, Sevondi and Lord Goring have always had eyes for Elendah's throne."

"The bride's a mere child."

"A half-faerie from Illialei."

"They say she's breathtaking."

Melia ruffled her feathers. What she heard fueled her own suspicions about the muannaye. He'd seemed attentive enough to Plantine at their little dinner, but who knew what he really planned?

Did it even matter?

Ever since Melia had arrived at the stronghold, a disturbing thought niggled the back of her mind. Every time she pushed it away, it came back.

Embril's potion wasn't changing Plantine. Umbra was. He fed her sister's raw ambition and made her ruthless. It was the only explanation for the alarming ugliness her sister displayed.

Melia searched the night beyond the courtyard's torchlight. Faerie's two moons shone in the sky. She flew toward the Great White Sea.

Ryder and Sinjiin had risked everything to search the north tower. She needed to find out why.

49. The North tower

Melia lifted into the ocean breeze. It carried her south. Circling back toward the Calashai, she arced toward the north wall. Damp, salty air drenched with the enchanted sea's mystic vitality cleared her lungs and rejuvenated her.

She executed a tight spiral upwards–and froze midair. An endless row of black-clad archers lined the stronghold's battlements. They'd been invisible in the night's shadows.

Did they have any of those guns?

She flapped her wings to regain altitude. If any of them cared for sport, she'd be an easy target in the light of the new moons. She swooped low and swerved as flush to the tower's stone wall as possible. Below her, waves crashed against the cliffs.

She pivoted. The infinite horizon of the Great White Sea stretched out before her. The vast body of water pulsed with subtle magic in the moonlight. She yearned to cross the sea and leave her problems behind. She wanted–

What did she want? The only thing she'd ever wanted was wings, and now that she had them from dusk to dawn, it wasn't nearly enough.

White foam roiled against giant boulders.

Ryder's face loomed large in her mind; his green eyes searched her soul. Gaining altitude, she spiraled into a cloud and lost the world around her in a dense mist. The Ryder she saw in her mind's eye wasn't the one who'd lost Koldis. Or the one who'd been thrown into a stronghold dungeon. It was the Ryder who'd reached out his hand to save her in her visions.

Where was that Ryder? She burst through the cloud's cottony barrier.

Straight ahead, the north tower's sheer wall rose flush from the steep cliffs of the Ruadain. Light glowed from the tower's windows; two of them faced battlements and archers, but the third illuminated rectangle faced the sea.

Melia flew across the water and cut back in a stealthy glide to the third window's ledge. She prayed it would be broad enough to hold her.

It did–along with a panel of iron bars.

She landed easily, inching toward the bars with excruciating care. If she moved too quickly her talons would scratch the stone. When she pressed her beak against one of the metal rods, she found herself staring at the back of the tallest muannaye she'd ever seen. His legs were endless. Yrrick's odd warning came to mind ... a big, black spider.

Enveloped by a curtain of grey mist, Goring leaned over a pedestal and chanted. Melia craned her head. Ormrun rested upon the stand. Her heart crept into her throat. The basin was right in front of her, yet the window's bars allowed nothing but her head to slip through. Iron bars blocked the other windows as well.

She strained to hear what the muannaye said. The only word she could make out was, "Elendah." He repeated the grey faerie's name over and over in a hypnotic hymn as he waved a silver hair comb studded with diamonds and pearls over the bowl.

The grey faerie wasn't in the room.

A single black-clad muannaye, half asleep, nodded against a tall wooden door. Torches burned in wall sconces. A table sat beneath one. Scattered sheets of paper, a knife, some ink pens, dried herbs, a handful of different colored pebbles, and a metal pitcher surrounded a thick leather-bound book.

A bleak flare of recognition jolted her. She'd seen that book before–in Achill, in her father's cottage.

The Book of Umbra.

A chill snaked up Melia's spine. Had Plantine been in this room? Had she gazed into Ormrun's depths?

The grey vapor shrouding the muannaye extended itself in fingerlike curls. The eerie tendrils unfurled; they pointed toward her. She knew what the searching mist was, having encountered it before in Flora's cottage. Panicked, Melia hopped backward before the serpentine fog could envelop her. Her talons scritched against the ledge.

The muannaye jerked from his trance.

She slipped from the balcony and fell several hundred feet before remembering she could fly.

"Who's there?" Goring's voice boomed above the crashing waves. The ocean's spray mizzled her wings. "Down there," he shouted, "shoot that eagle."

Goring's alert spread like wildfire. Arrows–no bullets–rained from the sky. Mad with fear, Melia searched for safety–a crack in the fortress wall, an open window, anything. When a sliver of light caught her eye, she slipped through a crevice to arrive in a deserted stairwell. The roar of the ocean and the shouts of the muannai were silenced by the stronghold's thick walls.

She peered down the staircase and followed the broad stone steps to their end. After surveying the empty corridor, she made her best guess as to the direction of her sister's suite.

Her eagle instincts served her well. Standing around the corner of Plantine's rooms, she tried to calm down. The guard outside her sister's room had fallen asleep, and she didn't want to risk waking him. His bulky form–stretched out in front of the door–proved Yrrick's point; the stronghold was no longer a place of refuge. Goring had turned it into his domain.

If Melia did nothing, Plantine would marry a monster. She had to try to use the Tasimas to take her sister home. Icy fingers pulled on Melia's tail feathers. She squawked and flapped her wings.

"Shhh!"

She spun around and found herself face to face with an ephemeral ghost-like Sinjiin. "What happened to you?" she whispered.

The mage's form shimmered. Tears burned her eyes. If he was dead, then Ryder ...

"You must find Tuck," the apparition said in a shaky whisper.

"Are they going to kill him next?"

"Kill? Ah, you think you see my ghost. No, I'm projecting myself."

Thank the gods of Azyllai. All day long she'd regretted cutting short her conversation with Ryder. Now her self-reproach quieted as she realized she'd have another chance to make things right with him. She wouldn't let it slip by. The next time she saw him, she'd find some way to tell him how afraid she was to live a life without ever flying again.

"We're locked in the Calashai's dungeons," Sinjiin said. "The tree elf can help you find the key to our cell. Tell him to use the wand if necessary."

"Is Ryder all right?"

The mage was having a difficult time maintaining the volume of his voice. "He's been better.

"Did they hurt him?"

"No, he's only disheartened."

Melia could hardly see the mage anymore; his image was so faint. "I flew to the north tower. Goring tried to have me killed. I can't let Plantine marry him."

"It's too late." Sinjiin's lemon-yellow turban and bright red pantaloons flickered.

"No," she said. "I'll use the Tasimas–"

"Your sister won't survive."

"But Embril's potion–"

The turban evaporated. A finger waved in the air. "The troll's potion is a mask. If you use the Tasimas, your sister will disintegrate. Traveling through the dimensions of time and space is only safe for those who are whole."

Melia trembled. "But–"

"Vows taken under duress are not binding in the enchanted world. Any marriage made while she is spellbound constitutes coercion in the grand court of Idonne, as well as before the Grey Council. Your sister can petition for freedom from either."

"What about the wedding's consummation? Will the court or council undo that?"

Only Sinjiin's voice remained. "We must get Koldis and Ormrun out of Faerie. Find the keys and bring the Tasimas to the dungeons."

Melia's gaze ping-ponged down the silent corridor. Sinjiin was gone.

She peeked around the corner. The muannaye guarding Plantine's door sill slept. It was a few hours before dawn. Maybe she could find a way to enter the suite through the courtyard and get a few moments of sleep herself. If she woke early, she could ask Yrrick to help her find Tuck before the rest of the stronghold stirred.

As soon as she entered Plantine's suite, Melia's fear of Goring resurfaced. Was Sinjiin right? Should she let her sister marry someone she didn't love in hopes that one day some distant court would free her when she realized she'd made a mistake?

–Or should she try to save her one more time?

50. The Grey Faerie

Melia woke up in the sitting room of Plantine's suites at dawn. After she shifted into her half-faerie form, she walked into her sister's private chamber and pulled her out of bed.

Plantine grumbled in front of an enormous mirror.

"Can you stop staring at yourself?"

The bride-to-be picked up a hairbrush. Melia grabbed her sister's arm and dragged her into the suite's main room, where there weren't any mirrors.

"Let go of me," Plantine said.

"What harm is there in seeing Tuck once?" Melia held up her index finger. "Only one time. He's come all this way."

Her sister's eyes flashed. "I told you not to bring him here."

They stood beneath a spiring tree. Melia smelled its leaves and bark, the rich loam its roots tunneled into. She loved the Calashai's living beauty. Compared to the ornamental tomb the Albiana's called a palace, it nourished life.

Glaring at her sister, she wished she'd come to the stronghold under different circumstances. "Goring tried to have me killed last night. He also tried to have Flora killed. Where is she, by the way?"

"Leave her out of this. Let her sleep," Plantine hissed.

"I want to know if she's all right."

Her sister's brittle laugh sounded like breaking glass. "You're so jealous of me."

Melia's head snapped back.

Plantine's eyes shined hard and bright. "You're jealous of everything I have. Mother's love, Father's love, Goring's ..." She plucked at her chemise.

"You can't even say it, because you know he doesn't love you."

Plantine's gaze shifted between Melia and the brush in her hand. Then she threw it. Melia ducked, but it grazed the top of her head. Speechless, she stood up. Plantine's hand covered her mouth.

"Marry him," Melia said. "You deserve each other. Tuck is too good for you."

Tatou flew out of Plantine's bedroom. "What is going on?"

Melia swallowed hard and stalked to the door. Tatou was already on her shoulder, stroking her hair. Melia would find Flora later. Right now she needed to get as far away from Plantine as possible. It was time to let her sister go and save her friends.

Save the Whole from the monster Plantine would become when she incarnated Umbra.

Melia headed to the guardhouse to find Yrrick. The morning was muggy, and she walked fast. Despite the gowns Plantine had showered upon her since she'd arrived at the stronghold, Melia still wore the clothes Gumf had given her at the Veil. The slacks and boots suited her; the long flowing dresses her sister encouraged her to wear didn't.

By the time they reached the black iron gate on the other side of the courtyard, sweat trickled down Melia's back and behind her knees. Yrrick wasn't in the building, but another muannaye offered to find him.

The remaining guards in the house stared at Tatou. You would have thought they'd never seen a pixie before. Then she remembered they probably hadn't. Pixies rarely left the enchanted gardens, and they never crossed the Maeldun Bridge.

A long line of delivery carts formed on the cobblestone road leading from the stronghold's gates. Two trolls hurled insults at one another. When they jumped to the ground and wrestled, traffic snarled to a halt. The guards shifted their attention to ending the brawl.

A few minutes later, a wagonload of white roses jostled by. On any other day their wafting scent would have refreshed Melia's heart, but this morning–as the cart's wheels creaked–all she could smell was the stench of Goring's effort to mask a horrid lie.

"The ceremony's going to be unforgettable," Tatou whispered.

The awe in her tone needled Melia. "The new Plantine wouldn't have it any other way." Her sweet sister was gone. Eaten away by Umbra, she presumed. A power hungry fae, determined to sit on a throne and become the Queen of the Realm of Faerie at any cost, had replaced her.

Tatou continued to stroke Melia's hair, but the half-faerie couldn't calm down. One of the guards looked in their direction. She pointed toward the courtyard to indicate they'd be waiting for Yrrick outside. The muannaye nodded before turning away.

The deliveries hadn't slowed for a minute.

When they were far enough away from the building that she was certain the guards couldn't overhear their conversation, Melia told Tatou about Ryder's and Sinjiin's arrest, the north tower, Goring's attack, and Sinjiin's apparition. Everything came out in a jumble.

Tatou seized on Goring. "We have to warn the grey faerie!"

The terror in her friend's eyes frightened Melia. "How?"

The pixie wilted. "I still haven't been able to see her."

"Have you talked to Flora?" Melia asked.

"She's had mixed results."

"Tell me."

"She found out the Glocks need to be loaded with bullets to kill anyone."

"What about Goring's threats?"

"Flora can't figure out if he's bluffing, or doesn't realize the truth. He sends trolls to the mortal world. They smuggle contraband into Faerie. They've brought back lots of guns, but no bullets. Or the bullets have gotten wet. She can't get a straight answer. Either way, it's driving Goring crazy. He can't figure out why the guns won't explode the way they do in the moving pictures."

"Moving pictures?"

"Don't you remember? Plantine told us about them. They're picture stories from the mortal world. I want to see one."

Melia raised her eyebrows. "So the guns are harmless?"

Tatou shrugged. "Flora couldn't flush out any evidence of Goring–or anyone else–shooting someone with one of them."

"That's good news. Okay, what's the bad news?"

Tatou patted her shoulder. "Nambrial isn't native to the Ruadain."

"Flora must be upset."

Tatou giggled with her hand over her mouth. "She went to the muannai valley for the seeds. She used the Tasimas."

"But I need it to free Sinjiin and Ryder!"

The pixie laughed a bit more before wiping her eyes. "Don't worry. She'll be back soon."

Her friend's assurance didn't soothe Melia's irritation. "If you were the one locked up in a dungeon, I don't think you'd find it so funny."

"You're right." Tatou offered an exaggerated frown. "It's not."

"Goring tried to have me killed. Without the Tasimas we're stuck here, subject to his lunatic whims."

"Melia, if I hadn't told you she used it, you'd never have known. I only thought it was funny she used a Rykkiel for a trip to the market."

"Ha, very funny," Melia muttered.

"Look!" Tatou squeaked.

Yrrick waved from across the courtyard.

"Finally," Melia huffed.

The muannaye's lean body moved with a dancer's grace. When he reached them, he was out of breath. "I went to your sister's suite looking for you. Not a very joyous bride-to-be this morning, is she?"

Melia tugged on her hair. "It's probably nerves."

"Follow me," he said.

The muannaye marched pass the guardhouse and didn't stop until he'd reached the stone staircase that led to the beach.

A horde of seagulls circled the cliffs. The flock screeched and dove into the sea for their breakfast.

"Every day, for as long as I've served her, Elendah has gone down to the inlet at dawn. Last moon cycle, she stopped going, but she's walking down there now. She prefers to spend her mornings in solitude, so I didn't bring you here."

Yrrick bowed and left before Melia could ask him where to find Tuck–or if he knew where the keys to the dungeons were kept. Ryder and Sinjiin would have to wait a little longer. This might be her only opportunity to meet the Calashai's regent. Perhaps when she told Elendah what Goring had done, the grey faerie would order the priest and the mage to be released.

Maybe she'd order Goring to be imprisoned.

Melia's heart hammered in her chest as she descended the staircase. She saw the regent before she reached the bottom step. Tall and lean, Elendah walked along the shoreline. Even from a distance she looked noble with her thick grey braids knotted on top of her head in the muannai style.

She wore black fitted breeches and an unusual lapis shirt. The gentle tide lapped at her bare feet. Awe of her paralyzed Melia.

"Don't just stand here," Tatou said. "We have to warn her that Goring is spelling her."

Elendah saw them. She waved as if she'd been waiting for them.

Melia forced herself to keep putting one foot in front of the other.

"I often walk alone in the early morning," Elendah said. "Come. Join me." She held out her hand. Tatou landed in her upturned palm. There wasn't a single wrinkle or line on the faerie's face. "You're the first pixie I've ever met," she said.

Tatou performed a graceful curtsey. "It's such an honor."

Elendah's deep grey eyes shifted to the half-faerie. "Are you the bride's sister?"

Under her gaze, something inside Melia untwisted. "Yes. But my sister is in love with another."

Elendah nodded. "The tree elf."

"You know him?" Tatou asked.

Elendah pointed a slim finger toward the Calashai. "We haven't met, but I can see this beach from my balcony. He comes here to seek the cove's peace. He's wise to do so."

Melia tried to tell the grey faerie about Lord Goring, but the words wouldn't form in her throat. Her tongue grew heavy and her lips refused to move. She gestured to Tatou. The pixie alighted from Elendah's palm to fly between them. She pulled on her bottom lip, but said nothing. Her warnings had been silenced too.

"Let's walk," the grey faerie said.

Melia and Tatou followed her along the beach.

Every time Melia tried to tell her that Goring kept the magical basin in the north tower, or that he didn't love Plantine, or that he'd locked her friends in the stronghold's dungeons, the same thing happened. Her mouth trapped the words.

That was Goring's spell. No one could speak the truth about him to Elendah.

Melia tripped over a piece of driftwood. She picked it up. She tried to write his name in the sand, but with every line she drew, the tide grew stronger, the waves more aggressive.

Again and again the lines Melia drew washed away. Her shoulders slumped. She dropped the piece of wood.

Elendah took Melia's hand and kept hold of it as they walked. "Life is a mysterious road which each of us walks alone. Moments unfold and we can never see what is waiting for us around the bend. So we must learn to trust our steps. That can take an entire life," she said. "But sometimes there isn't time." The grey faerie faced Melia as she reached into a deep rimple in her shirt. "I've been holding onto these, waiting for the right person to give them to, and the right moment in which to do it."

Melia couldn't breathe.

Elendah's grey eyes glistened. "You're the right person, and this is the right moment." She pulled out a handful of pearls and spilled them into Melia's upturned palms. "These are a talisman that will strengthen your heart. The longer you wear them, the easier it will become to discern your truth, separate from the needs of those around you. Use that knowledge to lead others."

Melia sorted through the strands. There were two bracelets and a necklace. She awkwardly slipped the bracelets around her wrists.

Elendah lifted the necklace from her hands. Melia bowed her head. The grey faerie dropped the beads in a circle around Melia's neck. She placed her hand in the center of the half-faerie's chest. "Dark doesn't cover light. Light is the center of dark. To know the light, one must travel through the dark. Shun that journey and you'll always be dependent on others to see. The only light that you know will be a reflection. Never your own." Elendah hugged her close, and whispered, "I'm at peace with the times."

51. The Mother of the Bride

Servants and wedding guests clogged the stronghold's corridors. The time with Elendah already felt as though it were a dream.

Melia rolled the pearl necklace the grey faerie had given her between her forefinger and thumb. No, it had been real.

"Will you be attending the ceremony and the feast afterwards?" Yrrick asked.

Melia guessed his question was a formality for the benefit of any ears that listened too closely to their conversation as they wove through the crowd. "If my dress fits," she said.

Plantine had demanded each of them–Tatou, Flora, and Melia–wear something appropriate on her special day. Melia had survived the fitting. Their gowns should have been delivered this morning while they'd walked with the grey faerie in the cove.

Yrrick's sideways glance was strained. "You're joking."

Her forced laugh came out as a squeak. "Of course, I'm joking. Who would miss the wedding of the century?"

Tatou patted the side of her head.

After Goring had tried to have her killed last night–and her nasty fight with Plantine at dawn–Melia had no intention of attending their fake wedding. She clutched at the pearl bracelets wrapped around her wrists.

Melia and Tatou had found Tuck after their walk with Elendah on the beach. As his condition to help them free Sinjiin and Ryder from the Calashai's dungeons, he'd demanded one last attempt to see Plantine. Melia had relented because, in her heart of hearts, she still hoped they could save her sister too.

Yrrick pasted a broad smile on his face, but his words came through clenched teeth. "Be careful. When Goring realizes how determined you are to stop him from marrying your sister, he'll have you arrested for treason."

Melia managed a more genuine laugh and fluttered her eyelashes. "Treason? Isn't that a bit dramatic?" Years of hiding her emotions from her mother and sisters made her play-acting easier.

"I've watched him for months now, and I know how he works. He'll accuse you–a half-faerie who changes her shape into a black eagle at dusk–of plotting against the grey faerie's life with black magic."

Melia's hands shook. She shoved them in her pockets while she showered the passersby with stiff smiles. "Elendah won't believe him."

"She doesn't have to. Goring won't ask for her permission to send you to join your friends in the dungeons." Yrrick pushed through the crowds.

She hurried to catch up with him.

When they reached the door to Plantine's suite, Melia crumpled to the ground. She clutched her stomach and moaned.

"Get Embril," Yrrick shouted to the guard.

He hesitated.

Melia moaned louder.

The guard ran down the hall.

"You don't have much time," Yrrick whispered before he hurried off.

Melia shot up.

"What do you think Plantine is going to do when Tuck shows up at her door?" Tatou asked.

Melia touched her pearls. "I don't know, but I can't stand another minute of this hideous mockery." Her fingers closed around the bronze door handle. "This is going to work. It has to."

✧✧✧

Pressina's lilac eyes glinted.

Her face was a beautiful, hideous mask that erased the grey faerie from Melia's mind. "When did you get here?" she asked her mother.

Tatou fluttered ahead.

"This morning."

An impulse to flee overwhelmed Melia. She pressed her hands against her thighs. Her mother and Goring lounged across from each other in the sitting area of Plantine's suite.

The muannaye stood up. He was so tall, and the grey at his temples gave him such a distinguished air. Tatou tried to distract him with a polite greeting, but his eyes never left Melia.

He wore a fitted vest, and his pants were so tight every muscle in his thighs was visible. His high boots outlined his calves. They were the same style as Melia's–the same style all the muannai wore. Except for Sevondi.

"I understand you and your friends haven't properly thanked your future brother-in-law for his hospitality," Pressina said.

Melia recognized the threat in her mother's tone. Memories from the afternoon she'd spelled them flooded her mind.

"N-n-no." Melia pressed her lips tight.

"Forgive her, Lord Goring. My middle child has always struggled with her manners," Pressina said. "You'd think I'd never taught her any."

Goring walked around the sofa and table. He made the beauty of the garden in the room look savage.

Melia stared at the hand he held out to her. Her arm was like stone; she couldn't lift it. They stared at one another. The muannaye leaned forward and crushed her in a hug. Melia's arms flopped at her sides. She couldn't force herself to respond, not even for the sake of her mother's performance.

Someone knocked on the door.

"Where is P-Plantine?" Melia asked.

"My bride-to-be is in Aldaine. A final fitting with the dressmaker before our special day tomorrow."

Tatou landed on Melia's shoulder. "Tomorrow?"

The muannaye's eyes never left the half-faerie's face. "Now that the mother of the bride has arrived, there's no need to delay," he said.

Tuck had been right; Goring had been five steps ahead of them all along.

The knock at the door came with greater force. Pressina stood up. Her ivory wings quivered. She looked so exotic in Tyrannis, where none of the dark faeries had wings.

"Let me get that," Goring said.

Melia closed her eyes as the muannaye walked past her. She heard the door swing open.

"Lord Goring." The shock in Yrrick's greeting was evident.

A shuffle of footsteps then deafening silence.

"Where is she?" Tuck.

Melia covered her eyes with her hands.

"You need to leave." Goring.

"She loves me."

Melia dropped her hands. A few feet away, Pressina's purple eyes turned black. Melia froze.

Goring laughed.

The dull thud of a body shoved against the doorframe. A crack of wood hit the Calashai's stone floor. The wand.

"How dare you attack me?" Goring wasn't laughing now.

Another thud.

Melia forced herself to turn.

Goring towered over the tree elf. He gripped Tuck by the front of his shirt. "She's mine," the muannaye said.

Tuck kicked, but he was no match for Goring. The elf struggled impossibly to grasp the wand. He stretched his fingers. The muannaye lifted him from the floor with one hand.

"Yrrick," Goring said, "there must always be a guard at this door. Call one, now."

Four cult members materialized from nowhere in less than a heartbeat. Two latched onto Tuck's arms. The other two secured his legs.

Goring released him.

Tuck spit.

The muannaye picked up the walking staff. Melia's heart pounded. She needed to protect the wand; she needed to fix everything their foolish plan had destroyed. Before she could think, Goring tossed the stick to one of the guards who caught it in one hand.

Goring straightened his cuffs. "Lock him and his crutch up with the others."

"You're going to destroy her," Tuck yelled as they carried him away. "I won't let you."

The muannaye brushed his hands. "What noble protests."

Pressina rushed to Goring's side. She touched his arm. "Plantine has broken so many hearts. That one used to come to our home, looking for her with flowers and books, but his persistence is madness."

A smile slithered across Goring's face. "She's quite the catch, your youngest daughter."

Was he glaring at Melia over her mother's head? Or was it only the light filtering through the garden that shadowed his eyes?

"Now that I've received your blessing" –Melia didn't know why he bothered to ingratiate himself further with her mother, she already fell all over him–"I'll announce our change of plans. The guests will never forgive me if I don't give them adequate time to prepare their attire."

As soon as he was gone, Pressina turned on Melia. Tatou landed on a tree limb. The pixie's wings jerked with distress.

"How dare you bring that tree elf to Aldaine!" Pressina's tone sliced, a sharp edge of broken glass. "And to encourage such an uproar! Melia, what were you thinking? And don't you dare lie to me! I saw your face when he knocked on the door. We're fortunate the muannaye is so devoted to your sister. What would we have done if he'd called off the wedding?"

Melia trembled before the force of her mother's rage. She glanced askance at Tatou. The pixie's face was a mask of shock. Pressina must have forgotten her friend was in the room. "Mother, G-Goring is spelling the grey faerie!"

"Please, Melia, stop it! You took your father from me. Will you take this from me too?"

"What am I taking from you?"

"The chance to be Luisa's equal," Pressina said.

"Have you even seen Plantine?"

"She was here when I arrived, looking more radiant than ever."

"It's the potion."

Pressina yanked on Melia's pearl necklace. "Where did you get these?"

"They were a gift."

"From who?"

"The grey faerie."

Pressina's lilac eyes flickered. She flung the beads against her daughter's chest. "You've never shown the slightest interest in jewelry before."

Melia pressed her lips together. The subject of Elendah made her mother uncomfortable. Pressina walked to one of the sofas and sank down. "Plantine was very upset when I arrived."

She let her mother change the subject. Pressina could only belittle Melia's experience with the grey faerie. "Maybe Plantine shouldn't exchange eternal vows with someone she doesn't love."

"Why must you always fight me on everything?"

"You gave Plantine a remedy: true love's first kiss. Goring isn't her true love. His kiss won't cure her. She'll have to take that potion every day for the rest of her life–or die. Is that what you want for her?"

"Anything would be better than the bitterness I've had to swallow my entire life."

Melia forced herself to walk over to her mother. This might be the only chance she would ever have to persuade her the wedding was a mistake. "Where is Flora?"

"I don't know." Pressina's mouth twitched into a frown. She looked beyond Melia, out into the courtyard. "Did Flora tell you about the time she found me wandering in the Balyudor?"

Melia sat down across from her. "Yes, and Gumf told me about the field of sapphire lilies."

Pressina released a brittle laugh.

"Mother, you don't have to let that monster marry Plantine to set things right. If we could convince Flora to return to Illialei–"

"A lovely thought, honey." Pressina pulled a slender brown stick from a crumpled package on the table. A compact metal object sat next to it. She picked up the silver rectangle and manipulated it with her thumb. A small flame shot out. She gripped the brown stick between her lips, lit its tip with the flame, and sucked. Smoke curled in the air. Her mother was smoking woodvine.

Melia sat in stunned silence.

"You need to understand something. A field of sapphire lilies is never going to exist again. Those days are gone. The sapphire lily doesn't call us anymore. My grandmother killed the spring faeries; we can't undo that. So Flora's not going to lift a finger to help us, no matter how much she's taken to you. And we shouldn't expect her to. We're Albianas. Daughters of Light. Born to rule. We have the power within us; you're too weak to embrace it, but Plantine isn't."

Melia couldn't sit with her mother any longer. She rose to leave.

"You're not going anywhere until you try on your dress for tomorrow. It's in the room across the hall."

Tatou returned to Melia's shoulder.

Pressina's face blotched with red. "I didn't know your friend was still here."

The pixie's silence was an icy condemnation.

Pressina recovered quickly. She pointed with the woodvine. "Both of you, go try your dresses on. We need to make sure they fit."

A wooden rack stood in the center of the room. Melia went to examine it. Only two dresses–one a miniature for Tatou–hung from the rods.

Where was Flora's?

Behind them, the door slammed shut. Melia ran to it. A key turned in the lock. She pushed on it. It didn't budge. Tatou hovered in the air beside her. Melia threw her weight against the door. Nothing.

"She's locked us in," Tatou said.

The interior room had no windows.

52. The Wedding

The next morning, two members from the cult of Umbra accompanied one of the Calashai's acolytes to their cell, as Melia had taken to calling it. The stony-faced guards set breakfast trays on the table but said nothing as the attendant helped the half-faerie and pixie with their toiletry. Goring's threat couldn't have been clearer. The wedding was going to happen, and the sister of the bride was going to attend.

Considering the circumstances, the attendant proved charming and patient as she struggled with their gowns and hair. An expert at applying cosmetics, she rouged their cheeks, darkened their brows, and painted their eyelids.

The guards led Melia and Tatou into the hall where her mother and Flora waited.

Pressina pinched her daughter's arm. "If you do anything but smile, you'll be brought back to this room by force."

Flora didn't say a word. Melia was crushed that the spring faerie didn't rise to her defense or criticize her mother for locking them in the room. Tatou stroked her hair, but it did little to calm Melia. She'd failed. Goring and her mother had won.

Plantine would marry today.

Black-clad muannai escorted them to the festivities. Outside the Grand Hall, the cult members melted into the shadows. Appearances were everything to Goring. Perhaps he wished to avoid the impression that the sister of the bride had been coerced into the triumphant nuptials.

Inside, Melia, Tatou, Flora, and Pressina followed another acolyte down a wide center aisle separating rows of round tables into long, twin columns. A multitude of eyes watched as Melia and the pixie trailed behind the spring faerie and the mother of the bride. Among the wingless muannai, Pressina and Tatou were the jewels that shone brighter than anyone else around them.

Flora waddled behind Pressina in a simple, green silk gown with black slippers. A flowery chiffon scarf tied at a dramatic angle around her head replaced the red-plaid kerchief she always wore. There was a bit of color on her lips and cheeks. The transformation was impressive. She looked almost spring-like. The rose quartz bracelet Aldous had sent with Melia and Tatou the first time they'd met her circled her wrist.

They reached the table reserved for Plantine's family and friends. It was in the front row, opposite the arching entryway. Pressina's stormy eyes followed Melia's every move.

Tatou landed next to an extraordinary spray of white roses in the table's center. The choices Melia had made since she'd seen those flowers delivered to the Calashai haunted her. She should never have agreed to let Yrrick bring Tuck to Plantine's suite. She should have let her sister go and saved her friends. Now, Ryder and Sinjiin were still in the dungeons while she was trapped in a different prison.

She touched the pearls on her wrist. Would the things the grey faerie told her about dark and light ever make sense? Would she ever stop drowning out the promptings of her heart with a million excuses? Would things have turned out differently if she'd been honest with Ryder on the beach?

Everything on the sage-colored cloth sparkled and shined–the crystal place settings, the polished utensils. Beauty's power to conceal ugly truth confronted her wherever she looked.

Melia caught her reflection in a golden knife. She considered grabbing the sharp blade and slipping it into the folds of her gown. She raised her hand over the shining temptation. She felt someone stare–her mother and a muannaye at the next table.

She dropped her hand.

If those who filled the tables in front of the hall were closest to the bride and groom, then Goring had stacked the tables with his faithful. Other than a few foreigners–she recognized a table of warriors from Morgannai by their coal-black curls, and picked out a couple of Huron knights–muannai surrounded them.

A stone's throw from where they sat, a magnificent grey marble throne was centered between two less ornate seats on a bed of white roses before a cascading waterfall.

Melia looked back over the heads of the hundreds of guests. She searched for the cult of Umbra's black-clad members. Her eyes drank in the pillars of redwood trees flanking the hall's east and west walls. Draped with garlands of more white roses, their tall tops towered beyond the room's high ceilings into wispy clouds. There was no sign of Goring's army, but she knew they were everywhere.

An ocean breeze blew in through high rectangular windows. The tang of sea salt rolled over the sweet scent of flowers. Once more, the stunning effect of nature contained within four walls had been achieved. Melia's heart ached. The whimsy of the grey faerie's castle was not suited to intrigue and war.

There were two empty chairs at the table. At least Tuck wouldn't have to endure the torture of witnessing this farce. But Ryder and Sinjiin's absence created an emptiness inside Melia that physically ached. Pushing the priest away had been a mistake. He would never have left her locked in a room. He would have broken the door down. When she found him–and she would find him–she wouldn't push him away again.

Melia prayed to the gods of Azyllai that Pressina would forget her middle daughter as soon as the ceremony ended, so she could slip away to the dungeons.

The half-faerie peeked at Flora. When had the spring faerie returned from the muannai valley? And why had she abandoned them?

Tatou flitted around the table in her lavender gown and tiny glass slippers. The attendant had curled her friend's gold hair and painted her lips the perfect shade of rose. The muannai at the surrounding tables kept sneaking glances at her.

Pixies remained effervescent no matter what disasters loomed.

Melia's gown was royal blue, cut uncomfortably low in front and back. The attendant had braided her hair and piled it high on her head in the muannai fashion. Gold combs held the plaits in place. Fearing the whole thing might come tumbling down, Melia moved her head stiffly. The strands of creamy pearls wrapped her exposed neck and wrists. Melia was surprised her mother hadn't taken the jewelry from her. She suspected Pressina's wariness of the grey faerie had more to do with her keeping her hands to herself than anything else.

The dulcet notes of a single flute silenced the noisy gathering. Several muannaye boys and girls, as long and lean as their elders, skipped and cartwheeled down the center aisle in skintight leggings and tops.

Melia gasped along with the crowd. A full-blooded mortal, recognizable by his musky scent, advanced behind the children. He trilled his silver instrument with a mastered artfulness.

A corps of drummers entered the hall next–dwarves dressed in matching vests and breeches. Their intricate rhythms echoed from the infinite ceilings and stone walls. When everyone stood, Pressina, Flora, and Melia followed suit.

Tatou flew above the crowd, clapping her hands. "It's Elendah." She pointed and waved.

Melia couldn't see a thing. Frustrated, she strained her neck. The crowd cheered. Then she saw the regent.

The grey faerie dominated the hall. Tall and slender, she moved like a jaguar. Her silver hair piled high on top of her head accented the grace of her feline movements. A platinum gown hugged her slim waist, its wide skirt flashing with each step. Diamonds dripped from her ears and encrusted the combs twinkling in her hair. She wore no other jewels, yet her presence was sovereign. A feeling of peacefulness preceded her.

The muannai curtsied and bowed as she passed by. They adored her.

The dancing children gathered to one side of her throne, the piper on the other. The drummer corps, divided in half, joined them. Elendah sprang up the steps, reached for a handful of rose petals, and turned to face the wedding guests. When she threw the silky white teardrops into the air with a wide arc of her arm, the muannai stamped their feet. The grey faerie smiled and assumed her throne.

Melia's fingers brushed her pearl necklace. There was no way to tell Elendah was be-spelled.

The crowd continued to roar.

The groom's head floated above the crowd. He wore his black hair as usual–pulled away from his face in a thick ponytail. His brocade jacket flared at the waist. The froth of his white ruffled shirt spilled over its lapels. His black pants, tucked into knee-high boots, gripped his lean legs.

When he was even with their table, he looked straight at Melia. Their eyes locked. Then he was gone. Fleeting sympathy for her sister touched Melia's heart; the muannaye was magnetic.

The drummers tapped the rim of their drums, the piper threaded a lilting melody through the sophisticated rhythm. Goring strode across the dais to stand next to Elendah's throne. They made a regal pair. Murmurs from the crowd moved in a wave from the back of the hall. Melia's hand rose to her lips as Plantine advanced down the center aisle. She wore a white silk gown, or was it the palest blue? For a moment it appeared as the color of sunlight before it transformed into the faintest shade of rose. Melia's breath caught in her throat; her sister's flaxen hair had been swept high and braided with strands of gold in the muannaye style. A simple diamond pendant graced the hollow of her throat. She didn't smile or wave to the crowd as Elendah had done. She kept her eyes focused straight ahead–on the groom.

Melia ground her teeth.

Until this moment she'd seen Plantine as Goring's puppet, but her sister had revealed no cracks in her façade. In one last desperate attempt, Melia called to her. *"Plantine."*

Her sister glided up the steps leading to Elendah's throne.

"Plantine," Melia called again.

Goring's head snapped. His eyes bored into hers. Flustered, Melia turned to Flora who stood on her chair, gaping like everyone else.

When the spring faerie caught her eye, she grunted, "It'll be over soon."

Small comfort, but she was right. Given the extravagance of the affair, the ceremony itself was brief. Vows were exchanged, and the rest of the hall cheered. Except for Pressina, their table sat quiet.

Female trolls wearing white caps and starched aprons darted among the tables with platters of food.

Flora encouraged one to fill hers and Melia's goblets to the rim. "She'll be fine."

The half-faerie stiffened, ignoring the drink in front of her.

Flora tilted the bottom of her glass to the ceiling, draining it in several hearty gulps. "Gumf should drink this. He'd never brag about the Veil's blackberry wine again."

Tatou begged Melia to join her in the grey faerie's receiving line. Melia acquiesced. It was better than sitting at the table with her mother, or watching the spring faerie get drunk. She tagged along behind her friend toward a long row of guests, waiting to exchange a few words with the Calashai's regent. The line already stretched to the arched entrance. Melia did her best to smile at the muannai who recognized her as Plantine's sister. If she didn't, the cult of Umbra might arrest her.

Shouts filled the hall. Wedding guests scattered.

Melia blinked in disbelief.

Sevondi, riding bareback on a monstrous black wolf–a turnskin, barreled into the hall. A second turnskin ran alongside them. Chaos engulfed the crowd as the dragonwitch and her black dogs charged down the center aisle toward Elendah, Goring, and Plantine.

Melia had to know if Sevondi carried Koldis. Tatou gripped the braids in the half-faerie's hair as she eased toward the front of the hall. Goring's black-clad cult materialized from behind the giant redwood trees. They'd been there the whole time.

Sevondi reached the dais. "What have you done, my lover?" The dragonwitch's accusing words rang through the hall, rising to the misty ceiling.

Plantine, seated at Goring's side, leaned forward. "Husband, why does this dark faerie call you her lover?"

The crowd twittered.

Plantine turned red-faced. "Zachariah, answer me."

Goring reached for Plantine's hand. Movement registered in Melia's peripheral vision. A dozen or so black figures wound through the oval tables toward the dragonwitch. Sevondi drew the blade in a wide arc.

Koldis.

Its incandescent blue metal shimmered in the waning daylight. Goring pressed his palm in the air; the guards halted their advance. Several already stood in proximity to the dragonwitch and her wolves. They baited the dogs with taunts and threatening hand gestures.

When the wolves snarled, the crowd, except for Melia and Tatou, retreated. The half-faerie took a few steps closer. Goring jumped from the stage.

He approached Sevondi. "My sweet."

The dragonwitch vaulted from the wolf's back. She twirled the sword, dancing for her lover with supple movements.

Sevondi was drunk on him, just like Plantine. Melia saw it in her eyes.

Goring snapped his fingers. The dwarves beat a low droning rhythm on their drums while the flute sent a haunting melody soaring through the room. Sevondi's dark hair swung loose and free, her gauzy skirt accenting her slim hips. Every creature in the Great Hall stared, mesmerized by the dragonwitch's seductive dance. The crowd applauded her frenzied gyrations.

When the drums tapered to silence, and the flute blew a final sonorous note, Sevondi stilled. Goring slid forward, his liquid motion surprising for one who stood so tall. He reached for Koldis. The witch bared her teeth. Her two wolves paced a tight circle around her.

"The blade is mine," Sevondi seethed. "And you made a mistake, Zachariah." She reached up with her free hand and feathered the muannaye's cheek with a single finger. "But I'll forgive you. Be rid of the half-faerie, and give us cause to celebrate together, you and I."

Elendah, who had remained silent on her throne, stood erect. "You're not welcome here, Sevondi."

"Grey Hair, your days are numbered," the dragonwitch challenged.

Elendah strolled toward Sevondi and Goring. "All our days are numbered."

In the light of the Muudron Stone, Sevondi had been the most powerful female Melia had ever seen, but Elendah displayed a different kind of strength. That of wisdom achieved through the passage of time. As the adversaries drew closer, the vein on the side of Melia's neck throbbed.

Plantine, still seated on the dais, glared at Goring. Melia heard her thoughts. *"Prove you don't love her. Prove you don't desire her."* The knuckles of Plantine's hands turned bone white as she gripped the arms of her chair.

Was it the falling light of late afternoon, or did her sister fade?

Elendah reached the threshold of snarling wolves. She held out a strong, slender arm. "As regent of the stronghold of Calashai, I'm the rightful protector of Isolt's blade."

Sevondi lunged toward her. "Koldis is mine," the dragonwitch hissed.

"Nych." Melia inclined her head. She needed Tatou to fly as far away from her as possible.

"Be careful," her friend said.

Melia had made up her mind. Koldis was not leaving the hall without her.

Goring nodded. The air charged with bewitchment as five of his black-clad guards shifted into fierce black wolves. They bared their teeth and growled but held their attack. Blue lightning erupted from Sevondi's extended fingers. The stench was horrendous, but no liquid mortar followed.

"You have no power here. Give me the blade," Elendah said.

Sevondi's impotence didn't inspire her to yield to the grey faerie's demand. "Your face may be smooth, but you're still a foolish old woman. He'll betray you, the same way he betrayed me!" She whipped around and whistled.

Goring's turnskins growled and snarled among themselves, but they refused to attack the witch. The biggest one crouched forward and flattened its belly against the ground.

Still wielding the blade, Sevondi leapt upon its back, squeezing its haunches with her knees. The beast sailed over the rest of the turnskins and raced to the arched entryway.

Melia was already running.

A single arrow sailed through the air. It hit its mark between Sevondi's shoulder blades. A spine-tingling wail pierced the hall. The dragonwitch slipped from her mount and landed with a dull thud on the ground.

Melia reached her first.

Shocked agony filled the witch's eyes. The blade, clattering luminescent blue steel, slipped from her grasp and slid across the stone floor. "Why, Zachariah?" she moaned.

"Who's the foolish old woman now?" Flora snorted. The spring faerie stood beside Melia. "Sevondi's no spring chicken, either. Two-hundred-and-forty-seven in mortal years. Never know it just by looking at her."

Melia's fingers bled as she slid them down the blade to grasp Koldis' ruby-eyed hilt.

"The Tasimas is in the chest in your sister's bedroom," Flora whispered. "Run like the wind."

With Koldis in her hand, Melia raced for the arching exit. Sharp teeth ripped the train of her gown. She needed the sun to fall from the sky so she could fly.

"Shoot her." Goring's voice rose above the melee.

Arrows whizzed past her ears.

"Duck!" Tatou shouted.

Melia lowered her head and shoulders. A sharp pain cut into her right arm where an arrow grazed her. She pushed her legs to run faster. Although the sword was light, its length felt awkward in her hand. More shouting and another round of arrows sang through the hall. Another sharp burst of pain erupted in Melia's left shoulder. She screamed when the third arrow pinned her back. Her body slammed against the cold stone floor.

She landed on the sword. Its hilt pressed against her hips. Grunting wolves circled her, snuffling and pawing the ground. Black boots stood inches from her face. Goring.

Every bone in her body ached. Her back and left arm burned with a cold fire. The sharp pinch of arrowheads embedded within her muscles made her lightheaded. She should have grabbed that knife from the table.

"Wait," Plantine's melodious voice reached her ears. The dainty patter of slippered feet followed. *"Give me the sword,"* her sister said.

"Nych."

"He'll lock you away in the dungeons."

The Great Hall remained quiet around them.

"With the rest of my friends?" Melia asked her sister.

"They aren't your friends. They only used you to get to me. And to the sword and the basin."

Sweat or blood, she couldn't tell which, trickled into Melia's eyes. She couldn't wipe it away without letting go of the sword. She squeezed her eyes shut. *"Don't go through with the incarnation."*

"This is not the time or the place for this conversation," Plantine said.

"Where, then? When?"

"You're bleeding. Let me help you." Plantine's words whispered through Melia.

"Flora," Melia gasped.

Plantine leaned over her sister. *"Leave the sword and the basin to me. Father wanted me to have them."*

Melia should have told Plantine about her visions. Then she would have understood why Melia fought so hard to keep Umbra in the Void.

"The time for a new queen is here—"

"Plantine, Mother is wrong. There is another way."

"*Give me the blade. Give me the blade. Give me the blade. Give me the blade.*"

Strength spilled from Melia's body, draining her will. *"Have you peered into the basin? Have you spoken to Umbra?"* She had to believe her sister was driven by something darker herself.

"Give me the blade. Give me the blade. Give me the blade. Give me the blade." Plantine's silent voice blew through Melia like a freezing wind.

Her mental defenses sagged. Soon, she'd be begging her sister to take Koldis from her. Where was Flora? Why was Ryder never here when she needed him?

Plantine reached out with pale translucent fingers. She was fading again. *"Give me the blade. Give me the blade. Give me the blade. Give me the blade."*

Melia's body rolled to the side, freeing the sword. Had she moved of her own volition? Hands were all over her, lifting her up.

"Take her to the dungeons," Goring said. "Let her rot there with the priest, the tree elf, and the cat."

Where was her mother?

53. Umbra's Influence

Plantine stood before Ormrun. Her father had spent his life searching for this bowl, now it belonged to her. This was her moment.

She brushed her hair from her forehead and smoothed the front of her gown.

Diamonds, sapphires, and emeralds circled the basin's rim, but it was the single ruby marking the beginning and end of the bowl's perimeter that compelled her gaze.

As she focused upon it, the red gemstone became a door that tunneled into the darkest place within her. It fueled secrets and desires which were improper to admit–how righteous she'd felt when Goring had announced that he'd locked the priest and his oversized cat in the dungeons; how willing she was to eradicate anyone who threatened her ambition.

She let herself slip into the black space as if it were a pool of water. She let the walls come down around her–the ones that shut away the single thing that threatened to undo her: the memory of Melia, lying broken on the floor of the Great Hall, blood streaming from three wounds.

Thank the gods of Azyllai her mother had come to Tyrannis. Without Pressina's strength, she might have faltered.

"Your sister has always been jealous of you," Umbra whispered.

Plantine stared harder at the ruby. It wouldn't do for guilt to rob her of her goal.

When the ruby had drained all concern and sympathy from Plantine's heart, her breathing came easier. She turned her gaze upon the tall muannaye standing on the opposite side of the basin. The one who'd made this possible. The one who'd chosen her over her mother and sisters. Plantine bestowed a smile upon her husband.

Did she love him?

Nych, his kisses repelled her, and they hadn't ended her mother's curse.

It didn't matter.

Of course, when he'd ordered Embril to stop giving her the potion that camouflaged her mother's curse on the morning of their wedding, she'd been furious. But Zachariah had stood his ground. "Umbra's embodiment will be traumatic enough," he'd cautioned, "without the additional complications of potions and opiates."

She'd used her increasing fragility to rebuff his every physical advance. He wasn't used to rejection, and his frustration delighted her. But she couldn't deny he'd been useful.

Plantine's smile froze on her face while her thoughts returned to her sister: The brave but foolhardy Melia, who'd come to stop her from incarnating Umbra. What had she been thinking? That she could steal Koldis in broad daylight?

Plantine frowned. Stupid, heroic Melia.

"Is everything all right, my love?" her husband asked.

She gave her head a vigorous shake as if she could toss every thought of her sister from her mind. "Of course, darling."

She hadn't seen her sister since the wedding, but she received Embril's reports on Melia's progress–they weren't good–along with Flora's grumpy admonishments when Pressina wasn't there to hear.

"You should be more caring of your kin," the spring faerie would say, and then wander off for more blackberry wine.

Plantine ignored her. All that mattered was that Melia remained incapacitated and unable to disrupt tonight's ceremony.

She tried to remember how she and her sister had ended up so at odds with one another. They'd never been close, but the night Melia had come home with that queer blue mark on her forehead had made things worse. When Plantine had touched it, she'd seen the Illustrator lying dead with her cat.

Plantine swayed and reached for the side of the basin to steady herself.

"Are you sure you're all right?"

Zachariah's voice came from far away. Plantine nodded but squeezed her eyes shut. She'd promised her mother and couldn't bear to let her father down. Umbra must incarnate. And if the grey faerie had to die, and the battle between Dark and Light had to follow, so be it. She raised her chin. Better to triumph as the new queen than drown in an undertow of regret.

"My beautiful wife, are you ready?"

"Yes, my love," she mewed.

Her gaze steeled on Ormrun's ruby. Once the strength of the dark master filled her body, and she commanded the cult of Umbra, she would banish her husband from Tyrannis.

"Then we'll begin?" he asked.

"You'll watch over me?"

"I'll be by your side day and night," he promised.

She didn't trust the silk of his voice, but their charade would end soon enough. She forced another smile.

Alrick handed a crystal pitcher to Zachariah. Her husband poured the liquid–water from the Great White Sea–into the bowl.

Plantine's heart emptied as freely as the glass vessel.

The basin absorbed it all.

Zachariah droned in the ancient mortal tongue scribed by her father in *The Book of Umbra*. She understood few of the words. A ghostly white film formed upon the still waters. She inhaled the heady scent of a million summer flowers. Her gaze wandered to the bloodroot candles circling the north tower's stone floor. Zachariah had encouraged her to pick the herbs with Embril and melt them into the wax herself.

"If you help make them, their protective shield will be far stronger," he'd advised her.

She'd believed him and had risen at dawn every morning since her wedding day to traipse down the mountainside with the troll until they'd gathered enough bloodroot to make twelve candles. They were the only flickers of light in the blackened room.

Beyond the Calashai's stone walls, the dark moon cycle had reached its zenith.

Zachariah fell quiet. His hand tightened upon Koldis. He held the shimmering blade high before he plunged it into the basin.

She half-expected a loud clang as metal struck metal, but the sword plunged deep into the Void. An invisible force sucked Plantine forward. She gripped the sides of the basin, resisting the strong pull from the Parallel of Shadows.

Zachariah had warned her the other dimension would call her. "It will be irresistible," he told her. "But you must withstand it."

The whirlwind of yearning begged her to release the basin, to allow herself to be drawn away into timelessness, infinity–an incorporeal existence with no material obstacles.

"Or material advantages," Zachariah had warned her.

Despite her fading state, Plantine resisted. The longing subsided as an icy wind blasted from the basin's depth. Physically cold, she shivered.

The sense of Umbra being born into her body began in her womb. A budding sensation swelled to bursting. Pure heat radiated through her arms and legs, it hummed within her lungs and chest. The feeling spread to the tips of her fingers and toes and exploded in her mind. She clutched her head and screamed.

Nausea consumed her as alternating waves of ice cold and searing heat coursed through her.

"Call Embril," she heard Zachariah cry.

His voice sounded far away.

Plantine lounged upon a chaise in the private garden outside her rooms. She'd never recovered from Umbra's initial assault on her body. Fever, chills, nausea, headaches, and blackouts plagued her disintegrating form.

Her being rejected Umbra's consciousness like a poison.

At least Zachariah had been attentive, coming to visit her several times a day, ordering broths and teas, massaging her feet–the only part of her body she would allow him to touch or see.

Where was he?

It was late morning, and he'd usually stopped by to check on her by now –always hopeful something had changed with her condition.

At the sound of footsteps, Plantine forced herself to sit up. She reached for one of the many shawls which she pulled on and off as her body cycled between extreme temperatures. She smoothed it over her gaunt legs and pushed her thinning hair behind her ears.

"How's the would-be queen this morning?" Flora's voice dripped with sarcasm.

Plantine let her body return to a shapeless mass. "Why doesn't Embril's potion work anymore?"

Flora swept past the chaise toward several pots of herbs which sat in a long row along the courtyard's retaining wall. "Can't hear you."

Plantine rolled over to look at the faerie. "That's not true, Flora. You hear everything."

"Hmmph. I could say the same about you." The spring faerie moved down the row of herbs, using the same crooked finger to dig a bit of dirt from each pot. Every time, she rubbed the soil between her forefinger and thumb before raising the small black clods to her nose.

Plantine pushed herself back up. "That's all you have to say?"

Flora remained focused on tending her plants.

Plantine picked up a crystal glass filled with water from the table beside her and threw it. White shards exploded at the spring faerie's feet. Flora whirled around and marched toward the chaise. Her body trembled. "Your sister's dying. That's what I have to say."

"So am I."

"Whose fault is that?"

Even though Flora came to the courtyard daily–some days more than once to tend her stupid plants–she usually refused to speak to Plantine, other than to make snide comments. This might be her only chance to ask the question burning in her mind. Plantine pulled her knees to her chest and tried to make the question sound casual. "Are grey faeries immortal?"

"They might as well be," Zachariah said.

Where had he come from? Plantine tugged one of the shawls from underneath her body. She was careful not to expose the ugly veins on the back of her hands as she covered every inch of visible skin.

"No one's immortal," Flora snapped.

Plantine gave her husband a wan smile. When he caressed her cheek, she forced herself to press her face against his hand.

"What is all this talk of death?" he asked.

Plantine shrugged. "Curiosity?"

The muannaye rubbed his hands together. He didn't seem displeased with the conversation. Maybe she'd misjudged his devotion to Elendah.

"Do they die of old age?" she asked.

"Not in my lifetime or yours," Flora said.

Plantine did her best to keep her voice calm. "Then what?"

Zachariah crossed his arms and rubbed his chin with one of his hands. "There is–"

"Leave it alone." The spring faerie shook her finger at husband and wife. "Both of you." The spring faerie bumped into one of the patio chairs as she turned to leave.

"What about your herbs?" Plantine called after her.

"You've upset her," he said.

Plantine curled her legs beneath her shawl. "Flora's moody."

The muannaye laughed. "Yes, she is. Mercurial like the spring. If she's upsetting you, I'll order the guards to keep her away." He pointed to the row of pots. "She can do her gardening elsewhere."

Tatou had tried to talk to Plantine several times after the wedding. When Zachariah had seen how much the pixie's visits agitated her, he'd ordered more guards for Plantine's rooms and given them orders to keep Melia's friend away. An army patrolled the halls outside her door now.

Plantine snuck a sideways glance at her husband. He'd handled the grey faerie's memory of Melia being shot and dragged through the stronghold's corridors by members of the cult of Umbra. He'd told her it had been easy to hide it in Elendah's memory of the dragonwitch's unexpected and unwelcome appearance on their wedding day.

"That's not necessary," Plantine said. The spring faerie irritated her, but in her self-imposed isolation, Plantine would miss her if she was gone.

"The pixie is making quite a splash in the Welcoming Hall's daily salon. I'm told the muannai adore her," he said.

"I'm sure she's quite the shining star," Plantine said.

"I'm surprised she hasn't returned to Illialei."

"She will soon enough," Plantine murmured. She had more important things on her mind. But before she confided in her husband, she needed to study her father's work.

Plantine leaned over the heavy leather-bound book.

"Do you need me to hold it for you?" her mother asked.

"If you could bring a candle to the table."

Pressina hurried to do as her youngest daughter bid. Plantine knew her mother had grown comfortable at the stronghold. And though she avoided Elendah and Flora, Pressina did everything in her power to please Lord Goring, despite his increasingly infrequent visits to her daughter.

Plantine seethed whenever she heard her attendants giggle and whisper in the next room. Everyone agreed Sevondi's recovery had been miraculous, and that her husband spent too much time looking after the dragonwitch. But Plantine was determined to show them all–especially Zachariah–who deserved to be queen.

It hadn't been easy to persuade her mother to keep her research secret, but if Zachariah knew what Plantine was reading, he might guess what she was up to. She wanted it to be a surprise.

It was strange how the rumors about her husband and the dragonwitch burned in her mind. Even though she didn't love him, she wanted to assure his devotion was to her alone.

Her mother had finally relented to her pleas and brought her father's book from the north tower. Plantine hadn't concerned herself with how she'd managed to get the book; her mother was sly.

Now Pressina's eyes glistened as she hovered over her disintegrating daughter. "Elynus would be so proud of you for continuing his work."

Plantine accepted the praise without comment. After lying in bed day after day, facing death, her view of the world had rearranged. Her mother's and father's approval had become meaningless to her. She no longer cared that love had driven them to Umbra, because something else drove her. The insatiable black hunger ate everything inside her.

She couldn't read with her mother buzzing around. "Go!"

Pressina reached down to squeeze her daughter's hand. Plantine let her. She watched Pressina leave. They never talked about Melia wasting away in the Calashai's dungeons. She sighed. It was a conversation too disturbing, even for them.

She opened *The Book of Umbra*.

Plantine read all night and into the morning of the next day. She didn't stop reading until she found what she was looking for:

The Flower of Isbelline: The perfume of the flower of Isbelline, while seemingly harmless to all other forms of life in the Whole, is believed to be lethal to the grey faeries. The blooms are reputed to be spectacularly striking: creamy white petals, vivid golden stamens ringed with coral, and thick jade-colored leaves abundant upon the length of the plant's stem.

Despite its beauty, the plant is left to grow wild by the healers and practitioners of magic in its native Tyrannis, as it is commonly considered to have no healing or occult properties.

Agile climbers may harvest the sparse blooms from high crevices in the northernmost sea cliffs of the Ruadain.

Comments: The source of this information, my colleague in Tyrannis, Lord Zachariah Goring, a muannaye, has charged me with confidence in this matter. He has assured me the deadly property of the flower is not common knowledge. Nor does he wish it to become so. (Note: His close friendship with Elendah, the grey faerie of Aldaine, is troublesome to me. In the final moment, can he be trusted to do what must be done, no matter how distasteful?)

Plantine paused in her reading. A rage burned inside her. Her husband knew about the flower. He'd almost told her that morning on the patio, but Flora had stopped him.

She plucked at her nightgown. Her father's question lingered in her mind. If her husband's friendship with Elendah was anything other than a façade, why would he spell the grey faerie?

For the time being, I will refrain from passing this information on to Pressina. However, if the day comes when necessity overrides such discretion, she must be made aware of all her options.

Plantine kept reading.

* * *

Elendah, the Grey Faerie of Aldaine: As long as Elendah sits on the throne of the stronghold of Calashai as regent, serving as sentinel upon the Realm of Faerie's northernmost shores, no war will come.

Umbra's incarnation will be 'the first shot' in the battle between Dark and Light; it cannot be fired as long as Elendah lives.

The murder of a grey faerie would be a heinous act; yet, Elendah must die in order for Umbra to incarnate. The idea is offensive. However, it must be considered–a noble sacrifice of last resort. (Reference: Idonnic Prophecy, i.e., "Cunning will test the Grey Sentinel's shield.")

It is common knowledge that Elendah arrived on the shores of Tyrannis as an orphan. Raised by a sylph on the peaks of the Ruadain, it is believed she knows (and cares?) little for the history or culture of her race. There are no records of her traveling to the Isle of Minnanon. Nor are there records of any contact between the population of those island faeries with Elendah. It is possible (likely?) she has no inkling of the flower of Isbelline's danger, and thus, could be deceived.

"Mother!"

When Pressina returned, Plantine pushed the closed book to her. "Return it to the north tower. Zachariah can never know you brought it to me."

Her mother didn't argue or ask questions.

The revolt Plantine hoped to command against the pureblood Albiana required three specific events to commence: the grey faerie's death; Umbra's incarnation; and the waging of the great war–the battle between Dark and Light.

During her long days alone, Plantine had had plenty of time to think.

It was the grey faerie's life force–not her own weakened state–that kept Umbra's consciousness warring within her body.

✧✧✧

"Chloe, I need an ingredient."

The muannaye curtsied, but Plantine sensed her repugnance. It seemed Chloe had no appetite for ugly, and Plantine knew her beauty faded. The physical deterioration of her body had gone well beyond the eerie lightening of her eyes and skin.

Dried and cracked, her skin revealed blue-purple veins, while streaks of her hair, bleached of their color, fell out in clumps. She hid her hands in the folds of her robe, and reminded herself that she was Zachariah's wife and this muannaye was her attendant. "It's for a surprise–something special for Zachariah."

Chloe's eyes narrowed.

"I want him to have it in time for the party he's planning at the end of the month."

Plantine caught the spark in Chloe's eye. It seemed the muannaye lived to please her husband. If Plantine hadn't been bedridden, or if she had any genuine feelings for Zachariah, she might have slapped the acolyte. But as things were, she gripped the cloth of her robe tighter and continued her ruse. She nodded to a box on the table beside her. "I'll pay you three gold pieces to bring me a bloom from the flower of Isbelline."

Chloe's eyebrows rose. "I've never heard of such a flower."

"Not many have. That's why I'm paying you to find it."

The muannaye hesitated.

Did she know the flower's power to kill the grey faerie, or had Plantine's generous offer made her suspicious? Elendah paid the acolytes who served the Order of the Calashai in room and board. Three gold coins was an extravagant amount.

Chloe's gaze settled on the coin box. "I know a troll who's wise about such things."

Plantine looked down at her bed sheets and smirked. Her father had been right. No one–besides Zachariah, and perhaps Flora–knew the flower was deadly to grey faeries.

"When it comes to foraging and finding things in the forest," the muannaye continued, "he's the most reliable."

"I've heard it grows on the cliffs of the Ruadain. Tell him to search there first. I need a healthy bloom as soon as possible."

The muannaye curtsied.

"If you keep this to yourself and my husband is surprised, I'll pay you a fourth gold coin for your discretion."

Chloe beamed. "You'll have your flower. I'll make sure of it."

54. Regret

"What's the news today?" Flora asked Tatou.

They walked through the damp passageways in the Calashai's dungeons.

Even though she carried a pail, and the pixie perched on her shoulder, Flora practiced her invisible glamour. She wasn't having much success.

Spring faeries were born with an ability to render themselves unseen at will, but it required an effort Flora had refused to exert for many years.

"Goring's grip on the stronghold grows weaker every day. The cult of Umbra is losing faith in him," Tatou said.

"That's good news for everyone." Flora's concentration wavered and her safeguard flickered.

"The guards are angry that he's kept none of the promises he made, and he's tried to have the sword and basin removed from the stronghold twice, behind Plantine's back. Each time, the person ordered to carry them died. No one thinks that's a coincidence. But since he won't try to take Koldis and Ormrun out himself, they're calling him a coward. Not to his face–"

"Not yet." Flora grinned. "It's the founding stone."

"What's that?" Tatou asked.

Flora scratched her eyebrow. "It sits beneath the north tower and marks Isolt's grave–and the door to her otherworldly prison. Ormrun and Koldis were forged in the depth of the mountain–to unlock that door. The basin and sword have come home. It sounds as though they don't wish to leave."

Her invisible shield slipped again. She couldn't talk and hold the glamour at the same time. It was disappointing. She promised herself that she'd practice again tomorrow. At least with Elendah's ring to shove in their faces, no one kept her from tending to Melia.

Och. Melia. Until the half-faerie had shown up at her cottage in the Balyudor, Flora's path had been clear: stay out of Illialei until the battle between Dark and Light began, then take a front row seat and watch the Albiana queens burn, along with their sugar-frosted Cathedral Palace.

Melia had changed all that when she'd heard the sapphire lily's call.

Was that why Aldous had sent her to Flora's cabin after Goring kidnapped Plantine? Had he really needed Melia to gather information from Flora, or had he meant the rose quartz bracelet to convey a deeper message–one she'd chosen to ignore? It's safe for the sole-surviving spring faerie to return to Illialei. One with Albiana blood who can honor the sapphire lily lives.

They'd reached the half-faerie's cell.

Tatou flitted through the bars; Flora pushed on the door. No one bothered to lock Melia's cell anymore. She wasn't going anywhere.

For almost an entire moon cycle, the half-faerie had hovered between life and death, most of the time so close to death, Flora had feared moving her.

Tatou hovered over Melia's face and caressed her cheek.

While the pixie shared an intimate moment with her friend, the spring faerie slipped her hand into her apron pocket and touched the pearls. Flora had taken them for safekeeping when Melia had been shot–in case she lived. Now, the spring faerie choked back her tears and went to work.

Tatou watched over her shoulder. "I forgot to tell you. This morning, Goring had Sevondi moved to his hotel in Aldaine, the Blue Mermaid," the pixie said.

Flora pulled a soaked cloth from her pail and squeezed out the excess liquid. "Then she must be doing better than this one."

When the spring faerie discerned the poison on the tip of the cult of Umbra's arrows had been brewed in Ormrun, she'd boiled seagull glands with four kinds of seaweed and black hellebore to make the nourishing wash that had saved Melia's life. Embril must have filched some of the medicine for Sevondi. Flora didn't begrudge the theft. She was rather fond of the dragonwitch herself.

The spring faerie pressed her hand against Melia's forehead. "Fever's broken."

"Will she wake up soon?" Tatou asked.

Flora draped the damp rag across the half-faerie's brow. "It's hard to say. She took three arrows; Sevondi took only one. The poison that tipped them went deep into her heart. Not sure Sevondi has one, but I don't think that's the problem."

"Then what is it?" Tatou asked.

Flora massaged Melia's left arm and shoulder where the arrow had pierced the deepest. "Her body is whole. It's her mind that refuses to return."

"Isn't there something we can do?" Tatou asked.

"I think it was the shock of her mother and sister leaving her to die."

Tatou settled on Melia's other shoulder and stroked her friend's hair. "She'll come back. She has to."

Flora darted from one arched doorway to the next. She was on the highest–and most heavily guarded–floor of the stronghold, headed toward Elendah's chambers. It had been too long since anyone had seen or heard from the grey faerie, and Flora was tired of asking questions that no one would answer. It was time to visit Elendah herself.

Tiptoeing past the guards stationed at regular intervals, she maintained her invisible glamour as best as she could, but it was a tricky business. *If I'd known I was going to be called upon to perform such cloak and dagger feats at my age, I'd have gone lighter on the goat cream and blueberry pie.*

She panted at the end of the long hall. When she heard footsteps, she sucked in her breath and disappeared into an alcove.

"What do you need, sir?" a gruff voice asked from around the corner.

"Come with me to the north tower." It was Goring.

Flora slipped the silver ring with the blue stone from her pocket. Elendah had given it to her long ago. "To cool your emotions," the grey faerie had said. But Flora enjoyed her need for vengeance and refused to wear it most days. She used it now to muster the self-control she needed to remain hidden.

"I'm going to give you *The Book of Umbra*. I want you take it to Sevondi at the Blue Mermaid."

"Aye, Lord Goring."

Flora recognized Pogo's rough voice.

The troll and the muannaye walked by her.

The spring faerie's blood burned. She'd finally grown enough Nambrial to brew a killing potion. As soon as she made sure the grey faerie was all right, she was going to make Goring pay.

She tiptoed around the last corner. Other than two black-clad muannaye lounging in a couple of wooden chairs in front of the door to Elendah's suite, the hall stood empty.

Goring must have exited toward the battlements–the shortest route to the north tower. After she checked on Elendah, she'd follow him.

Concentrating on her invisible shield, Flora tiptoed toward the regent's door. When she was about two feet away, a black dog she hadn't noticed napping between the guards growled.

"Aw, quiet yourself," one of them said. "There's nothin' for you to be makin' noise about."

Flora took two more steps toward the door. The dog jumped up and barked.

"Dumb bitch," the other one guffawed. "Look at her gettin' all riled up 'bout nothin'."

"She's usually not so jumpy. What's wrong, girl, see a ghost?"

The dog continued to bark. Flora forced herself forward. She couldn't turn back now. The dog's sharp teeth were inches from her face as she sidled past it. Reaching up, she slowly twisted the door's handle. Then using her back, she nudged it open and squeezed through before it could close on her.

In the hall, the dog's barking ratcheted up as wooden chairs crashed to the floor.

"Did ya' see that?" one of the muannaye yelled.

"Aye!" shouted the other.

The door swung open, almost knocking Flora flat. Breathing heavily, she scurried behind a tile wall separating the foyer and the sitting room.

"Chloe!" one of the guard's yelled.

Flora peeked around the tiles to get her bearings. One of the muannaye held his dagger at the ready.

The slim, brown-haired acolyte swept into the room. "Yes?"

"Anyone bothering you or the regent?" the guard demanded.

"No."

"Then this door opened by itself," the other muannaye said.

Flora heard the soft tap of Chloe's shoes as she crossed the room. "It must have been a breeze."

Thankfully, the dog had stopped barking. Flora crawled beneath a table, around an overstuffed chair, and behind a divan. She heaved a sigh of relief. The door to the grey faerie's bedchamber was cracked open.

Behind her, the acolyte and the guards bantered. The long window on the north wall of the sitting room was wide open; its sheer curtains fluttered.

Flora slipped into Elendah's bedroom.

The room's far wall, against which the headboard of an enormous bed rested, was carved into the mountainside itself. Everything else–the large bed, chairs, and table–was sculpted from massive blocks of grey stone. Luscious grass carpeted the room's floor. A single wide window faced north, overlooking the horizon of the sea. Seagulls perched in the window's frame.

Flora tiptoed toward the bed. Too short to peer over the high mattress, she searched for something to stand on. Spying a footstool shoved into a corner, she dragged it to the side of the bed. Made of solid stone, it was much heavier than it appeared. When she finally had it positioned, she climbed up on it to get a good look at the grey faerie.

Elendah's face was far too pale. Flora leaned over to listen to the rhythm of her breath. It was shallow and ragged, the tempo uneven. She reached for the grey faerie's wrist to check her pulse.

Flora recoiled. Her gnarled fingers cupped her weathered cheeks. She was too late.

A sonorous chime rang from the stronghold's bell tower as Elendah, the Grey Faerie of Aldaine, and regent of the stronghold of Calashai, drew her last breath and crossed the threshold of death.

A second mysterious and chilling note sang out.

Bewildered, Flora searched for some small way to honor her old friend. Something white caught her eye. She stared. Although quite rare, she recognized the flower of Isbelline's creamy petals and coral-ringed stamen. The spring faerie stumbled with shock, lost her balance, and landed on the floor with a thud. Her invisible shield slipped away.

"Flora!" Chloe shrieked. "What have you done?"

The stronghold's bell lamented a third time.

The spring faerie elbowed the acolyte's thigh on the way out of Elendah's bedroom.

"Stop her!"

The plaintive chimes struck closer together.

Flora barreled between the two guards and flung herself through the open door. She landed in the hallway, sliding on her belly. The dog was right at her heels. She scrambled to her feet and raced around the corner.

"Stop!" the guards ordered.

The chime of the bells rolled into an anguished melody.

Flora fled down the long, narrow corridor, dodging the clumsy hands of the few confused guards who'd remained at their posts. She could barely catch her breath and couldn't focus enough to invoke her invisible glamour. Digging her hands into her pocket, she came up with Melia's pearls. She ripped apart the necklace and tossed the beads behind her in a wide spray. They bounced and rolled across the stone floor.

The dog yelped as it slipped and slid. The muannai cursed as they collided into one another.

The hint of a smile parted Flora's lips. Spring faeries had quick reflexes, and even after all these years, hers were still intact.

Flora prepared herself outside the Welcoming Hall. She straightened her kerchief and balanced Hermes' Wand in the crook of her arm. Yrrick had found the stick half-covered in mud on the way to Tuck's cell. Thank goodness he'd had the sense and kindness to return it to her.

She twisted the blue stone ring from her finger and righted the wand. She brushed her damp cheeks with the back of her hand. She could feel the weight of the Tasimas in the pillowcase she'd slung over her shoulder.

Inside, the large hall was crowded. Usually, during the middle of the day, muannai from Aldaine lounged with foreigners on sofas and around low tables to discuss art, history, music, philosophy, and politics. For centuries, Elendah had encouraged the daily salons and the passions they nurtured.

The spring faerie had never cared for all the blather. She'd preferred the generous portions of sweet cakes, sticky buns, and jasmine pie served with steaming pots of aurora infusion and endless carafes of blackberry wine.

The tolling of the bells had become frantic. The butterflies–often perched on a shoulder here and there, or flittering through the room–were nowhere in sight. The muannai who remained in the room stood in loose circles. Alarmed voices repeated the same anguished question: Why do the bells toll?

Flora pushed toward the far corner where Tatou had held court since Plantine's wedding. "Out of my way," she grunted at anyone who dared notice her belligerence. When she spotted the pixie, she waved her hand. The ground rumbled beneath her.

Tatou hurried in her direction, fear etched on her face.

Flora couldn't meet her gaze. She knew how much the pixie loved the grey faerie. Elendah was practically all she'd talked about when she'd stayed in Flora's cottage–healing–after Melia had accidentally torn her wing.

"What's happening?" Tatou landed on her shoulder. "Why won't the bells stop ringing?"

The stronghold rolled.

"Why are the walls shaking?" the pixie asked.

Flora didn't have the heart to answer.

The bell's grieving song became deafening. Thousands of butterflies poured from the canvases lining the walls, as if the devastated fields of daisies had thrown the fragile creatures out.

The crowd moved as one toward the exit.

The sea of bodies caught the spring faerie up in its tide. She lost her footing. Where was Tatou? She used a table to pull herself up.

Above the crowds, the pixie darted this way and that.

Flora shook the wand as high she could to get her attention. Tatou returned to her shoulder. "We need to get to the dungeons," Flora said.

They split off from the crowd pushing out of the hall. Flora headed for the stronghold's kitchen. They faced another stampede of muannai, dwarves, and trolls. With any luck, the dungeon guards had panicked as well.

And maybe ... just maybe ... the grey faerie's death knell would call Melia back.

55. Aftershock

I squeeze my eyes shut because I don't want to see.

The ground is quaking and the world crumbles around me.

My eyes flutter open.

The sky is black and there is no sun. I push myself to my hands and knees to crawl.

Muannai, dwarves, and trolls scream.

A stone walkway has split in half, leaving a gash in the ground. I pull myself up a rocky shard.

I know all the winged faeries are dead.

I stagger. A fountain of blood shoots skyward.

Dazed, I wander to the edge of a cliff.

A black sea crashes below.

Dread racks my body.

Blood drips from my fingers.

I fall to my knees and weep. When my eyes are bone dry, I hear it. The faintest glimmer of song. I race along the edge of a sheer wall.

I see a stone stairway.

I descend.

The song grows louder. Others live. Their chorus calls me. I race across a sandy beach to a field of grass.

I charge across the meadow.

Deathly silence rolls toward me like morning fog.

My heart blocks my throat.

I can't stop now. I angle my body and run.

My arms pump, my hair whips my face. The terrain changes beneath my bare feet.

Death gives way to life.

A torrent of lilies erupts before me. A sheet of majestic blue. In their midst, a faerie, her back to me, leads a small army of elves. Those aren't elves. Short and thick, their arms and legs move in graceful unison. They perform a drill. They obey the commands of their leader.

Blond pigtails twine into a single plait down her back.

There is something familiar about the way her body shifts from side to side. I grab her shoulder. She turns.

I stumble back. My eyes grow wide, and my hand covers my mouth.

Years have been wiped from her face.

"A field of sapphire lilies bloom," she says.

I throw my arms around her neck. 'Flora.'

The world shakes again.

✧ ✧ ✧

"Wake her up."

"Make her drink this."

"We have to get out of here."

As Melia struggled to wake up, familiar voices swirled around her. Tatou. Flora. Ryder. How long had she been asleep? Why couldn't she see anything? Fingers pried open her lips. She gulped and spit the bitter drink pouring into her mouth until the ground lurched again. Her eyes were open, but the world around her was black.

"Tatou?"

"Bless us all, she's awake. Are you in pain?"

The ache in her shoulder was secondary to the world quaking around her. "Flora?" Melia called out to the darkness. "No, I'm fine," she lied.

"Melia!" Tatou's tiny finger's brushed her cheek.

"What's happening?"

"The stronghold is crumbling." That was Sinjiin.

"Everyone hold hands." Tuck.

Strong fingers gripped her right hand. Ryder? Tatou's slight weight landed on her shoulder. Flora's gnarled fingers curled around her left hand.

"Why can't I see?" she whispered.

"We're in the stronghold's dungeons. The torches have blown out," Tatou whispered.

"We're going to use the Tasimas to carry us to the north tower. Goring is there with Koldis. We're going to take the sword," Ryder said.

✧ ✧ ✧

Melia's eyes opened to daylight streaming through windows barred with black iron. The compressed journey had jolted her memory. She hit the stone floor prepared for a fight. Wolves. Muannai. Goring. The cult of Umbra. Her sister.

Crouching as her friends stumbled around her, she surveyed the barren tower. Goring wasn't there. Neither was the basin or *The Book of Umbra*.

The empty room swayed as repeated explosions rocked the Calashai. Melia ran to the barred windows and clung to them. A jagged furrow cut through the courtyard below. Its maw widened with each passing second. Muannaye, dwarves, and trolls scurried across the lawn. She could hear their screams as they dodged the bricks and stone thrown from the stronghold's erupting walls.

The bell tower had already fallen.

Melia spun around and almost tripped on the shredded train of her gown. She still had on the same blue dress she'd worn to Plantine's wedding. It was filthy. "What's happening?"

"The grey faerie is dead, and the stronghold of Calashai razes itself," Sinjiin answered.

Her knees buckled. Elendah was dead?

Ryder's arm shot out. His firm grip steadied her. "You've been sick. The tips of the arrows that pierced you were poisoned. Thank Flora for your life. Her herbs and potions brought you back from the dead."

She took a good look at him. Her jaw dropped. Purple-green-yellow blotches patch-worked one side of his face. A thick black scab crossed his forehead. A smaller line scarred his lip. Dirty grey cloth cradled his other arm.

Stunned, she searched her friend's faces.

Flora headed toward an enormous door. "Goring can't be far," she shouted. The spring faerie exited the tower before anyone could stop her.

The stone floor shifted. The Tasimas rolled across the floor. Sinjiin stopped it with the toe of his black slipper. Bits of rubble fell from cracks in the tower's ceiling.

"Stinking muannaye, get back here and answer for what you've done!"

Tatou pointed out one of the barred windows. "Flora's found Goring."

"Gutless coward!" the spring faerie screamed.

Sinjiin rolled the Tasimas to Tuck.

Melia lurched toward the door and tried to push it open. The last explosion had sealed it shut, its frame splintered. She turned sideways and rammed the wooden panel with her shoulder, then doubled over as a sharp spike of pain shot down her arm.

"Flora!" Melia yelled. Another boom reverberated through the tower. "We can't leave her here."

Ryder gave the wooden door a mighty kick, splitting it in two. Melia slipped through the gap.

Flora raced down the crumbling battlements, away from the north tower. Despite her short legs and stout body, she'd almost closed in on the muannaye. Melia felt a rush of warm air beside her. Sinjiin shifted into his tiger form. He leapt passed her and tore after Flora.

"Watch the Tasimas," Ryder told Tuck.

He kicked the remaining wood from the door and followed Sinjiin.

Melia scanned the sky–dusk was hours away.

More loud explosions shook the Calashai's stone walls. The eruptions emanated from the stronghold's center. Down below, another segment of roof caved in.

The battlements followed the fortress' perimeter. They had little time. Wishing for her soft leather boots and pants, Melia picked up her shredding skirts and bolted after her friends.

Sinjiin reached Goring first. Rising up on his hind legs, he roared in the muannaye's face and then shoved him against the battlement's stone barrier with his forepaws. Flora hurled herself against one of the muannaye's long legs. Goring unsheathed Koldis.

With Flora's arms circled around his shin, the muannaye arched back. He grasped the blade with both hands and poised it high above his head. A shimmer of blue plunged toward Sinjiin's vulnerable chest. The tiger twisted in time to dodge the blow. Goring threw his shoulder into Sinjiin's flank, but the tiger still managed to land squarely on four paws. Flora slipped, landing on her hands and knees. Goring shoved his boot down on her back. She flattened against the stone walkway.

Ryder edged closer to the trio. With one arm in a sling, how much help could he be?

Sinjiin shifted to one side of the muannaye, Ryder boxed Goring in from the other side with his vulnerable arm out of the muannaye's range. Goring whipped the blade in a figure eight. He feinted first toward the tiger and then toward the priest. The heel of his boot never left Flora's back. She kicked with her entire body to no avail.

Then she twisted.

Goring lost his balance as she bucked to the side. She rounded back to his leg, pulled herself up, and sunk her teeth into his calf. The muannaye screamed and kicked out with a brutal jolt.

Ryder lunged and butted the side of Goring's ribs with his head.

The muannaye jerked sideways and made an awkward twirl to land on the ground, flat on his back, gasping for air. Although he still gripped the sword's hilt, the blade lay flat on the ground.

Ryder jumped, landing with both feet on the shimmering blue metal.

While Goring struggled to free Koldis, Sinjiin sailed through the air, coming down on the muannaye's chest and pinning him to ground.

Flora wedged herself between Ryder and Sinjiin.

She pummeled the muannaye's ribs. "Why'd you sic your wolves on me? Why'd you order them to burn my home? Why'd you kill Elendah?"

The only thing Melia could catch hold of were the spring faerie's apron strings. She yanked on them as hard as she could. Flora twirled around with a high kick that connected with the half-faerie's chin. Blood ran down Flora's face.

Melia rubbed her tender jaw. "He killed Elendah?"

The spring faerie jerked free. "He's got to pay."

Another loud blast cracked the length of the stone pathway. It was only a hairline, but they needed to get back to the tower before the entire thing split in two.

"We have to get out of here," Melia said.

The crack widened.

"Only because I value my life," the spring faerie said. She hurried toward the tower.

As Melia watched her go, the heroic young Flora in Melia's vision became one with the much older faerie; the one who had fearlessly attacked an armed muannaye twice her size.

The half-faerie turned back to Ryder and Sinjiin. The priest had the sword, but the muannaye had Ryder's leg. Sinjiin gnawed on Goring's jacket. The tiger jerked his jaws and growled like a house cat with a field rat in his mouth. He managed to pull the muannaye off the priest and drag him across the stone tiles.

Free, Ryder ran toward Melia with Koldis in his hand.

Sinjiin spun, jumped over the muannaye's inert body, and roared.

"Is he dead?" Melia asked.

Sinjiin roared again.

"That means no–so, run!" Ryder shouted.

By the time they stepped through the broken doorway, she staggered.

Another blast sounded from outside.

"We must find Plantine," Tuck demanded with feverish eyes.

"No, we need to find Ormrun," Ryder said.

"They're in the same place," Flora said. "Give me the Tasimas."

Sinjiin kicked the yellow diamond toward her as the others drew close.

56. True Love

They tumbled into the inner garden of Plantine's suite. An acolyte screamed–the one who had attended Melia and Tatou for Plantine's wedding. She calmed down when she recognized them.

"Where's my sister?" Melia asked.

The muannaye pointed toward the courtyard. A tree trunk blocked their path. Tuck heaved against it.

Behind them, something sinister growled. Melia whipped around. An enormous black wolf straddled Ryder, its fangs bared. The priest held off the dog's ferocious bite with his good arm.

Koldis shimmered–inert on the floor–beyond his reach.

The acolyte screamed again.

"Quiet yourself," Flora snapped.

With her eyes locked on Ryder and the wolf, the spring faerie reached forward for the blade. Hefting Koldis with knotty hands, she paused to balance the sword's weight.

Tuck taunted the wolf with the wand. The black beast snapped at Ryder and the tree elf by turns.

Flora slunk between Ryder and Tuck, braced herself, then sunk the length of the sword deep into the wolf's belly. She pumped the blade. Blood spurted everywhere. It streaked Flora's apron and forearms. It speckled her face. "Damn you to the Void for eternity," she said.

The beast yowled as it twisted and jumped in the air. Ryder rolled out of its way. The wolf landed with the blade still pinned in its underbelly. Blood darkened the ground beneath it. The wolf rounded on Flora and snarled.

Tuck gave it a mouthful of the wand.

Sinjiin lunged and butted the hairy black mass. The wolf let forth a piercing yelp as it slid sideways and slammed against the tree trunk Tuck had wrestled with earlier. The force of the collision plunged Koldis deeper into the wolf's soft underside. Sinjiin leapt upon the inert predator and roared. The wolf shuddered and stilled.

Its furry carcass, wet with blood, smoothed and elongated. Melia watched, horrified, as it transformed into the dead body of Lord Zachariah Goring.

Flora scurried over and kicked the dead muannaye. "That's for burning down my house, and that's for killing Bella!" She kicked him again and again until she fell to her knees, sobbing.

Goring opened his eyes and gurgled one final time.

Melia jumped.

The spring faerie toddled away.

Melia ran after her. "How–?"

The spring faerie pointed to her right shoulder. A brown stripe stained her dress. "He clawed me when I picked up the Tasimas."

Beyond Plantine's rooms, more walls exploded.

Melia hurried toward her sister's private courtyard. She swallowed hard. Plantine stood in the middle of the patio. Ormrun rested on a pedestal before her. To the side, Pressina watched her youngest daughter with a blank face and limp hands.

Tears stung the back of Melia's eyes. She blinked them away. They'd left her to die.

Plantine screamed into the misty waters hovering above the bowl's rim. "Why do you reject me?" She held her golden hair, streaked with white, away from the vapors. Her frame was gaunt.

"Her mind's split in two," Flora said.

"What do you mean?" Melia asked.

Flora stabbed her head in Pressina's direction. "Her mother's curse has worn down her body. It isn't strong enough to integrate Umbra's consciousness, even though it cleaves to her."

Pressina's jaw tightened, but she didn't defend herself, nor did she express any relief or joy that her middle daughter lived.

Melia's face burned. She pointed to her sister. "There must be something we can do."

"Not we–she," Flora said. "Your sister must decide."

"Why does Umbra reject me??" Plantine screamed. "I've done everything–EVERYTHING–he's demanded!"

Flora stepped closer to Plantine. "You're weak."

Pressina's jaw made a hard line. "Stay away from her."

The spring faerie took another step toward Plantine.

Pressina was swift. Her hands were on Flora's shoulder.

The spring faerie was even quicker. She yanked Pressina's hands so hard her ivory wings quivered. And Flora didn't let go. She spun beneath Pressina's long arms in an angry dance. After she threw Pressina's hands back in her face, the spring faerie jabbed her finger at the much taller faerie. "Don't touch me."

Pressina stumbled backward.

Melia stared wide-eyed.

Plantine ran after Flora. She kneeled before the spring faerie, and begged, "I can't live this way. Umbra torments me day and night, but he won't embrace me." She grabbed at Flora's apron. "Brew a potion to strengthen me!"

The spring faerie ripped herself away from Plantine. "There's only one thing that will heal you, and I can't conjure it."

Plantine reached for her hand. "What? Tell me."

Flora shoved her hands in her apron pocket. "True love."

Plantine threw her head back and laughed. Her eerie blue eyes sparked with madness.

"It will break your mother's curse and cast Umbra out once and for all."

Plantine leaned over the spring faerie. "If you don't help me, I'll ... I'll ..." She opened and closed her fists.

"There's one other way."

Plantine grabbed her shoulders. "Tell me."

Flora shook free of Plantine's hands. "Plunge Koldis through your heart."

Plantine staggered. "Suicide?"

The spring faerie nodded.

Pressina rounded on Flora. "How could you tell her that?"

"Because it's the truth."

Plantine held her elbows and paced. She rocked herself and muttered. "Bring me the blade."

Pressina rushed to her. "No."

Plantine covered her ears and screamed. "Bring Koldis to me!"

Ryder was by Melia's side. He held the sword. "No matter what she says or does, don't let her have it," she said.

Ryder rested his hand on her shoulder and squeezed hard.

Tuck had already crossed the patio with long strides. When he reached Plantine, he thrust Hermes' Wand into her translucent hands. "Take this."

She pushed the stick away. "I don't want this!"

"Hold it, and tell me you don't love me," Tuck said.

"I won't."

"We were dear friends once, you and I. So do this for me–for those days when we were close."

Her fading blue eyes clouded. "I married another. I've taken vows."

"He's dead."

"You lie!" Plantine hissed.

The tree elf reached for her hand. He pressed the wand against her palm. "Tell me you don't love me. Tell me that you've never loved me." He held the rod with her.

"I can't love anyone," she spit the words out. A shining thread of light traveled from the wand's center to its ends. Plantine cowered from the truth. "I don't love you."

Tuck held her with his eyes as the wand's glow gained strength. Its sparkling rays of light showered them, the basin, Ryder, the sword, Flora, Pressina, and then the entire garden.

"You're lying," he said.

She lowered her gaze.

Tuck took her hand. "I've loved you from the first time you walked into the library and asked me to help you find a book of poetry."

Tears flowed down Plantine's face. "No, it's too late. You can't love me after what I have done."

"What have you done?" he asked.

Plantine pulled her hand from his.

"What have you done?" Melia asked her sister.

"I killed Elendah," Plantine whispered.

Melia's heart stopped. "It was Goring, not you."

Tuck's brow furrowed. Shock twisted Flora's face. Even Pressina's mouth fell open.

"You don't know what you're saying," Pressina said. "Everything you've been through since you were kidnapped has unbalanced your mind."

"You think I'm not capable of killing the grey faerie, Mother?" Plantine shouted. "I left my own sister to die!"

Melia gasped. Ryder took hold of her hand and held it tight.

Plantine pointed at herself. "I paid Chloe gold to bring me the flower of Isbelline. I gave it to Elendah, knowing its scent would kill her."

Flora's hands covered her mouth.

"What is she talking about?" Melia asked.

"I thought it was Goring," the spring faerie whispered.

"Wait–what is going on?" Melia asked.

Flora shoved her hands deep into her apron pocket. "She asked me if Elendah was immortal. I'd never thought she'd do it herself."

Plantine had killed the grey faerie. The truth cut into Melia's heart. Her body slackened. She let her back sag against Ryder's chest.

A few feet away, Tatou's tiny fingers dug into the scruff of Sinjjin's neck. How much had they heard? It hardly mattered. The grey faerie was dead, and her sweet baby sister whose laughter pealed like bells had killed her. Not Goring. Not Umbra–Plantine.

A storm gathered in Melia's belly. Ryder lifted her chin. It was hard to meet his frank gaze. He cradled her face in his hands. "We have the basin and the sword," he said. "Umbra's incarnation has failed, and at great cost to your sister. Whatever she's done, be sure Umbra played a part."

"Listen to him," Sinjiin urged her. When had he shifted into his mage form? "The dwarf magic in Ormrun is malignant. It poisons everything in its reach. Your sister is under its spell."

Melia's heart wrestled with their words. Part of her wanted to believe Plantine could be blameless for all she'd done, and that she was possessed, but another part of her would never forget lying on the Calashai's stone floor, bleeding while her sister walked away with Koldis.

Sinjiin spoke again. "Umbra's long shadow may cloud her vision, but the magic of the wand is stronger. She loves Tuck."

"Does that matter, when she's killed the grey faerie ... and brought war to Faerie? Because the battle between Dark and Light will begin now. Won't it?" Melia whispered.

Tatou settled on her shoulder. Melia cringed at her friend's light weight. "What has been done cannot be undone," the pixie said.

"Always the tiny philosopher, but what is in your heart?" Melia asked. "You loved Elendah. How can you ever forgive my sister?"

"She's dying. Tuck can save her."

"Look me in the eye, and tell me you forgive her."

Tatou treaded the air in front of her friend's face. Melia saw her quiet tears. "If it had been you–"

"I would never–" Melia stopped. What had her dark moon visions shown her she was capable of? The realization chilled her blood. She rubbed her hands up and down her arms as she faced her sister.

Plantine stared down at the tiles at her feet. Melia felt Ryder's hand return to her shoulder. Sinjiin nodded. Flora crossed her arms, her gaze askance. Tatou tucked a strand of hair behind Melia's ear. Tuck pleaded with his eyes.

"You can still love her, knowing what she's done? What she's capable of?" Melia asked the tree elf.

"Her whole life she blamed herself for your father's broken troth. After your mother spelled the three of you"–Tuck glared at Pressina–"she became obsessed with making things right!"

Pressina's face ignited. "Don't put this on me." She stormed toward Melia. "It was your obsession with stopping Umbra!"

Ryder shielded Melia with his body, but her mother's words had already hit their mark.

If her father hadn't died, he would never have sent *The Book of Umbra* to Goring. The muannaye would never have kidnapped Plantine, or had Flora's house burned to the ground. Elendah wouldn't be dead. It was a damning chain of events.

"Save your sister," Pressina said.

Pain spiked Melia's arm. She bowed her head. She didn't know the right answer; she didn't know what was true; she didn't even know what was real anymore. But Tatou was right. Plantine had to be forgiven–or at least not condemned by Melia.

Unable to speak the words aloud, she sent her sister a silent plea. *"Accept the forgiveness of those who love you, and come back to us."*

Plantine's blue eyes–dulled by their mother's curse–watered. She tried to pull her hand from Tuck's, but he held it firm.

A strange conviction flowered in Melia's heart. The pain in her left shoulder eased. *"Don't let him go."*

Plantine shook her head, slowly at first, then violently from left to right. "I've killed the grey faerie. I don't deserve forgiveness, or life."

Melia sent her sister the awareness dawning within her. *"Tuck loves you as his own life."*

Plantine raised her head and searched the tree elf's eyes. "You can still love me?"

He pulled her to him. His gentle kiss turned into a passionate embrace. Melia watched her sister return. The white streaks in her hair shimmered to lustrous gold. The skin of her hands became smooth and opaque. When Tuck released her, her blue eyes sparkled.

The speed of the transformation unnerved Melia. Would it be that quick for her? True love's first kiss and she'd never fly again?

Black clouds appeared from nowhere; lightning cracked in the sky. "She's pushing Umbra out! Open the portal!" Flora yelled to Ryder.

When he stepped away from her, Melia's heart felt raw–her body uncovered.

The storm thundered as buckets of rain poured down. A brutal wind frosted the falling drops. Ryder shouted words in a language Melia didn't understand. He aimed Koldis at the center of the basin and stabbed downwards.

Tuck guided Plantine through the maelstrom to Ormrun. She leaned over the bowl. A thick, inky fluid seeped from her eyes and ears. She convulsed and more of the dark liquid spewed from her mouth. Nearby, a stone wall exploded.

"Again," Flora commanded Ryder. "Close the portal."

When Ryder stabbed the bowl again, it sucked the thunderstorm from the sky, pulling the black and grey cyclone into its center. Flora hardly waited for the sky to clear before she grabbed Ormrun; Ryder still gripped Koldis. They dashed back into Plantine's bedchamber–Pressina with them.

When all of their hands were interlocked, and Tatou gripped the scruff of Sinjiin's neck, Melia commanded the yellow diamond to carry them to the Veiled Tavern.

57. The Founding Stone

They hit an invisible barrier and dropped hard onto grass. Melia inched forward on her hands and knees. She struggled to get her bearings. Koldis had slipped from Ryder's grasp, but Flora still hunched over Ormrun.

Melia stared at the stone wall in front of her face. It looked familiar.

A loud explosion sent tremors through the ground beneath her. They were in the courtyard of the stronghold of Calashai.

"Why didn't the Tasimas work?" she asked.

"It's the founding stone," Flora said. "I'd hoped the magic of the Tasimas was stronger."

"What founding stone?"

Tatou explained. "The sword and basin have come home. They don't want to leave."

"It's true," Plantine said. "Zachariah ordered Ormrun and Koldis to be taken from the stronghold. But each time, whenever the one who carried them reached the stronghold's perimeter, some tragic accident occurred. A muannaye broke his neck; another impaled himself upon his blade."

Melia shivered.

Plantine looked at the sky. "Thank the gods of Azyllai the Tasimas dropped us here, so we didn't die."

"There must be a way to break the bond," Tuck said. "After all, the sword and basin got out years ago."

"The answer may be in *The Book of Umbra*," Plantine said. "My father's research was thorough. It has the answer to ... many things ..."

"I saw the book in the north tower before–" That thought led to her sister and mother leaving her die, so Plantine could sit on a throne and be crowned queen. Anger and sadness writhed inside Melia like two fighting snakes. Her shoulder ached. She forced herself to refocus on the present. "Earlier, when the Tasimas carried us to the north tower, it was empty, and Goring didn't have the book with him."

"He sent it to Sevondi," Flora said.

"The dragonwitch? I thought she died at the ... wedding." Melia's left shoulder seared with pain.

"No, she survived," Tatou said. "Goring sent her to his hotel in Aldaine before Elendah died."

Melia fell back into the grass. Ryder had Koldis and Flora had Ormrun, but the founding stone wouldn't let them leave, and the dragonwitch had *The Book of Umbra*. "What now?" she asked.

"Plantine must seek pardon from the Grey Council. That can't wait," Tuck said. "She'll need a witness to vouch her actions weren't her own, that Umbra possessed her. As an apprentice to Aldous, I can accompany her to the Isle of Minnanon and provide the required testimony."

Pressina hovered. She smoothed Plantine's hair. "That won't be necessary. I'll go with her to the Isle of Minnanon."

Tuck rubbed his forehead with his fist.

"Your devotion to my daughter is admirable," Pressina continued, "but you should return to Illialei. I can take care of my daughter."

Everyone froze.

Melia's heart thundered.

Plantine took Tuck's hand. She looked radiant. "Mother, you can come with us."

Melia blinked. Maybe her sister's transformation was genuine. She scrambled to her feet just in time for Plantine to embrace her.

"Thank you for believing in me when I couldn't believe in myself," her sister said.

Although she wasn't sure that's what she'd done, Melia offered a wooden, "You're welcome."

Pressina looked away with her hand covering her mouth.

Tatou settled on Melia's shoulder. "Flora, don't you have something for her?"

The spring faerie fumbled in her apron pocket. She held out the bracelets Elendah had given the half-faerie on the beach.

When Melia reached for the pearls, the healing balm of Elendah's memory washed over her. The grey faerie had offered her a wordless forgiveness she'd desperately needed. Perhaps she'd been right to share a small portion of that with Plantine, after all. "Thank you," Melia said.

"It's all I could save," Flora said.

The half-faerie slipped the strands around her wrists. A weightless feeling lightened her heart. "It's enough."

Flora patted her back. "It's uncanny what grey faeries comprehend."

A tall, slim figure crossed the courtyard in their direction. Yrrick. "I understand Goring's been killed," he said.

Melia's protective instincts rose to protect Flora. The spring faerie didn't deserve to be punished for what she'd done. "It was a horrible accident–"

"I only wish you–whoever–had managed it before Elendah–" Yrrick turned away.

Tuck shielded Plantine.

When the muannaye faced them again, his eyes flashed toward the sword and basin. "The dwarf magic won't let you take them from here?"

"No," Flora said. "What do you know about it?"

"The power lies deep within the mountain."

"We need to take them to the Isle of Minnanon," Ryder said.

"I wouldn't risk it," Yrrick said. "Even though the stronghold is in ruins."

Not a single wall remained standing behind the muannaye, and the booms of the Calashai's fall had finally faded.

No one argued with his assessment.

"What are you and the surviving acolytes going to do now?" Melia asked him.

"The stronghold must be restored."

Melia's eyebrows rose. She looked to Sinjiin. "Didn't the stronghold build itself around the grey faerie?"

The tiger roared.

"The muannai need the stronghold of Calashai and its regent," Yrrick said. "With both Elendah and Goring gone, we're rendered leaderless. We must try to rebuild."

"Who will lead?" Melia asked.

Yrrick opened his hands wide. "My job is to serve."

The muannaye's humble stance struck her as both honorable and dangerous. Images of Sevondi flourishing Koldis in the Great Hall sprang to her mind.

"We'll help," Ryder said. Sinjiin lowered his belly onto the grass. "Until we find a way to take the basin and the sword to the Isle of Minnanon."

Yrrick bowed. "There's a lot of work to be done."

Flora barreled in front of Melia. "I'm staying too."

"And will you two stay with us?" Ryder asked Melia and Tatou.

"Tatou?" Melia asked the pixie.

"We need to stop the rumors before they cross the river."

"Rumors?" Melia asked.

Tatou tilted her head toward Plantine. "If we don't return to Illialei, and set the record straight–"

Melia realized her friend was right. "We should meet with Aldous as soon as possible."

"I don't want to let you out of my sight," Ryder said.

Blood rushed to Melia's face.

"Here we go." Flora picked up the basin and wandered after Yrrick. Tatou zoomed after the spring faerie.

As the others walked away, Melia watched her mother's stiff back without feeling. She risked looking into Ryder's forest green eyes. What she saw in their depths reflected her own strong feelings without the doubt. She raised her hand to brush a damp curl from the side of his face, then hesitated. The only thing he'd done since he'd arrived on the shores of Faerie was help her–and believe in her. Melia let her hand rest against his cheek.

He closed his eyes at her touch.

Even though they'd never used the word love, that's what standing here with him felt like.

He opened his eyes and pulled her to him.

This time her body relented. His fingers ran through her hair. She'd found the place she belonged: here with him—or wherever he was. Yet when he lowered his face to hers, Melia pulled away. It was a reaction. She couldn't stop herself. She wasn't ready.

It had happened so fast with Plantine.

Hurt clouded his eyes.

"When I get back from Illialei ..."

He let her go.

The release was jarring. "I'm so sorry—"

He touched her lips with a rough finger. "I wanted to help you save your friend and your sister. When I find a way to take the basin and the sword to the Grey Council, I'll do that too."

She opened and closed her mouth.

He dropped his hands to his side. "Dusk is coming."

As the sun sank in the sky, the desire to spread her wings fought something primal in her body.

Ryder turned and walked away.

Melia and Tatou were halfway to Illialei when a searing pain gripped her left wing. She landed clumsily on the limb of a tall redwood tree.

A sinister laugh echoed through her mind. Umbra. Released from Plantine's ravaged body, he hadn't wasted any time in finding her.

She lost connection to the outer world. Her consciousness spiraled into threatening terrain.

"Melia," his voice slithered though her brain.

She gathered her strength to shield herself. *"Your incarnation failed. Go away."*

"Don't make me beg," he said.

An invisible pressure squeezed her head. She searched for a memory, an image, something to feed her resolve. Flora entered her mind's eye. She saw the spring faerie fighting the muannai in her burning yard, running after Goring as the Calashai crumbled, and plunging Koldis deep in the black wolf's belly.

Flora would never let Umbra defeat her.

"You're so much stronger," the dark master cooed. *"That excites me."*

Winds howled and storms raged on the edge of Melia's consciousness. A scarlet coil of will formed in the pit of her stomach. *"Go back to the Void,"* she commanded.

"Come, come. Don't be hasty."

A sharp pain ripped through her left shoulder. *"You can't have me."*

"There are others," his menacing voice whispered like a soft wind.

Was he talking about Melusine–or the halves in the mortal world? Luisa's descendants? She fought back. *"You'll never find them."*

"Half-faeries, I'm sure they yearn for more than their mortal world can offer," he taunted. *"Never underestimate desire."*

Melia willed the most forceful, *"No,"* her mind could summon.

Nothingness answered back. Umbra was gone.

Tatou's bell-like voice pierced the dark shroud in her mind. "Melia!"

The exterior world returned. She couldn't believe it. She'd fended off Umbra.

"What happened?" Tatou flitted back and forth, a ball of light in front of Melia's face.

The thrill of victory faded. There were others out there, innocents, who didn't know what was coming for them.

She had to warn them.

Epilogue

Sevondi parted the thin metallic slats covering the window in her room at the Blue Mermaid. She'd never understood Goring's obsession with the mortal world. First he'd demanded their books to fill the library in his home. He'd only wanted ones with pictures. Then he'd marked thousands of pages, and commanded an army of trolls:

"Bring me one of those."

"I want this."

"And that."

"I don't want to hear any excuses."

At first he'd sent for small things the trolls could filch in their pockets, but then he'd demanded larger items. Furniture, building materials–things Sevondi didn't care for.

The Blue Mermaid was the jumble of mortal relics he'd compiled–his ode to the twenty-first century. Its neon-blue mermaid blinked in the night.

"Garish," Sevondi said.

Neither Pogo nor Moog, standing behind her, agreed.

The enchanted world's moons were full. Their white and lavender light bathed the jagged pile of rock that had once been the stronghold of Calashai. Goring was dead. She'd felt the life bleed from him.

"I want you both to go up there and nose around. See who survived."

She studied the twins' drawn faces. "So quiet tonight. Oh, you're sad about the grey faerie's death. How touching."

Both of the trolls frowned.

"There's no time to mourn. Koldis and Ormrun are somewhere in that rubble. I won't lose them again."

Pogo and Moog exchanged somber glances.

Sevondi clapped her hands. "What are you waiting for?"

They lumbered toward the door.

She locked it behind them before gliding to the large wood cabinet on the other side of the room. She opened its doors. A hard, shiny screen stared out at her–an oversized, rectangular eye. She ignored it and pulled out the middle shelf. *The Book of Umbra* rolled toward her.

Goring had sent it to her this afternoon before he died. Perhaps he'd loved her after all.

She let her fingers rest on the book's leather cover.

"When I find the key, I'll open the door. Then we'll be one," she whispered to Umbra.

Something dark rushed through her. It was good Zachariah had died–Umbra didn't like to share.

Thank You

I appreciate you spending your valuable time reading *Half Faerie*. If you'd like to share the story with other readers, please tell a friend, or post a review on any book-ish site.

I'd also like to invite you to sign up for my newsletter: http://eepurl.com/wWKUj. It's quirky–like me:D–and I confess, it comes out sporadically, but I send a variety of things, including some (hopefully) pleasant surprises along with updates on all my new releases.

Sincerely,

Acknowledgments

Thank you, to the original beta readers who helped so much: Kevin Sullivan, Ladonna Watkins, Stephan Gordon, Phillip Spencer, Steve Brady, B. Morris Allen, Sandra Ulbrich Almazan, and everyone else at the Online Writer's Workshop who read the original manuscript, *Half-Faerie*.

Thank you also, to the first readers who left reviews and helped me understand where the early editions fell short.

This entire project has truly been a labor of love. The *Daughter of Light* series is inspired by my beloved grandmother and the transformative effect she had on my life. If it weren't for my intense desire to create something which would touch readers with a bit of her magic, I suspect I would have been content to leave the original published version alone a long time ago.

Half Faerie is the first book of the series as it was originally envisioned.

I hope you love it.

Sincerely,
Heidi Garrett

About the Author

Heidi Garrett is the author of the *Daughter of Light* fantasy trilogy about a young half-faerie, half-mortal searching for her place in the Whole.

She's also the author of *Once Upon a Time Today*, a collection of modern fairy tale retellings for adults who have already left home. *The Magic Cupcake* series is paranormal romance trilogy she writes with Billie Limpin.

Heidi was born in Texas, and attempted to reside in as many cities in that state as possible. She made it to Houston, Lubbock, Austin, and El Paso. After spending a decade in southern California, she now lives in Eastern Washington state with her husband, their two cats, her laptop, and her Kindle. Being from the South, she often contemplates the magic of snow.

You can find Heidi on her blog.

Glossary of Characters and Creatures

The Albiana: Although they are of unknown origin, the Albianas are considered flower faeries. However, they are taller than most flower faeries, and their alabaster skin remains pale even when exposed to sunlight. They are the most beautiful of all the faeries.

Basil: The Grand Library's ginger tabby cat.

Brownies: Ruddy-faced, dark-haired, playful creatures, they usually stand about three feet high. Some choose to serve in the Cathedral Palace Guard.

Aldous: A wood elf, he is the head librarian of the Cathedral Palace Grand Library.

Anton: An Idonnai, Ryder's mentor, and the head of the Order of the Idonnai.

Ava Albiana: The second queen of Illialei, she was Gwyneth Albiana's daughter.

Captain Tom: Captain of the Lucky Seahorse.

Cult of Umbra: An army of muannai who will serve the incarnated Umbra.

Dwarves: Dwarves originally populated the planet Una in the mortal world. However, when Isolt of the Waters, an ancient water elemental, was banished from Una by her husband, the god Vulcan, the dwarves abandoned Una with her. Una became known as Earth, and the dwarves migrated from Earth to Misgradde by way of the Realm of Faerie. A sizable population of dwarves never made it to Misgradde. They remained in Tyrannis as chefs when it was discovered their talent for cooking was as great as their talent for metalwork.

Elendah, the Grey Faerie of Aldaine: The only grey faerie who does not dwell on the Isle of Minnanon, Elendah sits on the throne of the Stronghold of Calashai in Tyrannis. She is known as the regent of the stronghold.

Elynus: The Great Mortal Druid. Estranged husband to Pressina. Father to Melia, Melusine, and Plantine. Exiled to the mortal world.

Evangeline: A mermaid Melia meets in the mortal world.

Field Faeries: The faeries related to non-blooming plants. Typically, their physical appearance is plainer than that of the flower faeries. They have wings and are capable of short flights at low altitude. Average height is five feet.

Flora: The sole surviving spring faerie in the Whole.

Flower Faeries: The faeries related to blooming plants. Typically, the females are of great beauty. They have wings and are capable of short flight at low altitudes. Average height is five feet. Verbena, Clementine, Brigitta, Gisele, and Marguerite are flower faeries.

Garrick: An Idonnai and baker, husband to Shilda. He is like a father to Ryder.

Glow Sprites, Nixies, and Undines: The water creatures native to Tyrannis. They live in the Undine River.

Gnomes: Stand about two feet high and wear red hats. Native to the Ruadain in northern Tyrannis, they are taciturn creatures and not friendly.

The Grey Council: Composed of grey faeries and located on the Isle of Minnanon, it is the supreme ruling body in the enchanted world.

Grey Faeries: Wise and ageless, a small population dwell on the Isle of

Minnanon in the enchanted world.

Gumf: A dwarf, the proprietor of the Veiled Tavern in the Balyudor in Tyrannis.

Gweff: The dwarf who forged the magical basin, Ormrun.

Gwyneth Albiana: From unknown origins, she was Illialei's first queen.

Haff: The dwarf who forged the magical sword, Koldis.

Huron Knights: The fair-haired natives of Huros. Considered to be the most chivalrous inhabitants in the enchanted world.

Isolt of the Waters: An ancient water elemental banished to the Void by her husband, the god Vulcan.

Lilliane Albiana: Illialei's faerie princess and daughter of Queen Luisa Albiana.

Luisa Albiana: The reigning queen of Illialei.

Malachi: A cat-like creature. The result of one of Pressina's botched spells.

Melia: A half-faerie. The middle daughter of the mortal druid Elynus and the full-blooded faerie Pressina. She has no wings.

Melusine: A half-faerie. The oldest daughter of the mortal druid Elynus and the full-blooded faerie Pressina. She has no wings. Melusine's story was legend in 15th century France.

Mermaids: The water creatures native to Illialei. They enjoy traveling to the mortal world.

Moog: A troll, he serves Lord Zachariah Goring. He transports communications between the mortal and enchanted worlds for the mortal druid Elynus.

Morgannai: A warrior race, they are the dark-haired natives of Morganna.

The Muannai (singular muannaye): Tall (over five feet) and lean, they are the wingless dark faeries native to Tyrannis. They are the only creatures in the enchanted world who cannot travel to the mortal world.

Nandana: A mortal, also known as the Illustrator, she lives in Illialei. Her body art is popular among the faeries and elves.

Ogres: Huge creatures from Kyrakkos. They are strong, but simple-minded and slow. Often described as smelling of mold.

Olivia Albiana: The fourth queen of Illialei, she was Uriel's daughter.

She is Queen Luisa's mother.

The Order of the Idonnai: An order of priests in Idonne. They chronicle and observe events in the Whole. However, they do not intervene.

Pixies: The most petite faeries. They are approximately four to six inches tall and dwell in the enchanted gardens. Known to be mischievous.

Plantine: A half-faerie. The youngest daughter of the mortal druid Elynus and the full-blooded faerie Pressina. She has no wings.

Pogo: A troll and Moog's twin brother. He has served Sevondi's lineage for centuries.

Pressina: A full-blooded faerie. Estranged wife to Elynus. Maintains a private life in Illialei with her three daughters: Melia, Melusine, and Plantine. She studies and practices black magic.

Ryder: A young priest fleeing his duties as a member of the Order of the Idonnai. An orphan, he was abandoned at the priesthood's gates as an infant.

Sevondi: A dragonwitch. She is a muannaye. Her great-great-grandfather was a sorcerer from Kyrakkos.

Shilda: An Idonnai and skilled herbalist, wife to Garrick. She is like a mother to Ryder.

Sinjiin: A mage from the Hidden City.

Spring Faeries: A race of warrior faeries native to Illialei.

Tatou: A pixie. She is Melia's best friend.

Tree Elves: Thinner and taller than wood elves, they are native to eastern Illialei.

Trolls: Both the males and females of the species stand about three feet tall. However, the males tend to be balding, with swarthy skin and large noses, while the females–though often stout–have thick, luxurious hair, bewitching eyes, and cherubic faces.

Tuck: A tree elf, he is Aldous' apprentice at the Cathedral Palace Grand Library.

Typhons: Natives of Typhos, considered to be the enchanted world's best sailors.

Umbra: A non-corporeal entity dwelling in the Void. He is a growing mass of mortal psychic ash, a result of rapid population growth in the mortal world. Umbra has developed a discrete identity and seeks to incarnate in the material plane. He requires a living material person/creature as a vessel for his consciousness. He seeks to ruin and rule the Whole.

Uriel Albiana: The third queen of Illialei, she was Ava Albiana's daughter.

Wood Elves: Mostly rather round, they stand about four feet tall and are native to western Illialei.

Zachariah Goring, Lord: A muannaye, he collaborated with the mortal druid Elynus to incarnate Umbra.

Glossary of Places and Things

Achill Island: An island in the country of Ireland in the mortal world. Birthplace of Elynus and Pressina's daughters: Melia, Melusine, and Plantine.

Achill Head: The most westerly point of Achill Island.

Aldaine: A city in Tyrannis located on the highest, north most peak of the Ruadain Mountains in the enchanted world.

Ashleam Bay: The western coast of Achill Island.

Azyllai: A country in the enchanted world. Home to the gods.

The Balyudor: The wild woods in Tyrannis.

Bryndale: The largest city in Illialei.

The Cathedral Palace: The primary palace in Illialei. Gwyneth Albiana's husband, a lesser god, built the palace for her. She ascended the Cathedral Palace throne as the first queen of Illialei.

The Cimmerian Inlet: An inlet to the Great White Sea, located in northern Tyrannis, in proximity to the Stronghold of Calashai.

The Crossroads: A popular tavern in the seaport of Typhos.

The Danu Meadows: A large meadow in central Illialei.

The Enchanted Gardens: Home of the pixies. The gardens border the Sylvan Forest in western Illialei.

The Enchanted World: Known territories include: The Realm of Faerie, the Great White Sea, Idonne, Morganna, Typhos, Huros, Kyrakkos, Azyllai, the Isle of Minnanon, and Misgradde.

The Flower of Isbelline: A striking flower with creamy white petals that blooms on the northern most sea cliffs of the Ruadain Mountains.

The Footing Fields: The fields of Illialei where brownies roll ball and play other games.

The Glen: A wooded valley that lies between the Rolling Mountains and the Nyssalei in western Illialei. Home to the largest population of wood elves in Illialei.

The Grand Library: The library in the Cathedral Palace.

The Great White Sea: The largest body of water in the enchanted world. Reputed to have mystical and healing properties.

The Hidden City: Home to the most powerful mages in the enchanted world. Its location is hidden from all who do not dwell there.

High Hill: A large hill in Illialei.

The Hive: A cafe in Bryndale that caters to wood elves. Honey is an ingredient in all the items on the menu.

Huros: Home of the fair-haired Hurons. Huron Knights are considered to be the most chivalrous in the enchanted world.

Illialei: One of two countries comprising the Realm of Faerie. In older days, it was known as the Territory of Light. It is considered the heart of the enchanted world.

Idonne: Home to the priesthood of the Idonnai. Idonnai, who are not members of the priesthood, are considered to be the finest artisans in the enchanted world.

The Idonnic Library: The priesthood of the Idonnai's work and purpose for existence. Its pristine architecture is the seat of Idonnic power and influence in the enchanted world.

The Isle of Minnanon: An isolated island in the northern waters of the Great White Sea. The Grey Council and the largest surviving population of grey faeries reside on the Isle.

Koldis: The dwarf, Haff, forged the magical sword in the bowels of the Ruadain Mountains.

Kyrakkos: Considered the font of black magic, it is home to the most powerful sorcerers and witches in the enchanted world.

Lake Vivientiana: A lake in eastern Illialei.

The Maeldun Bridge: The iron bridge that crosses the Nyssalei River between Illialei and Tyrannis. It is an in-between place.

Mare Cliffs: (pronounced mah-**ray**) The high cliffs that follow the Nyssalei River as it runs through eastern Illialei. Sylphs from Tyrannis have been known to cross into Illialei to dive from the cliffs into the river.

Misgradde: The country with the largest population of dwarves in the enchanted world.

Morganna: Home to the dark-haired Morgannai. The Morgannai are the enchanted world's warrior race.

The Mortal World: Home to mortals. Although it is not part of the enchanted world, the mortal world and the enchanted world must sustain a dynamic equilibrium of metaphysical energies for the Whole to function optimally.

The Muannai Valley: Borders the Undine River in southeast Tyrannis. Home to the largest population of muannai. Where the Muannai Valley Marketplace is located.

The Muannai Valley Marketplace: A large market in the muannai valley.

The Nuada: The plains of central Tyrannis.

The Nyssalei River: The river that borders and runs through Illialei. It runs from Lake Vivientiana into the Great White Sea.

Ormrun: The dwarf, Gweff, forged the bejeweled basin in the bowels of the Ruadain Mountains to be used as a portal by Isolt of the Waters.

The Parallel of Shadows: The shadowy realm between the Void and the enchanted world.

Pebble Rock: A large boulder with a natural cleft comfortable for sitting. It marks the head of the most popular trail through the Sylvan Forest.

The Primal Essence: Where all life–mortal and enchanted–begins.

The Realm of Faerie: A single land mass in the enchanted world comprised of two countries, Illialei and Tyrannis. The Realm of Faerie is the only country in the enchanted world that shares contiguous borders of time and space with the mortal world.

The Rolling Mountains: A hilly mountain range spanning eastern and western Illialei.

The Ruadain Mountains: A seven peak mountain range in northern Tyrannis.

The Sapphire Lily: The flower that grew from the seed Gwyneth Albiana planted on the shores of Lake Vivientiana when she first arrived in Illialei.

Southend: Illialei's port.

The Stronghold of Calashai: The four-towered stronghold in the center of Aldaine. Elendah, the Grey Faerie of Aldaine, sits on the stronghold's throne as regent.

The Summer Palace: A smaller palace in Illialei, located on the shores of Lake Vivientiana.

The Sylvan Forest: A light-filled forest located in northwest Illialei.

Typhos: Home to the Typhons and the enchanted world's largest and busiest seaport, Maris. Typhons are considered to be the best sailors in the enchanted world.

Tyrannis: One of the two countries comprising the Realm of Faerie. In older days, it was known as the Dark Lands.

The Undine River: Branches from a fork in the Nyssalei River and flows through Tyrannis.

The Unknown Beyond: A place beyond the Whole, about which little is known.

The Veiled Tavern: A mystical inn located in the heart of the Balyudor. Gumf, a dwarf and devout epicurean, is the inn's proprietor. He employs a large number of dwarves at the tavern as they are reputed to be the best chefs in the Whole.

The Void: The realm of incorporeal existence.

The Whole: Includes: The mortal world, the enchanted world, the Void, the Parallel of Shadows, and the Primal Essence. (The Unknown Beyond is not part of the Whole.)